LOSING
LINDANI

A NOVEL BY
LEANNE MARSHALL

ISBN: 9798770727128

To my mum and dad,
Sylvia and Dave Marshall,
for believing in me
when I didn't believe in myself

Thank You!
Leanne x

1

'Where are you taking me?'

I pinched the 'Bigfoot' freshener as it dangled from the rear-view mirror, its pine scent catching at the back of my nose, triggering a sneeze.

'You'll see,' he said, simply.

I pointed across him, sensing the electricity between us. 'I can't help but notice that civilisation is forty miles that way!'

There was something in the way he looked at me. He squinted into the July sun, faint double lines appearing beside his brown eyes, and the shadow of stubble completed a freeze-frame of perfection.

He was the first man in years who had held my attention. After a few exciting dates and the proverbial tummy flip, I'd had no reason not to welcome another, and only now, with our eyes locked, did I realise he was hacking the system and making me *feel* again.

Do you feel it too?

We turned down a dirt track then, just as a punch of heat began to colour my cheeks. I was grateful for the distraction it offered. The path clearly wasn't intended for four-wheeled vehicles. The *No Entry* sign only served to confirm my assumption. I waited for Lindani to source an alternative route, but he didn't. If I was honest, his sense of adventure and strong-mindedness kind of turned me on.

Our bodies began to jolt fitfully against the interior of the car, the pebble-peppered dirt having turned into a succession of grassy verges. Lindani's head tapped the roof with an irritating persistence, whilst my breasts, too, fought to remain secured. I let go of the 'Bigfoot' freshener and tucked them back into their assigned cups. A sneeze shot from my nostrils and sprayed the dash of Lindani's Sportage. He didn't acknowledge my embarrassment. I chose to read the subtle downturn of his mouth as a silent admission that we were lost.

My dating years had taken their toll on me mentally, so much that I'd decided to avoid serious relationships altogether. After Titch broke my heart. I was just seventeen. Since then, I'd lacked the ability to interact with another man – truly, completely, the way you're supposed to. I was okay with that though, honestly. It was a decision that had helped preserve my sanity. However, acquaintances told me (annoyingly) that there would come a time when I'd have to stop approaching relationships with the same degree of caution exercised in a covert military operation. Perhaps that time was now?

'Earth to Lois!'

Liquid silk.

A familiar voice penetrated my daydream. 'Huh? Sorry I must have drifted off!'

'I think we're here.' He searched my face for confirmation, an alluring glint in his eye I was yet to interpret.

A wave of emotion engulfed me as I contemplated my surroundings. Not only was I relieved my gut hadn't surrendered to motion sickness, I was reminded of a very special time in my life. One that I'd always thought was mine and mine only.

Fields of green stretched as far as the eye could see, flooding my pupils. Tiny white clouds dotted the pastures facing us. A single track stood brazenly in division, penetrating the Yorkshire Dales. An alien world, unspoilt by the litter and pollution that characteristically follows humankind. I was home.

'Come on, my love.'

I guessed my starry-eyed expression told him we were in the right place.

My love. My love. It was the first time he'd referred to me in such a loving way. I liked it. *This could be it, this could be the one!* I tried to conceal the classic signs of excited energy that were so adamantly re-surfacing. My feet paddled for the ground as I exited, like a baby dangling from its bouncer.

'How did you know?' I scanned the familiar countryside, embracing the swirl in my stomach.

Lindani rubbed his chin. 'Well, it took a bit of guesswork, but do you remember our third date?'

We both laughed. 'Beginners Baking, how could I forget!'

He'd wanted to feed the creative side of me. I'd tried to impress him by inventing a plethora of hobbies – all artistic in nature, of course. *Creatively*, we'd managed to burn two crumbles, lose three macarons, and design the chocolate cage into a more disfigured version of Quasimodo. We laughed until the stomach cramps paralysed us. It was … well … everything a first date should be.

'You had this cute glow in your eyes – like a dreamy, far-off look – when you talked about this place. So I figured it meant something to you.'

There was a pause as I calculated how he knew to come to this exact spot.

'I know, you're impressed, right?'

'Literally not a soul knows I come here though, Dan? How did you know where it was?' I plucked a piece of skin from my thumb, hoping I hadn't come across unappreciative.

'I guess I'm a little too eager to please. So I pulled out a few stops. All above board, of course!'

A few seconds drifted between us as we walked a few paces from the car. *It doesn't have a postcode, nothing?*

'What's life without a bit of mystery?' he added.

I suppressed a rising bubble of uncertainty, literally, by pressing hard against my gut.

Don't ruin things now. You've found a good one this time.

'I used to come here a lot,' I said.

He spread a plain knit blanket onto the grass. 'Oh?'

'Yeah. I still do sometimes.'

'Who with?'

His sharp words took me aback. 'It isn't one of those places, if that's what you're thinking!' I said, interpreting his tone as inquisitory rather than accusatory.

We sat beside one another in the centre of the blanket. He batted a crowd of midges from his temple before the burnt shimmer of his eyes connected again with my own.

'Why then?' he said, a pair of deep crevices appearing between his brows.

I peeled an invisible insect from his left bicep. 'Oh, so apparently that *was* what you were thinking! Interesting!'

He tilted his body to face me, pivoting the point of his elbow into the raw earth. He nestled the flesh of his cheek into the support of his palm. It was a change in body language that offered the prompt I had been waiting for.

'I just feel connected with ... well, nature, I guess. Like it knows me. I can just be myself here. Hard to explain.'

'So, what do you do here? It's a bit out of the way to just come and do nothing.'

'It isn't that far out, you *did* bring us on the scenic route!'

'Oh good, that's a little less weird, then!' *Crap, he thinks I'm weird!*

'You can trust me, Lois. Tell me anything you like and I won't be shocked ... promise!'

You promise. Trust wasn't a concept that had been competently demonstrated by any of the men in my life, and there was little reason to believe this one would be any different. Except, I reflected, he *had* always followed through on his word. That was new. He'd always been his authentic, casual, consistent, funny self. Just Lindani. *Perhaps I can trust him?*

My lips ruched messily into one corner. 'Don't we need food for a picnic?' I said, indicating the empty blanket. Also deflecting the attention away from myself.

He smiled. 'Damn, knew I'd forgotten something!'

How are you still single? I smiled back.

I wanted to learn more about him if he was going to be a permanent fixture in my life, so I broached a topic he'd retracted as soon as he'd brought it up.

'What were you about to tell me, on the way over here?'

Lindani's jaw tightened as he tweezed a greenfly from my loose strands of hair. 'Your hair's beautiful, Lois. Have you always worn it this long?'

Why are you deflecting my question?

'You started to say something about Africa,' I said, using his own tactics against him.

I hoped I hadn't injected awkwardness into our silence, but there was silence nonetheless.

'Did I?'

I nodded.

'Anyway you still haven't said why this place is so special to you.'

What are you hiding from, Dan?

I did feel it was an explanation I owed him, after he'd brought me to an empty field in the middle of nowhere.

'It's just where I come to reflect,' I said, hoping my openness would trigger the same in him. But he didn't speak. Instead, his eyes bored into me so deeply they told me he wanted to say something, but that he couldn't quite bring the words to leave his lips.

'Do you ever think about people who aren't in your life any more? Like where they are now? If they ever think about you? That kinda thing?' I asked.

His hand stretched across both my thighs. 'Recently, there's been no one I think about other than you, Lois. The past is the past, I find it best to leave it there.'

'Fair enough.' It was all I could bring myself to say.

'Do you know why I knew you were different from other women?' he said, extinguishing my dejection.

'Nope,' I said honestly.

'I mean, apart from your shockingly poor interrogation tactics!'

Am I that obvious? My cheeks blushed. 'Ha ha, very funny!'

'That was the first thing. But what really did it was when you asked who Kylie Jenner was! Now that *was* a shocker! Quite rare in a woman of your age, in fact.'

'Oh my god, I thought you were going to say something *really* sweet and thought provo—'

'Eish, really?'

Lindani was mid-shrug when I dug my fist into his upper arm. We burst into synchronised laughter before he made slapdash lunges at the parts of my body available to him. I could feel his presence profoundly as our movements slowed down. His breath kissed the bare skin of my face, prompting goosebumps to rise across my body in defiance to the heat that was assembling within me. My senses tingled as he grazed the exposed flesh across my hip.

I couldn't isolate what had caused my eruption of desire. Perhaps it was the glint of mischief that spread with precise evenness through his pupils, or his schoolboy affront that confirmed his mutual affection. Whatever it was, I was surprised to find myself spreadeagled across his torso. Our mouths magnetically entwined. And it was the exact way I'd fantasied since the same tall, dark, mysterious stranger sat beside me on that memorial bench by the Wellwish Centre a couple of months prior.

If it weren't for his reciprocation, I would have drowned with embarrassment, compounded by my already crippling fear of rejection. It wasn't my usual approach, instigating affection, but there was something in the way he teased me.

Somewhere amongst the mist of pheromones I realised I was alone. His weight had lifted from beneath me and the deep, soothing tones of his voice had dissipated into the distant air, to reveal a disquieting solitude that sent a tremor through the matter in my chest.

• • •

I stood from the ground and called after him, irrationally hurt from his premature abandonment. The air had chilled noticeably and although my instincts told me this was just him playing around, I couldn't combat the fear that this man, too, had left me.

He was testing me, shit, I gave in too soon.

'Miss Lane?' His voice was musical enough to draw in a crowd. 'Over here! This way,' he prompted, as my head craned in the wrong direction. A wide smile freeloaded my cheeks, urging his image to appear with a desire comparable to a drug addict craving a fix.

I caught sight of the baby blue fabric of his shirt, smirking at the smudge of green earth that defaced his attire at intermittent pressure points. We must have tumbled from the blanket onto the grass at some point. Lindani's upper body arched into the driver side of the Sportage moments before a soft tune sounded from the windows. I recognised it to be the only song so far, in our entire spectrum of musical taste, we'd discovered we both loved.

He walked directly towards me, wearing an expression reminiscent of a groom approaching his bride. Both of us were mute but I was alive with a flailing of premature emotion that was encapsulated by my fingers moulding magnetically into his outstretched hand.

'At the risk of sounding like a complete old-timer, will you dance with me?'

My chest thumped so hard I was surprised it didn't explode. I wanted to savour every moment, especially since I knew it couldn't last long, this feeling, this bliss.

'I'm flattered, kind sir. To have been chosen to dance out of such an extensive selection of fair maidens,' I said, proud of my confident execution.

'Oh, you needn't be, Miss. You're Lois Lane, how could it *not* have been you?' *Where are you going with this?* 'After all, I am Superman.'

My eyeballs must have rolled back further than intended as his expression stretched to resemble Edvard Munch's *The Scream*, albeit a cheerier version.

'Oh okay,' he said. 'You'll see!'

My chest was close enough, I could feel the pulsing through his. 'You'll see,' he said, more earnestly this time, slowing down our movement until we were blended with the flow of nature itself.

Our bodies rested against one another as we slow-danced in the spot I'd frequented so many times alone. The air warmed then; the birds watched from their branches and the sky was injected with the same shade of pink that coated the surface layer of my skin. At least in my imagination.

I felt his cheek push into mine as he smiled, the sound of Sade's 'By Your Side' drifting through the air in perfect cadence with our mellow union.

'It doesn't feel like we only met a few weeks back. Not for me anyway.'

'Me either,' he confirmed. A moment of quiet ran between our thoughts. 'Why were you sat there so long?' he said.

'Where?'

'On that bench. When we met. You were there over an hour.'

I had been discharged from the Wellwish therapy centre after what turned out to be my last session. I'd sat on the memorial bench, just metres away, calibrating my new, forced freedom and what it would mean for my immediate future. Every anniversary, birthday, Mother's Day and Christmas mentally kicked my ass, and there was no one I'd allowed close enough to whom I felt comfortable offloading such down moments. If Lindani had been sat opposite me I don't think I would've noticed. Only when he asked if the seat next to me was taken did I dismantle my train of thought.

'Bloody hell, that isn't creepy, is it?'

Lindani laughed his deep chuckle. 'Who you calling a creep, you cheeky bugger!'

I laughed at his accented interpretation of the word bugger, but was impressed he'd used one of my colloquialisms against me.

My mind went back to our first meeting.

'I lost my mum when I was seven,' I confessed. 'And I don't have contact with my dad.'

He offered his full attention, pausing our impromptu dance.

'Is that why you had therapy?'

'What?' I died a little at his question, tact not being one of his plus points.

'Oh I just assumed … you were sat close to that therapy centre, that's all. Sorry. I didn't mean to pry.'

Deep breaths, Lois.

'I only went to a couple of sessions. Nothing too scary,' I said, hoping he wouldn't run off into the sunset without me.

'It'll get easier, my love. Trust me, I know.'

Ask him what he means by that – now.

We were deep into our choreographed routine when I really paid attention to the shiny, raised swipes that ran diagonally across his arms and clavicle. *How did you get those scars?* It was with more than just a fleeting curiosity I wondered.

Lindani kissed my forehead before leading me into a ninety-degree turn.

I couldn't bring myself to look him in the eye through fear he could read my thoughts. 'You okay?' he said, noticing. I nodded and smiled.

I felt his arm slither down my back until it found its home at the tip of my bottom.

The thrum of music weakened inconceivably as we found ourselves dancing under the tree I often daydreamed beneath.

My two fantasy worlds merged into a single land of make-believe. *Has he lost his family too?*

Our bodies swayed together, following a synchronised rhythm.

Just enjoy it, Lois.

It was right there, during the mediocre, demonstrative twirl of our dance, that a pain shot through my leg with an intensity to rival a cannonball blasting through a stone fortress. My already pale skin drained of its colour as I fell shamelessly from Lindani's grip to the ground.

'Jesus, are you okay? What happened?'

I couldn't respond, and instead looked down to see my left ankle twisted out of shape. Lindani's face bore an expression that mirrored my own, grimacing as if he himself were in pain.

Shades of black and blue made their slow journey to the surface. He steadied me whilst identifying the offending badger hole below us. Nature's little minefield.

'I'm so sorry; here, let me help.'

He drew me in, hauling my dead weight slowly up the length of him, until we were almost eye level. Sensations of both pain and pleasure pulled at my chest as I inappropriately detected the sinews of his masculinity.

'I got you.'

My feet swept the surface of the ground as I was lifted into the air, melting the tension that had crystallised during his approach. He placed me gently onto the passenger seat.

'I'm so embarrassed. That must have looked super attractive!'

Another shooting pain splintered my nerve endings.

'I'll strap it up and get you to a hospital. It looks like you've just sprained it.'

Beads of sweat appeared ceremoniously across my forehead and miniature ringlets glued themselves around the frame of my face. Suddenly a little more conscious of my faltering appearance, I tried my hardest to disregard a familiar crippling insecurity that threatened.

'I'm not sure. This has to be a third-tiered fracture or whatever you call them,' I said. 'I can't walk.'

'Trust me.'

There it is again. That thing I can never do.

'You stay here and keep as still as you can, I'll be back in a flash. Don't follow me, okay?' he insisted.

I flicked down the mirror, swallowing gulps of tepid air before looking fully at the image that reflected back.

Lindani appeared to have a life's worth of experiences that I hoped to learn about one day. For now I should just enjoy his rugged handsomeness and strong physique. Yep, that was enough for now.

My insecurities rose again, having failed to take my eyes from the mirror. My tidy, styled hair and 'natural look' makeup had frizzed and sunken into my pores respectively; plus, I'd amassed worldly experiences enviable by no one. *What could he possibly see in me?* A row of birch trees stood proudly behind our parked car. Only nine minutes had passed, however my restlessness made it feel much longer.

Both the pain and anticipation thickened too. My leg throbbed with an urgency I found difficult to ignore so I scrambled for pleasant thoughts. It was a technique I had developed in childhood to alleviate physical and emotional pain, but it rarely worked.

The sky had darkened somewhere amidst the chaos, which made me begin to worry not only for myself but for Lindani too. *Where are you?*

I squinted into the darkness until I made out a thorny, elongated figure through the branches. I swallowed hard, stumbled to my feet, and hopped as carefully as I could to the front of the Sportage, my arm shielding me against an irrational threat, the same way a dodgy actress would in an amateur horror production.

'Dan?'

Stop panicking. You're such a frickin' loser!

'Lois, are you okay?'

Lindani's voice penetrated the blanket of pain that consumed my lower leg. The intensity yet to subside, I decided to trust him in that moment – the moment I found I needed to. He was a good man, but I knew the loss of my dad had affected my ability to interpret men's intentions.

I skulked out into the open, slightly embarrassed, and hoping he hadn't noticed my hiding from him. The wild assortment of branches elongated his limbs, forming the same shadowy silhouette I had been hobbling away from a minute earlier.

'How is it?' he asked with an air of concern.

'It's okay,' I lied. 'Hey, how about for our next date we do something a little safer?' It was my way of checking he wanted to see me again. Something I wasn't sure of right now.

'Safer than dancing in a field?'

That smile, shit, I'm in too deep already!

'Touché!'

'It's broken by the way,' he said matter-of-factly.

He set his bush merchandise on the grass beside us and examined the swelling around my ankle. 'See here where it's swollen? It looks like your skin has stretched over a broken bone. And when I press down here …' He applied pressure to the misshapen ridge. I bit down hard on my lower lip.

'It hurts, right?'

I nodded mechanically, worried any fast movements would cause irrecuperable damage.

'The bruising would be worse, too, if you'd torn a ligament. I think we should make a move now.'

'Make a move where?' It was uncomfortable, being out of control.

'Hospital?'

'Umm,' I began. 'I'll check Google. Ouww!'

I watched him with intense curiosity between sparks of pain. Only a trained eye – which it seemed Lindani had – could decipher the raised balloon of stretched pale skin as a bone fracture. He was knowledgeable, that much was evident. He lined up three branches and peeled thin ribbons of bark from each. I quizzed Google about the nearest hospital. Bracken Ridge Hospital, fourteen miles away. Very apt, I thought.

Moments later, I peered down over my iPhone to witness a godawful contraption. Something that could easily be mistaken for a prehistoric torture device. Lindani presented it with the same pride you'd see on the face of a child presenting his parents with an indistinguishable finger painting.

I didn't say a word. I was taken aback by his impulsive decision and natural instinct to look after me.

'It isn't perfect, but it'll hold everything in,' he said, fastening the makeshift splint securely around my lower leg.

'Does it feel okay?'

'It's okay, yeah.' His efforts released a sensation in my gut I had never before experienced. This man cared about me already. Enough to try to dull my pain. And if there was anything I had sought since losing Mum, this was it. 'Where did you learn to do that?'

His expression told me he was touched by my white lie, before continuing, beads of sweat beginning to pierce his tough exterior.

'It's just something I picked up. Did a bit of survival training in the A.R...' He hesitated. 'In Africa.'

2

Kai stood from his play area then crouched into a low squat. He dragged his amateur Lego creation closer to the kitchen where his dad was setting up. Every day, Lindani allowed extra time for our little boy's ritual grab for attention.

'I can see it from here, son. Stay there, before you break it,' he said, peering up to admire the wall canvas of a smiling African lady – an image Lindani had insisted we hang right there in full view of the main seating area. He'd claimed she would bring us fortune and good luck. Lindani had been a shut case about his life in Africa, so I'd found it a sentiment that had endeared me to him.

The makeshift panda-nursery jolted harshly over stray plastic toys that hindered its path. No sooner had Kai been warned than a baby panda hurtled across the wood floor – thrown from its nursery by a collision with what appeared to be a minion gathering.

'Kai, what did I just say!'

He stopped dead in his tracks and asked his dad instead to come and have a look, excitement waning as he flicked his attention from the broken panda to his angry father.

With his knife, Lindani scraped the spring onions into one corner of the chopping board and transferred two heaped tablespoons of tamarind and fenugreek into separate bowls before rinsing his hands.

'I'm getting sick of telling you, Kai! That's the third Lego set you've broken this week.' He flung the tea towel over his left shoulder before sitting cross-legged on the floor halfway between Kai's play area and the kitchen. 'Let's have a look then, shall we?' he said, sitting beside his four-year-old. Almost immediately his phone rang out.

'—Hey, Rich, how was your weekend?'

'—Yeah she's doing fine, been doing more hours at work, but she seems to be enjoying it.'

Kai pulled at his dad's jean pockets.

'—Oh, hold on, someone wants to tell you what he's made today.' Lindani pressed the phone to Kai's ear.

'Okay let me take a look,' he said, resting Kai into his torso after terminating his weekly check-in phone call.

Lindani picked up a Lego figure, one which Kai thought looked particularly like himself. 'This is me,' he'd often say, as if each Lego-world reflected Kai's own personal interests.

He used his mini-me to explore every crevice of his newly created world, excitement infusing each and every action until he glowed with the animation of a first-time traveller.

Lindani beamed with pride at Kai's vivid imagination. His child's smile was an unconscious cue for he himself to smile.

After experiencing an entirely different upbringing himself, Kai's happiness and purity of youth were all that Dan had hoped for. He considered his son's expression of creativity to be the figurative cherry on top.

'This is brilliant, son,' he said, guiding the figure to the panda feeding station.

'Time for dinner now, though. Pandas have to eat, too.'

Kai reached from Lindani's chest to remove it from the feeding station, interpreting his dad's instruction as a request to cease play. Lindani watched in silent contemplation. How Kai's light, slender arms stretched to not even half the length of his own. 'How could anyone …?' he wondered, casting his mind back to his own life as a child, growing up where he did and with the immense danger that threatened him and his family.

A punch of gratitude reminded him how far he had come.

'I think this may be even better than the tree house you made last week,' he pronounced, brushing errant crumbs from Kai's cheeks.

'No pandas in the tree house, Daddy.'

'Maybe that's why I prefer this one,' he said with an overstated shrug.

'Right, boy, Dad has some very important business to attend to. I shall ask for your opinion after the event, deal?'

'No, Daddy, come play!'

'How can you help me with our TV show if you won't let me film it, son?'

Kai loved to tell anyone he met about his dad's TV show. In reality, it was a YouTube channel Lindani had started shortly after Kai was born. Within his two-week paternity leave, he'd stumbled across a hidden talent and seemingly a hidden passion. Cooking.

'So, I can help you, Dad?'

'You're chief taster!'

'Yay!'

'Good lad. Right then, off you go. You sit over there,' he said, nodding for Kai to occupy his own miniature version of a bar stool.

Taking the cue, Kai squeaked both tiny bare feet across the wood floor before sitting as steadily as his four-year-old instincts allowed. 'Mushed pa-tato, Daddy! We having mush pa-tato and turkey dinosaurs?' Kai's hands flailed into the air, as would a scientist having discovered a highly researched cure. The spiderman motifs danced across his legs and chest in response.

Dan switched to selfie mode, and shot Kai a demonstrative finger across the lip.

He put the phone out of view and triple-checked the list of ingredients for their African-meets-English curry that was on this week's menu.

'Right, little man, you know what to do.'

'Are you ready?' Kai asked his dad in his most determined tone.

Lindani began his recording with a chuckle he found difficult to suppress. Nodding approval, Kai lengthened his limbs as far as was required to reach the on button.

Hey Guys, thanks for tuning in. You're back for another mash-up of Afro-English cuisine with me, Dan Attah. And don't forget little man, Kai, who is again undertaking cameraman duty. I hope you've all built an impressive binder full of the recipes we've experimented with over the past twelve months. If not, then what the heck have you been doing? As I say at the beginning of all my videos, if you're looking for fancy one-hit-wonder recipes then our channel is not for you. Our goal is to share affordable, exciting, everyday meal ideas for the entire family. If you're a member of a mixed family as I am, and you've had many disagreements over whose signature dish to emulate, then fear no longer. Our meal ideas are guaranteed to satisfy all palates. Please continue to leave us feedback and if any of you have ideas for dishes you'd like to see me try out, then I'll do my best to oblige. Okay let's get started.

•••

The next day, a Sunday, we found ourselves back at the supermarket. The frequency of our food shopping had ramped up since Dan's new venture. It was no wonder I had come to detest it, especially on the days I was dragged out after finishing work.

'Careful, Mummy, I mustn't drop them!' Kai stared intently at the box of free-range eggs in his hands. I tussled his curly hair as he passed by me en route to the kitchen.

'What the heck is that, Dan?' I noticed an unfamiliar, oversized perishable poking from his bag-for-life.

'Apparently, this is what you get when you ask your inattentive he-child to pick up a sweet potato!'

'Why didn't you just change it then?'

'What, and dampen his creative spirit? We both know that experimentation is the very essence of the Attah shopping experience, don't we!'

Kai gave a secure yes in response.

I plucked the item from the bag before showcasing it between my forefingers, still assessing its structure.

My husband leant into me, kissing my forehead before handing over two bags containing the lightest goods. We locked up the Sportage and headed to the kitchen to find Kai attempting to switch on the camera.

'No, darling, were just playing around for now – you and daddy can film together another time,' I said, emptying some of the items onto the counter.

Kai slid his mini bar stool over to the worktop and approached the coordinated family aprons with the same enthusiasm he did the camera, waving to the African lady on the canvas as if she was his sole viewer. The fabric of his smaller blue apron pinched the tip of his ear, his wild caramel curls limiting available wiggle space. Half the loop swept across the curve of his opposite cheek, exposing only his hazel eyes, both of which were alight with merriment and showmanship. I knelt and secured the apron into position until the words 'Kai, Sous-chef' read neatly at my eye level.

I scanned the array of colourful produce decorating my kitchen, privately regarding most as unnecessary extravagance. I was intrigued nonetheless.

'Well, my friend, you've outdone yourself this time. It's a tricky bunch of ingredients you have there, ain't it!'

'Hmm quite right, chef, good observation.' He grouped a seemingly random selection of produce and marinades in three separate piles, after some intense deliberation with our son.

Oh my god, my heart! 'You two are so weird.'

Kai handed us our respective aprons proudly. 'Mummy, Daddy,' he said, in turn.

Dan stood back to observe their final choices.

'So, are we all agreed?' He scanned our faces for confirmation.

'Let me up, Mummy!' The miniature chef straddled my right hip as if wishing to achieve a higher viewpoint. 'Yep!' He threw his spoon into the air playfully.

'Brilliant! Sous-chef, please begin chopping!'

I swapped my child for a chopping knife and popped Kai on his chair beside me to help.

'So, I met this woman yesterday at work.' It was a rare admission of mine so it succeeded in attracting my husband's attention.

'Oh, nice.'

'We've arranged to meet for dinner this week, but I said I'd check first that you and Kai could handle a night without my expert input.'

'I think we'll just about get by, love. Only just,' he said, pinching together his thumb and forefinger, signifying a slim degree of chance.

Adopting an animated tone, he called over to Kai who endeavoured to chop artichokes with his plastic knife. 'Boy's night in, son, what do you reckon?'

Kai's face lit in response, insinuating a glint of mischief was to ensue, a sentiment signalled by an enthusiastic nod of the head.

'What's she like anyway, this woman?' Although he was feigning genuine interest, I was excited to tell him about her.

'She seems nice, interesting actually, and nothing at all like some of the cabin crew I usually come across.'

He sliced what I assumed was a root vegetable. 'Oh, yeah? How so?'

'I dunno, just a bit more upstairs, if you catch my drift! And d'ya know what, I've surprised myself in that I actually, genuinely want to meet up with her. She's training to be a pilot,' I added, filling the pause in conversation, as if evidence was required.

'Hmm, smart.'

Dan's knife slid effortlessly through the white meat on the chopping board. The initial pop of skin triggered the skin around his jaw to stretch slightly.

'Good for you, love,' he said despondently, resting down his knife before cutting away the first lump of meat. I watched him intently, soaping his hands and staring into the plug hole as if it was an insight into another realm entirely.

A knot tightened in my stomach. *Is it happening again?*

There were times Lindani seemed to drift off during the most menial tasks. As if he had tripped down a rabbit hole into another world. I had learned early on not to bother questioning him about it. 'The past is the past, it's best to leave it there,' was always his answer.

Instead I watched him closely, the way his lips strained against one another, how the suds from the water bound over the rough curves of his hands. *Is this enough for you, my love?* I didn't know that it was. *Are we enough?* Part of me didn't want to know. I just hoped I wasn't losing him.

I wondered if part of the reason he'd changed his career path was because people had begun to notice. Selfishly, I was relieved. He'd gone from a plush employment solicitor to a full-time social media sensation, and full-time dad in one fell swoop. I had observed my boys' relationship blossom exponentially as a result so I was completely at ease with having accepted a full-time position at the airport again. It was an added bonus that there were no more client meetings or office secretaries to worry about. No young, tight-skirt-wearing, fertile-looking women making a play for my husband. The ones all married women feared: girls that thrive on mastering their sexual control over men.

Lindani splashed cool water against his face. *Stay with me, there you go.*

'Do you need help, darlin'?' I said to Kai, exercising my right as a parent to demonstrate the proper way to chop vegetables, irrespective of how hard his pride rejected my offer.

'Hey, did you hear me? Dan?'

'So have you exchanged numbers and all of that?' he continued after a few quiet moments.

'Yup, numbers and all of that. Check!'

'Sweet, I'm glad you have a friend who you actually could genuinely want to see!'

My voice grew bubbly and I could feel my eyes crinkle in the corners. 'Think you're funny don't you, Attah!'

He finalised our rhetoric with a serving spoon against my rear.
'Takes some of the burden off me. Win, win!'

'Oh my god, you're gonna get it bad, you wait!'

'That's no way to talk in front of our son, Miss Lane, is it?'

Kai giggled at our faux conflict, remaining steadfast in slicing his
veg correctly.

'Anyway, I honestly thought you liked being a loner?'

I finalised my update with a kiss, hoping to terminate the conversation before I became irrationally offended. *Was I a loner?* I pondered
this for a moment.

'Mummy, what's a loner?' Kai poured an immeasurable cocktail of
herbs and pastes into a mixing bowl before adding the chopped veg,
and churning the sloppy mixture with his hands. A wide toothy grin
possessed his face.

I swept his fringe of curls back against the crown of his head. 'What
do you think it is, darling?'

'Mmm.' He paused, engaging his most advanced thinking processes.
'A girl all by herself? A lone-her?' he said, sounding it out.

The raw truth of his words triggered a moment of self-reflection.
I squeezed his shoulders between my tensed hands, hoping some of
the love I felt for him would infuse into his skin.

I swept some mixture from his fingers as he spread them wide to
show us what he'd made.

'Can you tie my hair up, love,' I said, turning to Dan, indicating
my freshly soiled finger.

Reducing the heat on the hob, Dan stood behind me. I tried to
ignore his breath on my neck and the feel of his apron against my
back. He pecked the side of my neck lovingly and scooped the hair
from both sides of my face. An inappropriate sensation caused my
underwear to pulse.

'Promise me you'll never cut your hair Lo, it's still your best feature.'

'Yeah, you *should* step away,' I said playfully, ignorant to his
compliment.

'Time nor place,' was all he said.

I'd expected to be led into another room so we could spend some quality time alone. Kai would be occupied by the *Beat Bugs* on TV just for a short while. I wondered privately if he had turned down any of his previous partners.

Kai scraped the contents of his fingers across the edges of the bowl. 'Time and place for what, Daddy?'

My husband scolded me with a cautionary stare.

'Nothing, son, don't you worry about that,' he said, allowing a knowing smirk to cross his lips.

'I'll send her a text,' I said, slightly embarrassed. It was an attempt to shake off my desire for him. 'See if she's free on Thursday.'

'Oh, that woman? Thursday is good with us isn't it, little man?'

'Yep.'

I aborted sous-chef duties and flaked out on the sofa to type a message. Moments later, my phone pinged.

'Great, Thursday it is.'

I noticed Lindani reach for his phone and type some text with his right thumb before allocating me his attention.

'Get back here, Missy. Don't think you're getting out of it that easily!'

Kai followed his dad's lead. 'Chop, chop, Mummy!'

I folded my knees to my chest, melting into the couch from their playfully coltish approach. 'I'll chop, chop you in a minute, cheeky monkey!'

Dan's limbs grew noticeably laboured after our exchange. And there was that rabbit hole again. *What did I say?* The words never found my lips.

Both sets of fingers were clawed in preparation for the tickle attack I had pulled away from, when a hidden affliction struck him. 'I can't!' he said, his voice at a volume that was at odds with the situation. 'I won't!'

'Won't what? What are you talking about, love?'

The three of us fell into a confounded silence, paralysed both in movement and in speech, before Kai broke the ice.

'What's wrong, Daddy?' I felt Kai's eyes lock onto me pressingly. Instead, I searched Lindani's face for discernment, for the clarity I felt I was owed, not just now but for countless times before.

A white powdery mist rained down overhead, breaking the lull in activity. *The flour!* It was Kai's failed attempt for us to resume sous-chef duties, duties I felt his father no longer wanted to continue with.

I scooped my son from the floor and swung him full circle.

Dan didn't elaborate on his feelings, despite my asking him to. It was an explanation he persisted to refuse. To refuse *us*.

Dusted with his stash of white flour, I carried Kai upstairs to wash up, leaving Lindani in the living area alone. He was silent. Silenced by whatever was troubling him. I made a mental note to give him the space he seemed to need.

The stickiness of Kai's hand blended into mine as I led him up the staircase. 'Daddy said it was okay to do it!' he said, seemingly unsure why the play-fight had ended so abruptly and perhaps why his mother hadn't the know-how to explain why either.

Kai, stripped of his soiled clothing, splashed up the few inches of bath water whilst with a soapy sponge I rinsed the remaining flour from his young skin.

Dispirited by Lindani's lack of transparency, all I could think to say was, 'It's fine, sweet pea, if Daddy says it's okay then it's okay.'

My words were as contrived as the handful of explanations Dan had enlightened me with during our entire relationship. What good, I surmised, came from questioning a man who had the power to break my heart? Anyway, things were perfect most of the time. For the most part.

For as long as he was present physically, there would always come a time for him to fully engage emotionally. He was a man after all. For them, such sentiments didn't establish themselves overnight.

I wrapped our son in a bath sheet, his teeny feet buried beneath the fabric, searching for an exit. 'Come on, darling. Shall we go and make Daddy his favourite drink?'

'Yep, hot chocolate!'

'You guessed it, clever boy!'

His head accidentally clapped into my chest with the excited lack of stability displayed in a newborn.

'Then he will be happy again?' The innocence of his statement stabbed directly at my heart. I answered with a single kiss to his forehead. For now, I hoped. At least, for now.

3

THEN

I was seven years old. It was a Wednesday, my favourite day of the week. From Thursday to Tuesday, I dreamt away the hours, all millions of them. And as I grew closer to my favourite day, I persuaded Dad to read my bedtime story early – sometimes as early as six. That way, the sun would rise quicker, and it would be Wednesday again.

Mum always warned me not to wish my life away. That before I could blink, I'd have grown-lady problems. I knew she was worried I would suffer the same fate as her.

Wednesday was when my dad took me swimming after school. It was when I did my best thinking. But, more appealingly, it was where I went to escape.

I imagined I was a beautiful mermaid, graceful and enchanting. My fuzzy brown hair transformed into luscious golden locks that trailed the entire length of my ethereal body. I glided through the water, my fins massaging the current, propelling me forward with every stroke. My young body weaved its way amongst the waves. The freedom was liberating.

The water was my home. It just so happened that other people were there, too. Strangers. Trespassing in my secret biosphere. I knew I had to share, and it wasn't that I was being unreasonable. It's just, they were different. They didn't cherish their time in the water like I did.

When I complained to Dad about them, he told me, 'There will always be people who don't see things in the same way you do. If you open your mind really wide, you could learn something you didn't know before.' I thought it a silly sentiment. Minds were only so big, after all.

I copied what the others did at swim class. I tried really hard to blend in, to be like the others, but I urged the lesson to come to an end every week. It was the time after the lesson that I longed for – when the instructor ceased to teach, and my classmates dispersed back into their respective changing rooms. Sometimes my mind wandered, and I sank into my dream world early.

My dad was the only person who understood. He knew how much I loved to swim, so he let me play in the pool afterwards. He called me his water baby, like the kid in that movie. Sometimes, after the lesson he came into the pool with me. It was our time together. The most precious of times. He would jump in the air and grab his knees close to his chest, piercing the water's surface. I watched him in awe, wondering how it was possible for someone to make such a magnificent splash. I cherished the days he swam beside me in my void, free of gravity.

We glided effortlessly, admiring the beauty of the coral. We danced through rocky arches and secret underwater alcoves. Schools of African cichlids and guppies parted obediently as we passed, forming a passage fit for royalty. I revelled in the performance.

I didn't tell anyone about our underwater kingdom. Dad was the only person who loved it as much as I did. I honoured it as our secret. There was one occasion, however, Mrs. Mandel (my swim teacher) asked me about it. I had given her a fright one afternoon because she caught me submerged beneath the surface while we were supposed to be treading water. She must have thought I was drowning. When I popped up for air, she asked why on earth I wasn't doing as the others were. I replied confidently. 'A reef shark swam directly towards me. Someone must have left the gates open. I had to stay still so it didn't bite.'

'Don't be so ridiculous, Lois. You're seven years old now, I'm not listening to another year of this fantasy nonsense,' she scolded. A pink blush heated my cheeks instantly. 'If you want to get your certificate, you must pay attention,' she continued.

I remember feeling humiliated and angry. She had managed to expose our precious world. Even worse, she'd tainted it with her ignorance.

My dad wouldn't stand for it. He would stick up for me and tell Mrs. Mandel that it wasn't nonsense at all.

I looked up to see if he was watching, half wondering why there was silence in the spectator stand.

That's when I saw them.

My throat burned as bile travelled from the pit of my stomach to my mouth. I had an overwhelming urge to spit it in the face of that vile woman who sat so close to my dad, Amazonian limbs draped possessively over his shoulders. Her straight-cut bobbed hair red like fire. Eyes burning into his grey-blue pupils. The flimsy off-white fabric encased her boyish lumps that rubbed against his navy polo shirt. Bare flesh poked from under her knee-length skirt, her legs crossed idly over his lap. Painted crimson lips glued to the speckled grey stubble that coated the lower half of his face.

I waited for him to push her away. Throw her ashen limbs from his lap. Make it known that he wouldn't accept such vulgar advances. But he didn't. I watched in horror as he pulled her legs closer into him, squeezing the top of her left thigh. He nuzzled his face into the crevice of her neck. Tilted her pale pointy chin down until they were nose to nose. He used his lips to seal the entrance of her venomous mouth. He caressed her cheek and lips with the same fingers he used to wipe chocolate away from mine. Then, he slid her knees from his lap and scanned the room with an air of caution demonstrated only by that of a guilty man.

The air grew thin. A sharp, icy gust robbed me of my ability to breathe. The echo of kids splashing in the water and Mrs. Mandel relaying instructions became background noise, sunken almost under a blanket of water. My torso felt light, my legs detached, and my hands blurred with an insatiable desire to keep the rest of me afloat. I watched the water as they splayed aside with a slow repetition, casting speckles of distorted polka dots just beneath the water's surface. I bore no shape nor weight, yet my legs continued to pump as if I still needed them. Engorged lengths of hair engulfed the peach of my bare shoulders, like tentacles intent on dragging me into their watery lair.

I looked over to the boy on my left to see if he was underwater, assessing whether the threat was real. I immediately noticed the twins by my right weren't submerged either. My nose crinkled with confusion. I realised then that it must be me. Except I was afloat, treading water the same as everyone else. Why did everything sound so strange?

Mrs. Mandel wittered on about something or other. She pointed me out in the crowd, holding my gaze. Seemingly expectant of a response, I was unable to decipher her words so failed to comply. I was aware of the mounting attention as well as Mrs. Mandel's annoyance. Time had frozen, leaving faceless buoys bobbing repetitively around me. I was suspended in that moment. Alone.

I had to get out of there. An overwhelming surge of restlessness engulfed me. My arms became heavy. A weight so strong, I felt someone dragging them towards the faux turquoise abyss beneath me.

I couldn't convince myself to move, yet found myself dangling from the side of the pool, like a fallen sailor would hold on to his boat. For the split-second time allowed, I was in the spotlight. I peeped up at the stand, through the gaps in my hair, hoping Dad would be sitting alone, cheering me on and preparing for our play time after the lesson. What I saw confirmed no such thing. It was all real: the woman, the kissing, the betrayal.

I climbed out hurriedly. My feet slapped against the tiles one by one, despite calls from Mrs. Mandel to come back. No doubt she would be furious that I was running on a wet floor. I didn't care. Not then. Not that time.

In a matter of seconds, I was standing before the little grey locker, glaring at its tough, shiny exterior.

A twinge of regret twisted in my stomach. Not regret for leaving the class early. Not regret for making Miss cross, and not even regret for running by the pool. Regret for looking up to the stand where my dad was. For looking up at the exact moment I had. For seeing what I knew deep down I could never unsee. The scene flicked through my mind with little respite. Against my better judgement, I experienced a strange urgency to revisit the scene, to witness again what I knew to be true. But there wasn't time if I was to make my escape without him.

So much had changed in such a short space of time. Everything felt different now.

Carelessly, I snatched the dry clothes from my spotty swim bag. Tossing my belongings onto the communal bench in the locker room, I hurriedly poked my head through the hole of my dress before peeling it down the length of my soaking body. I flinched as my drenched hair slapped against the back of my dress.

Leaving a trail of unnoticed belongings in my wake, I ran from the leisure centre with my eyes firmly fixed to the floor; ran all the way home. There was over a mile of ground to cover and despite the constant punching of the bag against my back, I made it home, successfully avoiding any unwelcome interactions along the way. More importantly, I had escaped a confrontation with my dad.

'Mum, I'm home! Where are you?' I slammed the front door.

I hurtled up the staircase then knelt by her bedside. Deep, heavy breaths illuminated my exhaustion. I was still damp to touch, and the outline of my swimsuit appeared through the fabric of my dress. The cool air had caused an untameable curly frizz across the entire circumference of my head. I pushed Mum's hand against my cheek, enjoying its trickle of warmth before sobbing uncontrollably into her nightdress. My emotions were a jigsaw of confusion. If I couldn't make sense of them myself, how was I going to voice them coherently to Mum? Instead, I sobbed silently.

She must have known I had run home alone. Mums know these things, don't they? It was evident in what she mustered the strength to say. 'Where's your daddy, sweet pea?'

'I don't know, Mum. I don't know where he's gone, but *I'm* here now.'

4

The tyres of Mila's white Mercedes bumped up onto the pavement, blocking the driveway of her circa 1890s semi. 'You're coming in, right?' She stared me into submission from the driver side.

'Love to!' It wasn't a lie.

My response was met with a warm smile. 'Is it even safe there?' she said, lugging six Zara bags from the boot.

'Jesus, don't you start!' I trailed her to the entrance of her beautiful Victorian home, holding some modest purchases of my own. Purchases I neither wanted nor needed. I did, however want to spend time with Mila and this week was her week to choose what we did.

'I assume so. It isn't Africa-Africa, is it?'

'Never been, to be honest.'

'Coffee? Or something stronger?' she asked, walking into her pristine but cosy living room. I set my bags down by the front door and slipped off my shoes, grateful for the relief my feet had been craving after the shopping trip Mila had insisted upon.

'Just a coffee for me. I want to get back to the boys in time for tea.'

'Remind me why you thought it was a good idea to give you a fake name again, please!' I blurted, only semi-rhetorically. Keeping up the lie was becoming exhausting, and the closer our friendship became, the more I wanted to bring her into my life. 'I messed up with this one, Mila!'

'Needs and musts, Lo. Needs and musts!'

I still couldn't believe I had agreed not to tell my husband that my friend 'Emma' was actually Lindani's ex-wife, Mila. But it was a necessary white lie if I wanted her to stay in my life. And I did.

Mila disappeared into the kitchen to attend to the drinks. Meanwhile, I sank comfortably into her blush velvet sofa and rested my pulsing feet on the matching footstool.

'Aw come on, Lo, live dangerously will you! They'll be too busy doing boy stuff to miss you just yet!' she called from the kitchen. 'No offence,' she added, appearing in the doorway of the living room, two white coffees in hand.

'Thanks,' I took one from her, cradling the cup between my knitted fingers.

I recalled the moment I had looked my husband in the face and lied for the first time. We were in the line to collect our cinema tickets. I told him that the woman I'd met at work just seven days before was called Emma. I needed the two hours of *Jurassic World* to process how I felt about my decision. I considered telling Dan the truth after the final credits, such was my moral compass. I would tell him I had misheard. That it was a silly, innocent mistake. I'd tell him Mila and I had had a good laugh about it when she'd realised herself.

But I didn't tell him. Not after the final credits. And not any time since. My excuse wouldn't work, because I'd completed her medical certificate with her full details – a blatant flaw in my plan. I had dreamt up a number of weird and wonderful excuses in my head over the next couple of weeks, but none rang true.

My potent desire to learn more about him from Mila was too strong. So, to Dan and to Kai, Mila was Emma, and that was the final decision.

'Are you okay today, Lois? You seem a little on edge.' She folded her knees up onto the sofa beside me.

'We have a big problem!'

'Hit me!'

'He wants to double date, Mila. Me and him, you and Tom. Well, Emma and Tom.'

I paused to compute Mila's horrified expression, waiting for her step-by-step itinerary of how to dig us out of said predicament.

'Oh,' she said, plainly, taking a sip from the coffee cup.

'Oh? Is that all you have to say?'

'That may not be a problem, after all.'

It is absolutely a problem!

'I broke up with Tom,' she blurted before I had chance to respond. 'I know it sounds crazy, he's a great guy blah blah blah, but I wasn't feeling it … not really. Anyway, I don't wanna talk about him, that's why I didn't bring it up.'

'I thought you were planning on moving in together?'

'I just don't know if I'm ready for all that, Lo. Can we just talk about something else please? Please, Lois.' *This is a mistake, Mila.*

'Hey, look at it like this. Your problem's solved! Job's a good-un!'

There was something unreadable behind her eyes.

'Anyway, has Dan come round to the idea of taking you guys to South Africa with him?'

An automatic puff of scented freshener spritzed the room, making me jump. A splash of coffee jumped from the rim of my cup. I smoothed it over before it reached the blush fabric.

'Kinda,' I said.

'What do you mean?' she said, intently, not bothering to switch on the sixty-five-inch television as she usually would.

'I still feel like he doesn't want us there.'

'Why? What has he said now?'

Lindani had tried a couple of times to convince me it was too dangerous for a young child to venture anywhere around Africa.

'Just the usual. It's too dangerous for kids, *and* for me now, apparently. How he'd just prefer to 'pop' over to check on his aunt, given what's happened.'

'Fair enough, if you ask me.'

An unusual quiet drifted between us. 'You sure you're okay, M?'

'Perfectly fine.'

'Well, the trip's booked now, and quite frankly it's tough. We're going as a family. I'm putting my foot down on this one, for once.'

'Just think about it. He's from that part of the world. He knows what it's like out there. I would hate for something awful to happen to either of you!'

'Trust me, the worst that's going to happen is one of us contracting a stomach bug and shitting all over the hotel for the duration. Anyway, he isn't from there. He's from Uganda. So I don't see the link that makes him an expert, personally. I mean, if it's glaringly obvious to you then please feel free to enlighten me.'

I paused to afford myself a moment of amateur dramatics, awaiting her admission, but she just blew at her cup, cooling the hot liquid.

'South Africa is a different state altogether,' I said. 'It's a massively popular tourist destination. I haven't had a holiday for three long-ass years, and this place looks stunning. So I'm going!'

'Okay, calm yourself,' she said, suppressing a heavy chuckle. 'I'm sure he'll keep you both safe,' she continued, thoughtfully. 'He was always very protective, from what I remember.' I felt her reading my reaction. 'Sorry, it's still weird isn't it? I'll shut up!'

It *was* weird, and I *did* want her to shut up. Being reminded that my husband used to be in love with my new best friend was something I'd got somewhat used to, but I still didn't feel completely at ease talking about it so casually.

'So, are you gonna call that guy from the store, given your new status?' I glanced at the Victorian-faced clock on the wall above the open fireplace.

'Probably not, he seems a bit up himself to me. What did you think?'

'I think you might just be the modern-day goldilocks. Is anyone juuuust right for Mila Sanders, I wonder?'

She threw a grey velvet sofa cushion in my direction, spitting con-taminated hot water from the corner of her lips.

'Bloody hell!' she said, unintentionally smearing the coffee deeper into the fabric. 'Hang on, I'll go get a cloth.'

I sat alone just for a few seconds as Mila left to gather cleaning supplies, allowing my mind to drift back to our previous conversation. *Why did she break up with Tom? Seems weird, she was totally smitten last week. What could possibly have happened since then?*

'There we go,' said Mila, to herself, having successfully extracted the stains and resumed her position beside me on the sofa.

I pressed send on the message that informed Dan I was at 'Emma's' and that I would be home within an hour or two.

'Have you cleared it with work, the time off?'

I steadied my legs and set down the cup as Dan's name flashed on my iPhone screen.

I nodded gently, before answering it.

'Hey love, everything okay?'

'Babe, sorry to interrupt but me and lil' man have an excellent idea we wanted to run by you.'

'Hit me!' I said, mimicking Mila's rhetoric.

Mila busied herself by re-plumping the sofa cushions then clearing away my almost empty cup.

I smiled up at her as a silent apology for taking the call, to which she responded with a dismissive waft of the hand.

'So, hear me out. Me and Kai swing by to pick you up and whisk you off to your favourite place in the entire world.' He paused, awaiting my answer.

'Bed?'

'Okay, second favourite place! We'll go grab some pizza at Bella Italia for an extra cheesy thin crust—'

'With extra mushrooms,' we said concurrently.

'Then drop Emma back home, plop Kai in bed …' I detected Kai's reservations in the background at the last part of the plan. 'Then me and you catch up on that serial killer doc we've been dying to watch? Oh yeah, Emma's invited too if you didn't pick up on that! Be nice to finally put a face to the name, plus Kai said she likes pizza, so win-win, right? Thoughts?'

Mila had returned to the living room and began sifting through the bags from our shopping trip.

'Oh okay, umm.' I stalled, thinking of how to reject his offer. *I wish we could do that.*

'Aw, darlin', that sounds lovely but I'm afraid we've eaten already.' I heard Kai complain in the background so I offered a more elaborate apology. 'It's hungry work is shopping!'

'Eish! It's only four o'clock,' Dan said. 'Can we not just class that as lunch? What if we swing by later, say around sixish? I can help you with your gazillion bags. Anyway, Kai's dying for you guys to come.'

'Dad is too, Mum, he's crying like a baby. He misses you!' called Kai before falling victim to a tickle attack that naturally followed.

A genuine chuckle escaped my lips. 'Oh, poor Dad!' I said, into the speaker. Hearing my boys scuffle and giggle among themselves made me regretful of lying about Mila. It was a lie I'd felt entitled to at the time, given Lindani's secrecy.

'Listen love, I'll call back in two, just have to ask Emma if she fancies it, okay?'

'Where is she? Just ask her quickly now and I'll leave you guys in peace, I promise.'

'Two minutes and I'll let you know.' I hoped that would be enough for him to concede.

'Okay, okay, permission to call back in two?'

'Granted.' My heart warmed and ached at the same time. I cherished my family above everything and everyone, but I also harboured deep affection towards my best friend.

My voice rang through the house as soon as the call ended. 'Mila!'

She had disappeared into another room sometime during the call but quickly reappeared, showcasing her newly purchased off-the-shoulder, merlot maxi dress with a slit that may as well have been all the way up to her neck.

'Oh my god, Mila, wow! That looks incredible on you.' Her black, paper-straight hair contrasted perfectly with the vibrant crimson of the fabric. 'Where do you plan on wearing that number?'

'Anywhere my future husband may be. I figure if I want to bag that million-dollar man then I have to look the part.'

You've just dumped him!

'Job's a good 'un then!' I said, rising from my seat as if in the presence of royalty. My eyes fixated on her striking beauty. Her slender, toned appendages and deep-set cinnamon-tinted irises sparked a twinge of envy within me.

'You really do look beautiful y'know.'

She wasn't at all like me, not even like the pre-childbirth me. Right there and then, in that dress, with the light reflecting in her eyes the way it did, she was the image of a woman I could only ever wish to resemble.

'You really think so?' she said, humbled by my compliment.

Stop it, Lois. I scolded myself, shooing away the pull of jealousy. Perhaps it was how she looked in that dress. Perhaps that, paired with the threat of my husband turning up, laying eyes on her and falling in love all over again. I couldn't be sure, but as if spurred on by the thought, I called Dan back.

Mila paraded over to the full-length mirror in the hallway and admired her reflection; she twisted her hair into a modest bun and pivoted her head. Unaware of my growing anxiety in the next room, she hummed dreamily to herself, nipping and tucking the fabric against the curve of her waist.

'Hey, babe. I'll be home shortly. Emma's meeting up with some guy this evening so it's just going to be the three of us I'm afraid.' Another lie spilled from my lips. I was good at it now. The lies came fast and thick. I was becoming a natural. *That should quash any opportunity for persuasion.*

'Huh? Does Tom know?'

Shit! 'He's not on the scene any more. Can't really say much right now though, for obvious reasons!'

'Oh yeah, course.'

'Tell Kai I'll see him soon.'

'All right, will do.'

'Laters!'

'Wait,' said Dan, moments before I cut him off. 'Are you gonna be okay with all your shopping if you get an Uber? Didn't think that one through today did you, my friend.'

'I only have a few things, it'll be fine.'

Mila would sometimes drive me home, letting me out a couple of streets away, but I'd decided this time to order an Uber, in the spirit of being truthful.

'Thanks for the cuppa, love. I'm gonna get off now, if you don't mind.'

'What's goin' on, everything all right?'

I gathered my meagre purchases by the door.

'It is if Dan doesn't act upon his spontaneous impulses by showing up to take me and "Emma" out to dinner!'

'Oh shit, okay, yeah you go.'

'Exactly! You can bet Kai suggested it, bloody kids!'

Please don't come with me, don't follow me outside.

I waited on the doorstep, swiping my flats nervously across the damp wood, urging my Uber to show up before Kai had convinced his dad to pick us up regardless.

Mila remained out of view. It was a relief. If Dan saw her again after all this time – with all bad blood forgotten, looking as beautiful as she did right now—I feared I could lose him to her. I'd challenge any man to turn her down.

A drum of worry rumbled through my chest as I stood on the wooden step in front of her home. I felt her watch me from the reception room window.

Did she hope to see him?

You're getting paranoid again, Lois.

5

Kai was almost seven. Lindani's followers continued to replicate daily, and the friendship between Mila and I had never been stronger.

The three of us were finally in South Africa. Kai, Lindani and me.

Dan still hadn't shared much about his family so I was excited to visit his Aunt Alice and dig a little deeper into my husband's elusive past.

The door lights flickered into action as I slid the key card into the slot. 'It feels so good to get here … finally. Doesn't it?'

He kissed my cheek before slipping past to check out the bathroom, leaving the bags by the door – a well-established ritual.

'D'ya think Kai's gonna be okay downstairs?'

'He's in the crèche with the other kids, he'll be fine.' His words were so casual, so confidently spoken. I wanted to believe him, even if it was just to get some time alone with my husband. 'Anyway, as soon as he saw that ball pit I knew we'd lost him!' Dan reappeared from the bathroom. 'Double shower in there. Sweet!'

My sex drive had dwindled down to nothing after Kai was born. The birth had taken a toll on my body. And my mind too, for that matter. It was as if I instantly saw myself only as a mum. Mum body, mum mentality, and an unwelcome bout of post-natal depression. It didn't help that everything on my body deflated and was used as either a baby feeder, pillow or plaything. I had constant tired circles under my eyes and an attitude to match my appearance. Needless to say, I wasn't the greatest wife.

I rejected the memories then opened Kai's *Beat Bugs* suitcase, plucking out fresh clothes for his evening meal.

Whilst I was pregnant, I felt desirable and adventurous. I'd evaded morning sickness and luckily I'd carried my bump well, too. Plus, I think Lindani enjoyed my extra voluptuousness. So for a short time, we exercised a healthy marriage again.

'What do you say we christen that shower tonight?'

Dan didn't answer. He stood in the wall-sized window, peering down onto the street below.

My heart.

The sun had begun its descent behind the flat-topped mountain. Indistinguishable pedestrians dotted the pavement, dewy, burnt-orange rays illuminating their miniature forms.

'It never fails to impress, does it, love?'

'What doesn't?' I said, hoping its beauty would strike up some romance between us.

He nodded towards the window. 'That view.'

'You and your pink sky,' I said, joining him by the window. I felt a glassy shimmer coat my pupils. My eyes were unable to leave the luminescent outline of his face. *You make me nervous, even now.*

He took a stride away from the window. A moment later I felt his arms snake around my waist, before linking across my curved stomach. I covered the fine hairs on his forearms, gently squeezing my fingernails into his flesh. My heart burned with a fresh wave of desire for him.

My head craned to one side with a magnetism I couldn't resist. Strands of dark chocolate curls cascaded freely by the side of my face, exposing the bare flesh of my neck. Lindani's full lips greedily marked their territory along the length of my translucent skin, stirring within me a deep yearning that consumed every living cell in my body. I didn't realise how much I wanted him until an inaudible whimper escaped my lips.

I cooed at my husband's touch as his fingers crept beneath the cream lace of my bra, cupping my generous breasts. My trousers buzzed impulsively from his hot breath thickening in my ear. I fought back weakly as the strength of his taut thighs forced my legs to widen their stance. It was a sexual tussle I was ill-equipped to fight. Surrendering to his advances, I pressed my silhouette into his torso, drinking him in fully. He folded me, tilting my vision towards the floor until I was fully at his mercy.

The dampness of his breath tickled my ear. 'I want you so bad, it's all I've thought about.' I was locked into his desired position, welcoming the tingle that ricocheted the length of my spine.

My heart thumped. My senses sharpened at the musk of his salty cologne, triggering bolts of electricity in my chest. It heaved visibly in unison with every burst of breath. I swivelled my body to face him, yearning for his lips until the heat between us was tangible. With an unmistakeable fire in our eyes, there was only one thing I felt the urge to say. 'Use me, Dan, I want you to use me.'

He groaned through gritted teeth in a frustrated display of repressed testosterone. His fingers stiffly gripping the flesh that covered my hips, hungrily exploring my shape. The indents from his prints highlighted his most recent exploits on my body. Patience grew thinner as he urged to be released from the denim in which he was confined. I caressed him, allowing only the most delicate skin of our lips to touch, before pulling back, enticing him to come closer. Refusing to wait for my lead, his hands slid to the zip that strained against his growing lust.

We were halted prematurely by an indistinct tune that rang out in the distance.

It grew in volume, piercing our sexual haze. The iPhone tune sounded from the sideboard across the room, reverberating a persistent thrum as it danced urgently.

'Stop,' growled Lindani, wishing away the caller.

I smiled, folding my arms around his shoulders, pleased he wanted to continue.

The phone stopped ringing, then after a few seconds started again. 'Go away!' I urged.

His grip loosened from my hips then, yet his forehead rested against mine, allowing him time to contemplate whether or not to concede.

'Stay right there, love, just lemme check who it is.'

I remained motionless, waiting for his return so we could assume our latest position. Watching idly, I covered my fleshy bumps awkwardly like a shy schoolgirl in gym class, as he rushed to the other side of the room, hoping to get back before the mood dulled.

'Damn, just missed it.'

'Who was it?' I said, feigning interest. I shielded my bare bits from view.

'An old friend from work I think.' It was a stuttered response. He stood a moment, waiting to see if it would ring again.

I remained across the room, noticing his fingers dance around the screen. His eyebrows furrowed, creating a deep gorge of skin between them.

What are you doing? I was growing impatient. 'Dan.' My stomach stirred subtly.

'Where were we?' he said, after an uncomfortable length of time. 'Come here.'

'Do you think we should get Kai now … before we get too carried away?' I said, my switch to paranoia deflating my arousal.

His eyes searched my face for confirmation. 'Dammit … really?'

I kissed him politely.

He peeled himself away, with an obvious reluctance, motioning for the door.

A mild giggle exited my lips.

'Laters!' he said, collecting his phone and key card, then performing a salute before exiting our hotel room. The lock clicked as it sealed heavily against the door frame. I couldn't help but feel a twinge of deep longing for him. Longing for our love to stay this way forever, but also longing to know why he left me with this ominous feeling of uncertainty.

I linked my phone up to the Bose speaker I'd just taken from my hand luggage and pressed shuffle on my Anthems playlist. A Prince song reverberated through the room. My long hair sprang by my shoulders as I lifted the grubby cotton shirt over my head, sweaty from a full day of travel. The beat pulsed through my skin, engulfing my bloodstream.

I headed to the shower, shampoo bottle in hand, singing cheerfully to 'Purple Rain'. My aching limbs craved respite and the warm droplets bounced off my curves, cleansing me from the day's grime.

My right hand massaged the side of my head, lathering my hair in slow motion whilst I mimed the lyrics, imagining the camera zooming in for a close-up.

My airtime was cut short by a knock at the door. I continued to rinse the suds from my head, assuming it must be Lindani being too impatient to use his key card. I went to apply conditioner when a second, more aggressive knock sounded.

Frustrated and irritable, I stepped from my cocoon of warmth, wincing at the cold from the tiled floor. I silently cursed whoever was trying to disturb my bliss.

Wrapping a white cotton towel around my breasts I made my way to the door, very aware of my nakedness, air conditioning erecting bumps on my skin. There were three hard knocks, rapid in succession.

I walked hesitantly to the peephole. Images from Stephen King movies flashed through my mind eye, but I tried my hardest to bat them away.

Everything's fine.

So why had that feeling of dread incubated in the pit of my stomach? I considered ignoring it. Whoever it was, they must know I was here. Did they know I'd be alone?

I peeped through the hole, only to be greeted with an image of room 253 directly opposite. Despite apprehension gripping my gut and twisting the fleshy mass into a string of nervous energy, I pressed down the handle.

For no other reason than curiosity and innate British politeness, I tugged the heavy fire door from the frame. My body hid behind the makeshift shield. A moment before I poked my head around the door, a voice called out, 'Mum, it's me.'

Relief restored my biology. A feeling followed immediately by confusion. When I saw the beige, pressed trouser leg in the corridor and a wide pearly smile, I began to feel silly for the melodrama that had played out in my head.

'Hi, darling. Did you have fun with everyone?'

I smiled gratefully at the receptionist.

'He did indeed, Mrs. Attah.'

Kai nodded in agreement.

'I apologise if we have disturbed you,' the receptionist said, referring to my loose wet hair and awkward stance behind the door. I shook my head dismissively, a slight pink blush heating my cheeks. 'It's just, my friend, the crèche is closing early today as one of our staff has taken ill. I assumed you'd be busy, so took it upon myself to escort him to you. Save you the trouble and all.'

'That's very kind, thank you. I've just asked my husband to collect him, so if you would be so kind as to let him know I have Kai, that would be great?'

'Of course,' he said, obligingly.

'I built a house for me and Ada, Mum,' Kai interrupted.

'Oh wow, that's great, sweetie. You could build a house for us too, when you're older,' I suggested as Kai slid into the room and climbed onto the double bed.

'Not a real one, Mum.' He giggled.

Where was Lindani?

'They took quite a shine to each other, Mrs. Attah. This one's going to be quite the heartbreaker,' the receptionist continued, confusing me for a split second.

'Oh yes, Ada? Please call me Lois. "Mrs." makes me sound so old! And if Kai grows up anything like his father, then I don't doubt it for a second,' I confirmed.

The receptionist flashed his handsome smile before turning to bid us good day. 'Sorry to ask again, but if you see my husband in the lobby, would you mind just telling him I have Kai?' I repeated.

'Sure thing. Enjoy your evening and keep an eye on this little Casanova,' he said, pointing to the six-year-old flaked out after his thirty minutes of intense play.

'Ba-bye.' Kai waved.

'What do you say, Kai?'

'Thank you.'

'My pleasure, lil' man,' the receptionist responded warmly.

I collected my favourite navy bed shorts and oversized white T-shirt from the hand luggage, in preparation for the ten-minute nap I was determined to take as soon as Lindani came back. I typed a quick text to him to update him of Kai's whereabouts.

I ruffled the dark curls on Kai's head as I passed. I treasured these days, before he became too tall for me to reach or too cool to be seen having hugs with his mum. He was hardly a mirror image of us, with his velvety complexion, buoyant curls, and deep hazel eyes. Even his aroma was his own. Sweet and smooth. He was my greatest accomplishment yet.

• • •

Awaking from the nap I barely remembered drifting into, I looked at the clock. 20:05. I'd been asleep for twenty minutes. I glanced down to see Kai tucked snugly in the space under my left armpit. I scanned the room sleepily. Lindani still hadn't come back.

Where the hell are you?

My body jerked upright quicker than I'd intended. I scrabbled on the bedside table for my phone, then pressed last dialled. A familiar voice rang out into the room.

'Hey, you've reached Lindani. I have caller ID so chances are I'm ignoring you. Just jokes, leave a message and I'll call you back. BEEP'

'Hi love, it's me. Just checking in to make sure you're okay. Kai's with me, so if you're down there panicking that you've lost our son, you're in the clear! Come back now so we can go out for food before it gets too late, love you.'

A mundane, ordinary message. The kind I would leave on any ordinary day. A day like when Lindani and Kai would walk to the corner shop and race back home. Kai always made it back first and insisted on mc calling his dad to brag about his win.

I was afraid the trembling of my arms would shake my son awake, so I clenched my muscles on the side he was strewn against and worked harder than ever to control the rapidity of my breath.

My stomach quivered with each failed attempt, and I glanced as perceptively as I could around the room for anything significant that he had left behind. His clothes were still there, bagged up and left by the door. He had taken his phone and key card. I choked back a lump in my throat. He should have answered, should have returned my call, should have come back to the room by now.

I need to do something. I thought about calling out his name at the top of my voice. Maybe he would come running back like a homing pigeon gone accidentally astray. *Stay calm, Lois, everything will be fine, he'll be back.* It was a mistruth I needed to feed myself, especially as memories of Dan's worries about coming here were beginning to surface.

I had to show my son I was in control of the situation and that nothing was wrong. Perhaps it wasn't. Perhaps I had misread the time difference or had become disorientated after taking my nap.

Concentrating really hard, I brought the digital clock close to my face.

Ten more minutes had passed. Ten painfully arduous minutes that may as well have been the entire holiday.

Aware of Kai's presence, I began to feel suffocated. Suffocated because I was unable to freak out the way my body was urging me to.

'Come on, sweetie, let's go get your dad.' I peeled his dozing body from the bed and sat him comfortably on my right hip. He slunk sleepily over my shoulder the entire way to reception.

• • •

'What do you mean you haven't seen him?' Panic further eroded my former nonchalance. 'We checked in less than an hour ago.'

The receptionist stared back at me blankly before tapping indiscriminately at his keyboard.

My toes slapped against the rubber of my sandals, causing a dull ache to splinter my calves. My fingers drummed impatiently against the desk. I shot Kai a concerned look. Attempted to counter it with a hopeful smile. But he'd already turned away.

'He came to collect our son from the crèche not long after,' I said. 'How could no one have seen him?' My voice reached a pitch the staff evidently weren't comfortable with.

'I'm very sorry, Mrs. Attah. We can send someone to help you look for your husband if you'd like? Could you give me a brief description?'

'A description?' I repeated. 'He was literally just here. We *just* checked in?'

What is going on, like seriously? I picked away the loose skin by my thumbnail before hovering over to the seating area and falling into the chair next to my son. My hand heated the bare skin of Kai's knee. He responded by raising my hand to his mouth. 'You've hurt yourself, Mum,' he said, referring to the spot of blood bubbling through the puncture by my thumbnail. He soothed it with a gentle kiss and told me how silly I was.

'Where's Dad? He knows how to make things better.'

I had no choice but to accept the hotel staff's offer of helping me look for him. But how would I do this without worrying Kai? A revelation hit me, though short-lived. Dan was a tall, strong, savvy man with the necessary street smarts to stay out of harm's way.

I considered the possibility of him having nipped to a shop to surprise us with something. Or maybe he'd arranged for his family to join us at the hotel and was helping them gather their belongings? Just maybe? Perhaps he knew Kai had been returned safely to the room and figured no harm would be caused by sneaking out for a minute or two.

I rose to my feet and picked up Kai, keeping him close. We were going to head back to the room and more than likely bump into Dan along the way. Everything would be fine, I concluded, hopefully.

Although there was no commotion to indicate foul play, the biology that rendered me human seemed to think otherwise.

Dan, where the hell are you? I mouthed softly over my son's shoulder. *Come back, I need you.*

6

'Take a seat, Mrs. Attah,' said the soft-spoken lady with the auburn-tinted hair.

I followed her invitation, pulling back the black plastic chair facing the investigating officer.

'Your husband has been missing for forty-eight hours now, is that correct?'

'That's right, yes.'

I detected the hint of a sympathetic smile. 'I can assure you we have done everything in our power to locate him.' The ageing male detective lifted his reflective sunglasses from his face and placed them on the desk beside the case file.

'You've done everything? It's been two days – how could you have possibly done everything?' I blurted, failing to repress my desperation.

'I'm afraid, thus far, we've been unable to ascertain Mr. Attah's whereabouts. We cannot fully rule out the possibility that he remained in the hotel at the time of the fire. If this was the case, it would be almost impossible to identify your husband due to the scale of the incident. Am I being clear?'

I nodded, secretly refusing to accept his insinuation. 'So, you can't even determine from camera footage whether he left the building or not. Is that what you're saying?'

'Unfortunately, the hotel surveillance system was undergoing repairs at the end of last week, which I'm afraid coincided with the date Mr. Attah went missing. We can only assume that your husband may have left the premises at or around the time the fire broke out. That's if he had managed to evade injury.'

'Okay.'

Questions loomed. They crashed violently against the very pores of my skin but never seemed to penetrate enough to allow the formation of words. My elbows drilled into the desk, face cradled into my palms.

'I understand you are going through a very difficult time, but please try to see the positive. If it's true that Mr. Attah left the hotel, then he may still be alive and well.'

'But that doesn't make any sense. If he managed to get out before the fire started, then why would he not come back to look for us? His son and I were still in there by ourselves. You'd think he would have made it to one of the fire points. He'd never not come to look for us.'

'I suspect only you have the answers to that question, Mrs. Attah.'

'What's that supposed to mean?' My hackles were rising. 'No. Something must have happened. Something unexpected, I don't know. Would he have even been allowed to come back in to look for us? That's where you guys come in, surely?'

The ageing detective ignored my outburst.

'Let's say your husband didn't leave of his own free will, or perhaps he did but intended on returning, we have to look at every eventuality under those circumstances.'

'Such as?'

'Mr. Attah's connections to South Africa. Family, friends, acquaintances, et cetera. Could there have been someone who intercepted his movements before Mr. Attah was physically able to reunite with you?'

My brows furrowed intensely as my brain dissected the possibility that any of those persons could have played an intentional role in my husband's disappearance. The room fell silent, save for the reverberation of my pulse upon the realisation that I didn't know any of them.

'Is there anyone who would want to harm your husband?'

'What, no … I don't think so, I mean, back home definitely not, but … no.' Silence filled the room once again. 'I think … I don't know, not really.'

The detective's eyeline shifted to his colleague and back towards me, noticing my obvious hesitancy.

'Who did you say you were planning to visit here in South Africa?'

'Umm, we were due to stay with some family of his, an aunt.'

'Can you be more specific?'

'I don't have all the details. Dan took care of all the planning this time.'

'Think carefully, did your husband mention names or addresses or give you any contact details for his family as a backup?'

'He didn't give me contact details, but his aunt's name is Alice Bekker. She lives in the Western Cape, Swellendam, I think. I might have her number somewhere, I don't know. You see, we've been in the hospital, me and my son, so I haven't been able to search our things for her details.'

The officer inscribed the name and location into his pad.

'Is Alice a blood relative, do you know?'

'I'm not sure, I would imagine she is, yes.'

'When were you planning to reach her?'

Frustration bubbled up inside me. There was such an influx of emotions, most of which I struggled to make sense of. Now there was some hope Lindani was alive, my sense of urgency was hard to pacify.

'We were just going to surprise her sometime in the next two weeks. We had already given Alice the dates, so she knew roughly when to expect us.'

'Which are?'

'Sorry?'

'The dates? What were the dates you gave her?'

'We landed on the fourth and were set to go home one week today, the eighteenth.'

'So, as I understand it, Mr. Attah's aunt was expecting you all? Yourself, your son, and your husband? Is that correct?'

'Yes, that's right.'

'And at some time between the fourth and eighteenth of January?'

'Yes. You don't think she knows something, do you?'

'We just need all the information to target anomalies that may become unearthed during our investigation.'

'How will we know if he definitely escaped the fire?' I asked, feeling a sense of inclusion that was out of my arena of duties.

'We have more interviews to conduct, and progressively we expect to receive more leads. These will hopefully shed some light on the situation … Now, what was Mr. Attah's general mood like before his disappearance?'

'He was cheerful, as he is most of the time. We were quite playful … I'm not sure what you were expecting, but he was just himself, more or less.'

'I realise how uncomfortable this may be for you, but it will help our investigations if you could shed some light of any minor detail that may have previously been overlooked.'

'Okay?'

Sensing my diffidence, he continued, 'Such as stressors, changes in behaviour. Had either of you received any news? Something that may have caused a shift in his mood?'

'Ah, sometimes he suffers from bouts of anxiety, at night mostly. He seems to have, I don't know what you'd call them … night terrors perhaps? Not frequent, but he did show signs on the journey over here.'

'He showed signs? Can you elaborate?'

'He was tense. Trying to sleep on the plane but struggled, so he paced around. He mumbled something I couldn't understand fully, but he does that when in-and-out of sleep.'

'Your husband is a Ugandan national, is that correct?'

'Yes.'

'What were these mumblings you overheard?'

'I have no idea. I didn't think too much of it if I'm honest, he was fine otherwise.'

I'd tried to limit my capacity to overthink situations. From when I was a little girl, I'd driven myself crazy trying to dissect every detail of a person's behaviour and body language. The tendency still seeped through at times. Old habits die hard. Knowing so little about his past was far less of a concern to me than having security in our future together.

The auburn-haired lady beside the ageing detective interrupted his questioning to offer me a glass of water. I declined.

'There is nothing else? Anything out of the ordinary? No unexpected calls, emails, social media posts, inbox messages? Had Mr. Attah had contact with anyone besides the person you've mentioned? Anyone over here who knew of your arrival?'

'No, I don't th— actually yes, we were in our room. Kai, our son, was still downstairs and Dan missed a call from a private number.'

'Can you remember what time the call was?'

'I'm not sure.'

'Just a rough guess?' he pressed.

'Evening. I remember now, he commented on the colour of the sky, so it must have been around seven-thirty or eightish?' The detective wrote something down. 'I wouldn't know about the other things, really. I don't have access to his private emails or social media accounts.'

I felt uneasy saying the words aloud, kicking myself at my choice of words. Who doesn't have access to their husband's messages?

'Everything okay?' asked the lady with the auburn hair. I crossed and uncrossed my knees before eventually sliding the tip of my behind to the very edge of the plastic chair. The officer's breath was a tepid mint. It served to mask the unmistakeable whiff of judgement that failed to elude me.

The overt scrutiny of my marriage shot my already high discomfort levels through the roof.

I answered as if it was intended as a rhetorical question, inside reeling at the glaring mistakes I had made by distancing myself from his private affairs. I searched the box room for something obvious to focus on.

'Not access … I mean, I've never asked for passwords or anything like that.'

An imperceptible tilt of the eyebrows confirmed my paranoia.

'You say you've overheard some of these number-withheld calls in the past?'

'Yes.'

'Can you recall who it was your husband was speaking to?'

'No one specifically. I mean he gets calls from other YouTubers sometimes and I do know he keeps in touch with a few people from his old job.'

'What kind of employment is he in?'

'He has his own cooking show on YouTube. He's had it for a few years now and has quite a large following. African/English fusion food.'

'I see.'

Assuming something felt very different to knowing who contacts your husband on his private number. Having been asked the question directly, I realised I didn't know who he contacted or who contacted him, not really. Everything just seemed to be in order. As it should be. I'd worked so hard to blindly trust my husband. I suddenly began to fear I'd made a terrible mistake.

'These online followers, have any of them exhibited odd behaviour?'

'Umm ... We've read comments together in the past, but I haven't noticed anything particularly unusual. Some have in-boxed him. Some messaged more than others but that's all really, nothing untoward.'

I lied. I had no idea if any of his followers had private messaged him or stalked him on his other accounts. In fact, it had been a while since we'd sat down together and read the comments. The novelty had worn off for me, especially when I started to grow tired from my increased hours at work.

Instantly, I felt a fraud. My desire to appear mindful of my husband's online goings-on was too strong. It wasn't a big deal, surely?

'Okay, we'll have our guys pull up Mr. Attah's accounts and take things from there. Thank you for your time, Mrs. Attah. We will be in contact as soon as we hear anything.'

I smiled a genuine smile, pleased the questioning was drawing to a close. Now I could focus on searching for my husband.

• • •

I latched on to Kai's hand in the waiting room and we walked the two blocks to our new temporary accommodation.

It was a step above squalid but a few beneath the room which, as fate would have it, had burned to the ground.

Back at the hotel, the fire alarm had sounded not too long after Kai and I returned to our room. It was a short-lived moment of repose I allowed myself, under the delusion that Lindani would walk through the door any moment and restore everything back to the way it was. The fire, however, had other plans for us.

We stood before the entrance of our new home, my fingers hesitating to contact the metallic door handle. Instead, I folded my knuckles and pressed them lightly against the glass of the door. 'It isn't hot, is it, Mum?' asked Kai. I paused to look down at him, absorbing the sucker punch to my chest. 'No, sweetie. It's a different building, isn't it? So we'll be fine, won't we?' I assured, unclenching my fists and reaching for the handle to demonstrate my point.

I batted away the flashes of memory as if they were a swarm of moisture-seeking flies in the Australian outback. Persistent and confusing. The heat of the fire, the calls of distress from my little boy, cries to return back home, cries for his lost father. The covert slither of chemical irritants that snaked under the door into our hotel room. That first sign to alert me to the danger that had befallen us. Realisation hit. My husband could have been trapped within the inferno from which my son and I had escaped.

'How are you feeling, my love?' I said solicitously, releasing Kai's hand into the room we had been allocated. 'I miss my dad,' he said, with cutting honesty. His eyeballs sank behind a salty moana as soon as the words exited his lips, triggered by his own flashes of memory.

My mind struggled to assemble an appropriate collection of comforting words. 'I miss him too, darling,' were the only ones that managed to gather momentum. It was a raw admission that I had so desperately wanted to offer since the moment I suspected Lindani wasn't coming back to us. It was at some point amidst my jumble of thoughts that I found Kai and I stood entangled by the door, bonded by a shared grief and an expended sea of tears.

An undetermined number of minutes passed before Kai flopped onto one of the twin beds, seemingly undeterred by the dated surroundings and partially cleaned furnishings. Undeterred by anything that wasn't as cataclysmic as the loss of his dad. It was all I could do to distract us both from his potential regression into reticence; focus on anything that summoned dissociated thoughts, thoughts unlinked to our new devastating reality.

'The sheets are surprisingly clean!' The maid had chosen wisely from her list of priorities and time restraints, I figured. 'Don't you think, son?' I said, in my lame pursuit of normality.

The nicked and stained cream carpet housed shoeprints, etching their existence into the very fabric of the present. Dark orange cloth hung from the curtain rails, specks of dust furring the cheap metal. All details that failed to irk me. Hotel rooms, no matter how shabby, always aired current news broadcasts, didn't they? That was my only requirement as things stood.

I sat beside my son on his bed, staring into the evident dejection I knew we both shared. 'You know you can talk to me about anything, don't you, sweetie?' Did I see an ever so slight nod of his head? 'You know, we don't always have the answers to things that happen to us. A lot of things don't make any sense, the good *and* the bad.'

'Where's my dad? Where did he go?'

I swallowed another fetid mass of despair then asked him to face me.

'See, that's one of these things I told you about. We don't know where your dad is. But I'm sure wherever he is, he's missing you like crazy and trying his best to get back to us. That I *do* know.' I detected a subtle sideways movement of his caramel curls. He didn't believe me. 'In the meantime, though, we're going to just have each other, okay?' I said, simultaneously relieved and pained that I knew a little of what he was thinking.

'But he said he would be with me, every day forever, best buddies, that's what he said!'

'You still are best buddies, darlin'. You always will be.'

'Then why isn't he here? Why did he lie to me?' he squealed, sounding like a child half his age.

As much as I tried to hold back, tears traced my cheeks, and only when my breath sucked the salty droplets into my mouth did I gain enough composure to speak.

'Oh, I don't think it's as simple as that, Kai,' I confided, pulling him into my waist. 'Your dad wouldn't lie to you. He loves you more than anything in the world. You do know that, don't you?' I searched his young, troubled face for signs of agreement but found them difficult to identify in his sunken body posture.

'What do you say we play a couple of games, take our mind off things, hey? That'll be fun, won't it?' I suggested as cheerfully as the pain between my ears would allow.

He moved over to the other bed and glanced at me. His face emitted the smallest flicker of light, or perhaps I was hallucinating. 'We'll make up a story and act it out together, like we do at home! Once upon a time …'

I awaited his rehearsed response (that's a girl's story and I'm not a girl!). But I was met only with silence, so I recited another line as if he'd responded the way I remembered. 'Okay, let me think …' I began, already feeling regretful of my fruitless suggestion. 'In a faraway land, there lived a village of trolls …' Again, silence. And if anything, Kai had sunk further into the patterned bedsheets.

I sat on the twin bed adjacent to him, possessing no power to heal his heart. I stared at the smooth, round contours of his skin, the tight ringlets that spiralled from his head and wondered what lies he would tell himself in order to drift into a peaceful sleep.

Eventually, fatigue asphyxiated Kai's ability to stay awake, so I gave in to my need to know more of what happened at the hotel.

The red rubber circle on the TV handset invited me to press it, despite my fear. The screen lit slowly, integrating some life into the otherwise drab, inky dullness of the room.

Flames burned into my glassy pupils. I hurriedly pressed down the volume in case Kai was to pick up any of what was said.

Perched on the very edge of my twin bed, I listened as intently as the blood rushing through my ears would allow, pushing away historic motion pictures of my son's newborn body clutched into my chest, his parents' pupils black and wide with sheer adoration in spite of the uncontrollable leaking of tears. 'After this, we have to keep him alive on our own!' said Dan before he sliced through Kai's umbilical cord. *Please say you're okay, Dan. We need you.*

I hadn't realised I was crying. The screen replaced my mental imagery with a painful strike to my gut, one which brought me firmly back into the present.

It was the venue at which our family had been torn apart.

I searched through the gentleman holding a colourful CNBC Africa microphone, as if he was a mere voice-over. It turned out to be the live news feed that merely served to convince me I hadn't been dreaming. Our hotel had in fact been set ablaze, along with our family.

I was desperate to offload the news to another adult, and one who cared about us enough to offer some form of comfort. I needed their clarity and logic, whilst my supplies were lacking, and to report to someone what CNBC News Africa expected me to believe to be true – that something as menial as an electrical fault had the power to destroy buildings, take people's lives and make others vanish entirely.

Suddenly struck by the desire to resume the life we'd had before South Africa, I returned the multiple calls I'd missed over the last two days.

'Mila? Are you there, can you hear me?'

7

THEN

'Darling, can you fetch your mum's juice from the table please?'

I did as I was asked, wincing internally at Dad's sickly-sweet tone, the falseness of which implanted an emotion in me I couldn't immediately describe.

It was Dad who had introduced me to magic. Not the tricky kind – that was for boys, he said. No, the kind that made animals talk and rule over humans. The kind that made genies and fairy-godmothers grant wishes. I used to believe it was true. That if you really needed help or really wanted something all you had to do was wish for it. It only worked for kind people though.

Magic isn't for me any more, I thought, at least I don't think it is. I'm not sure. It's just … well it hasn't worked yet. I've been as kind as I could too. I'm trying. I love Dad, it's just … hard to show it right now.

• • •

It was a Wednesday.

'We're going to be late if you don't hurry, Lois. Mrs. Mandel won't be best pleased if you show up late.' He tried another tack. 'You can't stay in the school toilet forever. What's really the matter?'

I listened to Dad call me for the third time but still I sat on the lid of the seat, insisting I wasn't well enough to go to swim class.

His voice grew louder, more insistent. As if he wanted me to go even though I was sick. Of course, I felt fine but I knew Mum couldn't swim because of her sickness, so it was the only way I knew how to get out of going.

'Come out right now, the teachers want to go home, you're embarrassing yourself,' he called from the other side of the door. I heard him apologising to one of them.

'I'm still sick,' I said, flushing the chain to convince them further of my affliction. I wanted to go straight home to see Mum, but it didn't seem enough to just ask for Dad to take me home. He had planned to meet that woman again, I just knew it.

'Darlin' if you don't feel well then surely you would rather be in your bed at home than here, wouldn't you?'

'I'm not going swimming.'

'Let's go then, Lois. Now!'

I stared at the back of the cubicle door, knowing I was about to hand myself over to his fate. It was my only choice because I sure as heck didn't want to sit on that cold, stinky seat all night and become the talk of the entire school the next day. This new worry – that I would be teased by the other kids for the rest of my school life – made me open the door.

'You look fine,' Dad said, reminding me that I actually didn't look sick at all. My eyes weren't red and watery, and my face was no paler than it always had been.

'I want to go home.'

• • •

Months had passed since my last swim class, but I was still trying to get my head around things. It had been tough with everything that had been going on at home.

'Thank you, honey,' he uttered as I handed over the carton of enhanced vitamins.

'Morning, Mum,' I whispered, as if speaking to an old person whose hearing aid was up too high.

She didn't answer.

I planted my best kiss on the side of her cheek.

I remember how it used to be. Mum would point to her left cheek, her right cheek, her forehead, then her lips, showing me where to kiss. I'd copy her and she would kiss me back before lifting me up in the air and spinning me around, both of us locked in a tight bear hug. A tear traced down my face, falling slowly by the left side of my smile.

I thought I saw her eyelids flicker and my heart skipped with a hope that lit my eyes.

Holding Mum's hand snugly, I counted the fingers on her hand like you would a newborn baby. My head rested on her stomach in a rare moment of nostalgia.

Dad sat silently on the wicker chair by my side, stroking my back as I visibly sucked in the sweet, summery scent of her.

It was odd to enjoy that moment, but I did. It had been a long time since we'd all embraced. Had all been connected and present together with no distractions. It was a special moment, only in that we were able to share it together.

A couple of years before we knew Mum was sick, we went to Magic Kingdom. Mum, Dad and me. They were convinced I'd have a better time if someone my own age came along, so we asked my cousin Beth. Secretly, I was pleased when she couldn't make it. I had been looking forward to spending time as a family.

I'd been on rides before, even the odd roller coaster, but never the ones with the big loops. How did you not fall out?

All I remember is us standing in the queue for Thunder Mountain, forming the shape of a human triangle. I kept hearing whispers of it going upside down. Mum and Dad swore to me they were talking about a different ride.

I informed my parents of my most recent observation. 'Mum, there's a loop, look.' I searched their faces in turn, waiting for an explanation.

'That's another ride. Don't worry, this one has no loops does it, Em?' said Dad.

'No, it's for that one over there, can you see all those people queuing?' Mum said, pointing too far off in the distance for me to be able to see, even if I stood on my tippy toes.

I took a confident stride closer towards the person in front. 'You promise?' It was an opportunity for them to subdue my fear.

'Promise,' said Dad. Mum smiled in agreement and cupped both her hands over my shoulders. My excitement flowed freely, as we grew closer to the end of the line.

They lied.

It did go upside down and that loop I saw did belong to Thunder Mountain.

As luck would have it, it was the most fun I'd ever had on a ride, so I asked to go around again and again.

See, sometimes trickery can be good. Just sometimes. Not the kind that Dad practised though. Maybe he knew Mum was sick, so found someone who wasn't? My flesh ached at the thought.

There was a knock at the door then. A polite one which signalled the nurses had arrived.

Dad asked me to go let them in. He was probably tired from the run he said he went on earlier.

I didn't answer with words, but I knew there was little use in not doing as he asked. He always got his way.

Two nurses entered Mum's bedroom. Dad's room was the marital one still, whereas Mum had moved into the back room to accommodate her hospital equipment.

'How's she doing?' asked the younger of the two nurses.

The fact that the question was asked gave me hope. I mean, she wouldn't ask if she thought there was no chance, right? Would she?

'Well, just the same as yesterday. She's still unresponsive.' Dad took on the role of concerned husband, even though *I* knew he wasn't.

'Has she managed to drink any Fortisip?' she asked, expecting him to have noticed.

'Very little I'm afraid. I don't know how to get it down her. She just isn't interested, maybe if I …'

The nurse with the bobbed grey hair replied. 'Not to worry, Mr. Hudson, if you just keep pushing fluids, we'll make sure she's comfortable and pain-free.'

Don't worry! There was everything to worry about. In fact, there was nothing worth worrying about more. How could she say that so casually? And how could Dad just accept it?

My fingernail nicked on the fabric as I pulled at Dad's T-shirt. 'Why aren't you helping her? Are you just gonna let her stay sick? Are you?' I cried, loud enough for everyone in the house to hear.

He went to pick me up, holding out his hands like that's all it would take for me to forgive him.

'I'd make her better if I could, Lois, in a heartbeat. Of course I would! Come here, darling.'

I found myself staring at Mum's lemon-coloured pyjamas again. A habit I'd developed recently. The weak rise and fall of her diaphragm comforted me and broke me, respectively.

'Your wife is a strong lady, she's hanging in there,' the nurse said, with an uncertain smile. She'd taken Mum's vitals a moment earlier. Whatever that meant.

The hands of the clock protruded from the glass casing, ticking loudly over the silence. It was an oppressive, definitive noise. As if the numbers formed smudges of other-worldly portholes.

'If it's okay, Kerry and I will prepare Mrs. Hudson to be washed and changed now. I'll give you a call when we've finished,' the older nurse suggested.

Dad nodded, then grabbed my shoulders as he always did to lead me out of a room. I shuddered slightly at his touch.

We stood awkwardly in the hallway, stock-still and silent. One of the nurses called us back, just a moment before the door closed behind us, yet it felt like we'd been waiting for hours.

'I'm afraid she seems to be losing a bit of strength. It might be better if you waited with her.'

Now? It's happening now?

I recognised the nurse's sympathetic countenance. The younger one nodded almost imperceptibly.

I'm not stupid, I could read between the lines.

I looked to Dad in the hope his expression would reassure me. He appeared visibly distressed and it was the first time I'd seen tears spout from his eyes. It didn't make sense, how he could care enough to cry but not enough to be a good husband?

'Lois,' he began, kneeling on the carpet beside me. 'Remember when we had that talk back at the hospital, that first time the nurses told us how poorly your mum would become? Do you remember?' Somehow I had left his side and found myself leant with my back against the bedroom door. 'That time,' he continued, 'remember, when Mummy would join your nanny and grandad in heaven … that time is now, sweetie.'

I felt him stare through me, but all I could do was stare at Mum, begging her to be the one looking back at me instead. 'We prepared for this didn't we, Lois?'

A moment slipped by. It was barely detectable, yet long enough for the last drop of life to escape the person I loved most in the entire world. I swear I'd only looked away for a second.

Something formed in my throat. As if whatever was being pumped around my body had gathered into a blockage.

I fastened my ear to the door almost immediately after I ran from the room. The sombre tone of the conversation between Dad and the nurses radiated through the wood. If I didn't see her chest stop rising or her eyelids stop twitching, then I could fool myself into believing she was still here.

White noise sprayed incoherently through my head, causing me to miss some of their exchange. I'd seen and heard too much already, so why were my feet rooted to the carpet? I wanted Mum to be the topic of conversation, while she was still with me. But I just couldn't be by her side, staring at the shell of her.

I waited there still. My ear pressed against the door, waiting. For what, I wasn't sure.

The nurse apologised to my dad, from what I could decipher. They'd let her die.

The maggots sprung to life then, devouring my organs slowly, as if they'd waited for confirmation to begin their feast. They took root in the muscle mass that pumped life-juice around my veins, destabilising its rhythm.

An icy wind claimed my attention. It swept through the hallway, taking with it the distant cluster of voices along with the current of energy I'd always known to have lived in this house. The power source to my life had been turned off, it seemed at the mains. The shift could be felt, inhaled. She was gone. And now it would just be us, me and him, forever.

The walls stretched into a tunnel with no visible end. I watched as Dad headed to the bathroom and locked the door behind him. His phone shook in his hand. I slid out of the way quickly and sat on the staircase, not knowing how to feel or how to react. Feeling certain only that it was too soon for an encounter with Dad.

I needed safety, familiarity. Two human necessities inextricably linked.

'That's it … it's over,' I heard him say.

'I'm okay yeah, I think … it's just strange … I dunno, I can't explain, it just hasn't sunk in yet.' I moved closer to the door, eavesdropping gradually becoming my default pastime. '… thanks, I'll be fine, I mean we were preparing for this, so it wasn't a shock.'

I could only make out Dad's side of the conversation. I hoped he would be informing some close friends or family, those who'd visited last weekend perhaps? But an unmistakeable shot of rage filtered into the pain of my loss. Could he be speaking to *her*? I dreaded hearing the words out loud. The words that would not only confirm that Mum was dead, but that Dad had replaced her already.

'Well, the nurses are still here but they've called the undertaker or whoever it is that takes dead bodies away … shit it feels weird saying that.' His voice possessed a bitter twang.

I imagined Dad was rubbing his temple like he did every time I saw him say the 'S' word.

'What? No, I haven't changed my mind. Look, I can't talk to you right now, I need to go check Lois is okay and just focus on her, she's my priority.'

I detected a lull of silence.

'Oh my god, are we seriously having this conversation? Nothing's changed. Everything's in place. I just need to speak to Lois, be with her for a while. I'll call you tomorrow.' He paused as the other person said something. 'It's okay, but shit, Hannah, be more sensitive will you? This isn't about you.' Another pause. 'Yeah yeah, you too … bye.'

Fury rose inside me as realisation hit hard. I didn't know I had the energy. The pain of the entire situation was so intense that I thought I might drop dead on the spot. My mind conjured pictures of how I imagined heaven to look. From what I'd heard, heaven was far nicer than it was here. Especially now Mum was there.

The bathroom door must have unlocked silently, or perhaps my attention was elsewhere. Either way as I peered upwards mechanically, there were two familiar green eyes staring back at me.

'Lois?'

So, this was how it felt to hate someone.

It surprised me how so many years of unconditional love and admiration for someone could be erased in a single moment.

The disgust. The hurt. The disappointment. The very blend of emotions that lead to hate.

'I was just about to come and look for you, darlin'.'

My eyes bored into his. I felt it to be important that he knew I knew. That he knew I hated him. An urge to vomit broke our stand-off even though the desire to stay put was strong.

I ran downstairs, sealing my mouth, in fear I would vomit all over him. There was no question that's what he deserved, but it would be worse to show frailty. To be on the end of any meek attempt of his comfort.

An explosion of sorts erupted from my mouth, from my eyes and nose too. The kitchen sink really had seen better days. As had the plates that waited their turn to be washed.

I didn't see anything, but in the distance, I heard him tell the nurses he would check I was okay. It was then that my anger manifested into a piercing scream.

I needed Mum.

I didn't recognise the woman as I charged past her on my way to the staircase. Hauling my sagging limbs up the steps, I burst blindly through the dark mist that had presented itself as soon as Mum passed. The door felt weightier, as if ten men were pushing against it from the other side.

'Mum,' I cried out, until there was an opening big enough for me to enter. 'Mum, I need you. Please don't go. Please don't leave me!'

I made eye contact with no one as I pushed as forcefully as my young body would allow, past those that blocked Mum's body from view. 'Mum, where are you?' I yelled, panic further poisoning my bloodstream.

I couldn't see her lemon nightdress. Nor could I detect her soft, veiny fingers that always waited, uncovered, at the edge of her bedsheet – the hand I always cupped within my own every day before and after school, the one she asked to smooth over my cheeks so that she could savour the memory of my face. She was gone, all of her.

I packed my limbs tightly until I lay in a foetal position. Remnants of vomit and snot lolled shamelessly by the holes from which they had leaked. I felt no shame.

Someone tugged at my arm, but I snapped it back defiantly.

Alien footfalls accompanied the echoes of male voices in my immediate surroundings. People sprinkled the house. Strangers. They'd replaced her, physically at least. Not only did they violate our home, but they'd removed her from it entirely … forever.

The dark-wooden grandfather clock chimed it's pointless, belligerent peal. How did it still function when the world had come to a standstill?

I ran from the house and flung my arms around her, having followed the procession of thieves that insisted on taking her away. I clung tightly to the thick plastic that encased Mum's shell. A deep guttural howl emanated from an unidentified part of my body.

'Lois,' called an indistinct voice. 'Sshhhh, come on, it's okay.'

I felt my grip loosen when two giant hands pulled my waist backwards towards the door. I'd lost contact. My limbs waved frantically as I fought to get back to Mum.

'We have to let her go, sweetheart,' said Dad between shallow sobs.

'No no no no no,' I chanted, staring off into the distance, sinking my face into Dad's chest.

Mum was right there, just a metre away, yet we may as well have been galaxies apart.

I unstuck my damp cheeks from the cotton of his T-shirt and scanned the same street that had housed our family my entire life.

Amongst the haze I noticed a woman with crimson hair peering down at us from the window above the corner shop across the street. Other people hid in the shadows. Unlike those familiar faces however, the lady with the red hair motioned an unusual gesture. Aiming it directly towards us. I watched through the reflective glass on the front door.

She trailed her finger across her chest in the shape of an X then held her palm flat between her breasts.

I felt pressure against my back as I stayed slumped over Dad's neck. His palm rested against me unnecessarily. I looked at his face to find what I already knew. He was responding to her signal.

8

Returning the missed call from Lois, Mila did a quick tidy of the car interior until the line connected.

'Lois, sorry I missed your call, what's going on?'

'Mila, he's still alive.'

'What? Are you serious?'

She let the words resonate for a minute. Lindani hadn't died in the fire, everything would be fine, back to normal.

Muffled sobs escaped down the line.

Mila looked towards the heavens, sharing a moment of relief.

'Lois?' It was spoken with a delicacy not usually associated with Mila.

'Well, they think he is at least. He'd left the hotel before the fire.'

Mila's ears pricked forward like a hungry dog being offered a treat.

'Okay ... so where is he now?'

'I don't know. I need to find him, I've been calling his phone constantly, but it keeps going to voicemail and I've emailed and in-boxed him by every means I can think of but ... nothing.'

'It's okay, everything will be all right.' She experienced a tug of guilt at hearing her friend's distress, not having given much thought previously to how Lindani's disappearance would affect her. She would be there for Lois now just as she was a few months ago.

'If he's lost his phone or left it then I guess he'd have to be at a computer. Are there any where you're staying?' she suggested, attempting to keep up her friend's spirit.

'Of course there is, everywhere. I'm really scared something terrible has happened? He could call from someone's phone or a hotel or shop, couldn't he?'

'Perhaps he doesn't know your number by heart?'

'No that can't be it, he's always kept it in his wallet in case of emergencies. Oh no, you don't think … could he have planned for this to happen?'

'Hmm.'

'Oh my god, Mila, it's bad, isn't it? I can feel it.'

'Not necessarily. Look, just take deep breaths and think why he would have been outside of the hotel at the time of the fire. Did you send him out for anything? To call anyone or for any other reason? And why the hell would he plan something like this?'

'I didn't think of that. Maybe he went out for a smoke, he does occasionally. But then what? I'm going crazy, no one seems to know anything.'

He smokes? thought Mila, in passing. 'How's Kai holding up?'

'He hasn't said much, he's just brooding and quiet. My heart breaks for him. I swear I have no idea what to tell him.'

'Is he with you now?'

'He's in the other room, we're in an apartment near the police station. Honestly, I don't know who I can trust. The hotel staff were suspiciously unhelpful when I told them Dan had gone.' There was a pause on the line. 'Do you think Kai knows anything? He spent a lot of time with his dad, perhaps he kno—? No, I don't know what to think. I just know I don't want Kai to think I'm blaming him for anything. Jesus, it's such a mess, I don't know what to do.'

'Lois, you've got this okay. You'll both get through it. Whatever has happened, everything will work out in the end, I promise.'

'You know his Aunt Alice don't you? Do you have her address and phone number?'

'Aunt Alice? Yeah yeah, I will have it somewhere, I'm sure. Give me a bit of time and I'll dig out her details and send them to you ASAP.'

Mila had cast some transient thought over why Lois referred to Alice as Lindani's Aunt. The first time her name was mentioned, she'd thought she had misheard but sure enough there it was again. There wasn't much her ex-husband had shared with his new wife, it appeared. How was Lindani going to explain that away when Lois and Alice met? Perhaps he'd intended to reveal everything to Lois after all, when they reached their destination? All the dysfunction, the trauma, the severed ties?

'Perfect, please hurry, I don't have a lot of time if I want to get him back. You know him as much as I do Mila, I need your help.'

Mila paused to think. It was an honest assumption. But Lois in no way knew her husband the way Mila had, she thought, applying a thin layer of strawberry lip-balm to her top lip then the bottom lip, before glancing briefly into the rear-view mirror. She was worried that the revelations about Lindani's life, if revealed, would destroy Lois. Mila had witnessed first-hand how Lois had suffered a breakdown because of the death of her mother, so many years after the event. Her mind traced back to how fragile Lois had seemed, curled into the cushions of her velvet sofa, draped beneath an oversized chenille throw with only the crown of her head poking through. Her demeanour saddened at the image of little Lois, with no mum and no friends, only a cheating dad who had left her with a crippling fear of abandonment. Mila stared back at the mirror more deeply this time, contemplating the woman gazing back at her.

'Soldier through until I get there, okay.'

She was grateful to end the conversation with Lois. If only to stop the prickly electrical currents seeping into her cheek from the mosaic of cracks on her phone screen. Hearing Lois distraught and at a complete loss inspired her to intervene, even if at that moment she was unsure how.

She dropped her keys into her mustard shoulder bag as she considered the dated paintwork flaking from the brick under her bay window. She made another mental note to get it stripped, then proceeded to the front door.

She steadied herself on the thick wooden step – the step she'd once thought was so quaint and American-like, until the English weather rendered it a slip hazard.

Upon entering her home, she scooped the letters from behind the door and walked into the kitchen. Mila poured a generous tipple of vodka into a glass, satiating herself as she sifted through the modest stack of mail. She mused over a small, padded brown envelope.

Her immediate feelings were of anticipation. The envelope was plain. No stamp, no return address, and no names or identification marks. She wasn't sure how it had been delivered to her, but she had an inkling of what it was. Taking a seat on the cream faux leather stool that dressed her kitchen island, she tore open the seal and peered into the opening.

• • •

Mila's office was modelled on décor she'd admired in classic movies. Her four-drawer mahogany desk stood impressively on the far side of the room without so much as a pen holder on display. Everything tucked away neatly, out of sight, achieving the perfect balance of traditional and modern. The glossy dark wood, polished to within an inch of its life, revealed no signs of activity, despite its antique history.

Sliding into the thick, heavy office chair, she powered on her laptop, clicked on compose and began to type an email.

I know it's been a long time, but I heard the news. I'm not sure if anyone knows you're okay but please give me some sign you're safe.
M.

She had to get to Lois. Her friend needed her.

Opening a new window on her laptop, she pulled up flights to South Africa. She clicked on a BA flight from London to Cape Town, completed the purchase and hopped from the screen. Attempting to subdue an impending feeling of urgency, she removed the mobile phone from the brown padded envelope and slid it into her pocket. A ping sounded from her bag, announcing a new message.

FROM: *Lois*
I know you're busy but would you mind checking for any signs of Dan at the house. Know it sounds stupid but just in case. Lv L xx

FROM: *Mila*
Sure. Key? Xxxxx

FROM: *Lois*
There's one in the back garden in a plastic bag in the BBQ under some coal. Thanks as always. L xx

FROM: *Mila*
Keep in touch. He must be somewhere, we'll get to the bottom of it. xxx

Mila switched her laptop to standby and left her office. She began to throw clothes from her wardrobe into the suitcase she kept under the bed, and ran a mental list in her head of everything that was needed. Passport, toiletries, underwear, clothes, shoes, phone, charger, pen and notepad, money and – lifting the cardboard back from the frame she removed the photograph from the glass – picture of Lindani.

It was a good job she'd kept one, thought Mila. She hoped Lois didn't think it was strange to still have a photograph of him. It was a picture that harboured her fondest memory of their early days together. She drew the shiny image closer to her face, smiling at Lindani's bewildered but joyous expression as he stood before the kitchen worktop, a rubber mixing spoon in hand, his nose dusted with a fingerprint of icing sugar. It was a clear (barring the sugar print), forward-facing shot that could also be used to identify him with. After their momentous break-up, Mila had held on to the photo, torturing herself on many a lonely night, infuriated by how he had let her get away after all the love and patience she had shown him.

Lifting out an old, dusty Rolodex from the bottom of a box, she flicked through to A and snapped a picture of the contact card before pinging it to Lois.

The wheels of the suitcase shuddered down the staircase, chipping fragments of painted plaster onto the carpeted stairwell. Mila often wished she had a man in her life, if only to assist with the logistical demands that she so strongly begrudged participating in.

The next task, however, Mila was content in undertaking alone. Everything packed and in place, she embarked on her drive to the Attah house.

9

I checked the address for the third time, hoping I'd missed some subtle detail. Holding up the text from Mila, I compared it with the road sign and door number. They matched. There was still no answer, even after knocking harder. I had rehearsed my speech on the drive over, hoping that when Alice answered the door, I would deliver a first impression that defied the crazy I was actually feeling. Here's what I'd do; introduce myself as Lindani's wife and ask to come inside on account of having important news. The way she responded would be an indication of her involvement, if any.

The landline number offered no means of communication, having been met with a dead tone each time I'd dialled. *Shit!*

'Hello?' I hoped to attract attention from anyone inside the house.

I noticed Kai cover his ears to drown out the noise so instead I poked my head through the front window. Ordinarily I wouldn't think to try the door handle without an invitation, but times were far from ordinary. Having assumed responsibility to stay alive for the sake of my child, I'd drawn a line against breaking and entering a stranger's home in the unlikely, but not unheard-of event I was met with an angry, gun-toting psychopath on the other side.

'Where are we? Who lives here, Mum?' A faint interrogation came from the back seat of the car.

'Kai darling, Mum will be back in a minute, I'm looking for your dad's Aunt Alice.'

'Where is he, where's Dad? He wouldn't leave us for another family!

He wouldn't!' cried Kai from the car window.

'Kai, darlin',' I began, poking my entire upper body through the open window towards him. 'Where did you hear that, sweetie, why would you think that?' I said, cursing myself for not having been more consoling.

'You!' he declared. 'I heard you say it, Mum. Dad is with someone else.'

I was mortified and all indications that reflected as much instantly appeared in the creases of my face.

'*I* don't know if that's true son, why would I say that?' *And the best mum award goes to ... someone who wouldn't accuse their son of being a liar!*

'I'm sorry you had to hear that, but the truth is, Mum doesn't know either, not really. That's why we're here, darlin'. To try and find out.' I dragged my weight from the car interior, not entirely sure he believed me.

I stood beside Alice's front gate, growing more and more confused from everything I thought I knew to be true. I swallowed a deep breath and turned to face Alice's house.

It was pretty and quaint, the house. It bore two large square windows, crossed in the middle by the wooden frame to form four smaller squares, bordered by a thick strip of fresh white. The soft green colour of the exterior intensified the fauna that surrounded it.

The neighbourhood was quiet, as rural as it was industrialised. It had a beautiful, calming feel to it with curved roads and a delicate selection of restaurants, decorated by fairy lights and olive bushes. It felt inviting and, dare I say, safe.

Further utterances emanated from the car. 'I want to go home now. Can we go home, Mum?'

The idea of turning the car around and driving all the way back to Cape Town was as disheartening as it was exhausting, especially returning without answers. How did I not even consider where we would stay if no one was home or if Kai and I weren't welcome?

'You want to go back to England, sweetheart? Is that what you meant?' I asked with a delicate edge to my tone, crouching slightly to align myself with Kai's window.

'Not without Daddy,' he said, a physical pain showing through the whites of his eyes.

I packed myself back into the car and stared at Alice's front door, willing it to open. I was becoming obsessed with the idea of meeting her. Even more now that she was my only link, aside from Kai, with my AWOL husband. I should have waited for Mila to arrive before searching for answers myself.

'Okay my love, what now?' I asked rhetorically.

He sat in the passenger seat, idly scratching his hand with his opposing thumb. If there was a word more powerful than heartbreak, I'd use it to describe the feeling I had, watching my son disappear before my eyes. His consistently vacant expression told me he wasn't coping with what had happened to us as a family. I turned back to face him.

'I know it's tough, but is there anything you want to get off your chest? Perhaps you could help Mummy know what to do?'

He appeared silenced by his demons as he struggled to fathom our new life. The life that had been thrust upon him through no fault of his own. Who knew what was on his mind, or how deeply this was affecting him?

'Talk to me, Kai,' I said, spilling my thoughts verbally.

I couldn't shake the feeling that Dan might have told him something inadvertently. Something that might shed light on what was happening. There was no way I would believe my husband had planned to abandon his wife and son. He had been hesitant to let us tag along and I'd put so much work into persuading him it would be okay. And now look.

An upsurge of pain flooded me. I had failed my only son. The one to whom I'd promised the most comfortable, happy, harm-free life. The child I loved beyond imagination. I'd already failed him.

'We need to find Grandad. He'll know where Dad is!'

Dry air slid through the crack in the window.

I didn't know how to take it. *My dad? What could he do?* My mind whirled with missing pieces that I hoped would naturally crash together and make some sense. How could my son think my estranged father would be able to help find my missing husband in Africa?

'How would Grandad help?' I asked. My body spilled into the back seat in anticipation, vibrating as it attempted to process the dominant sensation of hapless confusion.

'I don't know, he just might?' Kai was close to tears as he stuttered and shifted uneasily in his seat.

'Okay, son, good thinking … okay.' I praised him inauthentically, squeezing the plumpest part of his leg.

I had to think smart now. The sooner I restored normality to our lives, the better the chance we'd … I'd have to reverse the ill-effects that were certain to alter my son's DNA for the worse. The only way to do that would be to find Dan, bring him home, and begin the healing process as a family.

I considered following my six-year-old's advice and contacting the sperm donor (that was, my father). But the more I thought of it, the more I was convinced it could have been a normal thing for a child to suggest. Normal for him to assume the only other male figure in his life would have the answers. *Typical boy solution.* They hadn't spoken much, Kai and the donor. Just at holidays and birthdays, and I was always privy to what was being said.

My priority was to find a safe place for us to stay, since this idea had so epically fallen through. First, I was going to book us into a local B & B and – against my better judgement – allow Kai to play games on his iPad for as long as he liked. It would buy me the time to make a few calls and come up with a plan.

'Please find him.'

Ignoring the dull ache I felt for Lindani, I turned the key in the ignition and waited for the thrum of the engine. Comforted, strangely, by its pulse of life.

If there was ever a lie I wanted desperately to tell it was the one that was ready to springboard from my lips right now, but I knew from experience how detrimental the consequences would be.

'I'm going to try harder than I have at anything ever before, sweetie.'

TO: Dan <3
We need you Dan. Where are you? I can't bear one more night
alone, please come back to us Xxx

I knew better than to be hopeful for a reply. I'd left a torrent of messages and voicemails from the very first day he'd gone. Even before the police told me he may be alive. I switched the power off as I'd been doing after each sent message, that way I could trick myself into believing he'd responded. It was the way I had learned to reject reality, I guess.

• • •

I checked myself and Kai into a local B & B that same evening, hoping to achieve a better night's rest so that I could attack the day with an energy that was most definitely required.

I sank into a fitful sleep during the night, replaying what Kai had said. Memories and conversations with the donor and his connection to my family morphed into an elaborate and complex feature-length movie. *The Betrayal*, it would be called, should someone give it a title. How he had chosen a different life entirely to the one my mum and I had offered him, how he had replaced us when we were still available to love. Still available and in need more than ever.

Perhaps I hadn't considered the donor's involvement because I was unable to mend ties with him. All those times I tried to accept his invitations to dinner, for coffees to talk things over, to babysit when Dan and I had to work long hours.

The pain of hearing Dan's name in my head reminded me how nothing in my life could be repaired, not as things stood. But equally as jarring was how a missing husband could leave his wife so utterly clueless.

'Where are you from?' asked the lady who smelled of pomegranate, snapping me back into the room.

'We're from England,' I offered reluctantly.

'Oh lovely. I've heard a lot about England. Is it true it always rains there?' she asked warmly, placing the plate of poached eggs and toast in front of Kai.

I smiled in appeasement. 'It certainly does where were from. Manchester,' I added.

It took every grain of energy to paste a smile on my face and engage in small talk. Usually, I would have elaborated and told her how beautiful and homely her establishment was. Which it was. But I needed to be left alone until I had planned how to broach the topic that was on the tip of my tongue.

I'd taken a couple of local maps from the excursions rack in the reception of the B & B when we checked in. I intended to familiarise myself with the area and see if anything jumped out at me as a lead. I could then cross off the streets and establishments that I had already canvassed.

Perhaps someone he used to know had contacted Lindani when we were in Cape Town and then coaxed him outside? Surely though, the police would have bridged contact between us by now. Why hadn't Dan gone to the police? Too many questions.

If I could pinpoint the main highways and link roads, if any leads came to light at least I'd know the quickest route there. Wherever *there* was.

As much as I craved closeness to Kai, I simultaneously felt held back from conducting my DIY investigation. My fear that he was experiencing irreparable hurt only compounded the feeling that I was stuck. I couldn't leave everything up to the police. To them, Dan was just another stranger, but to us … well he was our everything. I did, however, report Alice Bekker as a missing person in the night. It was a presumptuous and premature decision, but there was no time to waste. The South African police accepted my report with little vigour, but she was one of their own. Perhaps they would be better inclined to invest their time in her?

I struggled to determine if it was more damaging for Kai to stay with me or if he would be better off in the care of someone else? Mila perhaps? My thoughts were so conflicted that my head was beginning to throb.

'Can I get you anything else, my dear?' asked the lady who smelled of pomegranate.

'No, we're good thank you. I hope you don't mind me asking, and this may sound a little strange, and I know it's a long shot, but would you happen to know anyone named Alice Bekker?'

'A guest, you mean? Because I'm afraid we are unable to give out personal inf—'

'Of course, I understand, but no, actually, I meant more in the way of local residents.' I sensed hesitation. The lady's smile lessened slightly. 'Unfortunately, I don't have much information to go on, I just know she would be roughly in her seventies and lives here in Swellendam.'

'Is someone in some kind of trouble?' she probed.

'It's nothing like that … just ignore me, it's been a long journey,' I said, hoping to bring the uncomfortable conversation to a close. I planned on returning to the house that morning and hopefully, then, Alice would be able to enlighten me about something crucial.

'Just because … if it's who I'm thinking of, I actually do know her. I mean, it's a small town, so everyone tends to know each other around here.'

I didn't have any questions rehearsed for this response. My brain energy pumped hastily through my impending migraine, clawing at the information I felt I had to obtain to locate my husband.

Before I had the chance to explain my situation, the lady who smelled of pomegranate began speaking in her delicate South African drawl. 'I was beginning to suspect you weren't here as a tourist – with the way you were circling random areas on those maps, you couldn't be!'

I felt slightly defensive, exposed even. 'So … I was just going to ask if you had seen Alice recently? I've been trying to get hold of her. You see, we were meant to stay at her house this week, but it looks as though no one's home. I mean, we hadn't arranged an exact date or anything so it's my own fault really for just showing up unannounced,' I babbled, leaking nervous energy like a poorly constructed dam.

She peered over at Kai, who was spooning small cuttings of egg and seeded toast into his mouth, then back over at me. No one was home? That seems strange, she expressed.

The lady's eyes darted back and forth between us both as if in consideration of something.

'Hmm.'

I was unsure how to construe her actions, so sat awaiting her conclusion.

'You're Lindani's wife?' she stated, delicately.

Whether it was the false sense of familiarity or just the mere mention of his name, I smiled and nodded softly, salty water lubricating my pupils.

'How did you know?'

Although unnoticed by the other diners, a heavy silence fell over the room during an extended pause.

'I can't believe it! That's wonderful! Please call me Sarah,' she said, holding out her hand in salutation. 'You stay here, I'll go tie a few things up and come join you, if that's okay?'

'Sure.'

I meant it. Now I knew someone with a link to Dan, I didn't feel entirely alone.

'Does she know where Dad is, Mum?' asked Kai, hope exuding from his pores, sending his cutlery crashing noisily against his plate.

Her company would be welcome, therapeutic even, for both of us. I stared with dwindling promise at the face of my fatherless child. We were finally getting somewhere.

• • •

Sarah pulled up a chair next to Kai and placed a complimentary pot of English Breakfast before me.

'I took a chance and brought you black tea with milk.'

'Perfect, thanks very much.' I was grateful for her initiative but Sarah's offering triggered an unquenchable yearning for my life before South Africa.

'I know, essentially, I'm no more than a stranger to you but believe me when I say I've heard so much about you all. Alice, well she was so excited to see her Lindani again and meet his beloved family. You're all she's been talking about for the last few months.'

My posture sharpened like a neglected flower in receipt of water and sunlight.

'I'm so pleased you decided to come. Alice had a challenge on her hands convincing him to visit, let alone bring his family.'

'Oh?' I said, hoping she would reveal more of said conversation.

'It was his Uncle Joe's passing that tipped the balance, I think. It's hit Alice hard, really. Harder than I think any of us realised initially. I just know she'll be back to her old self when she sees you all.'

Knowing Dan had talked about us to people he cared for cured the drumming in my head. It was the confirmation I needed to explain some of my dissension. It was replaced, unwelcomingly, with an anxiety that my husband could potentially be in some sort of trouble.

'Why would Lindani not want to come here? It's beautiful!' I enquired, covertly.

I sensed Sarah's hesitation. She mused over whether Kai's breakfast had been prepared to his liking, despite him having already eaten it.

'How's your tea?' she diverted again.

It was difficult to know what to believe right now, and god knows it was good to get some confirmation that Alice was expecting us. I pushed away the nudge of uncertainty that Dan had held information which Sarah somehow felt ill-equipped to relay to me.

Thoughts had crept into my mind on the journey to Alice's that I'd tried hard to suppress. At one point, I had convinced myself Lindani had made his relatives up to get us to come over here. For what reason I hadn't yet worked out. I'd forced myself to dismiss the thought just as quickly as it had arrived.

'I could give her a call if you like, let her know you're in town – she'll be thrilled!'

She awaited my response, most probably for longer than anticipated.

How could I let that happen? I smeared the perspiration across both palms. Alice would be expecting the full package, not only me and my son. I feared her judgement in the same way children fear disappointing a proud parent.

'So where is he? Is Lindani staying here too?' she asked.

'Umm, Sarah, before you call Alice, there is something I have to tell you.'

Sarah retreated into the chair she had begun to vacate.

My mind furiously flitted between my two options. Tell her the truth or say that he's visiting a friend. I hated the thought of spoiling this woman's day. It would be even worse if she felt obligated in some way to take care of us, or to help me look for him. Although, if I was being honest, selfishly I wanted and expected both of those things from her.

'Lindani's missing,' I blurted.

'Missing?' Sarah's brows furrowed instantly and she pinched her left hand against her sealed lips.

I filled her in on all the confusing details, at her own request, feeling the familiar twinge of guilt for exposing Kai to yet more dysfunction.

'Are you sure?' I nodded to confirm.

'Oh my god, you poor things.' Sarah's cinched brows told me she wasn't fully accepting of my declaration.

'We have to get to Alice and see if he's been in touch. Let's go together.'

Our hot drinks were left on the table, abandoned to grow cold, as myself, Kai and Sarah set off towards Alice's house. I sat with Kai close to me in the back seat of the Hyundai, cursing my agreeable nature. I'd handed over our fate to a woman I'd become acquainted with just a moment earlier.

I switched on my phone and stared at the white screen, waiting for it to load. We were a few miles into our journey when a message pinged, immediately after securing a signal.

FROM: *Dan <3*
Lois. I'm so sorry, I love you both so much, but I just can't.
I can't do this any more. I tried to make a clean break, but

I couldn't just leave you to think something terrible had happened. I haven't got time to explain now. Forgive me. Dan x

A battery of white noise assaulted my ears. The temperature shot to a thousand degrees. I stared vacantly ahead. The stranger in front formed a blurry outline, indistinguishable to my naked eye. Her characteristic scent of pomegranate adopted a bitter hint of musk as Lindani's message involuntarily distorted my reality.

10

She hadn't expected it to feel so strange. Mila looked through her windscreen at the driveway of her friend's home, the one she shared with Mila's own ex-husband. She'd assumed she would feel connected somehow, that there would be a deep sense of belonging that made her feel strangely at home, having shared so much of herself with both of the people who lived there.

It was quite the opposite, actually. It wasn't envy or jealousy that she felt, she told herself. Too much time had passed to have any lingering feelings resurface.

Mila had never driven past Lois's house before. She hadn't really been tempted, not even on the number of occasions when she had given Lois a ride home and parked two streets away to evade Lindani's eagle eye. The possibility of being seen by him had smothered any desire she may have had to see how and where they were living now.

Lindani and Mila had shared a one-bedroom flat together, back when she was new to air hostessing and Lindani was new to the country. They both had little money but tried to make the best of what they had together, at first anyway. Their modest standard of living had fuelled Mila's desire to find ways of acquiring more money. She had her ways and means, as she put it to anyone who was daring enough to ask how she could afford her costly luxuries and sought-after postcode.

It was a desire compounded even more now, having seen the life Lois was accustomed to after marrying Lindani.

By anyone's standards, Mila's ex-husband had definitely come up in the world. He had provided a beautiful, manicured home for his new family. The sight of which burned a little within the deepest parts of her.

To the untrained eye, it was your typical suburban home, but the inside was anything but common. The absence of neutral soft furnishings and divided living quarters showcased Lois and Lindani's unique combined style. This had to be his style, she mused, judging from the considerable canvas decorating the wall by the dining area: a portrait of an elderly African lady, her face lined with life experience, her smile tilted into a cheeky smirk and eyes glowing with warmth and kindness.

Mila stood for a moment by the door, taking in the semicircle of cream leather chairs, each connected by a tiny wooden table. They circled a large flat-screen pasted to the wall opposite, peering over a smooth polished floor.

Two adjacent kitchen worktops stood proudly behind the living area, a tripod and camera overlooking. Mila assumed that was Lindani's preparation space for the YouTube channel he'd made a crust from.

There was no cosy corner to snuggle in and watch movies on winter nights – just an oversized black divider on the far side, where one should have been, she thought. Thinking back to how she had clearly mistaken Lindani's love of their old cosy, bijou living room filled with soft fabrics and fleece blankets, Mila struggled to familiarise herself with the man Lois had married. That's if his home was anything to extricate any information from.

Upon closer inspection, Mila found a plethora of children's toys and games strewn over the snakes and ladders floor grid behind the divider.

It threw Mila off, having not had Lois down as an ultra-modern, sleek, clean-edge kind of woman. She, for sure, came across more of the cosy homemaker kind.

Lindani had never really expressed his sentimental side during their years together, Mila thought as she scanned the display of African woven fans and the geometric lion-head and tribal lady figurines that were spread proudly across a couple of side tables. Any items linked to his troubled past had hardly been treasured and were certainly not set centre stage in their flat. Nor had they been regarded as a symbol of any precious memories he may have held. It just went to show what comfortable living and mental stability brings out in a person, she reasoned.

It was obvious he wasn't going to be there, so she felt stupid walking into their home and calling out Lindani's name. Deciding to make it a quick visit, she made a start on what she had come for before heading to the airport. It was more important that she get to South Africa to keep an eye on Lois.

Mila checked the landline for missed calls and messages. There didn't seem to be any, so she headed up the staircase, after the lady on the canvas had released her from her strangely captive hold.

Upstairs it was cosy, carpeted with delicate pastel shades that also tinted the walls. It was slightly more reminiscent of the home Mila and Lindani had shared. Mila liked how it felt. She gingerly tweaked open a door, revealing what was evidently the master bedroom.

The room emanated a masculine ambience, although Mila struggled to put her finger on what it was that made her draw such a conclusion.

A Harry-Potter-shaped picture frame stood on Lois's bedside (Mila guessed the side with a pack of contraceptive pills was Lois's). She couldn't help but be drawn in by the wizard shaped structure, enthralled to unravel another snippet of their lives together.

She held the frame with both hands, staring at an image she'd once dreamt of capturing for herself. The scene came to life in her imagination. A family road trip, singalongs and car games, high-pitched squeals of laughter and excitement. A piggyback ride perhaps? A joyous mum and dad meandering hand in hand, consolidating their love through touch. The perfect child dragging them eagerly to anything in sight that demanded the attention of a young inquisitive mind.

She had no memories of Lindani holding her hand in public or singing in the car or offering a parting kiss on her forehead. She'd yearned for such physical declarations of love, almost for the entirety of their union, but he hadn't been prepared. Not prepared for any suitable degree of affection, nor for a romantic relationship full stop. So, Mila had had to teach him how to love her with just as much vigour as she'd needed to appease his demons.

Mila slid off her shoes and climbed onto the queen-sized bed, being careful not to remove her thumb from Lois's face. She lay still with the picture frame against her chest, aware of the urgency of the situation but unable to do anything about it. Emotional paralysis rendered her limbs immobile.

She noticed a pair of brown suede loafers by the bedding box. A black T-shirt emblazoned with the *Jurassic Park* emblem was screwed up on the cushioned floor next to it. If she hadn't known better, Mila would have been convinced that the Lindani Lois claimed to be married to was a different person entirely. There were no traces of the 'old' him in sight.

Lois's and Kai's faces jumped from the framed image on the windowsill. Their buoyant curls entwined during a remarkably staged spin on a characteristically pebbled English beach. An image captured by Mila's former husband. She thought of her friend, alone in a foreign country and with no one to turn to. No one yet, anyway. She had to get there quickly. Lois must be going out of her mind. Just like when Mila had had to ask her own husband if she could give him a hug, she expected she'd need to now inject some of this same sensitivity into her friendship with Lois. It surprised Mila how concerned she had become with Lois and Kai's well-being. And a surprise it certainly was.

Going through the motions, Mila returned the picture and put on her shoes. She popped her head around each door in a methodical manner. When content nothing else required her attention, she sat in the lounge area, on a cream leather chair, and switched on her phone.

TO: Lois
Lo, I'm really sorry, no sign of him here. Hope you're holding up okay? Thinking of you. Xxx

• • •

The seats were filled with an archetypal selection of long-haul flyers. Well-to-do families taking their children on the trip of a lifetime, adventure-thirsty couples and backpack-clad solo travellers.

The airport made her think of Lindani first stepping onto British soil. It still surprised her how long ago it was. Their eyes had met across the terminal as he was heading to the exit, just as she was emptying her toiletries into one of those tiny plastic bags. She recalled how strongly her body had reacted to the sight of him, the butterflies that had ambushed her stomach as they launched a full-scale attack, and how intensely the feelings had excited her. She knew how Lois must have felt.

'Would you like the chicken or fish?' asked the sprightly, light-featured stewardess.

Aside from gossiping with her colleagues, Mila had long ago lost the desire to stay in the cabin as crew. The tug of working up front in the flight deck was much stronger. She would think about pursuing that dream whenever things had settled down with Lois.

Dismissing her daydreams, she chose to rehearse what to say to Lois. They were tricky, these situations. Not that she'd found herself in one such as this before. It was going to be mentally taxing, she expected, for both of them. She would take everything one step at a time.

Mila wished she'd remembered to text Lois to say she was on her way over to South Africa. If she had to wait too long for support from her friend, Mila feared Lois would do something to accidentally throw them off track. Emotional control not being one of Lois's strong suits.

She wondered how she'd feel if she was still in a relationship with Tom and it was him who had gone missing. Where would she look? Who would she trust? What would she believe? That was it – how Mila knew she was going to be of assistance. If she could only put herself in Lois's shoes. Really experience her thoughts and emotions as much as her intellect would allow.

She must have been lost in thought as the stewardess asked again what she'd like as her meal preference.

'Chicken, please,' she said apologetically. The woman handed over the warm rectangular tray.

'Thank you.'

She tapped on the screen set within the headrest in front of her.

Flight time remaining 5 hours 12 minutes. ETA 1.03 a.m. local time.

She kicked herself for checking the flight duration. Why is it that when you're eager to get somewhere in a hurry, time adopts a much slower pace? She would make another attempt to watch a movie or start a new series to pass the hours.

Piercing a plastic fork through the creamy coated chicken then scooping up some green beans, Mila flicked through the selection of movies with her free hand. Overthinking anything at this stage would serve no purpose. With any luck, Lois would have calmed down by the time Mila reached her and they could dissect their way through the details together. What the police had suggested would only play into her insecurities. It was obvious Lois would think Dan had left of his free will and chosen not to get in contact. No doubt she would be connecting the dots by now. It must be torturous to experience such crippling feelings of inadequacy.

11

THEN

The effort it took to peel open my eyelids was herculean. There was no Mum, no 'Good morning, princess.' Not now and not ever again. I bit back the ocean of tears that threatened to drown me. I must have sunk into a black hole of epic proportion, because surely somewhere, just somewhere Mum could be found. I think that's why it hurt so badly – because I knew, deep down, she wasn't anywhere. There was only Dad, and what use was that now that he had *her*?

I found each drip of consciousness to be more painful than the last, as if the very oxygen was laced with nails and toxins. The pain being equally intense in my body and in my heart.

Hopefully next time I woke up it wouldn't hurt so much. I remember Mum telling me that time heals everything, but it was hard to believe that right now.

My fingers traced the darker patches of fabric that covered my pillow, wincing from its dampness. I was mesmerised by how one of the characters faded into the background, no longer entwined in the same tapestry as its surroundings. A separate entity, like Mum was now.

My dreams of her were sometimes shared with memories of my happiest times with Dad, too. It was my brain's way of telling me that Mum wasn't the only one I had lost, but for as long as I was dreaming,

I was experiencing joy in its purest form. My happiness during sleep was punished by condemning my waking hours to unbearable suffering, suffering that only my dad would be able to relieve. If only things were different, I wished, before drifting swiftly into my happy place.

• • •

'Lois, are we going to talk about this?'

He wanted me close to him, but I couldn't do it.

'I don't want to talk to you. There's nothing to talk about.'

It took a moment for me to realise why he'd come to sit by me on the carpet. My hand lay sprawled over the covers on her bed, as much due to habit as desire.

'It's clearly bothering you, pumpkin. Why won't you talk to me about anything?'

I allowed the tears to flow freely then, bitter in the knowledge that Dad could see how upset I was. The warmth of his body radiated near me, so I shuffled around to face the other wall, swapping which hand rested on Mum's bed.

'Because there's nothing to say!' I said through tears.

He drew in an exaggerated puff of air then blew it back out behind me.

Salty water rained down beneath us both. It was right then that I wondered how on earth I was going to get through the rest of my life, when getting through today seemed so impossible.

I freed myself from his presence. Be kind, I reminded myself. I had to be if this was going to work.

'Well, we both know that isn't true. Don't we, Lois?' I could feel his eyes on me as he paused for me to respond. 'Okay, well you know where to find me when you're ready to talk.'

He lingered in the kitchen, looking over at me every two or so minutes. I shook my head the next time I caught him looking. He wanted me to eat something, but I didn't want to have any food if Mum couldn't eat any more.

My instinct to curl up into a ball and fall into the same abyss as she had was a persistent one, but there was something I had to do. It was a huge task, and if it was to work, I'd have to do it quickly.

I searched my memory erratically. Where had I heard about them, the vanishing spells? Harry Potter tried one, didn't he? He wasn't real though, I don't think. At least that's what Dad said when he caught me trying to transform that monstrous daddy-long-legs into something less scary.

I skidded towards the cabinet beneath the TV and threw open the cupboard doors. My spell book and wand had been tidied away before I lost Mum. Flicking through the pages impatiently, I waved my wand, muttering snippets of spells desperately regurgitated from memory.

It was right there, on page fifty-two. A Reappear Spell. To my delight, the list of required items wasn't extensive. I searched the house for a red candle, a photo of me and a photo of Mum. The last item threw me for a second, then I slid open the box entitled 'The Most Marvellous Fantastical Wondrous Magic Tricks' and picked out the purple crystal.

I scanned the kitchen to find Dad had left the room, but faint mutterings drifted through the hallway so I knew he must still be nearby. I had to really strain my ears to conclude he was in the front sitting room. Perfect! I counted to ten. His voice wasn't accompanied by a female one so I decided it was just the TV.

I stretched the tendons in my feet to reach right up to the counter. A growl sounded in the base of my throat. The cooker hobs were powered by electricity. I had to adapt my methods, and fast. I remembered Mum used to put those little round tea lights around the bathtub sometimes, so I rushed upstairs to see if they were still there. Silence was key. I didn't want Dad to screw anything up, because he would if he knew what I was doing. He didn't care that Mum was gone, not the same way I did. He had *her* now.

I'd been told I was tall for a girl my age, yet I still struggled to reach the top cabinet in the bathroom. I had to place one foot on the lip of the bath and the other on the toilet seat to reach it comfortably. I squinted hard to hone in on the tiny box hidden amongst the face creams and deodorants, trying my hardest not to knock anything as I stretched over to retrieve it. A heavy-set perfume bottle clunked onto its side.

'Lois, what the hell?'

When the heck did he get there? Silence was key, but I couldn't even manage to keep quiet.

He stared at the box of matches in my hand. All I could do was tighten my grip and stare mutely back at him, wishing him away.

'Give me those, Lois. They're dangerous and they are *not* for children.'

I climbed down carefully and hid the box behind my back, out of view.

'Stop being silly, this is getting out of hand. Give them to me now, do you hear!'

I said nothing but was beginning to question whether I could get him to go away and leave me alone.

'Am I speaking to myself?' His tone was the same as when he called me for tea whilst *The Jetsons* replay was on.

'I'm not doing anything wrong, okay? I'm NOT!'

'You can't play with matches, Lois. I thought you knew better than that. You're behaving like a stupid child.'

'Just go away all right, get lost. I don't care what you say any more!' And just like that, silence was unachievable.

He must have known I was serious this time because he lowered his voice straight away then asked for me to come down and have something to eat with him. He had weakened and grown softer in the face and neck so it was obvious he felt bad for calling me stupid.

The air was thinning and he hadn't left enough space for me to exit the bathroom. I wished I knew a spell to make him move out of the way, I thought amusingly, a sly smile threatening my face. He was too big, he blocked too much space, so I didn't have any other choice than to hand the matches over to him. I scoffed as he accepted the box into his open palm.

'That's a good girl,' he said, smugly.

'Stop saying that. I'm not a little girl!'

The thrum of the TV took precedence over our exchange for an elongated minute.

'You know I love you, don't you?' he said, taking me by surprise. It was the first time he'd said those words since Mum had passed. They had the same depth of tone as before, but somehow, they didn't feel as soothing as they used to.

He must have sensed my distaste towards him and shifted out of the way. I walked downstairs sulkily then knelt by my spell book on the living room floor. On the way down from the bathroom I nodded in agreement to having a bite to eat. That was the type of kindness I had to show for my magic to work, so it was an easy choice.

Dad flitted around the kitchen, finding the necessary ingredients and cutlery for the ham and veg omelette that he had offered me moments before.

Wasting no time at all, I gathered the necessary items from my box of magic tricks and rested the spell book open between my crossed legs. *You just have to read it aloud, Lois. Read it clearly and she will come back to you. Okay, now why are you stalling? Ready ... one, two, three ...*

Ensuring Dad's attention was firmly on making lunch, I revealed the cluster of matches I had picked from the box and gave myself another mental pep talk to begin the conjuring process. I had everything I needed: the pictures, the candle, the spell book, everything. My left hand gripped around the crystal, as instructed, now all that was left was to light the candle. *Faster, Lois!* My heart sank. I was running out of time.

How did I not realise? I had to light a match first, that was very important. Nothing would work without it, but just as my ribs bubbled with anxiety I remembered how Mum always used to light them with that strip on the side of the matchbox. The box that Dad had taken away from me. My shoulders were yet again occupied by a familiar mass of worry. I closed my eyes and mumbled the passage quietly, hoping the sound of the TV would mask my voice from Dad's ears. Opening my eyes with a cautious trepidation, I scanned the room. It hadn't worked. Dad was still chopping veggies in the kitchen and heating up the frying pan, but there was no Mum. I wasn't sure if she would appear in front of me or in the last place she'd been, which was upstairs in bed. I couldn't risk going upstairs to check right now; he would be too suspicious. Plus I also couldn't risk coming down to him having cleared everything away. I would try the spell again, properly this time.

'Dad, when will it be ready?' I called, gauging the approximate window of time available to me.

'Two minutes, pumpkin.'

I scraped the bunch of matches along the side of the Magic Tricks box instead. Nothing ignited. I blew onto them heavily then tried rubbing them each separately on the carpet. Surely Dad would be able to hear the throbbing of my chest from the kitchen.

Tears of frustration pricked my eyes. I looked down to find my hands involuntarily clawing the bunch of matches against one another. My jaw was tight, teeth engaged in a private battle of tug-of-war. Blue wavy tubes bobbed from the skin over my wrists, temporarily distracting me from monitoring Dad. The tubes, they were strong-looking and determined, as if they were trying to escape the confines of my body. The spell was working. I was getting closer.

Please God, let this light. Little Jesus please just for me, for Lois, come on, just one final tim—

A spark!

'Is everything okay?' Dad called. To which I replied instantly, unsure if he knew what I was trying to do.

'Fine.'

My nostrils deflated as a fresh sensation of hope was born, born alongside the flame that was going to return my mum to me.

I hurriedly lit the candle and chanted the passage in a whisper. Three times. Sweat formed around the crystal that I held in my left hand. I opened my eyes, excited to see her again, to hold her and tell her all about the hell I'd been through this past twenty-four hours. We'd cry together and Mum would be so proud of me for using my magic to bring her back.

She must be upstairs, I reasoned.

My legs flung me around as if powered by a mystery force, like in those movies where people can fly. I was on high alert, searching every corner of every room as I passed.

The door banged hard against Mum's bedroom wall as I entered, still heaving with adrenaline.

I stared over at the empty bed, confused and in a daze, crumpling to the floor as the trembling of my limbs grew into convulsions. Voices echoed through my mind as I hooked my fingers into the crimson carpet, stained red from my tears.

No time at all had passed, except it must have. Because Dad was standing behind me as if he'd been there all along.

'She is gone, darling. I'm so sorry.'

I hate you! I can't have ONE thing, not even this. Not even Mum!

He must have carried me back into the kitchen because if I had known I would have resisted his efforts. Only when I came around did I notice I was tight in his embrace, sat upright on my stool with his shoulders hunched over the back of mine. It was with a forced supply of determination that I tried to push him from me, but he had too much power. Blue wavy tubes pulsed through the side of his head and in his wrists, like they had in mine earlier. He had won.

A plate filled with eggy veg sat before me on the counter, but I could bring myself to look at the pile of food no more than I could bring myself to look over at that lying, fake magic book strewn across the living room floor.

It doesn't work. Not even when you're kind. Nothing works.

A searing anger lit my eyes with a deep darkness. It was all there was to feel now. Anger. Because living in hope of another idea striking me was proving utterly fruitless. Until an idea *did* strike me.

I considered the possibility that I might have tried the wrong spell. Dad had been pestering me to speak with him about what happened, and he did say I could ask him anything at all, but in no way did I want him to think I had forgiven him for what he'd done to us.

'What were you just about to say, just then?' he asked, visibly relieved I was trying to open up.

'Nothing,' I barked, chopping indiscriminately at my omelette

'Come on, I know you wanted to ask me something then, I'm your dad, you can ask me anything.'

Like that was supposed to mean anything.

I stayed silent to put him off pressing for an answer.

He set down his mug of coffee and I watched his eyebrows dance as he searched my face for something I wasn't quite sure of.

'If someone goes invisible, how do you make them visible again?' I said, not taking my eyes from the plate of food in front of me.

'Someone as in your mum, you mean?' he asked softly.

I regretted the display of vulnerability my asking gifted him, and instantly became fearful the other woman would pop up from behind the sofa and try to claim me as her own, now that I had been nice to him.

'Oh, I wish it was that simple, Lois. Your mummy isn't invisible though, sweetheart. Not in the way you think.' Enough time ran between us for confusion to puncture my thoughts. 'I thought you understood,' he said to himself. 'She's gone, darling. She isn't coming back.'

I wished I'd never asked. No one could help me now and *he* probably wouldn't choose to bring her back even if he knew how.

Let me wake up. I need to wake up.

I sent my fists hurtling towards the counter until my fingers struck the hard end, sending the plate of food crashing onto the polished wood floor.

The memory of Dad's voice echoed dreamily through the fog, taking me back to when Mum first left us. 'She will always live in our hearts. We can look to the sky,' I recalled him telling me.

I finally understood. Mum wasn't a person any longer, she was an angel. God had taken her back.

I spat out the forkful of eggy veg that was sitting in my mouth, giving rise to the taste of bile that now coated my tongue.

'That's it, I'm done with your crap, Lois, up to your room, now!'

My ankle twisted over the modest pile of regurgitated food until each morsel split to form a lumpy paste that lined the grooves of the floor. I steadfastly maintained eye contact with him, before accruing more waste which was soon delivered from my mouth onto the sodden mixture.

He ran out of words then, just as I had run out of the ability to care.

• • •

'How much more can we endure?' Dad was saying to someone on the other side of the door. My flesh burned as I listened to his conversation and how he went on to refer to me as a little girl again. *I'm not your little girl any more!*

I tried my hardest to listen, but no other voice sounded. Then I remembered he'd mentioned his intention to call Grandad after I was settled back into bed.

My biology relaxed back into a more compliant state as a result. For how long I didn't know, but I was coming to appreciate those rare moments of manageable pain as opposed to the white-hot grief that lived in me the rest of the time.

He was right about something though, Dad. There wasn't much more I could take. I'd thrown up more times in the last two days than ever before in my life and there was seemingly no end to my affliction.

Gazing out of the window towards the darkening grey sky, I wondered if Mum was with other people she knew, people that God had taken away already. I hoped this thought would bring me comfort, but instead the pit of my stomach sparked with jealousy. She was *my mum*, no one else's. And who did God think he was, taking her away like that?

The loneliness was palpable now. Peeling back the covers, I remembered the little doll Mum had brought home for me one day.

She'd said to hold it close every night that I struggled to sleep or every time I felt afraid. It had helped her, she'd said, having something to cuddle up to when she was a young girl.

I climbed back under the covers and hugged the doll close to my chest. Its big blue eyes and wide smile emanated warmth and peace. The strands of yellow wool splayed across my shoulder in a protective act of affection. The loneliness trickled away, just enough to recall the words clearly.

Through the sniffles and sobs, an ethereal voice sounded around the bedroom, through the wooden door and into the hallway where my dad still stood. I sang loud enough for him to hear, for him to remember all that he had lost too. It was the same song Mum and I had sung many bedtimes before.

Sleep tight my darling, for you are not alone,
For times you cannot find me, she's here to make you whole,
The dreams they will become you, enchanted is your world,
You're a star amongst the stones, dear. A new page you too
shall turn,
Sleep tight my darling, for you are not alone.

12

'Stop the car!'

My desperation splintered the relative ambient calm. I felt Kai shudder as a direct consequence of my outburst yet was ill-equipped to offer even a mere acknowledgement of his discomfort.

'Lois, what is it?' said Sarah. Jolted too by my untimely eruption, she shared her concern through the mirror. Concern that would probably have been better spent allocated to the road.

'Stop the car! Now, I need to get out, please, STOP!' I repeated, making to exit in a way that only showcased my weak, uncoordinated fingers. They slipped against the release handle as I tried to open it.

Sarah nodded into the rear-view, and without contemplation pulled over by the side of the road. I got out.

I clasped the phone in my palm as tightly as my nerves would allow, my head wavering aimlessly. Sarah offered no consolation. I dialled back the number, again and again, only to receive nothing except Dan's voicemail. It felt like hours had passed since the ping of the text.

'Is he here? Was that him, Mummy, on your phone? Mum? Mum?' said Kai at a pitch that wasn't picked up by my auditory register.

Gone were the days I used to call Dan when I knew he was unavailable, just to listen to his dark, lusty voice and to laugh at his mediocre quips. Now his voicemail served as a barrier, a wall fifty-feet high that only compounded the mystery surrounding his disappearance.

I left another message. And another. Each one adopting the same sentiment. 'Why did you abandon us?'

My biology was as unsettled as I'd ever experienced. Matter flew in all directions, crashing into obstacles that had for so long rested peacefully in their allocated place within me. I clawed at my throat like a feral cat, desperate to relieve the constricting pressure from the loose neckline of my T-shirt. Kai! How could he do this to him? What would he think? My body shuddered with anger as instantly as the thought surfaced.

What kind of father abandons their child, and no less, in a foreign country! And what kind of mother was I to just meander blindly into his trap?

I was too distressed to shed tears, so I gazed out into the distance, yearning for someone to grant me the power to evaporate into nothing.

A truck blew its horn then, demanding I shift from the road as well as from my mental coma. *Deep breaths. Come on, you have your son to think about.*

Lindani's words flashed around my head like the tiny white flakes in a roughly shaken snow globe. I struggled to piece together anything by way of an explanation. He'd gone. He'd left us. Did he have another woman? Another family?

I sat in physical agony, finally making sense of my husband's admissions. He hadn't wanted Kai and me to join him in South Africa, not because it wasn't safe but because he wasn't planning on returning to us. And I was *still* chasing him, dragging Kai through more unbearable shit!

Sarah approached me, having left the car. 'What's happened? What's wrong?'

A single glance showed Kai's head in the same position in which I'd left him. The ache in my chest strengthened. Why the hell was Dan intent on destroying our family? We were a team, all of us. And just a text? It wasn't him. It couldn't be. I thought I knew Lindani better than that, but apparently there was so much more to learn about him.

'Lois? What's happened?'

'Don't leave him, please go back, I'm fine!'

I'd learned over the years to try and take a step back from painful situations. Learned to evaluate things more rationally before allowing myself to be swallowed into the abyss. I'd had counselling again, after my last break-up, to try and regain objectivity and trust. Mainly trust. I'd finally mastered the ability. At least I thought I had.

'I just need some air,' I said, neglecting to catch her eye.

Deep breaths, come on, you've got this!

My chest settled slightly. My plain white trainers were decorated with swipes of dirt from the debris I'd been scuffling by the roadside.

I recognised the street. It was dark when we'd been, but it was definitely the same street. That forest-green paint and large white window frames. It was where Alice lived.

A parental fear spurred me to hurry to the gate. My son was alone in the car of a woman I barely knew, in a country that wasn't our own. *What am I doing?*

My attention flitted between the car and the house. *I'll still be able to see him.*

I creaked open the green metal gate.

My ears detected soft bangs somewhere in the distance. *Quick, just get it over with.*

'Lois, wait a minute,' Sarah attempted to steer me back to the car, guiding me by touch. I broke free from her clutches, ran up to the door and rapped heavily on the hard wood. *I need to know where he is.*

'Hello … Alice it's Lois, Lindani's wife, is anyone there?' I shouted. 'Hello?'

I feared Lindani had been in touch and told her not to open the door, to save this nice old lady the drama he assumed I would bring to her doorstep.

I considered retreating but instead found myself trying the door handle. It was locked. There was no car outside, but I'd assumed that Alice, being in the latter half of her life, would have waived her right to drive.

Footfalls clapped heavily up the walkway to the house. It was Sarah.

'Lois, are you okay? What are you doing?'

'We almost passed it?' I said.

'Passed what? What do you mean?'

'I'm going back to Kai, stay there!' I said, my anxiety heightened. He was alone in Sarah's car.

The faint sound of clinking metal turned my head back to the front door. She was home. The handle made a downwards motion revealing a Welcome doormat.

'Alice?' I said, searching the woman's face for confirmation.

Alice wasn't at all how I'd imagined, her tender frame and youthful glow bestowing the looks of some classic Hollywood actress – albeit slightly plainer. An irrational stab of jealousy hit me at the thought of Dan growing up in a home with someone so beautiful.

'We're really sorry to bother you, Kate,' interrupted Sarah. 'I hope you and Esther are keeping well?' The beautiful woman smiled and nodded in reciprocation, sparing a fleeting look at the stranger standing on her doorstep.

'We're getting there,' she answered.

'Glad to hear it. We'll be on our way now, sorry again for disturbing you.'

My face struggled to hide my confusion. The woman at the door shot me a half-smile before wishing me a safe onward journey. I replied politely then met Sarah on the pavement.

'I know, given the circumstances, this is a silly question. But really, are you all right?'

'I don't understand, this is where Alice lives, isn't it?'

'No, why would you think that?'

'A friend of mine told me she lived here. I'm sure it was here.'

I'd grown used to seeing Sarah's brows furrow with confusion, even in our short-lived acquaintance.

'Oh, I see,' she said with an obvious reluctance that made me defensive. 'I'm afraid your friend must have been mistaken. I've never known Alice to live anywhere else.' Her slight glance towards the centre of my face told me she noticed my nostrils flare in retaliation.

'Kate lost her husband a few months ago to cancer, so she was left to take care of his bed-ridden mother … here, in this house.'

'That's awful,' I said, genuinely saddened but pushing down the pang of venom in the pit of my stomach. *At least her husband didn't leave by choice.* Stop it, Lois.

'How long have you been in the area?' I needed to know if there was a chance Alice could have moved house since Mila was last in touch.

'Little over eighteen months.'

I blew out a small puff of air, relieved to have dodged a potential curveball. Sarah's short local residency confirmed my assumption. Alice must have moved. If anything, I was grateful Mila hadn't intentionally given me the wrong address, a potential explanation that had begun to plant its seed.

'We can go back to the B & B if this is all a bit too much? I *am* sorry for dragging you round with me,' she said.

My thoughts distracted me from using words aloud, until I sensed the break in conversation grow awkward.

'Sarah, you've nothing to apologise for. I'm sorry for embarrassing you just now, it's just a lot to take in.'

'You didn't.' I was appreciative of her white lie. 'Anyway, Kate was probably relieved by the distraction,' she said after a brief pause.

'You're too nice,' I said, feeling thankful for this stranger's lack of judgement and her comforting tone. It was a sentiment I needed more than I'd realised.

We walked back to the car in silence, my feet quickening in pace. I couldn't wait to feel Kai in my arms again. He was the only reminder that I still had something worth holding on to.

'Kai, darling?'

The backseat was empty.

'Kai!' My voice pierced the stuffy air. Sarah's words echoed my own before confirming for herself he wasn't anywhere in the car.

'We were only gone a minute; he can't be far!'

Sarah scanned every car she passed, whether moving or parked. I dropped to the floor and checked the tarmac for a set of familiar boys' pumps but none presented themselves.

She canvassed the streets, knocking on doors, and recruited passers-by to help us search.

Each passing minute meant a decline in my motor skills as raw panic claimed my body. I strained my eyes to enhance their function, but images of kidnap and murder flooded my conscience instead. My heart thudded aggressively for what I hoped would be the last time. Seconds turned into minutes, each one as distressing as the last. *Think smart, Lois. He's just wandered off somewhere, he's okay. He has to be okay!*

I grabbed my phone from the back seat, swiping away the image of the last message I'd had the misfortune to read. How insignificant it felt now, having experienced something far worse. Anger flared again, each time with an alarming potency. Lindani's son was missing and where the fuck was he? Selfish ba—. A guttural growl seeped through the side of my clenched teeth as I scrambled to pull up a picture of the little boy I loved above all else.

Why did I leave him? If only I could go back in time, just a few minutes, is that too much to ask? Please just let us go back!

I tapped onto my calls list. *You will answer this time, you have to.* As I pressed the call button, I noticed an outline in the distance. The midday sun illuminated a small boy with familiar fuzzy curls and, by his side, an adult woman. As if by instinct my body exhaled with relief.

I sprinted towards them, but the thick, tepid air stifled the speed of my approach despite my rise in adrenaline. His torso crashed into mine as I swept my son from the ground, my arm flailing at the woman until she too was enveloped in our emotionally charged embrace.

It was the first time I'd looked at her long enough to determine her identity. Only then did I understand Kai's emotionless response.

'Mila, thank god!'

'Lois, I'm so, so sorry. I didn't mean to worry you,' she said, seemingly awaiting my reaction. 'I saw you just ahead and Kai, well, he needed to use the bathroom. And I figured we'd only be a few minutes.'

Tears pricked the corner of my eyes. *He's safe! Thank you God, he's okay.*

'As long as he's safe.'

I immediately sank into reflection.

Mila smiled and nodded agreeably, shifting her gaze to Sarah whose fast strides towards us informed Mila of our acquaintance.

'It's lovely to meet you,' said Sarah, still catching her breath but with a genuine politeness. She pulled my boy into her, respectively embracing him also. 'Kai, thank goodness you're okay!'

I sensed all of us were in a brief moment of reflection, save Kai who was giggling sheepishly.

'I guess I should make myself scarce now you're all together.' Sarah's head bowed ever so slightly as she shifted sideways, freeing up space between us.

'Actually, Sarah, if it's all the same with you, I'd really love for us to stay together? I could still do with your help … y'know, if it's on offer?'

'You know it,' she said, more to Mila than to me. 'Miguel can hold the fort until I'm back.'

Mila interceded with a promptness that came to my surprise. 'Sarah, that's hardly in your remit of duties, I can help Lois now.' Mila's words forced Sarah's gaze upon me. There was no time to deliberate.

'Thanks, Sarah, you don't know how appreciative I am.'

A reticent smile formed across my face. I was overwhelmed. And there was guilt. These two women were making sacrifices to join me on my torturous journey. And I wasn't being entirely truthful to either of them.

Now wasn't the time to divulge my message from Dan, not with what had just happened. Sarah would ask, at some point, what had sent me off into a frenzy, and perhaps I would tell her. There was little I knew the answer to right now.

My thoughts slid into reflection about the family I thought I'd had. Lindani had no reason to leave … I mean, not to leave like this. Perhaps during the gap in our sex life after Kai was born he'd met someone else, someone willing to put-out the way *I* used to do. It was just sex!

Could he have been acting the entire time? Playing the role of doting husband and loving father? I'd have to tell Mila about the text. Maybe she could shed some light on his behaviour. For all I knew, he could have done the same thing to her?

13

The street had cleared its gathering of spectators. The little English boy had been returned safely to his mother. Daily activities promptly resumed.

'Who was that woman at the door earlier?'

Sarah turned the keys in the ignition, pulling out into the road with an additional passenger on board.

'Not Alice. Apparently she doesn't live there any more.'

'Huh? I guess they moved after Dan and I split.' Mila shrugged. Sarah's posture shifted with this new information. I glanced at Kai in hope he didn't hear. 'Sorry, Lois, I feel awful I've sent you on some wild goose chase.'

'She still lives local, so it isn't a complete loss. We can head there now, if you're both feeling up to it?'

What followed could only be construed as an awkward silence. In reality, I was inaudibly weighing up the benefits of seeing Alice. I'd convinced myself she knew that Dan had abandoned us, and that she might lead me further away from him. I didn't know what she knew. And it was beginning to freak me out.

'Are you sure this is a good idea?' I asked, searching for outward confirmation.

'Well, it's entirely up to you. I'll help any way you'd like.' Sarah paused. 'Tell me if it isn't any of my business, but what's making you unsure?'

I was annoyed at how I'd represented myself to Sarah thus far. I hoped she could see me as something other than an ignorant, paranoid, over-emotional liability.

'Actually, there is something I need to tell you both. Look, I promise I didn't mean to be deceptive, but I was worried you'd both think I was wasting all of our time. Plus, it's humiliating. I needed to get my head around it.' I could feel the heat of expectation on me. 'You see, I got a message earlier … from Dan. I'm not crazy – I'd know if there was the slightest hint of something being *this* wrong in our marriage. I was a naïve teenager again, desperately persuading my parents that my sixteen-year-old crush would never leave me. 'At the same time, how much do you ever really know a person?' I ruminated. 'Especially someone who wasn't very forthcoming with his past.'

'What did it say, this message?' asked Mila, striking her fingernails against the bare skin of her forearm.

Why had I brought it up? Especially in front of Kai. Again, I was a pathetic reject in front of these two other women. But Mila's persistent gaze was a clear indication of her lust for information.

I brought up the text and handed the phone to her first, then to Sarah. Sitting in silence, I brushed the curls from Kai's cheek and waited nervously. I wondered how this poisonous little chunk of information would affect our plans moving forward.

'Wow, really?' said Mila, scoffing inaudible insults at her ex-husband. 'What the hell is he playing at? How could he do this to you? And to Kai?'

'Mila!' I interrupted, signalling for her to stop before the six-year-old on my lap twigged on to her muted outburst.

'Okay, so what are we thinking?' asked Sarah. 'You have a great marriage, right?' I take it you don't believe this bullcrap? Is there any way someone else could have sent it to you?'

I didn't believe it, but deep down I feared my denial was an affliction all of its own. Tracing the contours of the car, I recalled the time we had become stuck in a thick body of gloopy mud on our family trip to Flamingo Land. He'd insisted we follow directions from the satnav, even when it led us four miles off track and in the wrong direction. 'These things never mess up,' he'd gone on to say. 'Well I can't see any flamingos, Daddy!' Kai had responded, causing a wave of laughter to which none of us was immune. After collecting rocks to wedge under the car tyres, Dan handed me his phone to free his grip as he pushed us out.

I'd thought nothing of it. Not then and not the numerous times before or after. If he was developing a relationship with someone else, then why the lack of secrecy?

I was moved to tears, or whatever is considered the prequel to tears. Sarah was fast becoming a trusted friend and I was touched at how defensive Mila had become over me.

'That's a point, could his phone have been stolen?' I said. 'I mean, the police think he's alive so maybe someone saw their opportunity in all the chaos, and Dan didn't notice?'

I held my son tightly, cupping both his ears to stifle our commentary.

'Well, I guess. But he'd just have to go to the police and tell them what happened?' said Mila. 'Anyway, what kind of weirdo would send a message like that? They wouldn't know anything about you?'

'Unless they *do* know us?'

'Who, Mum? Who knows us?'

'I don't know, darling, I'm just thinking out loud, that's all. Come here,' I said, his body tightening and attempting to pull away from my hold.

'Is it possible that he believes you and Kai were, you know …' Sarah ended her question with a demonstrative finger across the front of her neck.

'Um maybe. The police think he was outside the building at the time of the fire, so he probably assumed we were still inside.'

'Even if he wasn't there when it happened, it's been all over the local news, so he'd know, right?'

'You think he'd just assume you guys were … gone? That he'd move on with his life, just like that?' asked Sarah, her expression showing she believed none of it.

I took a minute to assimilate what she was saying. She was right to question my logic. Even if he'd planned on running away with another woman, infidelity was a different ballgame to leaving your family for dead. And why did he send the message, then? If he thought we were dead?

'He wouldn't give up on you both so easily, surely. He loves you both. I just know it. The way Alice and Joe have spoken about him – and his family – over the years … they made you guys the envy of everyone around here, trust me on that!'

'She's right, you've always seemed really happy together,' added Mila. 'Plus, don't people who do shitty things like this always have a motive? Dan has no incentive to leave, does he?'

The speculation was tough to process.

'We were happy, but …' I dragged up the memories of our early marriage, privately. The dry spell in our intimate life, how he'd said he was getting tired of asking, tired of reassuring me I was attractive and desirable, tired of asking to let the baby sleep in his cot.

We all sat for a moment peering out of our respective windows. I assumed Sarah was wondering why the hell she'd got involved with us.

'Unless …'

'Unless what?' I urged, sensing Mila's reluctance to elaborate.

Kai wriggled in my lap, nuzzling his face into my neck, the same way his father used to.

'Actually, Mila, hold that thought. I know this isn't ideal, but I've been going out of my mind wondering how I'm going to be able to do everything. It just isn't working, having this one with me all the time. It isn't fair he's being dragged through the rafters. So, I was thinking perhaps you could take care of him until we go home?' My jaw clenched revealing the join of my teeth.

'Lois, if that will help then I'd be happy to.' I was pleased she seemed receptive to my suggestion. Usually I'd have given her chance after chance to decline, but I was out of options. 'You hear that, little man?' she said. 'Sounds exciting, what d'ya think?' She reached back to ruffle his hair.

I recalled the time when my biggest fear was exposing mine and Mila's friendship to Lindani. How my priorities had changed.

'She's really lovely, you know?' said Sarah through the rear-view mirror. 'His foster Mum. Joe was too. They really turned his life around.'

I felt a twinge of unease. 'Alice and Joe were Dan's foster parents?' I tried to dampen my surprise. He'd told me they were his aunt and uncle?

'Alice isn't the judgemental sort either. So whatever it is you're thinking, I'd bet money you needn't worry about meeting her,' she continued as if she hadn't heard my previous comment.

'Why did he need foster parents? Didn't he move to England when his mum and dad passed away?' How I'd had to ask such questions about my own family to these two other women sparked the heat in my gut to appear in red dapples on my face.

'He did lose his parents, that much is true. But probably not how you think. Do you really not know what happened?' Sarah said hesitantly.

I was sure Mila could feel my eyes burning into the back of her head from the back seat.

'Does this ring a bell with you, Mila?' How did these two women know so much more about my husband than I did?

'Um, I guess,' admitted Mila awkwardly. 'Lo,' she began, craning her neck to look me in the eye, 'it w-wasn't really my secret to t-tell, and anyway ...'

The word 'secret' jabbed at my nerves. Vetoing my initial response for the sake of Kai, I took in a deep breath.

'Yet something else he hasn't cared to share with me.'

'I didn't mean to start anything, guys, I'm really sorry. I just assumed you knew ... We're five minutes away, are we all good?'

Mila offered an agreeable nod just after detecting my own.

As memories of our friendship threatened to surface, they were interrupted by the generic ringtone sounding from my pocket. Kai sat up to allow me space to answer. As soon as I saw the number, my gut flooded with nervous energy, I considered ignoring it, in case of more bad news.

'Hello?'

'Is it Dad? Mum, is it Dad?' Kai probed, reaching to the phone with both hands.

'May I speak with Mrs. Attah?' came a male voice.

'Speaking.'

He began by introducing himself as the same detective I'd been interviewed by previously.

'Is this a good time to talk?'

Was there any good time to find out your husband was either lying in a ditch somewhere or planning his second marriage?

'Sure,' I said, opting to put myself out of my current misery.

'Some information has come to light regarding your husband's case. If you could come down to the station at your next available opportunity, to go over the details?'

'What information? Is he okay?'

'I'm afraid I'm not at liberty to divulge details over the phone. Are you able to attend?'

'Of course. I'll be three or so hours though, I'm in Swellendam.'

'I'll be waiting, just ask for me at the desk.'

I pressed the red button, ending the call, immediately giving way to a wave of nervous energy. Kai shifted on my lap, growing uncomfortable and restless.

'I have to go back to Cape Town, Sarah. I'm so sorry. You must hate me. They have information on Dan and need me to go.'

'No, no, it sounds important, don't worry about us. If it's all right with Mila, I'll take her and Kai back to the B & B until we hear from you?'

'Kai as well?' I took a moment, considering how best to navigate this.

I wanted my son with me for comfort, for his *and* my own, but even if Dan was waiting for us at the police station, there were things I needed to ask him privately before we all reunited.

'Is that okay, Mila? Would you mind?'

'Actually, he can come with me, it's best if we stay together ... I think.'

Mila scanned us both, slowly adopting a gentle, motherly approach in the way that her features widened, and her tone of voice informed me that our trip may not end with good news.

I pondered this eventuality as I tried to still Kai on my aching knee for a little longer. Her knowing more about my husband's previous life, and her current ability to assess the situation objectively, helped me make up my mind. With great mental persuasion from myself, I agreed to let Kai stay with Mila at Sarah's B & B.

Kai hadn't offered anything in the way of a protest, and this was even more painful than I had imagined.

'Be careful, Lois. Keep us informed, yeah?'

I offered a nod that served as both my answer and a thank you, and scooped Kai up into my arms, savouring the feel of him. 'I love you so much, darling. Be good and call me if you need me ... for anything, okay?'

We drove to Sarah's B & B before I continued towards the highway, the warmth of Kai's skin leaving a residue of heat along my body.

Now, if only I didn't have to fill the hours in transit, accompanied by nothing more than my thoughts.

14

The speed dial read ninety kph. I weaved through the highway traffic nervously, trying to escape the mental torture that revealed snippets of our happiest moments together as a couple. Past tense.

I feared what lay in wait for me at the police station. I feared no less my capacity to adapt to any further regression in circumstance. I only hoped I'd arrive to find my husband waiting with open arms and tear-stained cheeks. He would race over and embrace me with a deep, genuine longing before explaining away our separation as a terrible misunderstanding. But as I glanced in the rear-view mirror to the back passenger seats, I remembered the message. The single text that was simultaneously as baffling as it was life-changing.

Losing Kai was comparable to nothing else, I recalled. Not even losing Lindani. To have thought our son had been kidnapped, held prisoner to fulfil some pervert's darkest desires. I shook my head to dissipate the image, then suddenly felt more at ease. At least I'd dodged one bullet on this godforsaken trip.

It was encouraging to know the police had prioritised our case as they'd said they would. I was losing optimism in my chances of securing concrete leads or explanations on my own. I considered leaving the Cluedo work in their hands, at least temporarily.

It was impossible to recall how I'd felt on our journey over to South Africa. I must have resembled a normal, functioning human then, though I'd forgotten entirely how to mimic one now.

Cars cut across my lane recklessly, causing me to slam on the brakes a couple of times. In my haste, I'd adopted the local way of driving so was no longer sanctioned the obligatory margin of leeway. I dabbed the brakes and retreated to the inside lane.

I leered over at the terrain through my window, the beauty of nature stunting my breath. *Why do people think they have the right to destroy everything in their path?* To my left stood a sea of dilapidated metal structures, undulating along the horizon. Clusters of casually clad locals going about their daily business. Was Lindani amongst them? Had he been hidden in the shadows, observing us from a safe distance? Had he trailed our journey to Swellendam, or beaten us to it? Had there been someone else preventing him from reaching out to us, despite him having wanted to?

Thoughts of him became disjointed. If he was able to contact me once, then why hadn't he done it again? He clearly hadn't had second thoughts about his decision to leave. How sick would he have to be to think we could forgive him? The worst part was, I knew that I would, eventually.

Replacing the well-rehearsed habit of dialling my husband's number in times of distress, I tapped Mila's name on the screen set in the console, for no other reason than to hear Kai's voice.

A couple of rings sounded from the car speaker until I motioned to end the call. I'd overlooked a message, so tapped voicemail on my contacts list instead.

I listened intently, under the premise that there had been some kind of mistake. A man's voice reverberated through the car as if not a single day had passed since we had last spoken.

'Lois, it's me. How are you and Kai? Listen, I just thought I should check in with you as I had a strange call from Lindani a few days back. It cut off before he could say anything much, so I just assumed it was a pocket dial, or whatever you call it. Anyway, hope you're all okay and having a lovely holiday. I'm always here if you need me. Bye, darling.'

What the hell was going on with my life right now? My mouth shifted fitfully, as if swallowing an angry bee. The voice was unmistakably that of my father.

He'd had a strange call from my husband? Shouldn't the very fact he was calling have been strange to him? Had they even exchanged numbers?

The bond between the donor and I had dissipated when he'd decided to replace Mum, and at a time we needed him the most. Since then, each and every dip I'd had into depression was reminiscent of said memory. The consideration of obtaining contact with him came uncomfortably close during the dark times. But never close enough.

Bitterness was the fabric of our severed connection. If he had been present enough to support me through Mum's death, perhaps I would have learned how to work through my grief like a normal person; whatever that was.

I felt exposed, despite being alone. My body responded like that of a schoolgirl presenting her English homework to a room full of published authors.

It niggled away at me as I continued down the highway. Was Lindani on Dad's recent call list? But why? It could have been a genuine mistake? Could it? After the initial shock of hearing my sperm donor's voice again, I considered returning his call. It would be foolish not to, given the circumstances.

I feared crumbling into a heap of jumbled game pieces at the sound of his greeting, which would negate the purpose of my call. This time I wouldn't be calling to wish him a quick happy birthday or to allow Kai to thank his grandad for his Christmas gift. No, this time it would be a conversation built on sourcing information.

No pressure, Lois, deep breaths.

The conversation had to remain concise and to the point throughout; hopefully that would discourage general chit-chat. I didn't want him, for a second, to think I had forgiven him.

He answered after the first ring.

'Lois?'

'Dad,' I said, infested with awkward energy.

'It's so good to hear your voice … is everything okay, darling?'

I drummed my fingers across my temples, the action causing a dull ache behind my eyes. Something was off. His voice or projection or mood was different. Maybe I'd caught him off guard by calling back. Perhaps he'd anticipated me being annoyed for letting slip his contact with Dan? Or more likely, that witch of a woman was in earshot.

Which was it?

'Yeah ... yeah, I'm okay ...' My instinct was to ask him how he was doing, tell him I missed him and loved him like I used to when I was super small.

'I need to ask you something.'

'Sure. I assume you got my message?'

'About that, I need to know what you remember from the call.'

'Okay, it was really brief though, so I'm not sure if I can help much?'

'I just need to know exactly what you heard ... what did he say? Were there voices in the background, noises? How did he sound? It's really important you tell me everything.'

'What's happened? Is he okay?'

The infantile part of me craved his sympathetic ear. For him to tell me everything was going to be fine. After the affair, I'd felt I had to be bigger, stronger and older than my years, and I never did quite muster enough will or strength to forgive him, especially because of how and when it happened.

'To cut a long story short, there was a fire at our hotel. We were evacuated and Dan hasn't been seen since. There's reason to believe he wasn't hurt, but I have no idea where he is.'

'Jesus, Lois, why didn't you tell me? Are you or Kai hurt? I can fly out to you, just say the word.'

'Please, just tell me what you heard?'

'Are you alone? I'll get a flight right now?'

'No,' I said bitterly.

'I want to help you; this is torture, hearing you this way.'

I rolled my eyes at the windscreen. 'Torture for you, is it?' I said coldly, recalling the tight reins his she-devil still had over him.

'Have you been to the police?' he asked, drawing in his focus.

'Of course I have, bloody hell.' My fingers dug deeper into my flesh, both calves straining from the insistent tapping of my feet against the hard surface of the car floor.

'What did they say? Are they doing anything about it?'

'I don't know, Da—' I stopped myself just in time. 'I don't know, I hope they are. Please, I need to know what you heard,' I pleaded with a little more fire than I'd intended.

'Love, there isn't much to tell, there was just commotion in the background, muffled like his phone was under something. It must have lasted all of a few seconds. I wish I had more to tell you.'

'What kind of commotion?'

'Why don't I book you a flight to come straight back home? You and Kai? It's too dangerous for you both out there alone.'

If he could have seen how far my eyes rolled back into my head, perhaps he'd have realised how close I was to hanging up. 'Stop!'

'Well … it was background noise, scuffling … I'm not sure. It sounded noisy, like chaotic but quiet at the same time if that makes sense?'

'No, it doesn't. Scuffling? Between people?'

'I don't know, I'm sorry, it just sounded like he'd called by mistake, that's why I didn't initially think there was anything to it. I tried calling back a couple of times and I couldn't get through, so thought it best to check.'

I had eased off the accelerator without realising. My speedometer now read ten kph under the limit. I may not have noticed at all if it wasn't for the flashing headlights behind me.

'There must be something you remember.'

'Lois, I'm sorry, there really isn't anything more to it. I always try to reach him if I've missed one of his calls, so it really wasn't that unusual to me.'

So they were in frequent contact. My mind reeled. *Stay focused, Lois.*

'I'm just waiting to talk to someone at the bank, so I only have a couple of minutes, I'm really sorry, it's just not great timing.'

'When was it exactly … this pocket dial?' I couldn't keep the anger out of my voice.

'Lois, I'm not the enemy here. I'm genuinely trying to help you.'

Through clenched teeth I guided the conversation back to the matter at hand.

'When was the call *please*. What day and time?'

'Hold on, I'll check my call list,' he offered defeatedly. 'It was on the fourth of this month, eight thirteen p.m. Does that mean anything to you?'

I don't know, shit. Think!

'Did you speak much, before us coming here I mean?'

The receiver was silent.

'Are you there? … Did he tell you he was bringing us here to leave us? … Hello?' My gut told me this man knew more of Lindani's movements than I did right now. More than he cared to share with me.

'Sorry, love, I'm next in. I have to go for now, but don't disappear okay?'

'If you hear anything or remember anything tell me straight away!' I managed to squeeze in before we terminated the call.

'I will, darling. Please be careful.'

The line went dead, leaving silence to fill the car. I sat with both hands clenched around the steering wheel, staring at the junction I should have taken but had been too deep in thought to action.

I couldn't be sure who had hung up first.

There were so many things I needed to know. He wasn't giving much away and he sure as hell wouldn't tell me if Dan had said he had plans to go solo in South Africa. If they'd had regular contact, then who knew what had been discussed? Was it possible they were in it together? My dad hadn't been the best role model in the world … or even in my life. I'm sure he would have encouraged my husband to 'follow his heart' regardless of the shitstorm that would be left in his wake. But then again, why would he confide in *my dad*? Even the neighbours would have been a more viable alternative.

Dad and I hadn't had any one-on-one time together since my teenage years. I wasn't proud of my behaviour towards him since then. If anything, I'd made my life harder than it had to be. But he'd been the first man that ever broke my heart, and I just couldn't help but think everything would have been different if he'd been the man Mum and I thought he was.

The little cartoon car followed the blue line around the map in front of me. I decided I was going to ask the police to contact him. He knew more than he was letting on.

It was painful questioning him myself, and I really doubted he would tell me everything they'd talked about regarding our marriage. Getting the police involved really was the only way to surface anything he may be keeping from me. It couldn't be a coincidence that Dad had now tried to contact me, now he knew I would need someone to love me.

It was the only lead I'd had thus far. What else could I do?

15

THEN

I walked down the darkened hallway into Mum's room.
I really had to stuff my cheeks into the fabric of the duvet before
the last traces of her slipped away.

I pressed the face of the rag doll into the sheets and across the
pillows, scrubbing firmly back and forth until she possessed Mum's
humanly scent. It was more taxing than I'd expected, even the chill
of the night air failed to block the rush of blood that surged to my
upper body.

Satisfied my method had been a success, I dashed back down the
hallway and trapped the doll under my duvet, savouring her scent. I
would sleep better, knowing Mum was with me again.

The thought of her standing there all alone, silently waiting for me
to acknowledge her existence was painful. I clutched the doll close
to my nightie as more tears rained down. *What if Mummy was scared
on the way to heaven, or she was lost? No. Angels don't get scared
or sad, do they?*

How long did it take for someone to get to heaven anyway?

I didn't want to waste a second not knowing.

'Dad!' I barked his name urgently. 'Dad!' I slammed my feet onto
the carpet in a fit of rage.

'Lois, are you okay, what's wrong?' He came charging into my room, peeling the white T-shirt down over his torso, and made towards me in a panic.

My tantrum dulled at the sight of him, despite the anger remaining ignited. I shuffled my legs back onto the bed, clutching my knees tightly. Dad plonked himself beside me again and made to wrap his arm around my shoulders. I shuddered at the advancement and uttered a firm, 'No!'

He withdrew.

'It's four a.m., darling. You've just had a nightmare that's all, it's okay.'

Wiping invisible specks from the corners of his eyes, he explained how nightmares worked. How it was normal to have them, especially for children who had suffered a loss such as mine.

He really didn't understand. He didn't know how I was feeling. My entire life was a nightmare and sleeping was the only time I could fool myself into believing I was happy again.

I resented that he was the only person in the house now, too. It was a feeling that grew each time he tried to strike up a pointless conversation, one that would usually be full of lies anyway.

The energy I needed to respond proved too exhausting, so our exchanges only served to make me resent him further. The really urgent things though, I would have to swallow my pride. Just for the *really* urgent ones.

'How long will it take for Mum to get to heaven?' I blurted.

He rubbed his palms across those same blue baggy check pants. Goose pimples coated his forearms.

'Oh, well someone as special as your mum will be there already,' he reasoned, smoothing over the pimples with his fingers.

I smiled. She was okay then. If she was in heaven, she wouldn't be alone.

My eyes gradually gave in to the pull of sleep, imagining Mum floating like an astronaut through the clouds, weaving in and out of sight during a celestial game of hide and seek with Nanna and Grandad.

I looked around in the morning light to find Dad had already left the room. The doll lay facing me on the same pillow. I sniffed the top of her head. For the first time in a while, I felt strong enough to face the day. That was until a disorderly clunking of cutlery signalled that his replacement woman may be sat downstairs in our kitchen, and perhaps had been sat there all through the night as I slept. Invisible tears pricked my eyes, and with the same intensity my heart deflated. I envisioned how she would sit facing him, their knees reaching out towards one another from their bar stools. Maybe hers would be bare, not even covered by pyjamas. She would sit and giggle, staring into his face, cultivating the attention that should have been my mum's.

Fuelled by an insatiable desire to stop them once and for all, I flung my duvet aside and charged midway down the stairs, growling with rage, until I had afforded myself a shielded view of the kitchen.

• • •

He must have heard the wardrobe doors slam shut. I'd washed, brushed my teeth, and changed into my favourite pair of purple leggings with the butterfly T-shirt Mum had treated me to on one of our shopping trips. I was intending to go out to the back garden and play in my Wendy house in case he was to bring Mum's replacement home. I collated my pencils and began to scribble a few strokes onto a plain white piece of paper with my favourite shade of pink, but my thoughts flitted elsewhere, until they were utterly consumed with make-believe scenarios.

I had rehearsed what I would do if I were to stumble upon Dad's witch, either in the living room or if I opened the front door and found her standing there in front of me. I would slam it shut without saying a word and twist the lock so she would know she wasn't welcome. Just as she left, I would call out, 'Don't come back!' and if she cared anything at all about what she had done to me, she wouldn't.

'Lois, come down please, breakfast is ready.' His voice echoed through the empty house.

I was going downstairs anyway.

Dad smiled a wide grin as he saw me enter the kitchen.

'Good morning, sweetheart. French toast, your favourite,' he said, placing the hot food on my best Princess Belle plate.

It did smell good, and I sure was hungry.

He sat down on the opposite side of the kitchen counter. We usually ate meals around the TV with trays on our laps. Maybe he wanted to talk to me about something. The thought made me lose my appetite, even before I had finished deciding upon today's motive.

I gulped down the glass of fresh orange juice and planned how best to escape without him coming after me.

'How about,' he began, tucking into his breakfast, 'me and you get our swimming kits and head down to the baths? We could go straight after breakfast if you'd like. Might cheer us both up.'

A venomous sensation contaminated my blood flow.

'What d'ya think?'

She's there isn't she. You think I'm stupid. All those times I'd gone with him to the baths. All those times I'd been so wrapped up in my world, too wrapped up to notice. He knew how much I loved to be in the water, so it made sense for him to be the one to insist on taking me. All those weeks I hadn't noticed. A sinking feeling gripped my bowels. Perhaps it was *my* fault. Maybe if I had paid more attention to who Dad was talking to, he wouldn't have had the chance to meet this woman, and Mum wouldn't have had to feel the added pain of his betrayal.

This is why he'd made my favourite breakfast. Before, he'd always tell Mum to give me porridge or cereal instead of that 'greasy stodge'.

A crescendo of noise escaped my lips, reaching its pinnacle as I smashed the glass of orange juice against the kitchen worktop. I ran out into the garden.

I could hear Dad call after me, he was angry now. Angry I'd ruined his plans to meet that other woman. I would ruin his life, like he had ruined ours.

Throwing myself onto the beanbag cushion in my Wendy house, I buried my head pitifully. He thought I didn't know but I did. I knew from the moment I saw that reptile sinking her teeth into him at the swimming baths.

'If you don't open the door I'm coming in, Lois. You can't keep behaving like this.'

I ignored him.

All those times I thought we were bonding. Just me and Dad. I'd let him, *only* him, into my world and we'd shared it together. It was our special secret. He said he loved it as much as I did, but all along he had used me to get to her. And now, he wanted to do it again.

'Lois, I mean it. We need to talk. Come out here.'

I ignored him.

'I'm not leaving.'

He sat on the grass outside my makeshift wooden sanctuary.

'Okay, so we'll do it your way,' he conceded.

Part of me wanted him to keep trying, to keep talking to me. I still harboured hate towards him, but of course I felt love for him too. Either that, or his company took the edge off my loneliness. I found it easier to communicate with him out of view so decided to share some of the best memories we had of Mum. Remind what he had lost, the pain he had caused.

I remember the summer we hosted our own family Olympics. That was probably my favourite. Dad chose a song to choreograph our gymnastic piece too. Me and Mum both had the same one, so competition was thick in the air. She kept snooping in on my practice sessions with Dad, said she was a bit rubbish at generating ideas so wanted to pinch some of mine. They both commented how brilliant I was at executing the moves. I had all those dance movies to thank, plus I was naturally more flexible than Mum. I let her have one or two of them, but I'd still won in the end. Cleared the lead by five whole points. Dad even hosted an awards ceremony with medals and everything.

'Lois, are you listening?'

I paused my train of thought. I had to before the dominant bubble of regret popped and caused more undue pain. The sensation of loss resurfaced.

I figured Dad must have loved us back then. I wanted to share the

memories aloud. To remind him what he'd thrown away. I only noticed
my words were mute by his lack of response and his utter disinterest
to revel in the memories with me.

All was quiet.

I caught a flicker of movement from the corner of my eye. Where
was he going? Where would he possibly rather be? Then I realised. He
was on his way to tell that woman his awful daughter had scuppered
their plans to meet by turning down swimming. My innards constricted
enough to cause a curdling sensation in my stomach. I wouldn't allow
it, not this time, so I fought the desire to remain in the safety of my
Wendy house and instead batted open the heavy weight of the door – a
short-lived freedom before cowering back into its confines. I scanned
the grassy space between both fence panels and spotted Dad loitering
in the kitchen.

I was exhausted by my very existence. My energy supplies couldn't
meet the demand required to have it out with him.

I pieced the door back into its slot, attempting to redirect my frustrations. There was nothing to smash, nothing to throw. What good
did it do anyway. It never really changed anything, and I don't think
I even felt better afterwards.

Thankfully, the anger ceased to burn after only a few minutes.

I pulled over the pink plastic chair and began to arrange my coloured
pencils in order of which I thought matched best. It was as I flicked
through my colouring book that there was a knock at the door.

'Come in,' I said, immediately cursing my own instincts.

I felt a tug of resignation as Dad entered with two dishes of food
and pockets full of cutlery. He pulled up the remaining chair and sat
by me at the table. Not a word escaped his lips. I couldn't see any of
his pink chair at all from where I was sitting – his lumps had spilled
over on both sides of the plastic. All I could think of was how much
he resembled a giant from those fairy tales. Perhaps if I called out
fee fi fo fum he would remember how he used to pull me up the
staircase as I clung onto a twisted bedsheet, how Mum would give me

a pocket full of M&Ms, claiming them to be magic beans. Then Dad would shout those words before dragging me up to the giant's lair. I'd return moments later after tickle torture, having traded my beans for a multipack of Wotsits.

'Thanks,' I said genuinely.

A bottle of Tropicana found its way to my hand. He sat and unscrewed the lid slightly before picking at his bowl of porridge.

He'd chosen me over her. Just this once, he'd chosen me.

Gradually, my appetite returned as we sat together in silence. The French toast was hot and fresh, as if it had been remade especially. Dad's porridge, on the other hand, was beginning to skin over and creep below room temperature. I could tell by how gloopy it had got.

We each brought a mouthful of food to our mouths.

He must have heard it too. A faint voice rang out through the garden. Assuming it would be one of the neighbours coming by to bring us more casseroles, our food succumbed to the pull of hunger. That was until the name being called out became distinguishable.

His body jolted up from the seat, frantically sending the cutlery tumbling to the floor. 'Two minutes, love.'

I watched in horror, hiding myself from view the best I could.

I was wrong. He's chosen her.

16

'Do you recognise this username?' said the investigating officer, referring to the printout of online posts.

'YDTNM? I don't think so, should I?'

'We found a link between this username and Mr. Attah's channel. Do you have any idea who could be operating under this alias?'

The pressure rose in my chest. Why had I not accosted Lindani more about his work life?

'What kind of link?'

'Well, there appears to be a degree of reciprocity between your husband and this user.'

I fought back the shallow breaths and rapid heart rate. Bolts of lightning struck at my chest as I thought back to the weekend trips I'd demanded I take without him, how I'd craved respite from my compounding insecurities after giving birth.

'Look here.'

I followed his eyeline to the highlighted comments from the same user. 'As you can see, there are consistent posts from two thousand and fifteen onwards.'

'Okay?' I said, unsure of what he was hinting at. 'But don't people post stuff all the time? Why is that unusual?'

'If we take a closer look, we can see that not only do the comments grow progressively more familiar, but they also indicate a knowledge of Mr. Attah's whereabouts … to an extent.'

I took a closer look, tracing the text with my forefinger.

'But there aren't even any replies from Lindani, so it's more than likely he isn't involved with this person … no?'

'Well, ordinarily, comments become less frequent over time with an absence of direct two-way dialogue or when there aren't any new videos posted. As we can see from the printout, YDTNM has commented regularly on the last video that Lindani posted, which as you can tell from the date was back in January two thousand and nineteen. The comments have taken on a different nature. A simple heart or seemingly meaningless symbol, gradually omitting dialogue altogether.'

'So, it's probably some obsessed fan or something? A woman who fancies her chances and has taken to stalking?'

I picked the skin from my thumb, conflicted between disappointment at being directed to another faux lead and becoming desperately hopeful that it *was* just that, a faux lead.

'That's possible, however Mr. Attah's private messages were suggestive of further communication.'

The distance between the walls had grown narrower since the last time I was there. The white paint showed signs of wear, appearing more a dull shade of cream. I hadn't noticed the offensive smears defacing its overall uniformity, not until now.

'How?'

'Well, the user provided your husband with a contact number and expressed his or her anticipation to see him.'

I sat with bated breath.

'What did he say to her? I'm assuming it's a her.'

'Well as you probably already know, Lindani doesn't usually comment on his posts at all. He prefers referencing his followers at the beginning of the next video he shoots, as indicated by his past videos.'

I didn't know that, but it was a breadcrumb of relief I wasn't going to deny myself.

'We think he picked up communication covertly via the number that was provided.'

'Why would you think that – he hasn't shown interest in her from what

I can see? I don't understand.' I suppressed a thrum of worry in my throat.

'The last message, which was ten days ago, coincided with his arrival in South Africa.'

My courage grew enough to meet his eye. 'Okay.'

The officer covered my current pile of 'evidence' with a new printout, presenting the most recent inbox message.

FROM: *YDTNM*
I'll miss this. End of an era, I guess. Here's one for old time's sake. See you TOMORROW!! <3 xxxxxx

I was sure they were staring at the throbbing vessel protruding from my temple. When I used to approach Mum with an inventive theory I had about one of my classmates, she used to tell me that 'thinking isn't knowing'. The difference between thinking and knowing had never before seemed so distinct.

'There's more, Mrs. Attah.'

Way to kick me while I'm down.

'Lindani's email account showed he ordered from an online lingerie retailer three days ago. He'd arranged for there to be a personalised message on the tag. This confirmed our suspicions that the intended recipient was someone other than you.'

I held my bottom lip inside my mouth, shifting in my seat as pain seared through the skin that encased my organs.

'I take it you haven't received any gifted items from your husband over the last day or so? Mrs. Attah?'

Lingerie? I closed the lids of my eyes, preventing the spike in blood pressure from shooting them straight out.

'Mrs. Attah?' he repeated, this time a little more firmly.

'No! No, that can't be right, it's a mistake, someone has made a mistake I'm telling you!'

'Have you received any gifted items from your husband?'

I considered the possibility the items in question had been lost in the mail or were sent to our address back home and hadn't arrived in time before we left. Or perhaps he'd ordered them on behalf of someone else as a surprise.

I shook my head. The shock slowly transformed my physiology into a spectacle of impassiveness.

'What was the address?' I said with an air of calm I knew to be fraudulent.

'Excuse me?'

Was Alice the other woman? Was that the real reason he was so insistent that we didn't come to South Africa?

'These gifts, where did he send them? Who were they intended for?' I pressed.

Why was Sarah so seemingly helpful? Had Lindani recruited her to look after us and make sure we got home safely without him? Or was she intent on exposing them together? Hence her offer of taking us to Alice's.

'I understand this is very difficult to hear. I'm sure it would be for any of us. We'll give you a minute to process everything,' said the male investigator before beginning his exit from the desk.

Had their contact had been consistent throughout our dating? And I'd never so much as seen a picture of her.

'Who is she?' I asked, not fully wanting to find out, flitting my attention clumsily between the officers and my own thoughts.

I had to ask Mila if she had met this Alice woman before. I needed to find out if she was really his foster parent.

'We're not sure. The username showed up only on searches that linked communication between your husband's account and the user, exclusively. The phone number appears to be a temporary pay as you go SIM card, so the only thing we know is that it was purchased somewhere in the UK. We think when the dust settles on your situation, they will be more traceable, no longer feeling the need to cover their tracks, and so forth.'

'Can I see the number? Give me *her* number,' I pleaded as aggressively as my civility would allow.

'I'm sure you'll understand why I cannot do that.'

The tiny light I'd had left dulled again behind my eyes, but the fire in my gut flickered with the last signs of life.

'It isn't a question, it's a request,' I demanded, pressing my fists firmly onto the desk between us.

Both officers looked at each other, but something in their composure told me they weren't considering it as a viable option.

'Things work a little differently here than they do in England,' said the ageing male detective. My sudden feeling of insignificance reminded me that I was far from home, a realisation that again seared at my heart for Dan allowing us to come here in the first place.

'You'll understand we can't just hand over that information.'

'So that's it then? He's gone?'

The officers glanced at one another, as if contemplating how best to conclude the horror show that was my life.

'For a fee perhaps, and if we were to be called out of the room, the number could find its way into your hands? Am I making sense?'

Were back on! A sly smile crept across my lips. It was a proposition I'd seen in gangsta movies and TV shows, but never had I imagined I would partake in real life.

'What kind of fee?' I said, with hesitation, my nerves awakened by unfamiliar ground. Was I really going to consider bribing them to find out who this woman was?

'Ten thousand rand … minimum,' stated the ageing male, matter-of-factly.

The number didn't immediately equate in my non-mathematical brain, but I knew from handling our holiday cash there was nowhere near that amount now.

'Umm, I don't have that much money.' *I'm negotiating with criminals.* Our exchange added a new dimension to my already liberal concerns.

'Cash, now.'

I felt an unspoken threat looming over me as I sat mute, recoiling my limbs under the plain wood table. *How important is this number anyway?*

What would Mila say? Probably that it wouldn't change anything.

'I … don't h-have …' I scanned their faces for the most minute sign of concession.

'You lie to us?' said the rotund, expressionless female, suddenly growing animated.

'No, I just, perhaps one hundred rand would be enough?' I suggested, stupidly.

Sweat threatened to show through my T-shirt and I was growing afraid of what would happen to me, were I to challenge them further.

'She will go to the bank with you now and come back here with nine thousand, no less?' he requested, plumes of rage encroaching his pupils.

How did it get to this?

I had to limit their frustrations if I was going to see Kai again. 'I can't. I don't have enough,' I confessed, embracing my growing urge to leave the police station and return to my son. 'But it's okay, the number … I don't need it, it's all right. I just have to go back,' I said with my last remaining trickle of confidence. For the first time, I wondered if the police were responsible for Dan's disappearance.

I held eye contact with each of the officers in turn, scanning the confines of the room during any moment of transition. *Do they know something?*

'Unfortunately, in light of the circumstances,' said the man who'd initiated the offer, 'and the absence of any evidence of wrongdoing, we're no longer able to commit our resources to the investigation. In adherence with South African and European law, if an adult elects to leave his family and become untraceable, I'm afraid we're obliged to allow that person to remain untraceable. Am I being clear, Mrs. Attah?'

• • •

It was ten o'clock in the evening. I'd been sitting in my hire car for three hours, staring blankly into the darkness. My face bulged, sore from the avalanche of emotion that had seeped from my pores. I'd called Dan's phone repeatedly until the pain in my heart had seeped into every nerve ending, preventing my fingers from dialling. My head throbbed with a consistency comparable to water torture, each pulse of life supplemented by a vision of my husband with another woman.

I couldn't face returning the two missed calls from Mila. I wasn't ready to verbalise what I knew. That would only make it real, and I wasn't equipped to deal with my new reality yet.

Mila's judgement would exude from her when she learned I had failed. Failed at the only achievement I thought I had succeeded her in.

Images and shapes danced before me, until I was able to fix my vision onto the iPhone that sat insecurely in my grasp. I flicked through my pictures with a speed unworthy of acknowledgement, having not quite synced with the real world. I studied each image closely as it blinked on my screen, searching my husband's eyes for any hint of unhappiness or dissociation, no matter how minuscule – so much so that I began to believe everything was a clue I'd formerly ignored.

I was numb to the self-induced injuries that were making their mark on my skin. My arms and legs hit out recklessly at the car interior in expression of raw suffering and halted only when I noticed the image of my lost love falling into the blackness beneath me. It was cruelly apt. It too had fallen from my reach.

The weight of my loss was colossal. Hello loneliness.

• • •

The sound of sirens woke me from my troubled sleep, only to acquaint me with a new troubled reality. Cool bumps peppered my body to conserve any trace of warmth that remained inside me. I rubbed my upper arms desperately, slightly relieved I hadn't lost all ability to function.

The dial read 03:42. It was too late to find anywhere to stay for the rest of the night, so I switched on the car engine and dared to look at my face in the rear-view mirror. I was a mess. For sure, it had been a while since I'd really made the effort to look my best for him. If only I had realised when it counted, I could have done things differently. I clenched my stomach as a reflex to the regret that flooded me. Regret for insisting Kai and I accompany him here, for overlooking safety concerns that I'd even had myself but had ignored in order to feed my selfish desire for a holiday.

I immediately jumped into replaying moments Lindani and I had had together, every memory I'd misread.

The times his phone sounded during the night. He'd claimed it was comments being left on his cooking channel. How I used to interpret his hyper vigilance when on dates as people-watching. The time I drove twenty miles to surprise him – wearing red lace lingerie beneath my coat – for him to tell me he was visiting a friend who lived a few streets away. Too far, it appeared, to return home to welcome me in. He'd been deceptive from early on, but I was too blinded by attraction to accept it. Even at the hotel there were signs, when he'd rejected me to answer his phone. Work-related, my ass! I should have persisted. And the police … I saw the glances. It was obvious to them. I'd been so locked out of Lindani's affairs, I hadn't even noticed him actually having one.

I remained in the driver seat, disgusted at my reflection, half blaming myself for my role in his infidelity. If only he'd given me the chance to change, to show more of an interest in him, in his dreams, his goals. I couldn't remember the last time I'd asked if he was happy. Perhaps if I had, he would have opened up to me, and our marriage could have been repairable.

In a single movement, I swiped my hands across my face before twisting my hair into a messy bun. Absorbing each punch of intermittent emotion, I began my journey back to Swellendam. I knew I had to get out of there and into familiar territory. Though nowhere, I feared, would feel the same again.

17

Mila greeted me in the tiny car park of the B & B. 'Lois, thank god, what happened?'

I collapsed into her like a woman only half alive.

'Shh, there, there, petal. I'm here now.'

'Thanks, mother,' I joked, lightening my mood, but the question of what she knew about Alice had rotted in my conscience for much of the journey back and it was still nagging at me.

'Mila, what do you know about Alice Bekker?'

'What? Why, what did they say?' she asked, remaining still in her fleshy vice.

'Have you met her? Please think, I have to know if she's who Dan claimed she was.' I assessed Mila's body language and her inability to hold my gaze despite remaining in my direct eyeline.

'Um no, I haven't. But he spoke of her often back when we were together, so I can't see him keeping her on the burner all these years, can you?' she explained, finally.

'Were they ex-lovers, M?' I tried to control my instinct to interrogate her. 'Could they have been friends and developed into lovers, do you think?' I dropped my battered face into her bare shoulder for the second time since returning. The words flowed unwaveringly, becoming muffled as they journeyed through her T-shirt.

'I don't think so, I mean she seems more of a mother figure from things he said. More supportive than romantic.'

I absorbed her explanation without actually processing what it implied.

'But what if it was all a ruse, M? For them to keep contact whilst you were together? And Joe, is *he* real? Is he? It's funny how Dan only decided to visit after he's passed away, don't you think?'

'Just come in and settle down. You need to look after yourself and you can tell me what the police told you when you've had a cup of tea and something to eat.'

'Where's Kai? Is he okay? I have to see he's okay.'

I took a deep stride towards the B & B entrance, enunciating how I hadn't seen this coming.

Mila trailed close behind me. 'Kai's okay, he's been reading anything and everything. Found a really good app to keep him occupied with short stories, poems the lot. Didn't know he was a book worm?'

Silently nodding, I allowed time to flow between us. How much did she really know about Alice?

'What's brought on all this suspicion about Alice anyway?' she asked, rousing a further flicker of suspicion in me.

Not giving away too much of how I was feeling, I decided to tell her a simple truth instead.

'He's gone, Mila. It's true … there's someone else.'

• • •

'Were in this together,' I repeated to myself. It eased the burden slightly, the acknowledgement that I wasn't entirely alone.

I could only look at the modest stack of pancakes on my bedside table, having the appetite for neither food nor life. I sat on the bed instead, stroking Kai's sleeping head.

'At risk of sounding like your mother again, you need to eat,' said Mila. 'Open up!' My lips stayed sealed.

I still felt that familiar pang of loss, hearing the 'm' word aloud, making my desire to return back home and be a proper mother to Kai an overwhelmingly persistent one.

'You're still in shock. And quite frankly you look like shit. Food always helps.'

My cup of English Breakfast was fast refilled, as if to acquaint me with the comforts of home. I toppled a couple of sugars into the modest white ceramic mug and cupped it between both hands, seeking its warmth and comfort.

Ignorant to Mila's concern, my thoughts spilled into the public domain. 'I need to see him, just one last time. We need to look for him still. I can't go back to England alone, not without hearing what he has to say for himself.'

Her eyes portrayed a woman who was contemplating the least damaging way to stunt her best friend's meltdown.

'What am I meant to tell Kai in the meantime? He deserves to see his dad. He needs closure, and I don't know how to give that to him.'

'Lois, it isn't healthy, none of this … for anyone actually.'

'Do you think I don't know that? Do you think I'd put my son through this shit for fun?'

'That's not what I'm saying, and you know it. Listen, I have to tell you something.'

Blood gushed through my ears.

'While you were in Cape Town, I went to look for him. I showed his picture to anyone I came across in the street. I took it into local businesses, knocked on doors, the lot.'

'And …' I awaited the silver lining.

She shook her head. 'Not a single person recognised him.'

'He was a child though when people around here knew him, they probably wouldn't recognise a photo of him as an adult?' I reasoned.

'I guess, but it doesn't help us find him, does it? If no one knows what he looks like?' Mila paused and placed her hand on mine, her compassion seeping through my pores. 'He's made his choice … wouldn't it be more painful to have to see his face again?'

'Sarah seems to think everyone around here knows each other, so someone must know something?'

'It was a long time ago, Lois. It kinda makes sense there wouldn't be anyone who recognises him now. He hasn't any family left, and he never really spoke of friends over here. If you really think about it, it does make sense,' she explained in a sugary, delicate manner.

'Well teach me, then. Tell me all about his family, and who he does in fact have. Because I'm hitting brick walls every way I turn right now.'

'That's it, all of it. He doesn't have a mum or dad or siblings any more. He has a foster family that has dwindled down to Alice. That's all I know.'

I felt a ricochet of regret for my tone of voice. She had dropped her life in England to come and support me. 'What more could I lose?'

Silence drifted between us.

'You could lose yourself.'

Mila knew I'd lost the plot when Mum died and was admitted to a special care facility for two months. I had to move back into the family home with Dad and *her*, so things quickly spiralled. I started sticking pins into my wrists, pushing them all the way in until the tips were irretrievable. I liked it, the control. The pain, too. Before long I was seeing things, imaginary things.

'I was so young back then. It's different now,' I said, wondering really how different my coping skills were now.

I'd learned somewhat how to fight the effects of the feelings, but the feelings were as strong as ever. It was scary sometimes, how I was a slave to them. The dreams I used to lure myself into as a child after Mum's death had turned into nightmares as the years passed, leaving me with no respite from the pain that consumed every living moment.

'Just promise you'll sleep on it,' urged Mila.

The entire way back to Swellendam, I'd had a burning desire to hold my son. Now I was here, I was ashamed to admit, I wanted to avoid him. I'd had confirmation our lives weren't going back to the way they were, so his company only deepened my remorse for not having told him the truth, and not having given him the news he deserved. How could I possibly tell him the truth?

• • •

I'd sent a flurry of vicious messages to Lindani on the journey home. It was pitch black and the roads were clear, so I could really let loose with expressing my contempt.

I'd left messages by the bucket-load. Each voicemail alternating between sobs and screams.

Now I was back at the B & B, I was completely jaded. Worn out from everything I knew to be true.

Sarah hadn't come to greet me when I arrived. Mila mentioned how she, too, had been worried, so her absence hadn't gone unnoticed. In fact, I quite missed her.

Mila stayed perched cross-legged on the corner of the bed. She swept up the remaining syrup with the last cutting of pancake.

'Has Kai said anything to you?'

'He's coping. He hasn't asked anything really; he still seems to be in shock. I did catch him going through my case when I came back from the bathroom though.'

'Your suitcase? Why would he do that?'

'He said he thought it was yours?'

'Sorry, Mila, that's not like him. We lost ours in the fire, he knows that. I really don't know what to tell you. He was probably just confused for a second, I don't know?'

'It's fine, I didn't bring any unmentionables, so we avoided any potential embarrassment!'

'Did he say what he was looking for?' I asked tiredly, feeling obligated to address his behaviour.

'He started saying something about his dad, but I couldn't figure out what he meant, and I didn't wanna push him, so …'

'Ah man, things are really messed up, aren't they?' I pressed the pulsing vein back behind the skin on my forehead.

'There's something else,' she began, searching my expression for a sign of permission to continue.

Turns out I didn't have to use my words.

'There's a reason I shot out of the bathroom. Kai was whispering something. I think he was on the phone to someone.'

'Could you hear any of what he said?'

'Nuh uh, not a word.'

Mila hugged us both before leaving the room, recognising the necessity for me to spend time alone with my son.

'Thanks, Mila,' I said, lightly burying my earlier suspicions of her.

I kissed Kai's cheek and eased off his headset.

'How was your day, my love?'

He allowed me to bring his game to an end, experiencing the tug of mental fatigue, or at least so I assumed.

'You can tell me, you know, son.'

He shrugged. 'Tell you what?'

A seed of hopefulness sprouted within me. 'Whatever it is that you're thinking. All of it, or just a bit of it. It's up to you. It's all up to you.'

'I just want my dad.' It was harder than I thought, hearing those words. 'I'm just waiting for him to come back, Mum! We need Grandad to help, he'll know where Dad is.'

I digested his manner of certainty and childlike belief that his grandad would come to the rescue. 'Okay son,' I appeased, unsure why he'd assume his grandad would be our answer out of this. 'We can do that. But please know that whatever happens I'll always be here for you, okay? No matter what. Me and you.'

'And Grandad?' His youthful innocence stimulated my guilt reserves to release another load.

'Shall we get ready for bed now?'

'I'm tired,' he said factually.

Kai and I motioned the same routine we had since he'd grown old enough to brush his own teeth. The only difference being we were missing our third in command, our third musketeer, the chef to govern us sous-chefs.

• • •

The squeak of the old iron door jolted me awake. I clutched my child close and sprang from the bed. My heart throbbed through my chest, each breath coming more quickly than the last. I scanned the slit beneath the door for any signs of danger. Fighting the urge to call my estranged husband, I lay in wait, trying to assess what was required of me to save us both.

'Lois, it's Sarah. I need to speak with you.'

Making a conscious effort to restore my physiology, I took in long drags of air through my nose, releasing them back calmly into the atmosphere.

'Do you have a minute?' There was a sharp edge to her voice.

'I'm sorry, we were just snoozing. Come in, I'll be in the land of the living soon.'

'It won't take long.' The door slid open.

She glanced over our belongings, pulling at the fabric on her sleeve, awkwardly, neglecting to make eye contact.

'Is all okay?' I said.

'Yeah, no everything's fine. It's just, I know I said I could keep helping you guys, but it looks like I'm going to have to stay here instead. We've had a booking for a big tour group, and we need all hands on deck.'

Sarah's eyes shifted uncomfortably as she loitered in the hallway. I watched her carefully. Something was amiss. Since we'd met, she'd had an air of warmth and confidence about her that certainly didn't match the cold, skittish woman who stood before me.

'Are you sure everything's okay?'

'It is. I am. I hope you understand, I'm sorry to leave you guys hanging like this.'

'Oh, I see.'

'Mila mentioned that you wanted to head back home anyway.' There was a short pause, paired with an inhalation of air. 'She and I have secured some flights back to England. She's making a few last-minute arrangements in the lobby.'

'What?'

'Your flights leave at seven-twenty. From Cape Town.'

'Sorry, you've booked flights for us, without even asking?'

'Mila said she heard you mention you wanted to go back home.'

'Where was she last night? With her ears pressed up against our door?'

It was clear Sarah had run out of things to say.

'I guess I'll pack our things then and meet you both downstairs.'

'Fab, well if I don't see you before, have a safe trip, Lois.'

If I don't see you? She doesn't plan on seeing us off? *What the actual fuck is going on?*

I pressed the door shut, wondering what had changed since I'd been away. Why was she behaving so strangely? I searched my memory the best I could, given the fatigue that was so entwined in my DNA these days.

I hadn't a bad word to say about her, so nothing could have got back. Perhaps something was going on with her personally and she wasn't coping well. Surely, we'd built up enough trust for her to talk things through with me?

I typed a text to Mila, my rising anger seeking immediate release.

TO: *MILA*
Sarah just told me you've booked flights for us to leave. WTF?

A message pinged immediately.

FROM: *MILA*
Morning Lo, yeah thought I'd save you a job. Stopped by your room last night to tell you'd I'd found a good deal but heard you speaking with Kai and didn't want to interrupt. Hope that's okay? Thought you'd be pleased? xxx

I grabbed Kai's hand then led him into the empty hallway, calling out Sarah's name on our approach to the lobby. As we passed, a bedroom door jolted away from its frame. I steadied my breathing for the second time that day and apologised to the guest who was exiting the room next door.

'Do you need help with something, dear?' asked a petite, dark-skinned lady with kind eyes and a shaved head.

Embarrassed, I quickly declined her offer and apologised again for the noise.

Mila had sent another text, this time explaining why it was imperative for us to hurry – it had been a mini-miracle we got return flights at such a good price and at such short notice. Both things I failed to give a shit about, given the circumstances.

I scribbled a rough time under the check-out box by our names in the lobby and rested the pen between my fingers, finding it tough to finally admit defeat and leave.

I loosened my grip after a brief moment of contemplation. The biro rolled across the collection of names on the list, coming to a halt by one several lines beneath our own.

My elbows harnessed the backpacks that had slid from my shoulders, my chest vibrating. I recognised a name in the guest book.

Alice Bekker.

18

Mila scrolled through the images on her screen. No one sparked any interest, so she swiped left a few more times before throwing her phone onto the dashboard.

She cranked up the air-con and shot Kai a reassuring smile through the rear-view mirror.

'Auntie Emma?' began Kai, causing Mila to turn around and face him.

'Yes, lil' man.'

'My dad's at your house, isn't he?' It was a matter-of-fact statement that she sensed didn't require conjecture.

She looked at this little boy's face, confusion bleeding from not only his but her own pupils. Mila traced her memory back to any occasion that could have led him to believe this was true. Did he overhear her tell Lois about Lindani locking himself in the bathroom at her flat after a particularly bad argument? How he'd come out hours later and explained that he'd needed time to centre himself? Mila's chest began to thump out of rhythm.

'Is that what you've told your mummy, sweetie?'

She exhaled as Kai shook his head in response. 'We're going to go there though, aren't we? When we get back to England?'

She scrambled together an improvised response. It was something Mila strangely enjoyed, answering the many weird and wonderful questions asked by children.

'I don't think that's what Mummy has in mind. But it's okay because your dad wouldn't be at my house anyway, would he?' She was pleased with her response.

'Does Mum not want Dad to come back? Is that why?' Kai's brows furrowed deeper than those of a child his age should.

She bit her tongue.

'Of course she does but Mum knows your daddy won't be there, doesn't she.'

'Oh.'

'Kai,' she began, drawing his attention from the car window. 'What makes you think he's at my house?'

'Where is he then, if he isn't there, Auntie Emma?'

Where was Lois? She felt the heat of not really knowing the right thing to say.

There was no evident solution to Lois's predicament, so she figured, the quicker Lois got home and accepted her fate, the sooner they could all move on, and selfishly the sooner Mila's life could also resume. She had to study for her pilot training that was set to start in three months' time, after settling the first gargantuan payment.

She reached for her phone impatiently and typed out a prompting text.

The passenger door clicked open, just as she hit the send button.

'Finally, let's get your damaged ass back home,' she joked.

One look at Lois's face told Mila she wasn't up to receiving anything in the way of humour. Nor was Mila entirely up for delivering it either.

'Too soon?'

'You'll never guess what!'

'What could possibly have happened now?'

• • •

'Okay,' I said, 'I know I'm driving you mad with this. Bloody hell, I'm driving myself mad, but don't you think it's worth staying a touch longer? Alice is staying in the B & B.'

Mila's face gave away nothing.

'Mila she's here, now!'

'It has to be a different Alice. Plus, Sarah would have told you.'

'Sarah's creepin' me out, something's going on with her, which is another reason to hang around, find out why she's been frosty with me since I got back from Cape Town.'

'Oh my god, you need to get a grip! Your son needs his own home, his own bed back in England.'

Mila flicked her feet in rapid succession across the pedals.

'Well, I don't feel good, leaving without knowing what's going on in Sarah's head. And if I could only find out—'

'So,' interrupted Mila, 'hypothetically speaking, if you find out Sarah has a grudge against you, perhaps because she thinks you've lost the plot … will that make you feel better?'

'Well obviously not, but what's the alternative? I just never find out what's going on in my own life? Plus, Alice, she's finally within reach, she could still fill in a few blanks … then we can go back home, yeah?' I turned to my son, who clearly had a weight on his mind.

'Kai?' I pressed, lightly. He turned from the window and fiddled with the iPad on his lap. 'Do you want to go back home?'

It was a simple question, but the hesitation in his voice told me he'd found it to be more loaded than expected.

'I think so,' he said, searching for something in my expression.

Mila saw an opening to inject her interpretation of my findings. 'If Alice knows where Lindani is, and in my opinion she probably didn't even know you were coming in the first place, then do you think that will change anything? Even if you track him down and beg for him to take you back?'

'She did know we were coming, though. Sarah said we were all she could talk about. She was excited to see us. It has nothing to do with' – glancing at Kai I lowered my voice to a whisper – 'begging for him to take me back. I need a reason, some logic to explain everything.'

Mila frowned but didn't say anything.

'Then he's lied to Sarah too. His phone has been off the entire time, hasn't it? When would he have told any of us he'd run off with some bit of—?'

'Mila!' I exclaimed, signalling Kai in the back seat.

'Sorry,' she said with a hint of insincerity.

'Does this mean you're ready to leave?' said Mila as I entered the car.

I shrugged. 'You don't think he's coming back, do you?'

'I hate to say it, but the evidence is staring us in the face.'

'Okay,' I conceded, imparting a lingering kiss to Kai's forehead. 'Let's go home.'

I couldn't help but notice my declaration was met with a soaring 'yay' from the backseat. It was the first trace of joy I'd witnessed for some time.

• • •

Mila peered through the mirror in silence. She'd had her cue to leave, but delayed the process for a minute or two longer. She took in the image of this broken mother and son before her. The display of human strength and acceptance was heart-warming really. Mila couldn't take her eyes from Kai. He was truly innocent in all of this. She wondered for a brief moment how his future would be affected. If the cards he'd been dealt would come back to haunt him. She hoped not, for what it was worth.

A stab of emotion momentarily crippled her senses. It was one she hadn't experienced in some time. The pain of loss was numbing, she recalled. Lindani was now at the centre of Kai's world, just as he had once been at the centre of her own all those years before. She had chosen not to reveal the full extent of her love for Lindani during her friendship with Lois. It was a form of self-preservation that she'd needed to be able to form such a close bond with Lois, and now it appeared, Kai too.

• • •

I gazed at the B & B through the back window as Mila continued to accelerate towards the exit, contemplating how something that once symbolised hope and safety could morph into another facet of mystery and confusion.

Sarah's recent behaviour had had the same effect. Her actions, however, felt slightly less bothersome than noticing Alice Bekker's name on the sign-in sheet. Had it been the same Alice I'd been attempting to track down this entire trip? It must be.

'There she is!'

It was unmistakeable. Sarah was stood brazenly in the top far-right window of the B & B staring directly at us. Her expression was unclear. One of her arms rested around a petite woman with a shaved head, the other pointed towards our car. It was the same dark-skinned lady I had spoken to briefly in the hallway earlier.

I slid from the cheap fabric, the car still in transit. Releasing the passenger door into the warm South African air, I stumbled upon impact as my feet touching the gravel.

'Five minutes,' is all I could think to say.

• • •

'I thought it was you earlier,' confessed the dark-skinned lady immediately as I turned the corner onto the landing.

I was taken aback. 'Sorry?'

'My dear, you were due to stay with me, I was very much looking forward to meeting you both.'

A familiar bubble of emotion rose to my sinuses. I was already relieved by my decision to come back. One of my questions had already been answered.

'Alice?'

A gentle smile brought life to her eyes and a single tear to her cheek.

'My daughter said you were here. You're leaving today to go back to England, is that right?'

I nodded. 'We have to, my son has been through enough. He needs some normality.'

'Of course, my dear. Of course. Without Lindani, no doubt?'

I followed Alice's gaze downwards to my chest. I hadn't even realised I was clenching at the fabric that covered it.

'Wait, who told you we were here again?'

'My daughter, Sarah.'

Sarah must have watched me run towards her and made another swift exit. If she'd taken offence to something I'd done or decided she wanted me out, as it seemed she had, then why had she invited Alice? Had she expected our paths to cross?

'You're her mother?'

Alice nodded delicately. 'She's adopted of course, though I love her as if my blood runs through her veins.'

My mind raced.

'So Lindani's her brother?'

'Dear, they've never had chance to meet but I've told her all about him and his new life in England.'

I felt faint. Words escaped me as I tried to decide how this minor detail affected my recent interactions with Sarah. Could Sarah or Alice have reached him at the hotel? Did they want only him and not myself and Kai? And if so, why?

I didn't know where to begin, but was conscious of my limited time.

'You can't imagine how humiliated I am to have to ask you this, but do you know where my husband is, Alice? You or Sarah? Or anyone for that matter who might know something? Are there other siblings that could be involved somehow?'

'Involved? I know you're worried, my dear, but believe me when I say there is no one *involved*. As distressing as it is, families break down all of the time, this is nothing new.'

Her blunt words stung at the deepest level. First impressions told me Alice was fiercely protective of her family. If my sensitivity hadn't already rendered me feeling worthless, that sprinkle of salt certainly finished the job.

'Something just doesn't sit right. We've been together for a long time now, I know him well, Alice.'

'Do you, though? Know him I mean.'

What does that mean?

'You have proof that he'd met someone else?' she said, more as a statement than a question.

'Yes, I have.' I paused. 'He isn't a bad person; I know he isn't. I've met those kinds of men, but Dan was different, he was always … I don't know, just so different, y'know.'

'Of course he isn't a bad man. Only the Lord himself knows how much I love him. But I'm afraid, my dear, that I've had the misfortune to witness so much in my time that nothing has the ability to surprise me. Lindani is a very troubled man and that alone gives him the potential to do the unexpected.'

'Troubled? How?'

'It would be improper of me to divulge, dear. He wanted you to know nothing of that side of him. He prayed you would see him for the man he grew into instead.'

I locked onto Alice's eyes with a deep helplessness I hoped pleaded with her very soul.

'Perhaps he couldn't be the father and husband he always wanted to be. Pressure Lois, it can be crippling.'

'No, he'd talk to me about it, not just leave?'

'You see, he has many demons. Betrayal and guilt have a way of making people retreat entirely. His journey, no matter how far it takes him, may not yet be over.'

Alice spoke with a mysticism I had never previously encountered. I was hypnotised by her words and experienced a regret difficult to interpret.

'He is a slave to his past; he hasn't always made healthy decisions.'

My exasperated expression bore no secrets. 'We were such a close, happy family.'

'That may be why it has taken him so long to bring you here?'

My intended response was abruptly cut short by the horn of a car. I looked out the window only to be greeted with an angry Mila, flailing her hands in the air, and signalling to the invisible watch on her wrist.

'Lois,' Alice said, interrupting my thoughts. 'Before you leave, would you be so kind as to introduce me to my grandson?'

19

'Promise me you'll never cut it,' he'd said numerous times during our courtship. 'I've never seen anyone with such beautiful hair.'

'It's just hair, you big numpty!' I'd say, secretly flattered by his compliment.

I scoffed illegible words into my bathroom mirror, as if that had been Lindani's hiding place all along.

Slithers of chocolate curls danced their way to the white ceramic, as memories of our past rhetoric flooded me. It's true, the hurt was fading, even if only by the tiniest bit each day. The memories were bearable now at least. And for that, I was grateful.

I had seen Kai, too, talk aloud to his reflection. Sometimes asking his father calmly what time he would be back, as if he had only nipped to collect some groceries. I couldn't be certain who had imitated who or when it started for either of us. But more often than not I hid behind the bathroom door frame and peeped at my son's wistful presentation of his most recent Lego creations. Just that morning, I'd watched him walk his figure into a dense cluster of trees, only for it to be pounced on and mauled by a plastic lion. He called out for help a few times until a Lego man wearing a cape flew overheard and searched for a safe place to land. Kai's Lego figure peered up towards the flying man and called upon him for help. 'Dad, I'm here, help me!' he yelled, in whispered tones, only for him to reply unto himself, 'I can't make it, there's nowhere to land. I'm sorry, son.'

The scissors unceremoniously hacked away at the last five inches of the hair that had characteristically defined me my entire life. I hoped it would instigate the fresh start I so desperately needed.

For the first time since becoming a wife and a mother, I was going to feel free again. At least that's how I chose to interpret my trembling nerves and lack of foresight. An unfamiliar image reflected back at me then, hauntingly. This was it; it was done.

I called for Kai to take out the potato faces from the freezer then made for my straighteners in the bedroom drawer.

It lay brazenly in plain sight, yet didn't immediately catch my eye. I reached out for my hair straighteners but retracted the folded piece of yellow A4 paper instead. I unfolded its corners, recognising the handwriting without any doubt as to who it belonged to. A wild bird awoke within me. Its wings stroked the thick iron bars that surrounded it.

> *Dear Lois,*
>
> *By now you will have learned of my indiscretion. I'm ashamed to have disappointed not only you and our son, but myself by the way I have handled the entire situation. Please know that I have agonised over this decision for the best part of a year. Sadly, thisZ is the only option for us. By the hands I was dealt in life, you would think I could have mustered the strength and decency to discuss how I have been feeling with you in person. For not doing so, I am eternally in your debt.*

The wild bird circled its confines, batting its feathered appendages more rapidly now.

> *You're probably wondering why I have left? If I know anything about you, Lois, you will have driven yourself crazy over all these unanswered questions. Again, I am sorry.*
>
> *First, it is NOT your fault. You have been a model wife, a best friend, and a loyal companion. I sincerely thank you*

for that. There's nothing you could have done differently and likewise there is nothing you could do now to rekindle our marriage. I guess the heart wants what it wants.

I have been in contact with someone for almost two years. We actually met as youngsters, would you believe. They subscribed to my YouTube channel and from there we have built up quite a bond.

I could hear the thumping, feel the vibration. The bird's wings strummed across my ribs in its quest for freedom, delivering stomach bile into the pit of my throat.

Please be at peace in the knowledge that we had a beautiful marriage and don't be sad, as all good things inevitably come to an end.

My love for you will always remain and, of course, for our son. I will always be Kai's father and upon my return I hope you will allow me access. He will need his dad and I'm the only one who can properly make it up to him. I couldn't place this burden upon you and only you. In the meantime, I pray you don't turn him against me and have already dreamt up a logical explanation for my absence.

Anyway, I intend on staying here in South Africa for a short time, until we both get settled into our new lives. I can only hope you'll open your heart to your father. You'll both need him. We plan on returning to the UK very soon so that I can rebuild my relationship with Kai. I do hope we can be friends, Lois, for the sake of our son. If not, then I hope we can at least be civil.

For what it's worth, I didn't have an exact moment in mind to jump ship or however the saying goes. I hope I chose my moment wisely but going off my past behaviour, I don't hold out much hope. I can be certain, however, that I would have had

*a final moment with you both in some shape or form. I really
do love my family, although I realise that must be impossible
to believe right now. If nothing else, do trust in that.*

*I'll continue to write until I see you both again. Please be
happy and move on with your life.*

*Before I forget, I have enclosed the details for a bank
account containing £10,000. Use this money how you please.
It's the least I could do.*

*Please give Kai the tightest hug from me and tell him I love
him. If you need me for anything, just call.*

Hope in time you can forgive me.

Love Dan xx

Shrill squawks pierced into the space through the bars. The wild
bird heard the sound of its own pain reverberate back from the room.
It could be detected over the panic-stricken attempts to break free.
Attempts that were constant and numerous but futile.

Upon reading the last line my hand clenched into a fist, morphing
the paper into a ball. My nails dug into my palm around the news
that had concluded my former life. It was a pleasurable release, both
literally and figuratively.

It didn't even sound like him. *So this is who you are, is it? A selfish,
condescending coward?*

It was with a cruel twisted irony that I got the closure I wished for.

My legs hurled me downstairs to the kitchen where I last
remembered seeing my phone. I mentally configured a rough, albeit
messy speech before pressing call. The pounding of my heart thumped
with a persistent aggression, sending my breathing into an erratic stupor.

I pressed call and paced the room, trying to slow the shallow breaths
that had possessed me. It rang.

'When he returns? *We* plan on coming back?' The words echoed
in my head. Nice! I thought with uncontaminated venom. Wait until
we 'calm down' first before bothering to face us.

I awaited the voicemail greeting I'd been conditioned to expect, but it didn't come.

In my periphery I detected Kai kneeling on the floor in front of the TV, a *Beat Bugs* song ringing out over my noisy, shallow intakes of breath. He wasn't singing along like he always used to, so I decided I would instead, just the parts I knew. Perhaps he would see that it was okay for him to do the things he used to do before his dad left. I circled haphazardly around the kitchen island, dropping smiley faces onto the oven tray, waiting to be joined in song by my son. Nervous energy threatened to swallow my entirety. Kai didn't join me, nor did he acknowledge my terrible rendition.

The ringing persisted, as did my breathlessness.

Was Lindani staring at the screen just as nervously as I was? No sooner had the thought come to me than it left.

'I know you remember the words, pumpkin!'

He wasn't in the mood, he informed me. He only sang when he was cooking with his dad.

I gravitated to the front door as if that would somehow encourage Lindani to answer. The faint UV rays shone a slight reflection off something that lay half covered on the shoe stand. I brushed away the clutter to find an object I recognised. The screen lit up with each ring. Finally both handsets resorted to voicemail in perfect sync.

I clawed at Lindani's phone, desperate for access, for anything to shed light on who this woman was, or where they were staying. I glanced over to Kai, ensuring he hadn't noticed my discovery, or the feral look that had claimed residency on my face.

With an urgency that rendered me useless, I tapped every six-digit code that came to mind. Anything of significance – birthdates, lucky numbers, any combination that felt slightly familiar. Nothing worked. I had an idea. My number flashed up on the screen, so I swiped across to answer the call then cut it off. Access was denied as immediately the phone locked again. I growled a guttural rumble through the spaces between my teeth.

Kai's TV show had ended. He was staring despondently at the wall hooks that stored our matching cooking aprons.

'What's on next, Kai?' I enquired, my voice evidently startling him back into consciousness.

'I don't know, I was just thinking.'

'Oh? Do you want to tell me what you were thinking?' I placed the phone in my back pocket.

Minutes passed between us.

'If Dad isn't at Auntie Emma's house, then he must be here somewhere … yeah?'

If he isn't at Mila's house? What did he mean? I juggled the only options I thought I had. Either tell Kai his dad was going to come back, like he'd stated in the letter, or that he never was?

'Um, what made you think your daddy was at Auntie Emma's house, sweetheart?'

He answered quickly, as if he had been nurturing the desire to tell me. 'I saw a photograph in her suitcase. They were together, holding hands.'

Hacked, brown curls tapped against my cheeks.

I walked over to my son and balanced on one knee, bringing myself to his level. I folded my hands around both of his, clutching them tightly in the space between us.

'Do you want to know why I'm holding your hands?'

A twinge of pain told me he'd needed me all along, needed me to show him how to cope with our loss, with the confusion of our new reality.

His head dipped, but not too fast for me to notice the glassiness of his eyes.

'Because I love you, more than anything.'

Confusion bled into them. 'But Auntie Emma and …' he began, trying to understand how to connect the image with what I told him.

'There are different kinds of love, sweetie. See, do you remember that time me and Daddy picked you up from school and you ran across the playground pulling that little boy Jake behind you? You were so excited for us to meet him, weren't you? Do you remember what you told us?'

Loaded tears threatened, as I watched his face light up at a memory of happier times.

'I said, "This is my best friend, Jakey! He's new and he's from the same place as Harry Potter!"'

'That's right! And Jake's mum had to pry him away from you, do you remember? You held his hand so tight because you didn't know if he would come back the next day.' The thought that his dad might not come back to him splintered my heart into a thousand pieces. I absorbed the pain as invisibly as I could. 'As soon as you both let go, remember how Jake grabbed your other hand and me and Daddy had to promise that he could come to our house for tea one evening?'

Kai let out a wholesome chuckle, one that only just caused his diaphragm to vibrate. I hadn't realised how much I'd missed it until then.

'So, Auntie Emma and Daddy are friends?'

I was cautious. 'That's right. They used to know each other a long time ago, yes.'

I swallowed the temptation to have done with all the lies and tell him everything, to get it all out into the open. I feared Kai would find out for himself eventually.

• • •

I stood aside to allow her through. 'Thanks for coming by, Mila,' I said, curbing my inclination to come right out with it.

'New hair?'

'Don't even!' I said, half-heartedly digging into her bicep.

'It suits you, strangely.'

I returned a tilted smile like the lady on the canvas – her illuminating presence never failed to lure me into a comforting sense of security.

'Well first, the good news. Kai started eating normally again. He even asked me when he was going back to school, and not in an *I'm dreading it* kind of way either.'

'Oh nice, some good news!' she said. 'Where is the little guy anyway?'

We hadn't seen anything of Mila since returning from South Africa the week before, but she had been in almost constant contact via text – which at first I'd found to be infested with awkward energy at her forcing my early return home. But if truth be told, I was beginning to miss her.

'The bad news is, he did see something when you caught him in your things.' I had rehearsed my delivery, hoping to appear secure enough to discuss the picture.

'Oh shit, really.' Her phone tumbled onto the sofa cushion.

'I'm sorry, Lo, it was tucked away under some clothes. I didn't think he'd seen it.'

'It's okay. It's just, I was just a bit taken aback that's all.'

'Where is he?' she deflected.

'He's in his room, catching up with schoolwork. I don't know where he gets his strength, I really don't.'

A seed of embarrassment sprouted. I'd called Mila here to moan about recent developments. I was proud I'd managed to find peace in the time it took for her to arrive since finding the phone, and since Kai delivered his mini bombshell. That was a significant improvement in itself, so I attended the kitchen and poured her a white coffee before filling her in.

Mila's response was a mixture of confusion, irritation and a third unidentifiable emotion. Her eyes flicked erratically between invisible stimuli as she learned about the iPhone that had mysteriously appeared in my home.

'Did Dan just have the one phone?' she asked.

'Why would he have more than one?'

'Oh, *I* don't know, perhaps to secretly lure a random woman into starting a new life with him on the other side of the world?'

My teeth clamped my inner cheek.

'Look we need access to this phone. He mustn't be far, he must have come back and dropped it by mistake. Either that or I am way more irrational than I thought!'

'Just forget the phone, Lo, you're gonna make yourself ill if you carry on. He's gone, that's it, nothing can change that. Kai is muddling through well, given that you haven't exactly mastered how to protect him. Just move on, put yourselves first will you!'

Whose side are you on, Mila?

My head sank into my palms, affording me a bit more time to process Mila's outburst.

She must have recognised my resignation, so softened her approach. 'I don't mean to sound cruel, Lo. You know that, don't you? It's just, you're not a friggin' detective, so give it up!'

I knocked back the last puddle of lukewarm tea before deciding whether or not to tell her about the note.

'There's something you don't know, Mila,' I began, sipping the side of my empty cup. 'He left a note in our bedroom. Said to call him if we needed him, on his number. The number that just so happens to be linked to the same phone that's sitting in my kitchen right now.'

She patted my shoulder in an awkward display of affection. 'That doesn't make sense. You've been trying his phone constantly and it's been off or going straight to voicemail, right?'

'Exactly, and literally since I read the letter it's rung out.'

'What do you mean?'

'His phone, it rings out now, more or less almost as soon as I noticed the note in my bedside drawer. He's close, M. I just know it.'

'What else did it say, this letter?'

'Only that he's coming back here to make things up to Kai ... and with *her.*'

'He's back?'

'He must be, why else would it be here now?'

Mila's lips folded downwards as she computed the information. 'Unbelievable. Fucking hell, we know how to choose 'em, don't we!'

'There's something else.'

Mila visibly held her breath.

'He's left some money for me and Kai, as a sort of consolation prize, if you will.'

'Huh?'

'Exactly!'

We both sat on the chrome kitchen stools, our eyes penetrating the phone that lay between us, a moment broken only by my decision to fill the kettle again.

Mila smirked as if she'd discovered a lead in a missing person's case (which in some respect it was).

'What is it?'

'Your dad.'

I picked the skin by my thumbnail, instinct triggered by a single word.

'What do you mean?' Signs of discomfort infested my body language.

'He was involved with Dan wasn't he, behind your back?'

'Huh? How do you kn—'

'How would you feel if I arranged to meet him, see if he knows anything?'

'Mila, how do you know that? I need to know what you know!' My nervous system tingled.

She supped at her freshly filled coffee cup then slid out the strip of black hair from the crease of her mouth. 'It was you that told me, Lois.'

I glared at my friend, hoping she would impart some more wisdom, enough for me to uncover some truths about their relationship, if they'd had one.

'I don't think he'll want anything to do with us since I fed him to the coppers.'

'He'd understand? And anyway, nothing came of it in the end so it's still worth a shot.'

'I dunno, Mila. I think even after everything, he would have told me if Dan had been in touch, don't you?'

'Not necessarily. Like you said, you're not on the best terms. Anyway, even if your dad knew Lindani was back in the UK, he wouldn't know he lost his phone, would he?'

'A minute ago, you thought tracking him down was a bad idea. What's changed in the last few seconds?'

'Oh, it's an appalling idea but if I've learned anything it's that you're not gonna stop banging on about it until you've all the answers under the sun!'

It was impossible to oppress the urge of laughter, apparently for both of us. Pulling me into a bear hug she kissed my cheek affectionately. I thanked her again for her patience, even though I was under no illusion it had worn down to a thread.

'For no one else, Lois. Absolutely no one!'

'Take the goddam phone to that sperm donor and let's track this bastard down. Last favour, I promise.'

'Hallelujah.'

20

THEN

I had just turned seventeen. The birthday gift to myself was a new
address. I had worked tirelessly at a Manchester hotel and saved
up as much money as my active social life would allow. Before I
knew it, we – my boyfriend Titch and I – had saved the money for a
deposit and the first three months' rent. The pull of independence and
drive for freedom produced good results, I found.

'Lois, you're not ready, you don't know pressure until you have
bills to pay.'

'I don't care, I'll make it work, everyone does it. It can't be that
hard,' I bit back, petulantly.

'That's real mature. See what I mean? You're not ready.'

'You just don't get it, Dad. You don't know me at all.'

I was horrified Dad and that woman had stayed together for so long.
Seven years to be precise.

She hadn't moved into the family home, but we'd crossed paths
a dozen or so times. I did my best to avoid her at all costs, in every
circumstance, turning down dinner invitations, cards, gifts, the lot.
Every pathetic attempt to get me on side.

My preferred option was to stay away from home altogether, though
that wasn't always possible.

I had tea at friends' houses after school, hung out at the local park in the evenings. I was a teenage cliché. In winter, when it grew dark by four p.m., I skulked around my room feeling trapped. However, I disliked the cold of the outdoors more than I disliked the confines of my bedroom. If she came round to spend time with Dad, I'd be stuck upstairs for the rest of the evening.

Dad tried to orchestrate our movements the best he could. It would have made his life far easier if we both got along but that wasn't the dynamic I wanted. She isn't family, she wasn't then, and she never will be, God willing.

I had to get out of there before I lost my mind completely.

• • •

Titch and I had celebrated our first year as a couple. We spent most evenings scouring the net to find a place of our own, when on a particularly mundane Tuesday evening of gossiping (more me than him) over FaceTime, the perfect property papered his laptop.

The Victorian mid-terrace with beautiful bay windows and original features was impossible to ignore. By some miracle it was within our modest budget and located within four miles of The Masons Hotel in Manchester, where I'd worked as a waitress and maid since turning sixteen. Needless to say we applied immediately.

The moving date approached rapidly, and it was only two days prior to key collection that we realised our house came as a package deal. Cursing our youthful impulsivity, we found ourselves moving into the property with another couple.

A house share. Our room was within budget, but the house … we should have known.

So there I was, in the grown-up world, adopting the role of girlfriend and housemate in one fell swoop. Difficult considering the many years I'd spent alone and in relative peace. But I did it, and I survived my first month.

Titch and I were gradually exiting the passionate phase, or at least I thought. We'd had a few disagreements throughout the year where we'd stumbled upon our boundaries and stretched a few more to their max. The intensity was dulling slightly but our new joint venture served to liven the butterflies that lived within me.

The kitchen worktops were more cluttered than those at the old house. In fact, most things were littered with human paraphernalia, none of which belonged to me. Even Titch had taken to dumping his possessions in public areas, much to my annoyance. Both floors were in a constant state of disarray, to varying degrees depending upon whose turn it was at making dinner.

Fiona and Rafael, our new housemates, had welcomed us with open arms. We tried to comply with their routine and make little to no fuss, which at times felt impossible. Two days every week, Fi and Raf took it upon themselves to invite newly acquainted partygoers back to our house for drinks. The routine was becoming firmly implanted into consciousness, despite my reservations. At first, I slept clutching my most personal belongings to avoid them falling into the wrong hands, but the habit quickly grew tiresome.

Adding weight to us adjusting to our new accommodation and our new housemates, Titch and I were struggling to free up cash. We would be for a few months to come. On the other hand, it had been Raf and Fi's home for almost three years, and their relationship had survived roadblocks that some married folk had failed to endure. They were beautiful, exotic specimens, with their bronzed skin and sharp, symmetrical features. I learned from one of our drunken nights in together that Fi and Raf had been childhood sweethearts. They cared for each other fiercely but fought just as hard. It made me wonder how it was possible for them to appear so much in love.

They'd arrange a date night every Saturday, even if that meant staying in watching a movie with a bottle of wine. Friday was 'let loose' night, and Sundays they did the grocery shop together before preparing a traditional English roast back at home. They matched, both in interests, temperament and looks.

It was the 'looks' bit that formed a knot of anxiety in the arc of my chest. It began at our initial meeting, with a fierceness I found gruelling to conceal. A ferocity that made me want to go back home, as much as I would hate that.

• • •

It was Friday night. The venue was small and rustic with low lighting and tiled flooring. The polished bare wood tables each held a single lit candle, centre to the wooden chairs that orbited around it. Our elbows were in grazing distance of the darkened bodies around us. Jugs of sangria enhanced the Spanish authenticity the club aimed to achieve.

A lone spotlight lit up the stage, paying no homage to the figured shadows that were enough in number to reach capacity. Fiona was the exception.

Her clear, fluorescent skin was a beacon amongst the crowd. Perfectly highlighted caramel waves fanned from her face, hanging with a buoyancy witnessed only in elite circles. The petite, pointed curve to her nose drew shadows across her face, illuminating the highly constructed cheekbones concealed by her taught skin. The spotlight from the stage drew focus to the deep textured brown of her eyes.

My pulse quickened.

The spread of her rosebud lips revealed a depiction of pure white, pearly symmetry. A perfectly imperfect indentation made its appearance in the centre of her cheek as she smiled. As if aware of my adoration, a slim, manicured hand hooked a wave of hair behind her left ear, mocking my naked fingers by showcasing the rock that glowed, only to prove she was loved more than me.

I swallowed hard and tried to control the uneasy shifting of my gaze.

'Good, isn't it, darlin?' whispered Titch, leaning into me, flopping his hand drunkenly onto my knee.

I nodded and flashed a half grin.

I focused on the dancing, the dramatic flailing of the arms, the timely drumming giving rise to orchestrated shoe-tapping, the shifting of skirts and undeniable depiction of artful erotica in motion. Under any other conditions I would have been captivated. Instead, my heart kicked with the burn of jealousy.

The performance reached an intermission. Fi informed us, collectively, of her need to attend the bathroom. Titch sat beside me, taking in her shape as she stood before him. My innards felt singed as a result.

I smiled up at Fi and asked if she'd like us to get her another drink in her absence. I hoped to scrape back the chance of her not seeing me as odd or generally uncomfortable. I also wished for Fi and Raf to see me as the adult I felt I was, hence my underage drinking. Upon reaching my seventeenth year, I'd maintained a hundred per cent success rate of failing to hide the ugliness that were my emotions.

'Same again, por favor,' she responded, before swaying her shiny, leatherette-covered hips towards the far end of the room.

Titch volunteered to retrieve the drinks. Leaving the table and making towards the bar, he glanced over in the direction of the bathroom. I felt a flush of embarrassment. Did Titch fancy Fi? I wished for the ground to swallow me up. The pain of watching the boy I loved admire someone else was suffocating.

My twitching became noticeable then. I shuffled in my chair and pulled at the strapless top that was too formal and too tight on me. Hoping to widen the space between the fabric and my invisible lumps, I needed to hide all evidence of imperfection. Fi was a woman I couldn't compete with on any count.

At the mere thought of her returning from the bathroom, a wave of irrational dread encroached my sense of ease. The stretch of floor she'd have to walk would showcase her natural beauty and my boyfriend would be watching, admiring her form. It was humiliating and unbearable.

I watched Titch like a hawk, waiting for him to slip up so I could confirm my fears and decide how I would deal with him. Raf was playing on his phone, oblivious to my dread. I answered him when he asked if I was enjoying the show, then knocked back some more sangria. My less than sophisticated palette would be better suited to a Diet Coke, but adults drank drinks like that, didn't they? Especially when they were out at bars with their new twenty-odd-year-old housemates.

The night only progressed to make me believe I wasn't good enough. If Titch had met Fi before he met me, then I'd be left by the wayside. He kissed me on the cheek during the second act, only because he wasn't able to kiss her. I struggled to look him directly in the face. I didn't want him to assess mine, then Fiona's in turn. It was blindingly clear that he had chosen the less beautiful one.

He made no attempt to conceal his wandering eye. Every time she looked back to share a joke with us, and when she spoke with Raf in their native tongue, Titch couldn't take his eyes from her. I shook off the thought of her stirring desire in my boyfriend's nether region. Another thing I was in no position to compete with. No longer was I new, undiscovered, or unchartered territory.

Every grain of self-control was redirected to focusing on the show. I drank away the insecurity until I was able to stare blankly ahead, ignorant to the people around me. I stared over Raf's shoulder, past the flamenco dancers at the wall that I bore no associations with. I was aware of Titch's calls for attention but, deep in my feelings, rose to none of them. Ignorance was the only way I was able to stunt the flow of the heart-wrenching emotions. Then eventually, I hoped, it would stop.

There was idle chatter at the close of the show. And applause which I joined in with. I congratulated myself mentally for keeping it together for so long. My desperation since noticing his interest was a persistent crescendo.

Fi and Raf suggested we go to another bar before returning home. My heart sank. I couldn't look at her face a second longer. I waited for Titch's lead and for the first time that evening, he didn't disappoint me.

'Love to, guys. But I think Lois has had a bit too much to drink, she's a total lightweight! Another time though!'

We said our farewells, which were only temporary. My boyfriend's dream woman would soon be returning to the house which I wished I'd never moved into.

'Shit, Lo, you look awful. Let's get you home pronto!'

'You think that's funny, do you?' I slurred.

'Whatever, you weirdo. I've ordered us an Uber. No idea how to get back from here!'

'Speak Spanish now do you?' I continued drunkenly.

Titch ignored my illogical ramblings. It must have been a short ride home, because the next time I opened my eyes I was looking at the wall opposite my bed.

Flashes of memory from the flamenco bar sucker-punched me in the gut. I would wait until morning to talk it through with Titch.

He crawled into bed beside me, a feeling I was becoming accustomed to.

Where he'd usually pull my body into his chest and kiss the side of my cheek, he instead adopted a solo position, firmly on his side of the bed. I assumed a foetal position on the other. Was he pissed at me or something? I peered slyly over my shoulder. He was staring up at the ceiling.

Fantasising about precious Fi.

Fire whipped my chest as we both lay in dour silence.

21

I hadn't heard from Mila since Tuesday. I'd tried both numbers – hers *and* Dans – multiple times over the last few days. It was enough to know she wasn't going to answer. Perhaps I should have been worried, as it wasn't like her to ignore me. But my gut told me to give her some space.

Her break-up with Tom had only been a few months prior. It was her longest and healthiest relationship since I'd known her and although she *seemed* okay, Mila was also skilled at compartmentalising – something I admired her for.

On closer inspection, I settled on the assumption that rather than genuine concern for her, I wanted to lessen my own guilt for having been so selfish. I ignored the very real possibility of Mila also having suffered a kind of mild trauma herself.

I'll go see her. Perhaps surprise her with some flowers or at least a bottle of bubbly to say thanks for all she had done for us. *She must have met with my dad by now.*

I was waiting for Kai in the lounge at Spring View Centre, when I decided to pop by the shops after his appointment and pick up a few high calorie treats for her.

Mila had suggested for Kai to meet with a counsellor. I protested initially but he did need help, even if I felt equipped to support my son without it. I was hesitant at allowing my child to discuss private matters with a stranger. It all felt too intrusive, too much like a personal attack. This woman, this stranger, would be allowed access to all areas of our lives. Learning how Kai had interpreted this entire matrix drowned me with dread. She would see how much of a failure I was, in the two roles I held in highest esteem. Wife and mother. It wasn't about me though, was it? My ego would have to repel the beating for the benefit of my son's happiness.

So I found myself sitting in the waiting room of a converted townhouse, my son in the room next door. Closed off from me. What was going on in there? No doubt she'd be calling him 'Sweetie' and asking him to draw things, paint things. Things that would reflect what I knew he wasn't comfortable telling me. He would need more than coloured pencils. He'd probably just roll them around the desk, gazing longingly at the box of Lego instead.

A well-turned-out lady in her mid-twenties approached me in the waiting room. Her paper-straight yellow hair rested immaculately beside her lightly contoured cheeks. Her wide, toothy grin and large blue eyes emanated warmth and transparency. The disruption in the pit of my stomach settled slightly, being in the presence of another gentle and kindly woman entrusted with the care of my son. She bore an air of familiarity.

A delicate, manicured hand invited my own into a greeting.

'Mrs. Attah, you're welcome to come through now,' the young lady said warmly.

'How is he, did he open up any this week?'

'Well, we've explored some of Kai's thoughts and feelings about the changes in his life, and how these are related to his actions. He seems receptive, as though he is processing what we discuss.'

'That's good, surely. Has he told you how he's feeling or if he understands what's going on?'

'He seems quite withdrawn right now. He hasn't divulged too much personally but it's very normal when children suffer a trauma such as this. It often takes some weeks to really get a grasp of how the child is coping, after a greater degree of trust is built up between us.'

I struggled to believe many other children had to cope with 'a trauma such as this'.

Wendy, as she introduced herself, held open the slick, white door for me to enter.

'Kai, your mum's here.'

I smiled my most loving smile, simultaneously widening my arms to invite his embrace. A brief moment of inner panic struck as I silently begged for my son to respond lovingly. I stared at his innocent caramel face, the essence of purity, urging him to love me. The idea that these two lovely young women – who were at the beginning of their lives and careers – may have already labelled me a neglectful mother, pained me.

Kai responded with a slight upturn of the lips and lazily fastened himself around my waist. He was wistful somehow, pensive. I kissed the top of his head and asked how he was feeling. His shoulders shrugged against me.

I found it frustrating that nothing of Kai's progress had been divulged to me thus far. I was desperate to know what was going on in his head. An ability I apparently lacked, both with my husband and now my son. Wendy and Gina, Kai's therapists, had assured me they would try their utmost to encourage him to express his feelings to me directly. They advised me to encourage creative expression: drawing, painting, singing, dancing, anything that would allow him to tell his story. With this in mind, I found it telling how Kai had been using his Lego sets to communicate with his missing father.

I had assumed therapy would help restore my son to the child he once was. Now I couldn't help but feel more locked out than ever. So I was going to utilise his Lego to help the both of us.

• • •

There was a crisp chill to the air as we stood on Mila's doorstep, but it was Kai's hand in my own that triggered a deeper state of cool within me. Here I was, dragging my traumatised six-year-old around the streets when the boy I used to know would have rather been tucked up at home with a hot chocolate and a Disney movie. My bag of tat swung in the air as I rapped on the door for the third time.

'D'ya want to tell me how things went with the ladies you spoke with?' My grip tightened around his fingers. Nothing. 'What about if we go straight home instead?'

The therapists had warned me about probing him too much. It would cause unnecessary 'damage' they said, in no uncertain terms.

I'm only giving him the chance to open up.

Dozens of families passed us in their family-sized vehicles, chatting, laughing or singing along to music. Envy engulfed me. Envy of almost everyone who wasn't stuck in the hell that had been thrust upon us.

'I don't think Mila's home, Mum.' Just the sound of his voice melted my insides.

'I think you're right. Let's get out of this wind shall we.'

Our family hatchback still housed the residual scent of the departed. Lindani's reading glasses and a pack of cigarettes sat unapologetically in the lift-up compartment between the driver and passenger seats. I was cruelly reminded of his decision to leave. How he'd found it easier giving up his family than giving up a habit that may well kill him.

'So how about we go home, devour these snacks and watch Peter Pan under the duvet. I might even treat us to a takeaway for tea?'

Kai began to ask something, but stopped.

'Go on, son. What were you about to say?' I shifted the car into second gear.

'Today Gina asked about something.'

Here we go! 'Okay?'

My bottom lip folded into my mouth. *Come on, son. Talk to me.*

'It doesn't matter.' He picked at the skin by his fingernail the same way I did. A habit I assumed had gone unnoticed.

'Do you want to tell me what she asked you?'

'I don't know.'

'That's okay, just take your time, peanut,' I said, proud of the only semi-successful interaction we'd had of late. A couple of minutes passed.

'I'm scared you'll be upset.'

You're scared? How could I have so epically cocked up, that my own boy was scared of upsetting me? *Don't overreact, Lois, hold it together.*

'Oh darling, you could tell me anything and I wouldn't be upset with you. You do know that, don't you?'

'Well, Gina …'

'Mm hmm.'

'She asked about Nanna and Grandad.'

'There's nothing wrong with that, is there?'

Why would she do that?

'Okay, well that's fine too son.'

'Gina said …'

I wondered how long it'd take for those words to start pissing me off. How qualified was Gina anyway?

'She said to ask you if I wanted to see him.'

'That sounds fair. Is that what you're thinking? You'd like to see your grandad?'

My avoidance had been more overt than I'd realised. The mountain of excuses I'd used over the years had masked my desire to stay away from him.

'I'm so sorry, my love,' I said, suppressing the urge for vindication. 'I don't want you to feel like you can't talk about him.' Kai's expression lifted in a way only a mother would recognise. A reminder I hadn't lost him altogether.

'So can we? Can we see him?'

I stared back into the hopeful eyes of my six-year-old, voiceless to his request before scolding myself for my selfishness.

Forcing a smile, I said the only truthful thing I could think of. 'Your grandad's gonna be over the moon.'

A familiar pull away from my dad ignited again. My knuckles, white with tension, clenched inwardly against my chest. It seemed there was nobody left who needed me any more. I still wasn't enough.

'Can we go see him today, Mummy?'

It was the 'Mummy' that did it. If I'd learned anything from this sham of a marriage, I'd learned not to sweep the needs of my loved ones under the rug.

'Sure, sweetie. We'll go to your grandad's now, see if he's home.'

22

Mila knew it was the right thing to do. Yet those four missed calls were making her reconsider. She sat and watched the last one ring out, frozen in her attempt to respond. Perhaps this entire mess was unnecessary after all?

She splashed cool water over her tired skin and wrapped the elastic around her hair, a couple of attempts until she was satisfied with her high pony. She squeezed some cream from Tom's Moisture for Men and spread it over her cheeks generously.

Staring at herself in the reflective glass, she became fearful. Had her clarity been clouded by this new development?

She'd had to end it. Or so she'd told herself countless times during her and Tom's on-again/off-again relationship. Their courtship hadn't had a clear-cut ending. Not like her relationship with Lindani. What effect had their abrupt divorce had on her? Perhaps the sleepless nights, endless answerphone greetings and blocked messages had caused her so much unaddressed trauma that she was left with a residual fear of being locked out of Tom's life for good too.

When she saw he'd tried to call, it came as something of a surprise. The break-up had been civil, despite her having made it clear during their last rendezvous that she had to end it for good.

Mila had wanted to respond to him; old affections resurfaced every time he'd reached out to her. Seeing him again would satiate her mounting need for love but also, she feared, would make her feel vulnerable again. It would, at the least, be some other-worldly time out from the emotional bruising of being pulled into other people's drama. And that's how she found herself standing outside his apartment block, waiting for the click of the door.

· · ·

Leaving Tom's apartment, she made her way to the white Mercedes, contemplating her next move.

Sex with Tom had stirred in her a fresh wave of desire for him as a lover but also as a partner too. She'd hoped her feelings of longing had subsided since their last meeting, but that hadn't happened. Mental images plagued her thoughts, of how Tom had pushed her against the wall before sharing even a single word. How he'd bound her wrists firmly with one hand, pinning them above her head, against its unforgiving firmness. Their breathing synchronised, growing shorter and stronger with each inhalation. The dampness of the air engulfed the narrow space between their faces, a mist of desire that soon mounted into an animalistic eruption of energy.

Mila shook her head as if that in itself would erase the memory. She couldn't afford to get sucked back into a relationship. Things had become too complicated.

Something drew her attention from fantasising about sex with Tom. Something was missing, literally missing. How stupid! Lindani's phone had been thrown carelessly onto the passenger seat on her way to Lois's dad's house, she was sure of it. She hadn't planned, however, on making a detour to Tom's on the way over. Now look what had happened!

She flicked open the glove compartment, folded down the visors, and searched desperately in the footwell before discovering it wasn't under the seat either. She called Tom. Between short breaths she asked if he could see another phone anywhere in his apartment. The sound of him shuffling items of furniture penetrated through the car speakers. She cancelled the call after his firm 'No' and midway through his joke about her having two phones.

Cutting through the panic, a tune rang out again through the speakers. Answering it instinctively, she hoped it would be Tom telling her he'd found it.

'Hello, Mila?'

She cursed herself for the timing.

'Lois, listen I'm so sorry I've missed your calls, I just needed a bit of rest. I crashed out after seeing you. I've been in a daze all over the Bank Holiday weekend. I was just on my way to your dad's but ... don't be mad at me.'

'Mila, it's okay, I'm not mad at you.'

Mila gurgled an indecipherable response as her focus remained on finding the missing phone.

'Are you there?'

'Yeah, yeah, so where are you now, Lo?'

'That's what I wanted to tell you. I'm at Dad's. Kai wanted to see his grandad so, well, so we're here.'

'Wow, I didn't see that one coming! Are you sure it's Kai whose been to therapy, and not you?'

'Very funny, no. Listen I have to go, before I change my mind. Haven't got round to knocking on the door yet, but just wanted you to know I'll handle it. The Dad thing, yeah? That's if you haven't beaten me to it?'

'Oh okay, no, I was literally just on my way.'

'Fabulous. Listen, you stay put and get some well-deserved chill time.'

'I don't mind coming, Lo. You sound a bit loco right now!'

'I know! I'm just nervous, but I want to do this. Stay home and rest up, okay? And wish me luck.'

'Okay, I will. Well try not to get too heavy in front of Kai, yeah? I'm happy to ask all the uncomfortable stuff.' Telling her what to do with Kai was probably not the best move. 'Good luck!' she added, noticeably sensing Lois's hesitation.

'Laters!'

She didn't seem offended, good!

Mila knew she'd been foolish. Men were just an unnecessary distraction. This was just another example of what can happen when you take your eye off the ball. Look what she'd lost. Plus, there were very important matters to discuss with Lois's father.

Mila considered herself a creative type, a problem-solver, ever since she was a little girl. At bedtime, her mother and father used to take turns reading to her. Mila often figured out the endings, sometimes as early as midway through.

So her struggling to find this phone only served to irritate her.

If she hadn't misplaced it, then perhaps someone had taken it? The vein in her neck pushed through the skin. This entire shitstorm was wearing thin on her. There was already too much to do, too much to think about, and now this. She climbed out of the car and looked for signs of entry. Chipped paint, dented metal, or fragmented glass. Nothing. To her knowledge there wasn't a second key either. Nothing else in the car had been taken, not even the fifty pounds cash she kept in the glove compartment as an emergency fuel stash.

Returning home, Mila continued her search.

• • •

It wasn't anywhere. Not on her driveway or on any of the counters or worktops. It wasn't even in any of the nooks and crannies she used for storage.

Part of her felt a flicker of relief. It was gone, out of her hands. True, Lois wouldn't be happy, but it would force them all to move on?

She tried to push away the urgency the situation demanded. As long as Lois didn't have the phone then what was the worst that could happen? She had to find something to do to pass the time. To keep her mind occupied until some information came to light.

Mila tore out a page from her diary. She did so often, when she found the entries difficult to read back. She re-read the paragraph, contemplating every line, every detail. It was an entry from a couple of weeks back. Just before she went out to meet Lois and Kai in South Africa.

Mila had moments where she felt just as determined as she did at the very beginning. When they first boarded that plane, but this was not one of those moments. Kai had crossed her mind then, he wanted to go back to school, Lois had said as much herself. She knew nothing of school timetables and kids' holidays but it didn't take a professional to know that Kai wouldn't be returning for a while yet.

She knew of his creative side and his love for reading and writing. Lois had told her previously how good he was at spelling and how he had mastered the art of the English language better than most in his class. At first, Mila was sure it was merely a symptom of an overzealous mother claiming bragging rights about her genius child. Mila had to admit though, having got to know Kai in recent weeks, she found him to be as bright as Lois had claimed. She watched him give special attention to anything that contained written text. From the hotel menu to road signs and safety notices. Nothing went unnoticed.

It was only when Mila really paid close attention, did she notice him seeking solace in words. Those car journeys in South Africa, that time when his mum lost the plot outside that poor woman's house. He was either reading signs or something on his iPad.

She couldn't be sure of the exact moment it happened, but Mila had actually grown fond of the boy.

She thought back to the moment her fondness of Lindani had grown into a deeper adoration. It was roughly fourteen winters ago when his tall, broad shadow decorated the tiny glass panel of her front door. She was touched by his willingness to spend time with her on the anniversary of her father's death.

Lindani was stood wincing against the hail that whipped at his wide, open smile. Icy white balls peppered the black shadow of hair that surfaced his head. He had a holdall full of wrapped items, items that concealed everything a loving couple could possibly need for a cosy, romantic evening – complete with a memorial candle engraved with her father's name and date of passing. The memory warmed her.

Pouring herself a glass of bubbly, Mila listed the numbers one to twenty in a column. She wanted to compile a spelling list for Kai. The next time she visited Lois, she could keep him occupied and out of earshot.

Experiencing a misplaced sense of loss herself, she opened her WhatsApp and began to type a message to whoever had taken Lindani's phone.

TO: *Lindani*
Cheers for stealing my phone. What a decent human being you must be.

23

He answered on the second ring.

'Dad, it's me,' I stated sharply, before allowing him the opportunity to speak.

There was a hesitancy during which I instinctually hoped the call would be terminated.

'Lois, darling. What a bloody lovely surprise!'

A short silence replaced what should have been my reply. 'Thanks,' I said, pacing the pavement back and forth as if stuck in a boxed room with invisible walls.

'Umm well I was just ringing to see if you …' The words faltered for a moment as flashes of his betrayal struck me again.

'Lois?'

'… if you wanted a couple of visitors? I was ringing to see if you wanted some visitors. It's fine if no—'

I spoke through gritted teeth, stunting his pseudo concern. They were words that made me visibly cringe. But to the same degree they made me feel prideful of having managed to get them out in the first place.

'Wow … Lois,' he interjected. I imagined his eyebrows rebounding from his hairline. 'Yeah, yeah of course I would, in fact I'd love nothing more. When were you thinking?'

Is it too late to get back in the car and drive off?

Kai was standing beside me as my animalistic gait subsided into stasis. We remained hand in hand, directly facing the black wooden entrance to our family home. I swept aside some grit with my suede ankle boot, staring down at the ground. Kai on the other hand stood tall and strong, awaiting the door to open with a light in his eyes that told me I had made the right decision by bringing him.

'That's the thing. We're actually outside yours.'

'You're outside the house? Now?'

My tongue furled the enamel of my molars. 'I know it's last minute and I shouldn't have just turned up but, well, Kai wanted to see you, so … here we are.'

'Oh shit! I'm not home but give me twenty minutes and I can be!'

I imagined he'd raised his hand against his forehead as he swore, like he always did when I was a child.

'Um well, twenty minutes?' I hoped for Kai's sake I could remain receptive to the visit for that long, but wondered too if he was cavorting with his witch of a woman.

'I guess, yeah,' I conceded after a moment's thought. 'Actually, Dad,' I said, indicating my swift change of heart. 'Would you mind coming to our house instead? I can make us some food maybe?' I felt the transfer of my son's luminosity reveal itself on my face. We turned back to the car in one synchronised movement.

'Yesss!' said Kai, letting out a hissing sound and clenching his fists.

'Okay, darling, that works for me. I'll see you very soon in that case.'

There was still time to retract the invitation. 'Okay, see you.'

'Fast as a mouse, Grandad!' shouted Kai into the mouthpiece as I occupied the driver seat.

His grandad chuckled down the phone, triggering a minor tremor of exposure within me. It was too familiar. Too soon.

'Lois … I can't tell you how much I'm looking forward to it.'

I said nothing. Kai reached over the centre console and tugged at my cardigan, prompting me to start up the car.

'Kai is too. Aren't you, Kai!'

He nodded enthusiastically, widening his grin in the same swift movement. Light reflected from his pupils. Just in that moment, they shone with the joy of a 'normal' boy his age.

• • •

I poured my second glass of Pinot, sucking in the rich scent of beef stroganoff as it simmered away peacefully on the hob.

'Mum, what time will Grandad be getting here?'

Kai guided himself down the stairs slowly enough to showcase his favourite Avengers jumper.

'Not sure, my love. But shouldn't be too much longer.'

It was a taste of how life used to be, only I'd substituted one cheating man for another. Perhaps this was all Kai needed for now. To connect with a grandad he had only seen over video call. Not months upon months of therapy.

The clock told me it was seven p.m., approximately an hour later than I'd expected him, but my expectations of him were low enough to forego the shock his late arrival may have otherwise induced.

Kai raced to the front door as a silhouette of my father appeared, no sooner had the thought crossed my mind.

They greeted each other warmly, with billowing arms and wide smiles, but I sensed the donor was nervous too.

We engaged in the usual small talk of strangers, from which I quickly learned he was now single. I wasn't at all concerned with the details. The fact they were no longer together was enough for me to be civil, so he soon moved on to complimenting my youthful appearance and the unique décor of our home – to which I replied rhetorically with another question.

'Nice picture,' he commented, allowing the dominant canvas of an elderly African lady to draw his gaze.

I attended the hob without comment, sliding the wooden spoon in circular motions until a few minutes later my attention was drawn to their conspicuous game playing.

Kai's body was tossed into the air as if he was a human volleyball, his head almost touching the ceiling before clumsily landing back in his grandad's arms.

Kai and I had adopted new roles. I had occupied the role of shy, unsociable child and Kai had taken the role of host and entertainer.

They were clearly comfortable around each other. So much so that I wondered how it was possible for Kai to display such ease around him after their relative estrangement. I wasn't sure if I should be impressed, relieved or perturbed.

'Grandad? 'Member the peg men I told you about? They're over there, come look,' he said, tugging at the donor's blue knit jumper.

I don't know if it was the sight of my dad indulging Kai in all his boyish imaginative games that triggered it, but strangely I felt ready to move on. Maybe it wouldn't be such an epic struggle after all. Kai's smiling face was a reminder that I had so much to push forward for. One thing I was certain of, Lindani had lost more than I had. *Remember this feeling, Lois.*

The topic of Lindani had been broached already in my head, from the moment the donor stepped into my home. But having witnessed Kai's excitement at seeing him in person, I couldn't bring myself to do it, and nor had there been an appropriate time to accost him about everything since.

I was the guilty party, it appeared. The one responsible for the state of our current family dynamic, for depriving Kai of making memories with his grandad for the past six years.

The thought caused a surge of panic to shoot through me, the wooden spoon slipping from my grasp.

I had replaced his blissful childhood memories with ones of neglect, had I not? I found solace though in the consideration that perhaps I was protecting him from potential betrayal. Who's to say the donor would have been a consistent fixture in Kai's life had I not protected him?

The lines were blurred in my mind, between allowing their relationship to flourish naturally and remaining loyal to my late mum. I stared at the stroganoff, hoping its sporadic popping and bubbling would shift my thoughts from everything to nothing.

'Tea's ready, guys. Come sit down.'

I lifted two scoops of fusilli onto two of the plates, one scoop for Kai, then slathered a ladle full of stroganoff onto each. I positioned Kai's plate between ours at the breakfast bar, dipped the pans in the sink to find, upon my joining them, they had sat down.

'Wash your hands, Grandad. C'mon, we forgot,' demanded Kai, leading him yet again to another area of the house.

Life had changed dramatically since I was a child and, if I was really honest with myself, I struggled to remember why I was convinced Dad had been responsible for Mum's death. The cheating and betrayal still festered inside me, but he hadn't *caused* her to die. It was the cancer, not her broken heart. The surge of loss was overwhelming at my childlike misinterpretation back then.

'Lovely this, Lois, thank you,' he said, looking across at me with a loaded fork.

'You're welcome,' I said reservedly. I sensed he wanted to connect with me over more than just a hot meal, but I'd already decided we'd speak about the more pressing matters when Kai had retired to bed.

'Did you bring the jeep, Grandad?'

What jeep? Perhaps the conversation would come up sooner rather than later.

'What jeep?' I asked, scanning both faces with a suspicion that leaked from my open mouth.

'You said you'd bring the jeep after my holidays.'

'Don't be so cheeky, please,' I scolded. 'Now what's this you're talking about, Kai?' I added, swallowing my current mouthful of stroganoff.

'You said didn't you, Grandad, weeks ago, that after my holiday I could play with the jeep you bought me.'

The donor's face flushed as if he was a child caught shoplifting.

'Didn't you, Grandad!' persisted Kai.

What the hell? When did this little arrangement come about? My mind raced backwards, and in circles like a dog chasing his tail. It must have been at least eleven months since they last spoke, for Kai's birthday. They couldn't expect me to believe he'd remember after all this time … could they? Plus, we'd only booked the godforsaken trip a couple of months ago.

'Son, eat your food then get yourself off to bed, okay. I'll come tuck you in.'

Grumbles and moans occupied the air around him, which I found surprisingly easy to ignore.

I stood loading the dishwasher when Kai came hurtling towards the kitchen, having too ignored my instruction to get into bed. He was wearing a makeshift spiderman mask and holding a long piece of string. I traced the trail only to find my dad's stripey socks protruding from behind the screens of Kai's play area.

'What have you caught?' I said in dulcet tones, whilst sealing the dishwasher door shut, feeling a little lighter of heart.

Kai was too engaged to answer. He tugged at the string until it snapped and he slipped onto his bottom. He shielded his face from the capture of his grandad who was rapidly approaching, having broken free from his restraints.

'Mwahaha, I've got you now, laddie. That was all part of my evil plan.'

Their exchange was punctuated with laughter and giggles.

I watched the scene unfold, having silently banked a mental reminder to accost my dad about the jeep later on. I had enjoyed seeing their interactions after tea and hoped something more of their clandestine relationship would reveal itself naturally.

What's wrong with me? I interpreted my mixed feelings as petty jealously, it must have been. I so desperately ached for Kai to smile at me in the same way.

My dad approached me in the kitchen with Kai dangling freely down his back.

'I believe this is yours,' he said, indicating said child.

I turned his shoulders to the side manually, examining the load in question, remembering how I'd once flinched at his touch.

'Hmm, I don't think it is, no,' I said with a faux seriousness.

'Oh well, in that case I'll have to dispose of him as he so evidently poses a threat to society.'

'So be it!'

Kai laughed in a way I hadn't heard since before South Africa.

My dad lifted open the bin lid and dipped Kai's feet into the bin. Kai screamed and giggled, limbs flailing wildly like a caged hen.

I had decided. Kai would only go to therapy when he was feeling particularly down, and I would try to maintain a healthy relationship with his grandad. Kill two birds with one stone. Hopefully that way, some of that normality would rub off when it was just us on our own.

It was well past Kai's bedtime, even for a non-school night, so I encouraged the process that would usually involve him reluctantly dragging himself off to bed.

After ensuring he had drifted off to sleep, I came back downstairs to find my father sitting on a kitchen stool, visibly exhausted.

'I hope you don't mind me putting the kettle on? I thought it would be nice having a brew on our own.'

'That's fine,' I said defeatedly.

'Some boy you've got there.'

I took it as a compliment. It was clear he already adored Kai, and I had a feeling it was mutual.

Switching back to my role as host felt uncomfortable. I'd actively rejected engaging with this man in conversation most of my life and now I had to embody the adult I was, which meant actually discussing our issues.

'He's the best, honestly. Always has been. It's just lately, with what's happened, he's been a bit withdrawn … actually, massively withdrawn … from me, anyway. It's like banging your head against a wall at times,' I admitted, welcoming the shred of relief it gave me.

We both stared despondently into the space between us, connected over the same boy, even if just for a brief moment.

'That's why I called you earlier. Thought it might help for the two of you to get to know each other properly.' It was only a small lie.

'Well, it did that all right! I haven't had that much fun in years, since ... well since you were small.'

A moment of reflection triggered quiet. I noticed then that he looked like a different man to the one I remembered. Even from seeing him on FaceTime. He was more imposing somehow, similar to when you see up close someone you've admired from afar.

He began preparing our cups with tea and coffee, stunting any awkwardness.

I reflected on our evening as I watched him shake surplus coffee granules from the teaspoon. How ironic that for one night I had got my son back, and I owed it to the man who had caused me so much lasting pain.

'Bloody hell, Lois, you must really not trust me!' he said out of nowhere, his expression masking a grimace.

'What do you mean?'

He motioned towards the camera that remained set up in front of the kitchen worktop. I still didn't understand what he was referring to.

'Recording me, were you? When you took Kai to bed?'

'What are you talking about?' I was genuinely perplexed.

He must have read the confusion on my face.

'The red light's on.'

Impossible! 'Can't be, there's no way he would have left the camera on before going away for two weeks!' I walked nearer to check the bulb for myself. I found it difficult to darken the feng shui of my home by saying my husband's name aloud.

'That's odd,' he conceded.

'It is ... very.'

I watched him replace the milk in the fridge door before setting down a fresh cup of tea next to his stool.

Irritation pricked me. I wasn't ready for the familiarity he seemed to be expecting, so I swiped a lick of dust from the top of the camera. The action was mundane enough to restore some perspective. I would try my best to offer the same back … for Kai.

It was getting on for eleven p.m. and although we were both shattered I considered it one-on-one time that was long overdue, particularly since I had so much to discuss with him.

I recalled some memories I'd shared with Kai, all the while trying to leave out Lindani. There were very few I'd had without him so I'd stumbled over my words, trying to edit the memories. I talked about Kai's achievements and hobbies, which of course were as ample as they were impressive. To a parent at least.

I sought out gestures that could incriminate the donor. Subtle glances towards the ceiling or a discreet scratch of the chin, anything that may confirm Kai's earlier reveal of them having spoken privately. It made sense all of a sudden why Kai had been so insistent on seeing my dad. Of course, they had been in touch. I'd only needed to read how they greeted each other to determine that.

My hopes for the evening had been appeased – that them spending time together would lessen Kai's sadness – and for that I would consider the evening a successful one for now. But utilising the fresh current of determination that was tapping against my vocal cords, I opted to speak right there and then before the fire inside me weakened.

'Sit down, Dad,' I began, swallowing the anxiety-infested marble that had appeared in my throat. I noticed the skin around his lips cinch at one side, an indication he was chewing on the flesh inside his cheek. It was also a sign of trepidation, I recalled. Like the time Mum requested he bring home some lady products en route from my friend's birthday party. I shook the image so as not to become distracted by the good times. I had to find out what role he had played in my husband's life … and now my son's.

'It might do you some good to get out there and start dating again. Have you met anyone you like the look of?' he said, with ill intention no doubt.

I did not have the strength even to talk about dating again, let alone consider actually doing it.

'I take that as a no then?'

'No. I mean, yes … it's a no … obviously.'

That familiar pull of anger attached itself.

'All right, Lois, I was just asking.'

I had rehearsed this conversation in the mirror countless times over the years, should I find myself in such a situation. Now perhaps wasn't the most appropriate time, but I didn't care.

'Look, just because you can move on from someone at the drop of a hat, it doesn't mean we're all the same.'

My mind trailed off on a tangent. I wasn't sure if he'd responded but it was irrelevant if he had.

'I couldn't even do that to the man who has just abandoned me and his son, let alone to someone who was sick and who I claimed to still love!'

'Okay, my fault, forget I said anything.' A concoction of venom and pain poisoned my gaze. 'I have a distinct feeling this is about me and your mother, not you and your husband.'

Well done, Poirot. 'How could you have done that to her? What kind of sick, selfish arsehole could physically betray us like that? All those dark nights Mum waited up for you to come home from one of your drinking sessions or golf trips or poker stints. She wouldn't sleep without knowing you were back safe.'

He rubbed his temples, allowing his head to drop a little too weightily into the palms of his hands.

'She was exhausted, Dad, exhausted from looking after me and the dogs and her parents. And you were probably—'

He interrupted my harangue.

'Lois, darling … can I speak?'

I found myself near Kai's play area, shuffling toys around indiscriminately, like someone with social anxiety in a room full of people.

'You're making me sound like a real scumbag, Lois. Cheers for that! If you remember, the "drinking sessions" were once a year at Christmas. And the poker nights, well they were meant to be for couples but your mum wanted to stay home with you instead, so she sent me to represent our family. She hated the idea of everyone slagging us off for being so "flaky" all the time.'

A pause filled the gap.

'And I agree it was stupid to even care what they thought, but your mother did, too much! She didn't want the other kids calling you names at school or treating you differently. You don't remember darlin' because you were a child,' he stated, confidently. *Why did you not take me with you?* I wondered if there were other kids there.

The pace at which I was tidying Kai's toys reduced noticeably.

'The golf trips, fair enough. But I hoped you'd be proud of me, or at least though it might inspire you to follow your dreams, no matter how old you are ... that obviously backfired!'

I couldn't make eye contact, not yet. Part of me needed to hear this, so I listened, feeling the errant molecules of my heart binding together slowly.

'You're forgetting the times you and your mum used to come and caddy for me. Surely you haven't suppressed or *repressed*, whatever it is, all our good memories?'

My blood pulsed erratically at his recollections, but I had waited too long to not say what I had needed to say for so long.

'I know you only used to take me swimming to meet *her* ...' It was an accusation that had sounded a lot less petty in my head. His expression faded into one of contemplation. 'I thought it was our time and you destroyed it. I could never go back there again. Mum was dying and you used your own daughter to go out and pick up another woman!'

'What the hell are you talking about?' his voice became louder then.

I didn't know what kind of reaction I'd expected, nor did I know what I'd hoped to gain. An apology of sorts perhaps? He placed his half-drunk coffee down and approached me in an awkward gesture of comfort.

'So that's why you stopped wanting to go? I thought it was because she passed away and you felt guilty or something for carrying on ... I dunno.'

'Me? *You* should have been the one feeling guilty. I was just a kid. Do you know what that can do to a little girl, seeing her dad – the

most important man in her life – betray her family? And even worse
… she felt she was the one who enabled it to happen. Do you?' I was
shouting now.

I waited through his self-induced silence.

'It can cause twenty years of abandonment, apparently.'

'I want you to leave!'

'I'm sorry, Lois. I'm just tired and irritable.'

He brushed a damp salty palm across his forehead.

'I just want to be on my own right now … okay?' I said.

'Okay. But promise me we can sit down and talk about everything soon.'

I nodded reluctantly then motioned for the door.

Twisting the key in the lock behind him, a thought occurred to me.
This was going to be harder than I'd thought.

24

THEN

Titch's tone informed me I'd taken it too far. 'Lois, what the hell?' 'They're not throwing a party *for* us. They wouldn't even notice if we weren't there,' I said with an air of desperation I tried my hardest to conceal.

'They want us to meet their friends, so that's what were gonna do. End of!'

I switched tack.

'But we haven't had a minute to ourselves since we moved. It's supposed to be me and you living together, remember.'

'No chance, we can't change plans last minute, it'd be such a dick move.'

'I know, I know, I just want us to spend some quality time together, just me and you. How good would it be to go on a road trip and stay in some swish hotel overnight, get ourselves a full body massage or something … you do love a good pamper!' My eyes illuminated with a persuasive energy I was desperate to convey.

'Lois, stop it. Fi and Raf are hosting a party … for us. We're staying put,' he demanded with unshakeable finality.

I bit the gaping skin from around my thumb, relinquishing my urge to persist.

'Fine. Just trying to do something nice for my boyfriend, that's all,' I said.

'You couldn't have worse timing Lois. Anyway, we'll be together at our little party, won't we.'

'Suppose so.'

He kissed the hand I was chewing. Surprisingly given the mood I was in, I didn't pull away.

'I'm intrigued to see what their friends are like anyway. Be nice to widen our social circle, ay?' he added.

My turn of feeling reverted back to default, with a reminder of why I was so hesitant to begin with.

I knew exactly what their friends were like. It only took a few Facebook and Instagram searches to find out. My innards hissed at the thought of having to stand by and watch my boyfriend lust after even more exotic beauties. If Dad had taught me any life lessons, that was certainly one.

'I guess, but what if they don't speak English?' I queried with only a grain of enthusiasm.

'I think we'll get by, Lois.'

Planning for another social event with Princess Fiona was enough to break me. I wanted to sleep it off and repair the colossal eye bags I'd grown in recent weeks.

No doubt I would have to spend a rehearsed two hours holding unsuitable outfits against my frame before tossing them onto the floor disapprovingly. I'd have to pray for a good hair day and re-apply each unsatisfactory layer of makeup. Needless to say, I was absolutely dreading it.

I'd been dragged to lunches and drinks a number of times since the flamenco club. Titch was becoming quite close to Raf, as I was to Fi. Our faux friendship, on my part, was hindered by the realisation I couldn't relax in her company without the inducement of alcohol.

I dabbled with Baileys at our 'panini lunches' and graduated to hard liquor in the evenings. It wasn't without unanticipated benefits. I'd managed to convince Fi and Raf I was a 'fun-loving party girl'.

Titch could see through my lush-like behaviour and had collared me on occasion because of it.

My options were simple, I figured. Either I convince these strangers of my extrovert personality or reveal the unstable, bubbling cesspit of childhood insecurity that is Lois.

The months since the flamenco club had worn heavily on me. My reaction to dealing with uncomfortable situations mirrored my behaviour as a child. I dealt with negative feelings the only way I'd learned how. By running and hiding from them entirely.

I'd come home from work late, offering to take on overtime and cover for anyone who wanted to take a day off. Titch had noticed my reluctance to stay home and thought initially it was due to his and Raf's incessant 'Call of Duty' playing. He confessed he hadn't even noticed I was working longer hours for the first week or so.

Fiona's movements had not gone unnoticed, though. I listened to him grilling Raf about their relationship and Fiona's family. Her background, their interests, and the like. Fi lost her purse, a few weeks into our cohabitation. *My* boyfriend went out of his way to look for it, even opting to drive her back to the supermarket where she thought it'd slipped from her pocket. Why she couldn't drive herself there was beyond me.

I came home one night after taking the scenic route back from work to find Fi and Titch sitting at the kitchen table having a late supper together. Raf was nowhere in sight. Fi had wanted a man's opinion on why Raf had delayed coming home. Titch led her to believe that he was likely picking up more shifts to build up some cash so he could treat her. A holiday perhaps, since their anniversary was looming. That would be no less than what someone as perfect as Fiona deserved, of course.

My instinct was telling me he was playing the field. A young, attractive man like Raf must have his pick of women. Although he didn't particularly strike me as the cheating kind, if there was such a thing. He had never given *me* the flirty vibes, but then again why would he? I wasn't exactly an upgrade from Fiona.

Raf spent most of his social time tapping into his phone. Perhaps his disinterest in his surroundings was in fact a sign he was playing away. There must exist more appealing girls on the internet *somewhere*. The motive was lacking, but I doubt men innocently became distant as a result of planning huge surprises, as Titch had concluded.

I wondered if I was shooting myself in the foot by staying away as much as I had. Plus, whenever fatigue hadn't dulled my senses by itself, I was often drunk. Fi and I were beginning to spend less time together. Titch having gradually taken the place of two in our four-way friendship.

It crossed my mind that I would be pushing them together, particularly now Raf was more absent than I'd known him to have ever been.

I sought advice from online chatrooms. Apparently I was expected to 'look the other way' when Titch obscenely eyed her up. It was normal male behaviour and there was nothing I could do to change him. I considered moving out, with or without Titch. It would be a true test of his loyalties. I knew he loved living in the city but if he chose to follow me rather than stay with her, then I could begin to forgive him.

I approached the weekend tentatively. The two days it took to get there were effortful. I secretly hoped something would happen to result in Fi and Raf cancelling the party.

As my luck would have it, nothing caused such an outcome.

25

It was a beautiful day, the perfect temperature to get outdoors. It had taken serious effort, but I'd finally managed to drag our bikes from the garage, which proved a much easier task than dragging my reluctant child from his room. After some convincing, we rode side by side in relative peace, passing dozens of people who'd had the same idea. We dodged the multiple potholes that characterised the mossy lanes on our doorstep.

Kai wasn't overcome with joy at our endeavours. It was a blow I'd have to ignore for now. Baby steps, I reminded myself. At least I'd got him outside. He used to love playing outside with his dad.

It was nothing like I'd imagined. Nothing like it used to be once upon a time. There used to be singing, joking, trickery. Never silence and boredom.

'Which way?' I said as we approached a sharp fork in the road.

He indicated right by sticking out his right arm, neglecting to accompany his choice with words. I followed his direction, hoping that at some point in the day I could bring a smile to my son's face. We'd been riding for almost an hour already. Hope was fading. I was never going to be able to help him alone, was I? It was a sentiment that terrified and devastated me.

'Hold up a minute.' He was a few metres ahead, swaying idly across lanes.

I pulled to the side of the path. A deep ditch sat to the left of us. I'd recognise that bright, warm face and paper-straight blonde hair anywhere. Wendy. She was alone.

'Hi Wendy, what a nice surprise.'

'Mrs. Attah isn't it?'

'Lois, please call me Lois.'

She smiled pleasantly. 'How's Kai getting on?'

'He's doing okay, thanks. Thought getting out and about would do him good, hence the bike ride.'

'I'm sure that will help him a lot.'

'What are you doing around these parts anyway?'

'I just came out for a quiet walk with the weather being so nice, but think I've drifted. I'll ramble back if you could point me in the right direction?'

'Sure can.' I demonstrated rough directions towards Sale, where I knew the practice to be.

We exchanged quick goodbyes, and I assured her Kai would be back for another session soon.

I caught up with Kai. From the look on his face, I hazarded a guess he wasn't enjoying himself, not even the slightest bit. I rode ahead revelling in my new-found validation, courtesy of Wendy.

I rode off ahead.

'Mum! Mum!' he yelled.

My tyres skid to a halt, spraying up rubble from the path. Why hadn't he followed?

'Everything okay?' I called, pedalling back towards him.

'Can I see Grandad?'

Another punch in the gut. I didn't know how much more rejection I was expected to digest.

'That came out of the blue? Are you not having a good time?' I was merely stating the obvious.

'It'd be better if Grandad was here. We are going to see him again, aren't we?'

'Do you not like spending time with me any more?' I blurted, petulantly. It wasn't the most mature approach. 'I know you've been through a lot, more than most boys your age, but you still have me. I'm always gonna be here for you.' It was a gamble as to whether Kai found them to be words of comfort or dread.

He climbed from his bike and sat on the dirt path, legs splayed over the slope of the ditch. I guessed the latter.

'Come up from there, Kai.' There was no shift in his posture. 'Are you listening?'

He stared at his feet; his brows pitched steeply, forming a frown.

'I'm sorry you have to put up with me, but you're going to have to learn to deal with it. Do you hear me?'

'I want Grandad,' I heard him say under his breath.

'Fine. Let's go then ... Let's go!' I shouted.

He rose from the ditch reluctantly, brushing debris from his trousers before climbing back onto the seat of his bike.

The cycle home was tedious. My mind agonised over our exchange. How could he choose his grandad over me? His dad abandons him, his grandad is absent most of his life, but it's me who he can't stand to be around. I was aware how my actions over the last few weeks could have changed things between us: searching for his dad, leaving him with Mila. *I swear I give up.*

I almost pressed Mila's name on my call list, but wondered for how much longer I'd be incapable of dealing with my own shit. Plus, she clearly needed some time away from me. I knew I'd worked her nerves down to a thread. *Deep breaths.*

I weighed up my options. Call Dad and appease the child who demanded to see him, then gradually weave him back into his life, book him another therapy session pronto or put my foot down and make Kai endure the torture that was being in my company.

If Kai wouldn't talk to me about what was on his mind, perhaps he would speak to someone else.

I tapped 'Sperm Donor' on my calls list.

'Dad, it's me.'

26

Gradually, snippets of Kai's former self resurfaced. I unquestionably had his grandad to thank for that. Their encounters were having a therapeutic effect. Consequently, the pull to find Lindani had weakened. My once utter desperation had morphed into a rational choice rather than a burning necessity to locate him.

I soon, however, found myself ruminating about Mila's whereabouts, as well as her state of mind. I knew she had never been to visit my dad, but even the mysteries surrounding Lindani's phone began to lose some of its appeal. I was now only mildly curious if the phone had been contacted since I'd given it to Mila. She would usually have informed me either way but, uncharacteristically, I hadn't heard a peep from her.

It was a great sense of relief then, when she stopped by the house to bring some things for Kai. A relief not only born from confirming her safety but also from knowing that she hadn't abandoned me too. Something I was becoming rather paranoid about.

'So, it's just gone?' I said, my chest warming into a blaze.

'Apparently so. I've looked everywhere, but it must have been stolen. Lo, I'm so sorry, truly I am.'

'I don't get it. Stolen from where, by who?'

'I left it on the front seat of the Merc, I think. Then when I got back it was gone.'

She shifted awkwardly, unable to meet my eye.

'Was your window smashed or anything?'

The whites of her eyes expanded. 'No, nothing, it was the weirdest thing.'

I picked at the skin beside my thumb, scrambling for a suitable response. Something about our exchange was unsettling. It wasn't that I didn't believe her. But at the same time, I wasn't certain I did either. *Weirder things have happened. I was living proof!* I reassured myself, batting away the buzz of doubt. Opting to let the news sink in, Mila lifted a notepad from her bag and took to the stairs, stating she had some reading for Kai she'd forgotten about.

I tidied away the pots from the dishwasher, all the while contemplating the possibility that Mila had lied to me. She was more likely to have lost the damn thing than to have lied about it being stolen.

Rationally I knew the phone couldn't possibly be on the stand by my door but I double-checked, regardless.

Whilst approaching the stand, I was startled by the appearance of a shadow behind the front door and experienced a swollen pang of grief. A deep yearning for my husband to take the place of any one of these visitors I'd had lately.

I peeled it open. 'Wendy!'

'Lois, hello. Apologies for stopping by unannounced.'

'That's okay. Is something wrong?'

'No, no, nothing like that. I've been trying to contact you, but I haven't had any response.'

I hadn't missed any calls. I was sure of it.

'Oh, that's strange, I'll have to confirm my details at the next session. I haven't had any notifications,' I said, having no real intention of returning Kai to therapy before the effects of having my dad around were proven to be futile.

'That would be great, thanks,' came Wendy's reply.

I considered the intentions of the woman who stood before me. If she was here to give me a nudge to bring Kai in for another session, I'd have to think of a convincing enough reason to turn her down.

There was an awkward pause.

I doubted my justifications for keeping him away would be accepted by her or Gina, but they didn't know what we were dealing with. The thought of Kai sharing with them the extent of his secret contact with his grandad worried me now. More than it had before I knew there had in fact been some. Therapy would only encourage Kai to keep yet more secrets from me, resulting in yet more secrets I'd have to unravel in the long run.

'I was just popping by to offer my help, that is if you needed any?'

At a loss as to how to answer, I contemplated inviting Wendy inside. My mute response prompted Wendy to continue.

'I see from the weekend that Kai is doing better than before. So I guess it's more of a courtesy visit than anything. Well, that, and to encourage you to continue with the good progress.'

'Thank you, I appreciate that, Wendy.'

Her lips rose into a polite smile, head dipping slightly into a dated farewell.

'So, I'm not a complete failure then?' I said, seeking reassurance like an insecure child.

'You're certainly not. These are extraordinary circumstances. I'd say you were doing just fine. And don't forget, I am here to support you too.'

Before I could muster a response, she offered a parting wave and disappeared into the tangle of streets.

I sealed the door behind her, as bewildered as I was comforted, partly wishing to disappear with her into the distance and talk away my troubles.

• • •

'So what's it like being duped for the umpteenth time?'

'What are you talking about?' My mind reeled as Mila revealed the screen displaying zero funds in the account that my ever-so-generous husband had set up for his son.

She slid a kitchen stool towards my legs, catching my overstated fall. I slumped onto it, not realising I was crying.

'Take it easy, Lo, deep breaths,' urged Mila, noticing the signs.

'Are you certain you typed in the right details?'

Mila zoomed in on the login information and account number, then shifted the screen into my full view.

A primitive shriek permeated the hollow living quarters of my home, ricocheting from the high ceilings and bare walls. All bare except for the single, oversized canvas Lindani cherished so dearly. Without a pause for hesitation, I flung my carcass over the furniture, scraping at the fixtures that served to seal the image firmly in place. It hurtled clumsily to the polished floor, scoring slices into the varnish.

'What the hell are you doing, Lois, calm down! Kai will hear you.'

I dragged my aching limbs to the canvas, along with the Santoku knife I had released from its block moments earlier. With an attempted serenity that betrayed my outburst, I sat on the wood floor with the image cradled over my folded knees. With the blade, I picked at the woman's features gently, as if instead yielding a needle and thread. I punctured the skin of the canvas steadily. It restored a sense of familiar calm within me.

'It's just money, Lois, that's it. It's nothing. Can you hear me? Are you listening? Lois!'

The thrum of Mila's voice buzzed through my head, implanting a pulse of pain through my temple.

'Stop!' I yelled, after muttering the same request repeatedly under my breath. 'Everyone just stop!'

Silently, I rose to my feet and brushed my jeans free from debris, abruptly exiting my mild episode of psychosis.

'Ibuprofen,' I said. 'Can you get me some?'

Mila sifted through drawers and cupboards with no clue from myself as to where they were stored.

I replaced the knife into the wooden block before resigning myself to the sofa. Decades passed between me swallowing the pills and me mustering the strength to speak. Mila having sat beside me throughout.

'It isn't the money,' I said timidly.

Mila placed her hand on my knee, the heat of her skin prompting me to continue.

'We've been dancing to his tune this entire time and I can't allow it any longer. I thought that this once, maybe he would demonstrate the ability to possess a single shred of decency, if not for me then for Kai.'

Mila, sensing that my recitation was only beginning, smiled and nodded.

'I wanted to make his birthday special this year, with everything he's going through. I wanted to buy him anything he's ever wanted, everything that we were too bloody principled to get in the past. To really spoil him, ya' know.'

'It's just stuff though, Lois. I think you guys have raised him better than that. He'd probably be happy with a pen and paper and a mum who isn't thoroughly miserable.'

'You're starting to sound like Wendy,' I asserted unfairly.

'It's better than sounding like *him.*'

My heckles spiked the same time my limbs furled into my torso. 'What are you insinuating Mila?' I asked over the grinding of teeth.

'Well you are starting to sound like our ex-husband.'

Ex?

'In that shitty letter he left you, can you not hear yourself? As if money and toys can heal everything Kai's been through … is *still* going through … just like that!'

'Shit, Mila, obviously I didn't think it would solve everything, did I? I mean what else can I do right now? … And it's his birthday for god's sake!' She stared down at her shuffling feet as I spoke. 'If you have any better ideas then feel free to enlighten me,' I said rhetorically.

'Actually, I do!'

'Huh?' Trepidation modified my tone to a lower pitch.

'How would you feel about hosting a birthday party, say, next weekend? Invite your dad?'

We connected eyes for an instant, allowing silence to lend me the right answer.

'Oh no, I'm not sure. I mean, what if he isn't ready for all of that yet. It could be a bit too much for him.'

'Too much for him or for you? He loves having everyone around, he told me as much earlier.'

I exhaled, having already partially conceded.

'What harm could it do, having a few more people here to make a big fuss of him?'

'Okay, okay, as much as the idea terrifies me, it's his day not mine. You have to help me decorate, though!'

'Brilliant!' said Mila, beaming proudly.

Shortly after, we began discussing themes, props, gifts, and entertainment. I was already lighter inside from partaking in something so ordinary. It wouldn't be Kai's first birthday party but would certainly be the first without his dad.

The remainder of the evening flew by without any hiccups; the three of us tucked into our Domino's order and shared ideas of how to transform our home into an indoor *Jurassic World*.

Kai's excited laughter coursed through the house as ideas flitted from the predictable to the absolutely outrageous. We were still a family and his smiling face served to remedy any ill feeling I'd had regarding hosting a birthday bash for him.

We only had one thing left to decide upon. The guest list.

27

'Where's the birthday boy?'

My dad's eyes lit animatedly as he crossed the threshold. I beamed at him with a growing adoration that was still paired with a degree of discomfort.

'Sorry, Dad, I've packed him off to bed. He said he wasn't feeling too well.'

'What? Talk about bad timing! He can't miss his own party!'

'It'd be typical though, wouldn't it! He should be fine after a little rest.'

'I'll have a man-to-man talk with him later and get him in the mood. Leave it with me.'

I felt relief born from having so many other chores to attend to.

'Wow, you score a strong ten out of ten for this. Good work!' I said, noticing the wide selection of tat poking from the opening of his re-useable bags.

'Like music to my ears that, Lois!'

Relieving him of the merchandise, I nosed a peak before splaying the contents onto the living room floor.

'I haven't played this since I was a kid! Does anyone actually play pass the parcel these days?' I pondered aloud.

'It's a classic, why wouldn't they? Wait until we start with musical statues, the kids are gonna go nuts.'

'There'll be no one moaning at my song selection for a change,' I said, my mind trailing back to before South Africa. The recollection triggered only a lick of pain this time.

'*I* can moan at your song selection if you like?'

'Oh no you're okay, it might be a nice change,' I said hopefully.

'Glass half full. Good girl! What do you need me to do now?'

'Hmm if you take out the sausage rolls and minis from the oven, I'll finish the party favours.'

A seasonal themed melody echoed through the house.

'I'll get that,' I said, as Dad motioned towards the door.

My chest grew with anticipation. It wasn't really my forte, hosting parties. Even ones for kids. Not without Lindani here to entertain the guests.

'Is it just me or has the entire population of *Jurassic Park* spawned all over your house?' jested Mila, poking her face through the door.

'Where's Alice?' I said, looking past her.

'In the car, she'll be here in a minute.'

'Cool isn't it?' I said after a slight pause. We looked towards the giant velociraptor that was bursting through the partition wall of Kai's play area.

'Yep! Authentic, too. Especially the floating T-Rex heads! It's like being inside Kai's head.'

'I wish that was all that was in there!' I proclaimed, wrapping Mila into an embrace. I was thankful she'd offered to collect Alice from the airport. If truth be told, the idea of seeing Alice again sent an added flutter of nervous energy through me. I wondered how she would perceive our home, our lifestyle and, well, my parenting … me as a woman, even.

'Is there any more food to come out?' I called across the room. The donor split warmed edibles between a row of foiled dishes.

'That's everything,' he said between chews, small bullets of pastry flying from his lips.

Alice's impending approach to my home triggered anxiety until the entrance of a rogue breeze indicated her arrival. *Everything's fine.* My hair parted at the nape of my neck, until both halves straddled my cheeks. *You got this.*

'Dear, your hair?'

Her voice radiated through my spine as I made for the kitchen area, despite not having been summoned by anyone.

I turned around just as slowly as my lips stretched into a smile.

Alice sucked her teeth upon entering. She followed Mila into the entrance hall. A heavenly glow surrounded her as if the sun itself had trailed her movements all the way overseas.

'I had a fight with the scissors I'm afraid. Needless to say, I lost,' I said, amused by my own wit.

Alice seemed distracted by my new haircut, more so than the twenty-plus imitation dinosaurs residing in every crevice of the living room. Her hair fixation served to remind me of my transition, as well as remind me I was at the mercy of her judgement.

'Oh, you and me both dear,' she said, rubbing a hand across the stubble on her own head.

'It was a temporary slip of sanity that's all.'

'You still look very pretty, Lois. And it will grow back.'

'Fast too, with any luck!' I responded, triggering a new insecurity. 'So how was your flight?' I asked with genuine interest. 'I hope you were treated to extra leg room and something interesting to watch?' I was deflecting from my fear of exposure. Fear of what Sarah may have told her about me crept into my consciousness. I was overcompensating.

'It was wonderful, dear. I do appreciate you flying me over, it was just the loveliest gesture. The best news I have received in a very long time I must admit, since Lindani—'

'Pleased to hear it,' I said, splintering my thoughts of him.

'Sorry, dear, I can be quite clumsy with words these days,' she said, realising she had brought up Lindani's absence too early on. 'I do hope you don't think me insensitive.'

'No, no, don't worry. I know how that feels, Alice, believe me. Did you and Mila have a nice catch up on the drive over?'

'We did, actually. I was pleased to hear you know of Mila and Lindani's late marriage. I was ever so worried I would reveal that to you in a moment of carelessness.'

'We realised more or less as soon as we met. It seemed a shame to let that kibosh our friendship though.'

'Sure. How strange it is how things work out sometimes. Perhaps your friendship was the very thing that was meant to come out of your acquaintance with him?'

'Who knows.' I admitted honestly.

My dad held up drink options from the kitchen area. 'Can I get you something to drink?' I offered. 'The other guests should be arriving soon so feel free to make yourself comfortable before the good seats are taken!'

'Whatever you're having would be lovely, dear, and thank you.'

I placed Alice's patterned knit shawl onto the hanger in the hall, secretly questioning whether my taste in beverage would match hers. The uncertainty ignited a brief flutter of panic.

My instinct to revert back to insecure teenager was never too far away. I had learned however from the pain and exertion I had endured my entire life from countless futile attempts to fit in.

It's just a drink, grow up!

'Is a Diet Coke okay, Alice?'

'Splendid,' she acquiesced.

It had taken a good portion of my savings to fly her over to us, but it was a decision I didn't question, even for a moment. I beamed at the guests as they trickled through the door one by one. Some offered condolences for the 'loss' of my husband, others outright slated his very being, whilst my preferred guests merely ignored his existence entirely.

As it happened, I wasn't too clued up on the order of events at kids' parties so I had little choice but to ad-lib most of the day. Lindani had always accompanied Kai to school gatherings in the past, allowing me some much needed 'me' time. A flicker of something travelled through me, as I wondered briefly if that's where he had met his new lady friend. I pushed it away.

More guests streamed in.

'Michael and I have been praying for you both, Lois. For you and that sweet boy of yours. I do hope he sees sense and comes back home with his tail between his le—'

'Thanks, Cheryl, can I take your coats?' I offered, hoping she would decline in favour of leaving her son at the party unattended. My neighbour's blunt expression of ill-informed sympathy threatened to spark my anger.

Cheryl peeled off her coat and handed it to me, along with her daughter's.

'Kai should be down soon, he's just getting ready. Help yourself to drinks and I'll be with you all shortly.'

I had laid out Kai's party outfit prior to setting up, but suddenly hoped he would remain upstairs with his grandad for a little while longer, rather than risk walking into a room full of people speculating about his father's fate.

I noticed my dad's striped socks occupy the centre point of the stairs. 'Everyone get ready for the birthday boy!' he said, attempting to hype up the crowd.

'Happy birthday, lil' man!' I called out, watching Kai clunk robotically down each step, his smiling face poking through the toothy jaws of his Dilophosaurus costume.

Scanning the room for my location, he came crashing over to the living area and dived into me with a warmth that I no longer recognised. My heart throbbed with a pride I selfishly revelled in, a feeling compounded by being in full view of my friends and family, especially Alice.

'Look at all these people, they've come to celebrate your birthday.'

'I really love it, it's so cool, thanks, Mum,' he said, drinking in the explosion of prehistoric paraphernalia.

Alice rose from her seat to embrace Kai with an air of politeness not usually demonstrated between grandchild and parent. I listened in, as he spoke animatedly about his costume, the gifts, and the *Jurassic World* cake he confessed he couldn't wait to tuck into. He went on to show Alice who his best school friends were before relaying tales of their mischievous antics.

I hadn't before contemplated how Alice would feel, spending time with Lindani's family but without the man himself, especially staying in his home for the duration of her visit. I only hoped she would be able to reconnect with him sometime soon. Perhaps, even, her presence may lure Lindani back home? It didn't seem fair for her, too, to lose him amongst our domestic affairs. *How far I've come!*

It wasn't long before my dad had engaged everyone in a game of musical statues. Mila had embraced the role with full enthusiasm, dancing around in a sea of primary schoolers with a competitiveness that ill fitted the occasion.

I poured myself a Diet Coke and carried it over to where Alice was standing.

'How're you feeling?' I asked, standing shoulder to shoulder in full view of the antics taking place before us.

'I'm well, dear. How are you feeling now?' She sought physical contact with her free hand.

I should have seen it as an opportunity to give my story a voice, but I only wished to savour watching my son enjoy himself. Those moments being far and few between now.

'I'm doing well, Alice, thank you. As well as anyone could hope, anyway.'

'You have done a blessed job for the boy, dear. Just look at his face.'

For all the doubts and fears I'd had in anticipation of her arrival, our ability to connect over Kai's well-being had enabled me to lay them to bed. Alice being close made me feel as though Kai's father wasn't so far away either, and this way his close proximity – imagined or not – couldn't bring us any more undue hurt.

Before long, the house was filled with ample guests and a healthy stack of gifts to match. A handful of parents chose to stick around to accompany their children whilst most opted to drop them and leave. There were kids from Kai's school and friends from the airline industry who I had grown close to over the years.

They enlivened the ambience with healing bouts of laughter and chatter, spraying life over the deep cracks in our foundations. The flurry of children was a welcome distraction to the mundane, and on occasion prying, adult talk. I was becoming increasingly at ease as the minutes passed. The Caribbean Rum pierced through my glass of Diet Coke, restoring my demeanour to pre-South Africa days.

After a few games, where Mila crept to the top of the leader board, I coaxed Kai into opening gifts. He'd already opened his main presents from myself and his absent father. He thanked his friends collectively, then his grandad held out a large rectangular box, concealed beneath a shiny dotted covering. Kai peeled away strips of paper methodologically, wishing to make this present last as it was his final one. The words 'The Most Marvellous Fantastical Wondrous Magic Tricks' were revealed one by one, sending a shot of electricity through my chest.

I watched my son tamper at the same box I had centred my childhood around.

'You kept it?' I whispered, in a daze.

Kids' limbs flailed dramatically in imaginary warfare as their attention waned from the gift-giving. The sprinkling of girls however, clustered around Kai to witness the final reveal, having struggled to find their place amongst the boys' amateur dramatics.

'Thanks, Grandad, its brilliant!' pronounced Kai as he picked at its contents excitedly.

'Dad?' I said.

'It seemed a shame to part with something you loved so much. What better than to pass it down?'

He turned to Kai and explained how he had replaced some items as well as sourcing some new ones to 'keep up with the times'. 'It's very important you look after it, champ. Perhaps you'll follow in your mum's footsteps one day?'

'Did Mum used to be a magician?' he asked curiously.

'She did, little man. Around the time she was your age, too.'

I fought a private battle of instincts. On the one hand I yearned to question Dad's motives for dragging up the past, but just as aggressively

I aimed to avoid conflict with him altogether.

'Oh, Lois, how wonderful! I know a thing or two about sorcery, dear,' added Alice.

Great!

Kai beamed up at me with a new appreciation. A gesture I had longed for tirelessly. I was stunned into silence, suppressing the urge to come clean as a fraud. I was never a magician. And Dad knew it all too well, so why was he telling my son otherwise?

I felt uneasy. Hoped Kai wouldn't follow in my footsteps by trying to conjure up his father with a few pieces of plastic. I hoped, in equal measure, I wasn't going to dampen his passion with my own cynicism.

I reflected how I'd once believed magic held enough power to bring back my dead mum. It hadn't worked of course. But I did irrationally consider whether it had the power to conjure my living husband.

'Okay everyone, who wants to play pass the parcel? Adults, too. I won't take no for an answer!' And with that, the guests joined us in the lounge, assuming their positions in the circle.

28

THEN

There I was, dressed in my most striking attire, only to stand in the same kitchen I usually frequented in my pyjamas. My heels welded themselves to the tiles, as did the wine glass to my hand. I was relieved no less about my good hair day than I was about my empty stomach. It churned angrily at the reduction of food I had delivered to it over the last few days. As a result, I'd managed to shimmy the leatherette trousers relatively easily over my hips. To my disappointment, they didn't quite emanate the same sex appeal as they did when Fiona wore them.

Titch was mingling enthusiastically. Only the first wave of guests had arrived and already he was engaging in friendly introductions and small talk. I followed his movements closely, hoping no one else would notice my eagle eye. My fingers drummed the wine glass involuntarily, leaving a faint watery silhouette.

Fiona was equally as comfortable as Titch. She sauntered by the door, hurrying guests up the path before clutching them against the red ruffles on her chest. I scanned the immediate area without being able to locate Raf and wondered for the first time if maybe we had something in common.

Every bit of floor space was occupied by a mixture of English and Spanish millennials. It was ten p.m., and I'd finally migrated to the living room after an uncomfortable two hours circling the breakfast bar, concealing my imagined bloating waistband.

Titch and Fi had coaxed me to join the friends that formed a semicircle around our fireplace as if we were witches about to cast a hex on someone. I'd been told there was a theme we were to comply with, to wear white, hence my choice of top and shoes. Scanning the room, I questioned my memory but concluded there was definite talk of a 'white' party. *Why was no one wearing all white?* It stung. We had been tricked into some spectacle of initiation. How could they do it to us and think we wouldn't notice? All of which could have been avoided if Titch had chosen to spend the weekend with me instead.

It was evident from Titch's continued conversation with a pretty blonde girl that he hadn't noticed we'd been victims of a childish prank. He was more interested in his new acquaintance and hadn't wasted time to approach her during my only trip to the bathroom.

A dull ache entered my stomach. This entire 'new stage' of my life was hardly working out the way I'd hoped, and I couldn't decide if the sensation was a result of that or my growing hunger. The idle chatter of our new 'friends' was only background noise whilst I fought again with the rise of jealousy. *Turn a blind eye*, I recalled.

I knew from a glimpse in the bathroom mirror that fatigue had noticeably loosened the skin around my eyes. I'd considered climbing into bed to sleep it off, whilst I was out of view. I yearned for repose, but my thoughts had lately deprived me of the rest I needed.

I was becoming exhausted with tracking Titch's eye movements and body language. Only a fraction of my flesh, it seemed, remained healthy. I'd anticipated the pain all week, and I'd prepared myself well this time, but there was simply too much competition in one room.

I decided I was going to leave this house and everyone in it. I'd waste no time in trying to find somewhere new to live. I'd be away from fake people and selfish boyfriends.

In turn, I smiled warmly at everyone who caught my eye. A smile that masked my satisfaction of having decided upon my next move.

It was self-preservation.

I was vaguely aware, then, of questions being directed towards me. Titch, being Titch, took centre stage and answered on my behalf, noticing my disinterest. He lapped up the attention. I was out of my depth. The realisation triggered an overwhelming sense of numbness. But I recognised his behaviour still required my attention, right now before he could deny my accusations later on when they were out of context.

The music achieved a much higher volume than moments earlier, and I noticed Raf swaying by the houseplant, wincing at the thud of the bass. He was flanked by two other boys I recognised from previous nights out.

A vaguely familiar girl dressed in a fitted black jumpsuit reached for the flesh of my upper arm as a delicate grab for attention. 'Hey, how you doin'?' I mouthed whilst continuing my approach to the corner of the room. The air was so thick with cigarette and marijuana smoke that the confines of our high-ceilinged dream house were not only constricting the dimensions of the room but also my ability to breathe.

I cursed again at the discomfort of my outfit. The strain at its seams had to be as noticeable to everyone else as it was to me. The knowledge sent a surge of insecurity to my cheeks as I crossed the room in full view.

I peered over my shoulder subtly to check Titch's location. I couldn't immediately trace him but could hear whispers of his laugh amongst the crowd. The point of my heel caught on the living room rug as I turned back around, causing me to sway and stumble. An action only serving to represent the drunk I'd evidently become.

In my slow, blurry descent to the floor, a bolt of anger shielded me from impact. 'We'll be together at our little party,' he'd said. He could barely bring himself to stand by me, let alone introduce me to blondie.

He'd made me feel special before we moved in together. But now I realised it was all fake. I was a place filler. It wouldn't have surprised me if he'd known we were moving in with them from the beginning.

What he didn't know was that I was going to leave him. There was no going back now. His deception was the final twist of the knife.

I lay on the makeshift dance floor in the recovery position. Although

soberly aware of descending faces I remained simultaneously unconcerned. There was a buzz of commotion in the air that I wasn't a part of.

Ignoring the thrum, I pleaded with unknown forces to transport
me to bed, only to be craned back onto my feet by Raf and Titch. My
arms webbed loosely around their shoulders, causing the white fabric
to reveal the area around my navel. I wrestled to free my arms from
embarrassment, with an intended force I failed to muster. Fi was the
lead in guiding us to the stairs. She cleared away anyone who stood in
our path. Her assistance conveniently serving to minimise the humiliation she felt by blocking me from onlookers.

The party was in full swing and attention had thankfully moved
from my tumble to the lines of white powder that decorated most
surfaces. I had never been around drugs before, not in real life. I had
seen enough on TV to recognise them though. It was a surreal moment
for me. The lines were glowing and impossible to miss. The same as
when you see in the flesh someone from TV.

I suddenly felt a pang of longing for my life before I'd lost my
parents. I wondered what Mum would think if she could see me now. I
hadn't turned into the woman she would be proud to call her daughter,
not one bit. I had to change. Change into anything else but this.

Despite my adolescent curiosity, I was going to leave the drugs
alone, and the alcohol. Things in my life were to straighten out as
soon as I was out of this toxic environment. Cocaine acting as the
perfect alibi. One of the boys Raf had stood with earlier offered Titch
a rolled-up five-pound note. He stood aside and motioned for Titch to
occupy his spot. To my utter shock, Titch swept up the white powder
like a professional, splattering the larger chunks into dust with another
boy's driving licence. He wiped the remainder across his gums to
signify the end of his turn before handing the apparatus to the blonde
girl he'd been talking to earlier.

I disguised the disgust to the best of my ability, not wanting to
draw further attention to myself, nor to the glaringly obvious fact
that I absolutely did not belong. Meanwhile, Titch had morphed into

someone I couldn't recognise, and my lack of food intake had triggered dizzy spells to the intensity that would almost certainly cause me to take another untimely tumble.

Fiona must have noticed the blood draining from my face and signalled to Titch, as he almost immediately appeared at the kitchen worktop I was leant against.

'Lois, we need to get you some food.' He turned to the jumble of people. 'Hey guys, what do you think about ordering pizza?'

I wondered at what point Titch had become so integrated in Raf and Fi's friendship group to initiate the next course of action.

'I'm okay, Titch, you go and do your thing. I'm gonna lie down.'

'Lois, you haven't eaten properly for days. What the hell were you thinking, throwing that much booze down?'

Oh you remember my name now, do you!

I was taken aback by his tone, my mouth open aghast.

'Was it really worth it, Lois? All for the sake of squeezing your ass into those stupid pants?'

Frantically, I urged him to shut his mouth. He was humiliating me in front of everyone, more noticeably his perfect harem of women.

'I'm gonna get you some food, okay? I am not taking no for an answer.'

With that, he exited the room.

Fiona quickly moved towards me and poured herself a glass of Brancott wine from the bottle next to my elbow.

'Are you really okay, Lo?' I understood her to say through a slurred, thick Mediterranean accent.

'I'm sorry, Fi, I have to get out of here. I can't bear it any longer.'

'I'll come out with you, get some fresh air,' she suggested, wrapping her arm around the small of my back.

'Please don't,' I said, a comment infested with deeper sadness than this evening alone had warranted.

With an expression that only barely defied tears, I stepped away from her embrace and made for the front door.

29

Mila froze when she read the label. 'Lois, you might want to see this,' she said, having stripped the parcel down to its final layer.

'What's the matter?'

'It's for you.'

'Huh? That's impossible, I wrapped them myself … Just open it please,' I asked, refusing to remove my finger from the play button.

Mila held my gaze wearily. 'No. You have to see this,' she insisted.

I picked at the skin around my thumb. Alice shifted uncomfortably on the sofa cushion.

My pulse quickened then, as I recognised from a distance the curves of the letters that formed his name. I shot Kai a look, salty beads forming on the surface of my skin.

My dad, noticing my alarm, pressed for the game to continue. 'Push the play button would you darlin'?' he instructed, as if nothing untoward had happened.

I did as I was asked, thankful of his attempt to divert attention. The clattering in the background signalled the guests were continuing with pass the parcel. I didn't even notice the eyes of my colleagues tracking my movements.

I plucked off the label and tossed it in the pedal bin. A singe of regret followed.

Mila pulled up the stool beside me. I felt her arm warm the centre of my back.

'You don't have to open it, you know. You can just throw it in the bin, like it never existed.'

'That's probably what I should have done,' I said.

A dark wiry material enveloped my thumb inside the opening.

'He always gave me a present on Kai's birthday,' I volunteered wistfully.

'That was then. Let's not let him win today, okay? Not on Kai's birthday.'

I fully agreed with Mila's rationale and nodded to demonstrate as much.

'I'm just curious, Mila. It means nothing.'

I felt the guests' eyes lusting after its contents.

My thumb scored further into the wrapping, forming a wider opening, from which I extracted the gift.

I should have listened to Mila. Had I done so, I would have avoided the humiliation of what came next.

'Why would he do that?' said Mila, outwardly grimacing in disgust.

I churned the bile over in my throat, tears threatening my eyes. It shouldn't have hurt but it did. *I can't let him win, not today.*

'He always loved my hair, that's why.'

'So, what, he just wanted you to know that he doesn't like you with short hair. Fucking joke, he is,' barked Mila. 'Sorry,' she said in a lowered tone, acknowledging the party demographic. 'I told you, you should have thrown it out.'

I stormed through the house, as composed as possible, exited through the back door, and dropped the long brown wig into the dustbin. I took a moment to compose myself, despite the fact my 'missing' husband was clearly watching my every move. I just needed a minute, I reasoned.

The games were in full swing. I walked back to the house to see Kai clutching a dinosaur-themed craft set. He was happy, that was all that mattered. In hope of not spoiling the mood, I detoured to his bedroom, taking solace in the knowledge I still had *him.*

So what if Lindani had sent me a stupid wig! So what if he was trying to show me up in front of everyone! So what, I maintained. He wasn't mine to impress any more. I shouldn't care and I wouldn't. I did wonder, however, who had wrapped and delivered it. I detected my name being called, or at least spoken about inside the house. It matched my dad's voice.

I fingered my shortened hair. It had to be someone at the house as the pattern on the paper matched the kind I had used on everything else. Perhaps someone from work was the mystery woman? I searched my memory for any possible link between Dan and each guest. I lacked the fire in my tummy to find out. Cruelty I believed wasn't in his composition, but I guess if he had no issue with letting his family think he had perished, nothing was out of the remit of possibilities.

If Lindani was going to come back to his family, he would have done so already. And as things stood, my desire for that eventuality had died. I did, however, have the desire to weed out the snake in my home.

Alice and Mila bore the obvious connections and were both out of the house immediately before the other guests arrived. As was my dad. I still hadn't questioned him on the extent of his and Lindani's contact, and so far he had excelled in distracting me from providing the answers he knew I required. Could he have brought the 'gift' on Lindani's behalf, as a favour perhaps?

I opted to lay low and monitor everyone's behaviour covertly. I wasn't going to rule out the possibility that it could have been delivered and wrapped by Lindani himself. He had a house key and he'd only have to look in to see when the coast was clear to make his move. It would also prove I hadn't completely made up the entire spectacle of his phone turning up randomly in our home.

• • •

And just like that, the wig was the least of my concerns. I noticed a small pile of lined paper, clumsily strewn over Kai's bedside cabinet. I sat upright, intending to straighten the pile or tidy it out of sight altogether, recognising the sheets as his spelling practice.

A yellow corner caught my eye. It peeped from behind the collection of children's stories that Kai and I knew by heart. Removing the book from its resting place, I relocated it to the floor. It produced a thud as I lost my grip around the same time I noticed the familiar scribbles of Mila's handwriting. I recalled the moment she'd told me she had something to give him. I was distracted with having been visited by Wendy and had neglected to look at what she was talking about.

It wasn't only the content of the handwritten spelling list that implanted an uneasy feeling in the pit of my stomach, it was the colour of the paper that caused my nerves to tremble.

Yellow paper. I certainly hadn't ever purchased any, nor had I bought any for Kai. Falling victim to a sudden wave of panic, I thrust open the drawers in his room, flicked through colouring books and plain paper pads in hope of finding the offending merchandise. I repeated the procedure in my marital room as well as the spare bedroom, flitting away the apparent link between Mila and the same paper that had been used to deliver news of my husband's abandonment.

The drone of the party persisted beneath me. Youthful giggles and adult laughter sounded as more games ensued. I imagined her, currently engaged mindlessly in the festivities, revelling in the success of her sick plan. She would raise a glass with Dad, unable to believe her luck that he had come back into my life, offering a well-timed distraction.

There was motive. Mila had been married to Lindani. She must have still held a flame for him and couldn't bear the idea of him being happy with someone else. Surely that was enough to ignite a bolt of jealousy strong enough to trigger such a domino effect.

I kicked myself for not having told Lindani I was friends with his ex-wife. If I had, she would never have been able to get so close to my family. He certainly wouldn't have allowed it.

Instead, I thoughtlessly shared anecdotes of Dan's loving nature as a best friend, a husband and a father.

The desire to hold someone accountable grew, the more I allowed my mind to wander. I needed to blame someone, other than a mystery woman who was likely never to cross my path.

Part of my theory felt forced as I grew increasingly aware of my desire to cast blame. Part of me hoped I was connecting the dots incorrectly. I relied on Mila's friendship now more than ever, and to find out she too had betrayed me, really would break me to the same degree Lindani's betrayal had.

As a last thread of rationale, I trudged through the reasons why she could not have been responsible for the note Lindani had left in my bedside drawer. The handwriting, for one, was distinctly his – the exaggerated curve of the S and crossed strokes of his Ls were his only.

In no way had Mila shown any signs of jealousy towards our relationship either. Plus, she had loved Tom throughout our entire friendship – it only breaking down as a direct result of her irrational fear of being hurt. Which all of a sudden felt as contrived as it did unbelievable. Despite the assumptions, I *knew* her. She had supported me unquestionably, responding to my distress calls at the drop of a hat. She had even come to South Africa with little to no hesitation.

My mind was a runaway train of questions. Did she want Kai? Was that her plan all along?

I applied pressure to my forehead, forcing back the drill of pain that threatened. If Mila had decided to sneak off to see Dan whilst we were away, Kai would have either had to go with her or be left in someone else's care. He had never so much as hinted at her abandoning him whilst I was at the police station, or having stayed with anyone else whilst she sneaked off to meet his dad.

Having possessed the natural instinct to consider both sides of a story, memories trickled back that jumbled my outlook.

Alice did say, 'Sometimes good people do bad things.' Had that been a hint as to Mila's involvement? Was it even conceivable that my loving husband would leave his son to go back to his ex-wife? I tried to recall what had caused their disentanglement in the first place. Scraps of memory surfaced. They had grown apart, that's what he had said. Neither had betrayed the other or had done anything unforgivable.

I slumped onto the carpet in Kai's room, at a loss where to check for evidence that would serve as a reasonable explanation. Yellow paper, I thought again, wondering if I had attached too much significance to my finding.

I dragged the storage box from under his bed in anticipation of clearing away the rubble. I tapped the cluster of papers against the firm of the table, aligning its edges.

As I motioned to insert them into Kai's storage box, a glow of words served to incriminate someone very dear to me. I stared at the highlighted words from the torn-out diary entry. They were words that mirrored those on Kai's home-made spelling list and simultaneously exposed Mila for the sick, manipulative, deceitful monster she was.

The evidence I had exhausted over whipped me in the face.

It had been her all along.

30

Ownstairs, impeccable, perfumed tentacles sucked at the soul of my son's birthday party. They belonged to a creature that slithered amongst the crowd, down the walls and across the furniture. A creature that weaved through parted feet, invisibly licking at the skin of its potential prey. Its stomach satiated from its most recent meal. A meal born from an attack of savagery usually witnessed amongst the most hideous of creatures. But instead, it bore polished features with perfect edges. A welcoming smile and a lure of which to be envious.

A creature I had consistently invited into my life and entrusted with the care of my beloved son. I had shared my darkest secrets with it, no less. The partner I had devoted thirty years to finding.

I paced the confines of the first floor, heart quickening uncontrollably as the jagged pieces firmly sealed into place. My clothes nicked onto edges I'd never before noticed, compounding my agitation. My mind began to process the level of deceit that was insinuated by my finding. I recalled dates and times it could have been possible for their courtship to blossom. Opportunities had been available in abundance.

I tore what little skin I had left on my reddened thumb. It triggered a shot of pain, releasing a trickle of blood that cascaded to the carpet below. A shred of relief travelled through my veins as a direct consequence.

I held my position by Kai's bedroom door, guarding his innocence from the evil that had already seeped through the slits in the wood.

It was my job to protect him from harm. To protect him from abandonment, pain, suffering, from cruel intent. Just one role. I sank my fingernails deep into the paintwork on either side of the door frame, my face pasted onto the wood as I wailed silently. Smears of salted crimson coated the white wall as I scraped hard into the plaster.

I had only recently become accepting of Lindani's infidelity, but this …

The realisation that we'd have to recover from yet another cruel twist of fate immediately caused a dark fog to settle overhead. I allowed snippets of displaced laughter from the party to penetrate my consciousness, to diffuse through the toxic smog. I begged for Kai's ignorance of what I could only speculate were Mila's attempts to instil into him the venomous truth. That Mila had stolen his father.

I was momentarily crippled with dread at discovering the extent of Kai's interpretation of mine and Mila's involvement. I was equally as overwhelmed with the responsibility of unravelling the truth from the lies. I had to restore Kai's ability to feel safe and to trust again. An instinct that revealed itself by the urge to fly downstairs and push a blunt instrument into her chest.

The unadulterated violation seared my heart. I questioned if we, as a family, could ever restore some semblance of normalcy. Casting my thoughts back to before South Africa, before that godforsaken day in the Medical Examiner's office where Mila and I had met. I had been filled with gratitude for having secured a beautiful, healthy, loving family. An achievement I had previously attributed to other people. One I never would have anticipated this sweet, interesting woman would have vowed to destroy, nor would I have thought myself capable of encouraging their union by having secretly invited her into my life.

The sugary smell of icing would have teased my nostrils if the wolf amongst the sheep hadn't shown itself. I thought I heard distant voices calling everyone to regroup but remained in my wayward state of shock.

I imagined myself in therapy then, sat opposite a warm, kind lady who oozed sincerity and genuine empathy. She would guide my actions by teaching me how to calm my thoughts. How to rationalise and to not act on emotion. A teaching I felt was finally taking effect. Wendy's face came to mind. Something about her eyes bore an honesty I found soothing.

The sound of muffled footfalls grew louder, interrupting my calming process.

'Lois, where are you? The kids want to cut the cake?' Its voice mirrored the timing of the same footsteps I'd noticed moments earlier. My pulse punched through the skin of my chest. I imagined it to destabilise her, reaching far enough to send her plummeting back into the abyss from which she'd crawled.

A stab of sadness conflicted my intentions. I was losing a friend. And what if I was wrong? It was a hell of an accusation. One we wouldn't likely recover from. I looked down again at the sheet of paper I held in my right hand, confirming her guilt. Hiding it from view, it appeared I had decided what I was going to do.

Like many times before, I told myself to regain composure, take a deep breath and stabilise my chest.

Our eye level matched. I swallowed for the fourth time since hearing Mila's footsteps approach me. I thought I saw a hint of realisation creep into her expression. The tremor in both knees told me it was more than just my paranoia speaking.

I scraped at the recollection of what she had previously said, not wanting to seem preoccupied.

'Are you feeling any better, Lo? It was just a silly wig. This is what he wants, to make you feel like shit, with or without him.'

Oh, the wig. It had slipped my mind entirely. She had exposed herself with that comment alone, I thought. Lindani had never set out to make me 'feel like shit'. Never intentionally. Quite the opposite. She had slipped up.

Playing along, I used the wig as a perfect scapegoat. 'You were right, Mila, I should have just left it alone like you said to. Instead, he got what he wanted, again.'

'Well, it's done now anyway, not to worry. Everyone is waiting for you downstairs. And when I say everyone, I mean a gaggle of sugar-deprived children.'

'I'll come and dish it out shortly,' I said. As Mila turned to leave the landing, I stopped her.

'Mila, is Kai okay? Has he said anything to you?' I asked with a new dynamic of intrigue.

'He's fine, hasn't said anything, just asked where you were.'

Had one not known otherwise, it would be easy to overlook her wrongdoings – given how the syrup gold of her eyes shimmered hypnotically when she'd had an idea, how when she broke into a smile her pearly teeth commanded the attention of all in the room, including myself. Her alluring ebony hair shrouded the poised elegance of her sculpted neck which housed an alternating collection of delicate gold necklaces. Her glossy smooth skin, barring a few sporadic imperfections, must have borne the weight of more layers than the naked eye could see.

'Okay that's good, just give me a minute and I'll be down in two.'

'Will do!'

Her serpent-like features were visible to me then. Gigantic suckers exuded from her thick flesh; her claws sharpened into a point. I folded my evidence into a perfect pocket square and slid it into the back of my jeans. I sure as hell was going to 'dish it out' I mused, lifelessly.

The sound of children playing made me question my intended course of action. The party had been going on for close to two hours. The kids, at their age, would already be growing tired. There was no harm in concluding things a little early. I was going to hand out the cake and goody bags and ask my guests to leave.

'Who wants cake?' I declared as I reached the ground floor.

Wails of excited chatter broke out without hesitation. Dad shot me a smile from the living area before joining in with the kids, to which I responded with a shaky, interpretive grin similar to someone suffering from motor neuron disease.

I took a moment to assess the scene that centred my world right now, taking in the small cluster of faces that surrounded me. I chewed on the gristly mass of realisation that my circle of friends had shrivelled into nothing other than a theoretical notion.

Before too long, everyone had tucked into their dessert and been gifted a party favour. Some children had already been collected after my contacting the parents, whilst the remaining guests were preparing to leave.

I spied Mila speaking to Kai by the front door. She tussled his hair, her face alight with an animation appropriate for the occasion. I didn't notice any reluctance in Kai during their interaction. *Good, he doesn't know.* He didn't flinch or appear upset in any way. I hadn't really believed it when I'd thought earlier how Mila wanted to take Kai from me, but that same seed of doubt was beginning to sprout for the second time. Dismissing it may not be an option. Few guests remained, the ones that did were a couple of work acquaintances, Alice, Dad, one of Mila's friends and the seductress herself.

I helped Dad with clearing Kai's toys back into his play area and thanked him for everything he'd done to help. Kai was clearly thrilled to have him around.

'Dad, would you mind doing one more thing?'

He was visibly exhausted, if the deep-set rings under his eyes were all telling.

'Of course, my love, what would that be?'

'Could Kai come to your house for a couple of hours? Maybe you guys could watch a movie or something?'

My expression froze, in hope that his hesitation was due to fatigue rather than his suspicion of my intent. I chose to believe the former, before advancing to the next stage of persuasion.

'I'll literally be a couple of hours. Kai will be shattered so you can just chill on your couch with him until I'm done here, that's if you don't mind?'

Something was on the tip of his tongue.

'Okay. But you will be okay, won't you?'

'I will,' I answered, attempting to conceal the grin that repelled my cheeks from one another.

'Lois?'

'I will be. I promise.'

'You look pale and you're sweating, darlin'. Are you sure you're feeling all right?'

'I always look like this, Dad. It's called parenthood,' I joked.

I awaited his scolding reply, but instead received something that was more malleable to my foul mood. 'Okay then, can you get me his coat and shoes, and I'll give him the good news.'

'You're the best, thank you,' I said, kissing his cheek in gratitude.

Mila motioned to leave as I collected Kai's coat and shoes from the entrance hall.

'Where are you going?' I voiced, blocking her exit.

'Lois? Are you okay?' asked Mila, reacting to my tone.

'I will be,' I said coldly.

Proceeding with the most pressing task at hand, I called to my son, 'You're going to Grandad's for movie night! I'll pick you up later, okay?' I stood blocking the door.

'Cool! Can I take the rest of the cake?' he said.

No sooner had he been dressed to leave than they were on their way, extra cake in hand. My penetrative stare held Mila inside as they left.

Alice appeared purposeful, imparting her wisdom to the audience she had acquired by the seating area.

'New underwear, Mila?' I asked rhetorically, referring to the lush red lace that penetrated her white camisole.

She knocked the umbrella stand clumsily, sending it to crack against the floor.

'What?' she said, dragging across her blouse in concealment.

'The red lace, you didn't purchase it as a little treat for yourself, did you?'

I noticed Alice in my periphery, stuffing the scarf that had been draped around her shoulders into her bag, cramming it over something else I couldn't quite see from my position.

'You're right, I didn't. But I' – the glitchy shifting of her neck made me aware that Alice's gaze was flitting between Mila and me – 'don't see how that's appropriate to share with a room full of kids, still. And what's with the fascination with my undergarments, all of a sudden?'

I allowed time to silently gather my conclusions.

'Give it up, M. The cat's out of the bag, don't make it more embarrassing than it has to be,' I said with diminishing confidence.

I sensed Alice rise to her feet, presumably waiting for the perfect time to intercede before things escalated, or perhaps she had a confession of her own to offer to the room?

'The lingerie that my husband ordered just so happened to find itself on your body, did it? Is that what you'd like me to believe?'

'Lois,' said Alice. 'Mila, just go dear, just leave.'

'You've got it all wrong, Lois,' Mila claimed, sliding the umbrella stand back upright.

'No … no, Mila will not be leaving.' I read Alice's response through her expression. The sucking of her teeth was accompanied by a deliberate refusal to meet my line of sight. 'That is unless you know something you need to share with me, Alice?'

Mila too lent Alice an extended moment of her unwavering attention.

'Anyone, if there's something you need to tell me, I suggest now is the time,' I commanded amidst a flurry of movement in my gut.

I scanned the faces of everyone in the room, my guests clearly stricken by the same mysterious paralysis as the vocal cords of these two women. Alice and Mila were deeply connected, as if both were assessing how much of the tele-prompter they were able to read aloud.

Alice broke the mould and stepped towards me, parting ways with her possessions.

'There is nothing I have to inform you of that pertains to Mila, if that's what you're suggesting … I was just thinking about something else, which is why I didn't speak upon it just then.'

The paper, Lois, don't let her get away, not now.

'You have some explaining to do if you expect me to let you walk out of here any time soon,' I continued, plucking the yellow square from my back pocket.

Alice folded her rough, veined fingers around my wrist before I'd had the chance to reveal its contents, so I slid it back from where I'd retrieved it. Her nutty, woody scent wilted my posture as if the very essence of her had the power to drain my energy source. 'What happened to the photograph, Lois?' she enquired, the same endearing warmth she usually emanated also draining before my eyes.

'What photograph?' I asked, leaking genuine confusion.

'It was Yetunde,' she stated, calmly, as if her declaration was to mean something of significance to me.

Although infested with an urgency to present my evidence to Mila and find out why she wanted to destroy my family, Alice's name-drop implanted a curiosity all of its own, one that with any luck could enlighten me with much-desired information about Lindani's past. Perhaps then, Mila's alienation – and mine – wouldn't turn out to be so entirely catastrophic.

I was firm in my request to know what Alice was referencing.

'It was a picture I gave to Lindani. He kept it close to him after escaping the A.R.M. and then again when he decided to start a new life over here. It was a part of his history, Lois, to remind him how far he had come.'

The colour must have drained from my upper body as waves of chilled pimples replaced my former ruddy glow.

'Escaped … what?' Invisible beads of sweat pierced the pimply masses.

Alice continued to fill my confused silence with an explanation of why Yetunde was so significant to them both.

'This lady founded the foster agency that brought him to me. "Mother has come back", that's what her name means, Lois. Lindani was delivered to me from God himself. He knew Yetunde was destined to become a saviour from the moment of her birth.'

Not only had I not, to my knowledge, possessed a picture of this woman, but I neglected to trust Alice's intentions for bringing her up at such a critical time – at the precise moment I was about to incriminate Mila. Why was Alice trying to protect her?

'What the hell is A.R.M., and why did Lindani have to escape from it?' I asked, my mouth buckling under the heightened demand of questions that sought issue.

'She saw the damaged canvas, Lois,' spoke Mila out of turn.

'Yeah, thanks for that, Mila, I didn't ask you.' I wasn't going to betray Kai or myself by giving her the respect she thought she still deserved.

I began to unfold the yellow corners slowly and methodically, buying some necessary time for my brain to catch up.

'Explain this to me please, best friend!'

'Why did you destroy it, dear?' interrupted Alice again, this time with a quasi-gentility.

I reflected how Lindani had hosted a reveal 'party' just for the three of us when we moved into our new home. It was the first image to decorate our walls and it was an event all of its own.

'Wow, it's ... big,' I'd said, standing back a few strides to drink in its presence. 'It certainly commands the attention of the room,' I'd said, with my shoulders slumped heavily from the pull of my baby's weight.

'Do you honestly like it?' was all he'd replied, a glow of pride lighting his face to such an extent that it even managed to bring a twinkle to my own.

'Her smile brings such a warmth to the room, don't you think?' I'd said, before retiring Kai to his bouncer below the wall on which the canvas hung. I'd hoped the swathes of maternal joy that exuded from her picture would instil a blanket of security into our home. I thought of the times I had sat before her image and begged to be released from the entrapments that motherhood had claimed over me.

'This is insane. You can't genuinely believe I'm the other woman?' declared Mila, interrupting my ghostly recollections. 'Oh my god, you're serious aren't you? You think it's me?' she repeated, interpreting my unfaltering glare as perseverance.

'Just tell me one thing,' I said, subduing the harried flare of my nostrils, having grown tired of delaying her accusation. 'What more could you possibly want from us Mila?'

31

I read the diary excerpt aloud, hoping she felt backed into a corner enough to offer a confession.

I am an actress. Not in the literal sense. You will not find my photograph in glossy magazines nor will I be invited to any fancy galas or awards ceremonies. People don't stop me in the street and congratulate me on my latest role. Lo—

'That's enough Lois, for fuck's sake just stop before I say something I regret.'

Lord knows I am not on an actress's salary, but that's what I am, an actress, in the true sense of the word. I am a rabid mixture of good and bad, fact and fiction. It is a skill I have had to acquire. So far it has served me well.

'Very cryptic, Mila. Do you think I would be so stupid as to not see right through your inscrutable confession,' I said.

'Lois, just stop before you make a fool of yourself. They're just words, they don't mean what you think they do. This is one huge misunderstanding.'

I scoffed in response. 'You're no stranger to those are you? So they're words that just so happened to have found themselves on my son's spelling list, that you—' I stopped. 'What did you just say?' I digressed, accosting Mila on a whole other level.

'You always get the wrong end of the stick, Lois! Come on, it's nothing new, is it? We both know that.'

Stay focused. 'What do you mean by that?'

Mila sat down on one of the kitchen stools then pulled out another, gesturing for me to sit by her.

I declined the offer.

'What exactly have I misunderstood, Mila?'

Alice sucked at her teeth impulsively. 'Come on, dear,' she interjected. 'What is it that you are implying? And think very carefully before you speak. Words are impossible to repossess, my child.'

I shrugged off Alice's comment, irritated by her untimely input. 'My child?' It was a term I may have once considered charming but in this context it oozed with superiority. I hoped she had read my thoughts, despite the effort it took to prevent them from possessing my face.

Mila remained on the kitchen stool, but her eyes danced to the same tune as my body.

'Well for one, you thought Sarah turned on you for no reason at all. She was actually one of the few people who wanted to help you, imagine that!'

I searched the ceiling for the appropriate memory and for a split second considered her statement to be true, but the gravity of our last exchange was still pasted against my conscience.

'I won't fall for it, Mila, not this time. So, what do they mean, these words on your little innocent spelling list?' I demanded, not wishing to displace my anger onto Alice just yet.

'They're nothing. Can we not do this, please? Not in front of everyone.' She exuded an air of desperation that appealed, only for a split second, to the best friend in me.

'No. I'm not playing this time. If you had nothing to do with my husband's disappearance and you care about me as much as you claim, then you'll tell me the truth.'

She glanced over at our friends who were sitting frozen on the leather couches, their gaze shifting from her eyeline awkwardly.

'Why are you looking over there?' I yelled, hammering my fist onto the counter. 'It's me you owe an explanation.'

I was possessed with an assertiveness no one in my circle had ever witnessed. I could tell it unnerved Mila. She knew how to handle the desperate, lonely, insecure Lois. But not this one.

'It was just something stupid scribbled in a diary. I write stuff all the time. None of it means anything. Do you think I'd be that careless if it was so incriminating? You think I'd purposely write Kai a spelling list, painting myself as some kind of mastermind? Even more ridiculous, you think I'd do that, knowing you'd find it?' Mila scoffed, appalled by my accusation. 'How could you even think, for a second, I could be capable of doing that to you, and to Kai? I love you both like you're my own family. I thought you knew that.'

My chest flexed at her choice of words.

'Well, Mila, as it turns out, I don't know you at all. Maybe you wanted the attention, or you wanted your husband back, your old life when you saw how happy he was in ours?' Mila bit down on her lower lip, chewing the words that were evidently attempting their escape. 'How am I to know, I don't have the mind of a sociopath do I?'

'Woah, that's enough now. You've had your say, can we just take it down a notch?'

'She said she didn't do it, so that's the end of it,' said a friend of hers.

'She didn't do it? She didn't just steal a tenner from my purse, she stole my husband and tried to ruin my child's life, I absolutely will not take it down a notch!'

'It's okay, Caroline, it's fine,' assured Mila. 'Lois,' she continued, drawing a deep breath, 'it actually breaks my heart that you think I could be capable of something like this. Did it not cross your mind that I simply wanted to give him something nice, something I knew he'd love? So what if I've made the spelling list from some crappy creative writing piece. It was never meant to imply I've been fake with you and your family all this time.'

Her words were calm and collected.

'That's bullshit. I don't buy it, Mila. I feel it in my gut, I know I'm right about you.'

'What's changed? I don't get it. Aside from this stupid misunderstanding, what has actually made you think I'd take your husband? Assuming that I actually could in the first place!'

'I don't have to explain anything to you, not any more.' I paced the floor, containing my bubbling frustration, but only succeeding intermittently. 'It wouldn't surprise me if you only befriended me because you knew I was married to your precious ex-husband,' I said, hoping she'd choose to terminate her interrogation. I had the proof, there was no way I would allow her to gaslight me. 'You even convinced me Dan would force us apart if he knew, as if you knew him better than I did.'

'If the shoe fits!'

Her friend joined us in the kitchen, upon detecting our flaring tempers. She stood beside Mila, protectively. 'You don't have to listen to this, Mila, it's insane.' She continued, this time addressing me instead, 'Lois, we're all so sorry you're going through this crap right now, we really are, but you're going to have no one left if you carry on like this.'

'Who will I not have left? Because as far as I can see, I don't have any friends. Not one of you believe me, do you?'

No one responded. Nor was there one gesture of comfort or signal that reflected allegiance. I was in a room filled with the opposition.

'Look, I know how it all sounds and trust me I wish I was wrong, but I'm not. She fooled me too, it's what she does. What did you do with Lindani's phone, Mila?' Her nose scrunched mechanically. 'You know, the one you so kindly volunteered to keep hold of until you found a way to hack into it. The one which just so happened to get stolen.'

'It did get stolen, it must have. It was an accident.'

'Or maybe it fell from your pocket as you were sneaking out of my home? Is that the accident you were referring to? And who bought you that slutty red underwear you've been flaunting all afternoon? And the wig, Mila. Nice touch!'

'You sound paranoid, Lois, you really do. It makes sense now. You always saw me as a threat, didn't you? You were the one who decided to lie to Dan, and you alone.'

I couldn't process what I was being told. It was Mila. Mila and her insistence that Lindani would freak out if he knew about our friendship. 'That's a hundred per cent false, and you know it is.'

The remaining guests turned into each other, speculating in hushed tones about her connection to Lois's missing husband.

'It isn't though, is it, Mrs. Attah,' she goaded. 'You've always been the same. A jealous, insecure wreck. Of course, you were going to use a fake name for me if it meant protecting your marriage.'

'Eish! What's the purpose of all this, ladies?' said Alice.

'It's from Tom by the way, the red lace,' she said, exposing the floral strap of her bra. 'I screwed him the day I lost Lindani's phone. Believe it or not, it wasn't the most pressing thing on my mind at the time.'

'*Lingene!* Both of you. Stop this,' interrupted Alice, spewing Africanisms more forcefully this time. 'May I say something?'

She allowed for a brief silence.

'It may not be my place to speak, but I have known you, Mila, for a long time and I believe I know you well. Lindani, at some point in time, chose to be with both of you. Neither of you are bad people. So why on earth are you behaving as though you are?'

Mila and I surrounded the kitchen island, looking at the floor, lost in our own thoughts as Alice scolded us in turn.

'Lois, dear, I don't know where Lindani is or who he is with, but please do not turn your back on those nearest to you. From what I gather, she is very much your only true friend.'

Who do you think you are, Alice? The potential truth of her statement induced another dimension of pain in my chest.

Caroline began, 'Mila has never badmouthed you or your marriage to me, Lois. She's been worried. Truthfully, she never said so much as one bad word about you.'

'Do you all expect me to believe that this was just an innocent fluke, that Mila's twisted confession found its way into my son's bedroom unintentionally?'

Much of me hoped for proof I'd been mistaken.

'It was just the list, I swear. I must have dropped the rest without knowing. Must have fallen out of my bag or something, I don't know.'

'I'm glad you did leave it, Mila, otherwise you may never have been exposed for the snake you really are.'

Alice extended an offering of affection to me by cupping my face in her hands. The feeling soothed something within me.

'Lois, dear, you are a beautiful, strong, brave woman. Above all, you are a wonderful mother and certainly Lindani thought the world of you. But there is no way Mila would do such a thing. She was his sole support when he was at his absolute worst. This behaviour you're accusing her of, it just isn't in her nature.'

I wasn't really sure what Alice was referring to. Nor did I understand what she meant by Lindani being at his worst. I had to get all the information out into the open and see if that would change her opinion of Mila. Perhaps then would the sprinkle of doubt I'd experienced from Alice's announcement dissolve.

'Before you all jump into camp Mila. There's something else,' I declared.

Mila chewed on her bottom lip anxiously, before asking Caroline to pass her a glass of water.

'What's the matter? Scared of what dirt I have on you?' I said, enjoying my new-found confidence.

I poured myself a glass of bubbly before gushing it down my throat, restraining myself from the desire to drink more.

'Yellow paper, Mila? You weren't even discreet about it. How many people do you know who use yellow paper?'

I cursed inwardly at how petty and mundane my declaration sounded.

My work friends joined the interrogation then. 'I have no intention to take sides but logically, any of those kids could have had it with them. Perhaps it came from one of Kai's colouring pads? Why does it even matter?'

'Let me tell you why it matters,' I proceeded, like some Agatha Christie detective pinning the crime on the murderer in the room.

'I'm not listening to this, Lois, you've gone mad. Don't bother calling me, I'm done helping you.' Mila stood from her stool authoritatively and began gathering her things, all the while uttering words of vexation.

'When we got back from South Africa, I found a note that was left in my bedside drawer. It was from Lindani stating why he had left and what he planned on doing next. A goodbye letter essentially.'

I felt the tension in the room thicken.

'It was written on yellow paper.'

Mila's friend began gathering her things, trying not to seem as though she was listening to me explain my evidence.

'So, if Mila can get hold of yellow bloody paper, then other people will be able to get hold of it too,' reasoned Caroline.

'I've searched all our supplies, I've searched *his* things, too. Not a single piece. You were the only one who has been in my house. Did you put the letter there for him? Do you remember when I asked you to see if he'd come back home? Is that when you left it?'

Mila lost her temper then. 'The only thing your half-wit theory proves is that I wasn't in the goddam country when he abandoned you. Honestly Lois, you are more stupid than I even thought. I was in England and he was on holiday WITH YOU! DO YOU UNDERSTAND?'

It was an act of humiliation that I wasn't about to stand for, not in my own home. The skin strained against my jaw. My knuckles whitened and sharpened respectively. I pushed away Mila's reasoning to focus on the facts. There had been nothing left in the drawer prior to leaving for South Africa. I remember because Lindani asked me to retrieve his phone from it, moments before we left the house. Mila was the only one I knew to have entered my home unsupervised.

The only thing that triggered confusion was the handwriting. It was unmistakably that of Lindani. It was too distinct not to be. I thought back over the timing of his disappearance. I had stayed away from home for a couple of weeks, technically, allowing him time to come back and leave it himself. It had been written, though, as if he hadn't decided how and when to leave. So why the hell bring us with him then, no matter how hard I pushed for us to come. It would be easier for him to disappear if he was alone.

Somewhere amidst my thoughts, Mila flew towards the exit, cursing on her approach.

A sharp knocking sound signalled someone was waiting outside.

It couldn't have been worse timing, I thought. Although I was ready for Mila to leave, part of me knew she would make it impossible to regain contact with her. There was too much I needed to know, and I hungered for a confession, even more than I hungered for revenge.

My jaw gaped to the floor when I saw her. The guests, and myself included, circled the entrance to my home.

No words escaped my lips as I stood facing the woman I instinctively knew was responsible for stealing my husband's affections.

'I'm afraid we need to talk,' she declared through her still perfectly formed rosebud lips. She brushed past me, crossing the threshold in the same breath. My only option, amid a modest audience and a scorned best friend was to confront my past head-on.

'I know who you are, don't I?'

32

THEN

I couldn't tell if it was the fierce hunger pangs or chill of the morning air that woke me. I peeled my head from the internal plastic of the car door, the left side of my neck screaming with the pain of stiffness.

It had served as a refuge the night before, but now stirred only feelings of regret. Loneliness was palpable, so much so that I was willing to wipe the slate clean, forget all the drama and head back to my life with Titch. I would apologise for being too sensitive then everything would be okay again.

I pieced together the jumble of memories from hours earlier, not really wanting to acknowledge what had actually happened, and more so, the role I had played in it all. The shame was tepid, so much that it laid sour eggs in the pit of my stomach.

Pleasantly surprised, however, at not having lost my phone amongst the chaos, I scrambled through the messages noticing, first, that I hadn't had any missed calls from Titch *or* Fiona.

I tapped the WhatsApp icon. His face popped up at the top of the list. I didn't recognise his profile picture initially. I was expecting the same one we'd both had just hours before – the cute selfie of us both on last year's birthday outing at La Tasca. Titch had looked super handsome; he wore a tight white shirt tucked into his belted jeans and the candlelight reflected favourably onto the contours of my face. We both beamed with happiness.

I looked at the image to find it had been replaced with his solo portrait. Fiona's face was visible in the forefront, having photobombed the image. My gut told me the two messages he'd sent weren't going to be of an encouraging nature. I scrolled up through the list to pinpoint where the evening's messages started.

FROM: *Titch*
R U alive?

FROM: *Titch*
Uv bin online so assume ur ok, here goes. I hate to be a dick and do this over text but I'm just gonna say it. I feel like it's the end of the line for us. Do you agree? I do care about you a lot but uv bin unhappy for months now, in fact we both have. I honestly don't know what happened to us, but I know I can't fix it. I've tried to be understanding and patient but I'm out of ideas. You're always mad about sumfin Lois, obviously I'm not the right guy for you. I understand if you want to stay in the house, I'll move out but knowing how funny you get around Fiona I assume u'd rather move back home. Let me know if I'm wrong. Anyway, don't worry about the bills and all that shit, I'll sort it. Take care of urself Lois and thanks for the good times. Maybe we can be friends one day in the future.

He was last online at seven a.m. I waited for another message. One to tell me he didn't mean what he'd typed. I held on to the hope of another message that would take back his decision when he realised through sober eyes that he had made a terrible mistake.

How had I been so unbearable that he'd want to leave me? My empathy flitted between us both, attempting to gain an objective stance. Surely, we had both been to blame?

I tapped on the reply box, deliberating how best to respond. His name flashed up online as I was about to ask if we could talk. At the very next glance, his status and image had disappeared, in exchange for a faceless thumbnail. This was it, I thought with a heavy heart. I was completely blocked, and it bothered me even though being with Titch was tedious and exhausting. Even though I was healthier without him.

I was delirious. The effects of another abandonment toyed with my ability to ascertain peace in any one of my living cells. In my haste, I logged onto social media. Facebook, Instagram, Twitter … anything that connected us as a couple. He'd cut off all links. We were no longer friends on social media, and he'd even gone further and set all his accounts to private.

The shakes flooded my nerves. I wasn't comfortable to go back to the house, yet. Everyone would still be at home and the humiliation of being dumped would be too great to withstand. I had to clear my thoughts, then sneak in for my things whilst everyone was at work.

I would wait, play him at his own game. We had done this dance before, a handful of times.

The white fabric of my top lent itself as a tissue with which I wiped the mascara-stained tears from my cheeks.

Starved of my appetite, I struck up the engine and began to drive South to the sperm donor's house.

Days later, I knew that I would never hear from him again. I should have known it all along, ever since the day we moved into the house together. Since the moment the door peeled open to reveal the woman I felt I'd had to compete with. It was Fiona he had wanted. And now I was out of the way, he was free to secure her as his own. The knowledge stung. It caused a swelling that remained visible for an undetermined length of time. One I was incapable of abating by myself.

33

'Fiona?'

'Lois? It's you?' Her elbow tapped against the wall as she stumbled a few paces backwards, tripping over the rubber of her shoe.

Mila looked us both up and down from the corner of the room. We were centre stage in what had turned out to be a real-life disaster movie. The current atmosphere of the house masked its former role as children's Jurassic wonderland.

'How did this happen?' I said, mainly to myself. The emotion I had already expended was quickly regenerating. The puzzle of my life had exploded into a thousand pieces. I was now challenged, yet again, to reconnect it.

I heard echoes in my periphery. 'You know each other?' mused an unknown voice.

Her attire was casual. Black, fitted leggings that formed a perfectly symmetrical heart shape from her waist down to her slender ankles. Black high-top trainers elevated her a few extra inches, which served to showcase the delicate curves of her perfectly proportioned body. Time had been kind.

'I came for his phone, Lois, and to give you this. It's from Lindani,' she said, following me to the living room.

I watched her pull out a large, decorated box, papered with animals in party hats and sealed with a green bow. On it was taped a card enclosed in a yellow envelope.

'It's for Kai. For his birthday.'

I asked her to confirm the obvious. 'You're the other woman, aren't you?'

She nodded, her words muted by our unanticipated reunion. I still admired the unspoilt beauty of her, in spite of my burning envy and pain not only at her having crossed paths with the man I loved, but having lost him to her, too.

My knees buckled under the weight of knowing I had made a grave error of judgement. 'I need to lie down. I don't feel well.'

'Is it the pain of your conscience kicking in?' said Mila, scornfully.

'I … I'm s—' I started to say, laying on the sofa with my legs draped over the armrest. 'I don't know what to say, I'm so—'

'You had plenty to say earlier though, didn't you!'

'I don't understand what's happened, I was sure …' I didn't know where to begin.

I plastered the skin around my eyes with the smooth of my palms, too pained and regretful to make eye contact with anyone, but detecting the amber, woody scent of Alice nearby.

What have I done?

I sensed the cushion above me sink with her weight, as her worn fingers swept the short, loose curls from my face. My heart cried out for Mum. I was never going to stop needing her, and the knowledge seared in the deepest parts of me.

'Please let me have his phone, Lois.' The light from the glass reflected kindly across the contours of her cheeks, just as it had years before. Although now, the area above her brows and cheekbones demonstrated a lack of expression one would associate with artificial enhancement. 'Then I need you to leave us alone,' she said with a final twist of the knife.

Fiona's reference to them as a partnership strummed aggressively at my heartstrings. I could have sunk into my self-induced coma quite wilfully, having lacked the physical strength to take so many blows in succession of one another. I did, however, have a desire strong enough to find out why and how this woman had built a relationship with my husband right under my nose.

I soothed the sting of the memory of her with the realisation that neither my innards nor appearance withered in her presence. Still, she bore the same beauty that had lured Titch and, now, my husband into her arms.

'I don't have his phone,' I said, calmly.

'He dropped it somewhere around here when we came back to get some of his things,' explained Fiona, as she would on any ordinary occasion to a friend. 'It has to be here.'

An awkward stillness engulfed the house once again as my next move was anticipated by those around me.

From her unprompted speech, I figured she mustn't have planned on staying long. 'You need to stop calling us, Lois? Stop emailing, texting, in-boxing, all of it. He shouldn't have to keep his phone switched off for hours, sometimes days at a time.'

'Is that right?' I said coldly, steadying my breathing with a silent number count.

'He's already told you he was going to get touch when he was ready, when you stop freaking out, when he's ready to see Kai again.'

I rose then, like a mummy from a forgotten grave. 'You can say what you like about me but do NOT bring my son into this. You're nothing to Kai, do you hear me? You're no one.'

Any restrictions I'd had before now were overruled.

'Fine, if I'm no one, then you'll leave us alone. Be careful, Lois. Someone could come and take Kai away from you too. Just be careful.'

The heat from an instant hot flush powered me upright and into the same space as her un-minted breath. Her flaws revealed themselves to me then. The undetectable pink bumps poked through a creamy layer of tan, and the flat, ordinary tint of her pupils mirrored a true reflection of what lay behind their outer facade.

'I want nothing to do with either of you. And I don't have his stupid phone, so congratulations, tell him to get a new number and both get the hell out of our lives.'

'I didn't come here to fight with you, Lois. He just misses his son. He needs to see him. It isn't fair to keep them apart.'

'You ever speak my son's name again, you watch what I'll do,' I threatened. 'How dare you even breathe a word about taking him from me. How dare you!'

Mila and Alice watched Fiona attentively, as did the rest of the room. The whites of their eyes wide with alarm.

Mila broke from the modest crowd and approached. 'This is all getting out of hand now, Lois. Just let her leave. He's moved on to his next victim, that's all that's happened.'

'If you expected me to take pity on him when he didn't even have the balls to face me himself, then you ought to adjust your expectations, and quick,' I said.

'We don't want your pity. That isn't what this is about.'

'Just STOP Fiona. I mean it. Just stop!'

Alice was pottering around the kitchen, emptying a cupboard of its contents. She switched on the kettle as if she was home alone. I would ordinarily have been amused by her stereotypical peace offering. But it wasn't the time.

'Please just stop what you're doing. This isn't a communal event. I need to speak with Fiona alone, please … Thank you, though,' I added to limit the damage to my reputation.

'No, you won't,' interjected Mila, 'You'll have it out with Fiona until everyone in this room is satisfied that I was in no way involved with what Lindani did to you.'

Fiona's eyes locked onto Mila as she learned of my earlier ill-guided witch hunt.

I let out a guttural scream, alerting the neighbours to my distress.

'Oh my god,' I heard someone say, through the mist of emotion.

'STOP! JUST STOP!' I continued to shout, even as I felt Mila's arms wrap around my shoulders.

It was what I'd needed yet I sensed her resistance.

'Sshh, it's over now. We'll leave … okay … is that what you want?'

Silence filled the gap of undisclosed time that lapsed between us.

'I'm sorry,' I said through tears. 'Please forgive me, I don't know what happened.'

'I should be going. I only came to drop off the birthday present,' Fiona said. 'It wasn't my intention to cause such a fuss, I apologise if I did,' she offered fruitlessly.

I ran my sleeve over both damp cheeks, tucking the remaining hair behind my ears.

'I don't know how I can make this up to you, Mila, but I will somehow.'

The room fell dead, save for my unrelenting snivels.

'What a lovely man you have, Fiona,' I called out, demonstrating a replenished confidence. She stopped, offering me the attention I required. 'How nice it was of him to send you here alone, knowing he was thrusting you into a potential war zone.'

'Whatever, Lois. I've done what I came to do. I'm leaving.'

Mila walked ahead and reached for the handle, guiding her out.

'You really ought to work on keeping hold of this one, Fiona. It won't be long before you lose your appeal and someone else is cast for the role of seductress. Just watch your back with Lindani though, you won't know of his deception until it comes crashing down on you all at once.'

'Lois, you have it all wrong.'

How I had come to loathe that phrase, I thought.

'Nothing ever happened with me and Titch back then.'

'Just tell me when it happened, Fiona,' I interrupted, suddenly unconcerned with the past.

Mila was right to tell me to move on, what good could any more information do? I knew who the other woman was now, and although there were still gaps of knowledge to fill, I questioned how much suffering my body was able to absorb and whether what I may learn about my husband was worth the extra anguish.

'Who messaged who first? When did he decide he was going to leave? I need to know everything, Fiona. Then I'll leave you alone.'

'Okay,' she said. 'That's fair.' She took the seat that Alice indicated to her and prepared to speak, scanning the room indiscriminately.

Her choice of words aggravated my nerves, but I remained composed in order to get the closure I wanted.

'Can you tell me one thing first?'

She nodded.

'Has Kai been around the two of you together?'

'No, I've never met your son. That's why Lindani thought it best I come to drop off his gift.'

I breathed a sigh of relief, however small. 'Okay … Now can you start from the very beginning.'

Alice placed a cup of herbal tea on the worktop for each of us.

'So how long has it been going on?'

My phone buzzed. I ignored the initial thrum, in anticipation of hearing what Fiona had had to say. But before she could answer fully, it rang for a second time.

Recognising the name on the screen as my dad's, I dialled back immediately, noticing also that I'd had an earlier missed call from Wendy.

'Darling, I need you to come down to the hospital. Try not to panic. Just come as quickly as you can.'

'Oh my god, Dad, what's happened? Is it Kai? Is he okay?'

I strained my ears to make sense of the chatter behind him, beeps and the sound of moving traffic pricking my ears further.

'We're in the ambulance now. I'm sorry, Lois, everything was fine one minute then …'

'Dad! What's happened? Is he okay? Please tell me he's okay.'

I heard him ask the paramedics how far from the hospital they were.

'Dad, talk to me please,' I pleaded.

'I don't know what happened, he was fine.'

'Dad!' I said, piercing the bout of induced quiet.

'Just meet us there, darlin', and I'll explain everything when you get here, I promise. I have to go now, I'm sorry. Please drive carefully.'

I raced to the door, leaving the women to decide their next course of action amongst themselves.

I was operating on pure adrenaline born from unadulterated panic, but the guilt for feeling torn splintered the fear that battered me.

The tyres screeched from the driveway and slammed against the tarmac of the road as my thoughts flitted from the horrors I had yet to uncover in my home, to what fresh hell awaited me at the hospital. What had he done to my son?

34

The smell of airborne sickness permeated the blanket of disinfectant. I regarded it an odour that characterised the very essence of the accident and emergency room I found myself in. Emergency practitioners busied the floor in a chaotic, orchestrated fashion, seemingly in constant demand by the intensive care that was required by the high volume of patients.

'I don't know what happened Lo—'

'What have you done?' I said, accusingly, screwing his jumper at both shoulder points.

'Me? No, no, no' he said, resting his palms over my clenched fists.

'Don't insult me, Dad. What did you do to my son? Where is he?'

'I've done nothing, Lois. One minute he was okay, the next he was all confused and pale looking. He felt dizzy and tired, his head was on fire.'

'I need to speak to someone right now.' I needed to know he was out of the woods before I tore into Dad as I felt I needed to.

A flurry of people buzzed around us. I reached out to the closest one.

'Will he be okay?' I asked.

'Someone will be with you shortly.'

I fought the urge to demand instant confirmation or breathe life back into him myself. Instead, my only option was to look on helplessly as my son's fate lay in the hands of strangers.

It wasn't long until the triage nurse greeted us with a concerned smile.

'Is he conscious? Can I see him?' I blurted, desperate to know I hadn't lost my only son. She explained the tests that were being carried out, but had little else to offer. There were no physical signs of injury, so Kai's bloods and urine had been taken and there was talk of him going through for an X-ray in as soon as a few minutes' time.

A monumental silence passed between me and Kai's grandad. A silence detected only by the two of us.

'He's going to be okay isn't he, Dad?' I conceded after confirming Kai's affliction hadn't been caused by my father.

'Of course he will, love.'

'I probably should apolo—' I began, adopting the demeanour of a timid child on their first day of school, but he cut me off.

'No need. You're under a lot of stress, darlin'. Sometimes things get said …' We pondered on the sentiment of his words for a moment. 'But I would never hurt that little lad, or you, never d'ya hear?' Before long I found myself curled into his chest, my extremities tucked tightly between his shoulders as he shielded me from an uninhabitable environment.

We rested beside the IV infusion stand that continued to drip life-juice back into my son's young veins. If only upon opening my eyes, this flaccid, pale body would have transformed to the vivacious, healthy boy he deserved to be.

'I shouldn't have left him, Dad,'

'Shush, don't say such a silly thing, this would have happened no matter where he was.'

'But I should have been with him, I'm his mother,' I said, as if our earlier altercation had never happened.

'He knows you would do anything for him. You have to stop being so hard on yourself.'

The oxygen mask that cupped around Kai's cheeks only served to make him appear more fragile. The abnormal paleness to his skin, save a slight tint of yellow, tore at my stomach aggressively. There were signs of life – a flicker of the eyelids and flexing of fingers – but no sign substantial enough to warrant promise.

'Excuse me,' I asked, grabbing the attention of another passing woman, one in purple scrubs this time. 'Why is he that colour?' She responded accommodatingly and placed a comforting arm on my sleeve.

'Wendy?' I declared as she turned to face me.

'Lois, love, leave the poor woman alone, can't you see she's busy?' Dad said, scanning her name badge for confirmation.

Wendy took the brief distraction as an opportunity to disappear amongst the sea of brightly coloured uniforms.

'That was Kai's therapist, I didn't know she worked here too?'

'Come on, love. Maybe we should go and get you a cup of tea and wait outside until we know more. Kai's in the best hands. Let's get out of their way, shall we?'

'No way. I'm not going anywhere until I know my son's okay.'

'Don't you think we should go outside, and you know … let his dad know?'

My gut spiralled into an even tighter helix of tension.

'I think you would have a better chance of reaching him, don't you think?'

I considered demanding once and for all he tell me everything, perhaps then I'd know how to find him myself rather than having to cause so many rifts with every person around me.

'Will you come with me?' he asked, choosing to ignore my bitter tone.

'Did you know that he planned to leave us, Dad?' I said, delaying contacting Kai's donor.

'This is all I have to tell you, pumpkin. And it's the truth.'

I swallowed deep and hard as I waited with mounting impatience to be told the full truth.

'I spoke to him every now and then, that's all. He copied my number from your phone and texted me, back when you were pregnant with Kai. He seemed to think you were never going to be open to the idea of letting me back in. God knows why, but he was certain of it.'

I held my tongue if only for the knowledge that my son was sick in a hospital bed.

'I have no clue where he is now, or why he took you both with him to South Africa if he planned to, well … do what he did. I still struggle to believe it myself. But that's all there is to know, love.'

I wasn't sure how I was expected to feel, but the relief I experienced wasn't as fulfilling as I had imagined.

'Will you come outside with me please?' he asked for the second time.

'I just realised, you won't be able to call him. He doesn't have his phone any more, remember.'

'Oh, shit you're right,' he said, raising his hand to his forehead. 'Do you really think your friend has it? Maybe it's worth asking her again, given the circumstances?'

'I don't know, and I don't even want to think about any of that right now. Let's just get Kai better. He's the only thing I care about.'

I loosened my grip of Kai's hand as a tall, stoic man dressed in maroon scrubs approached us.

'Mrs. Attah?' He introduced himself with a handshake. 'It seems Malekai has suffered a severe episode of haemolysis. The CBC test indicated clear signs of haemolytic anaemia.'

His name badge told us his name was Tohid.

'Now in its severity, this type of anaemia is quite rare. It's a blood disorder that has caused his red cells to break down much quicker than they would normally, therefore rapidly depleting his oxygen levels. Do you understand so far?'

'Um, when you say severe, it *is* something you expect him to recover from, isn't it?'

'Right now, he is stable and receiving oxygen therapy and will continue to, until we administer a blood transfusion.' The doctor paused to look us over. 'So, we'll require you to sign a few documents to give us written consent before going ahead, yes?'

Stunned into silence, I nodded.

'What's caused it?' I asked, sensing my dad shuffle next to me.

The doctor obliged immediately. 'Any number of things. Medications, certain foods, an infection even. The information Mr. Hudson has provided doesn't point to an obvious cause. Sometimes the patient experiences a rapid onset for no reason at all. Before we begin, are you sure there's nothing out of the ordinary that Malekai could have taken?'

Both myself and my dad shook our heads.

'Okay, someone will be with you shortly with the paperwork, and ...'

His voice trailed off amidst the blur of information. I promise if you get through this, son, I'll be the best mum you could ever wish for. I swear I will.

'Perhaps it might help to get some fresh air, take it all in. You're welcome to stay with your son when he settles onto the ward. He'll be taken to the Paediatric Intensive Care Unit on the first floor.'

Three weeks after Kai's birth I'd noticed a severe change in my mood, I was trapped in an endless cycle of dirty nappies and night feeds. Worse still, I had been stripped of my freedom whilst his dad experienced nothing in the way of change, nor did he seem to care that my life had transformed so catastrophically. My pain was invisible, marred by the incessant routine of keeping a newborn alive. But my avoidance of and bitterness towards him were surely not.

'Okay. Thank you, doctor.'

I hovered over Kai's face, releasing short bursts of kisses, urging his swift recovery and whispering regretful notions of love and promise, stifling my own tears at the memory.

We followed Kai closely on his journey to the children's ward, ignoring the doctor's suggestion to retreat outside for fresh air.

A wave of activity flowed through the A and E as we exited. I hoped it was the last we'd see of it.

• • •

'Mum, when can I come back home?' asked Kai, eyes wide.

'I'm not sure, son. When the doctor says it's okay, I guess.'

'I'm bored, I want to play with my birthday presents.'

'I can ask your grandad to bring some into the hospital, if you like.

In the meantime,' I began, reaching for the remote control, 'You can watch as many episodes of *Beat Bugs* as you like. That'll be good, won't it?'

'Yep, can we watch it now, and get Grandad to bring my presents later?'

'If we must,' I conceded, happily stroking a stray curl from his forehead.

It was Kai's third day in hospital and seeing him almost back to his old self made the trauma of the last few days pale into insignificance. I'd had messages from Alice and Mila to check on Kai's progress since he was admitted, and I was optimistic I hadn't completely severed our friendship forever.

I pressed the arrow button on the remote control, trying to find the channel that played Kai's favourite shows.

'How come Dad isn't here?' he asked in a hushed tone.

I was caught off guard, even though I had expected the questions to come rolling out sooner or later.

I set the remote control by his mixed fruit juice on the table. 'He came to see you when you were poorly, darling.' It was a lie I owed him so he didn't feel entirely abandoned by his father.

'Does he not want to know me any more?' he said, not trusting my disclosure as the truth.

'Of course he does. Why would you ask that?'

'Because he never FaceTimes me any more, and he doesn't even come to visit. I didn't even see him on my birthday.'

'He hasn't wanted to wake you, that's all. You were sound asleep when he visited. Oh and I forgot, he brought another present for you, Maybe we could ask Grandad to bring that one too?'

Lindani and I had always given joint presents for birthdays and Christmas. Although I had still signed my husband's name on our son's gifts, I suspected Kai would see through my deception.

'Mum ... Please don't let me fall to sleep, even if I'm really tired, okay?'

I swallowed back the lump in my throat.

'Come on, let's go ask the nurse to find *Beat Bugs* for you, shall we?'

'He is coming back, isn't he, Mum?' he asked with a raw edge to his tone.

'He'd be crazy not to,' I replied after a timely pause, realising he'd already considered every eventuality.

• • •

A fitful tapping on metal jolted me awake. Reserving a moment or two to gather my composure, I smoothed a knuckle across the fold of my lip, clearing it of any loose saliva.

The tapping lent itself to a blurred movement of the blank framed contraption before me. Hospital! I was in hospital.

'Kai!' I called, recalibrating to my clinical surroundings.

My sharpening focus revealed Kai to be convulsing in his bed. His perfectly delicate features lolled back and twisted as if fighting a severe cramp that attempted to claim his upper body.

'Please, come quick. I need a doctor, NOW,' I yelled. 'Something's happening. I think he's having some kind of fit. Please hurry, anyone!'

Hospital staff surrounded Kai's bed within seconds. I found myself standing on the wrong side of the curtain, straining my ears, desperately trying to hear what was happening.

Another practitioner attended the scene, carrying with her an oxygen mask and canister. She sealed the curtain, leaving only a slither of view. Numbers were called out intermittently, which I could only assume were reflective of his vitals. My distress hadn't gone unnoticed. Another staff member guided me reluctantly through some double doors into a private seating area. I broke down weeping, barely recognising the lady to be Wendy.

Five torturous minutes passed before I was told Kai had experienced a strong reaction to the 'universal' blood type he had received in his transfusion. I glanced down at the warm paper cup I was holding in my right hand, unaware of when I had accepted a drink of tea.

'We have administered intravenous drugs to counter the reaction, but our next challenge is to find a specific blood match.'

'A blood match?'

'Yes, the ABO test showed Kai's blood as the Ro subtype. Given the severity of his body's reaction, we would only use a perfect match if we are to do another transfusion.'

'Can you take my blood? It would be the same, wouldn't it?'

'We can certainly try. However, a successful blood transfusion relies on sameness. Because Kai's blood type is over ten times more likely to be found in black males, the odds would suggest that your blood also won't match.'

'So, what now? There are donors, right?'

'Well, our options are limited right now, I'm afraid. We can take a sample from yourself just in case. But realistically, we'll likely have to approach his father's relatives. Unless of course we receive more donations from the general public. Is approaching his father's family going to be a possibility?'

Oh my god, no, no, no. Help us please!

'Earlier, someone mentioned that surgery may be an option, is that right?' Sensing my panic, he confirmed with little hesitation.

'With some people who suffer from haemolytic anaemia, it's possible to perform surgery, but only to remove the spleen. In Kai's case, tests show his spleen to be functioning normally, there's no signs of disease or deformity, so a blood transfusion is really the only viable option for now.'

Shouldn't that be a good thing?

'Will he recover from just one or will he need more?'

'It differs greatly from person to person. His anaemia could only last for a few months and correct itself with dietary changes et cetera. Or it could be lifelong. In some cases, it goes away quickly but returns further down the line. It really is difficult to predict.'

'So let me see if I've got this right. For Kai to be healthy again, I need to find an absolute match and you currently do not have enough supplies?'

A short silence followed. 'I'm afraid that's correct, Mrs. Attah. Be reassured though that we will be appealing for Ro blood type donors and Malekai is at the top of the list, him being so young.'

'Alice,' I blurted. 'Alice Bekker, she'll be a match, I'm sure of it!'

'Even better if Kai has a blood relation willing to help. If you kindly ask her, or anyone who could be a match, to contact us, that will certainly speed things up from our end.'

'No, wait,' I thought aloud, cursing Lindani for not having told me anything about her directly. 'Blood, she isn't blood related, I don't think. She wouldn't be, would she?'

The doctor watched patiently as I recalled what information I had about her.

'She's his dad's foster mother. Shit, she can't help, can she?' I asked, panic-stricken and wanting someone professional to assure me that Alice's blood could save my son.

'I'm afraid not, Mrs. Attah, I'm sorry.'

35

Dad and I were reunited back at the hospital.

'Oh my god, I've got it!' I said, hoping I'd found a way to track down Fiona, the woman who'd apparently lured away my husband. If I could reach her, she would tell me how to find Lindani so we could use him as Kai's blood donor.

My dad stared at me, chewing aggressively at his bottom lip. He implored my face for an answer as I tapped on the name that read 'Fi' in my contact list.

I had already briefed Dad on how events unfolded after he left the party, to which he responded with more relief than I'd anticipated. It was knowing, without doubt, the reason for Lindani's disappearance, he'd explained. I presented him with a raised hand as I lifted the phone to my ear, stunting any further dialogue between us.

There was a short pause before I detected any sound that wasn't the drumming of my swollen pulse.

I urged for something to happen, and quick. For someone to say something, or to be diverted to voicemail. Anything that would demonstrate my fate wasn't to explode from surplus tension.

'It's dead, shit!'

'Keep trying. You never know, love.'

'Dad, it's dead. It's not the right number,' I stated factually, searching his eyes for something that told me he knew what to do next.

'There has to be a way to get hold of her?'

Dad tapped at his screen until Lindani's voice sounded through the speaker, the rehearsed script signalling its disuse.

'Tell me we can do it, Dad. We'll do it, won't we?'

'We have to. Listen, worst case scenario, we can appeal for people to donate. We might not need him. Everything's gonna be fine. Baby steps, yeah?' he said, emitting an air of certainty I knew to be fraudulent.

'We don't have enough time to take baby steps. I'll message everyone who knows him. Maybe the news will get to him in some roundabout way?' The gentle rise of his eyebrows told me he concurred with my suggestion, so I held my tongue, hoping he'd add to it with a suggestion of his own.

I thought of all the unanswered questions I'd had over the years, imagining the heart-rate monitor that had beeped and flashed with a terrifying intensity. The times Lindani's vitals had fallen outside a healthy level, leaving me confused and powerless. A Rolodex of such occasions overwhelmed my mind's eye. The unexplained sickness, stochastic bouts of chest pain, and the persistent headaches I'd chosen to soothe with pills and kind words. The times he would clutch at his chest when we'd had to take the lift up to my flat instead of the stairs, his outright refusal to shop on the World Foods aisle at the supermarket, and my persistent effort to secure his agreement in adding the African element into his 'African-meets-English' fusion food cuisine. It was an ignorance born from complacency on my part. A complacency I was certainly paying for now.

'How could he do this to us?' Tears welled up behind my eyes with a fervour that threatened to propel them from their sockets.

Words evidently failed my dad as he stared vacantly at the floor, attempting to soothe my growing rage with a gentle fatherly shushing.

If there was ever a time I had to prove myself able to overcome the incessant desire to give up, this would be it. If it were not for the clatter of nurse trolleys, electronic beeps and the thrum of miscellaneous devices reminding me that maintaining human life was their sole mission, I may have done just that.

Instead, I searched Fiona Rivera on Facebook and Instagram,

disregarding dozens of thumbnails before stopping to enlarge an image that bore her familiar face.

I tapped the send icon after composing a brief message that informed Fiona of the importance to contact her boyfriend.

'There's no way I can just sit here and stare at my screen,' I said, hoping for a reply. 'If I go to her old apartment, will you stay here with Kai? I know it's a long shot, but even if she doesn't live there, someone might know where she went … right?'

Knowing better than to challenge me when I was hell-bent on an idea, my dad nodded and asked me to call him when I knew anything. I kissed Kai instantly upon getting his approval, then ran towards the double doors that signalled the exit.

The sliding doors parted frustratingly slowly, injecting me with the chance to change my mind. But the opportunity for escapism ignited its gravitational pull. No sooner had I wondered whether or not to fight against it than the glass doors sealed shut, blocking my route back into the hospital.

Fate had dictated my next move and it was one that would propel me forwards.

Time to track down Lindani and Fiona.

• • •

TO: *Mila*
Do you think Fiona's gonna come back? xxx

I was desperate for some form of communication. For some sign we were still friends.

FROM: *Mila*
No idea, why would she need to? I can hang at yours with Alice if you like, in case she does? Still have your key. Have you tried messaging her on Instagram?

TO: *Mila*
Would you? Need to pop back for some clothes to take to
hospital so will see you at some point. I have, but no reply
yet. Thanks a bunch. I owe you. Xxx

It was the response I hoped for. A little colder than normal but I'd take it, given the circumstances.

I checked in with the hospital. Kai was breathing and sleeping comfortably, which I considered the best scenario given my current absence. I had to busy myself so the fury of Lindani's unavailability couldn't consume me. Fiona's reply was yet to come through. Re-sending the same message only served to notify me that she had already received and opened it the first time round.

I considered the possibility she'd forwarded it to her boyfriend, who would now be tearing up the streets in pursuit of the hospital where his son lay deathly ill. I called my dad to check, only to find I was wrong in my assumption. I scrolled through the pictures on Fiona's Facebook, hoping to recognise a landmark or housing complex that would show her current residence. There was nothing familiar, no link to Lindani's page and no location update.

It's definitely her. I fixated on her image. My mind reeled with confusion. I scrolled past a recent photo of the same Fiona on holiday in Brazil with her fiancé. A catalogue of images flashed up, all of which portrayed Fiona to be in a blissfully happy relationship with a man that wasn't my husband.

Was she cheating on him too?

I searched for any mention of Lindani on both accounts, failing at every click. If they had been dating for two years then surely he'd be on her social media somewhere? A small mention or tag, something? I considered the likelihood he was kept out of view in case word was to get back to me too soon.

I parked on Bale Street where we used to pass back then, when

Dan and I dined at Don Giovanni. Maybe he would take her there too? A man and woman passed me, both wearing a see-through dress and too-high heels. *She's out there somewhere.* I scanned everyone who passed, like a peeping Tom. I was torn briefly between devoting another chunk of time to my stakeout or heading back to the hospital. Twenty minutes passed without seeing her so I decided upon the latter.

I still had to swing by the house to pack another bag of fresh clothes and snacks so I could return to Kai and release my dad from care duty. I searched again on social media for any live updates.

Beneath Fiona's relationship status ('Engaged to Luis Baute') was her occupation. Perhaps it had no bearing or relevance in the slightest. Perhaps it added nothing to my search. But my gut told me it did.

She's an actress!

A link to her business page revealed her availability to be privately hired for an abundant choice of roles, 'Fake Girlfriend' included.

Since when is that a thing?

I was caught in a tailspin. How was it possible that this could have happened to us? What kind of person would actually hire someone to be their girlfriend?

I typed another message, this time to her new account.

SEND TO: *Fiona Rivera*
What's the truth Fiona, about you and Lindani? The whole truth this time.

36

There was no blood donor, no Lindani and no word from Fiona. I sat by my sick boy's hospital bed, scribbling notes onto a tiny, lined pad that I'd picked up from the crappy in-house supply shop. The paper absorbed every punch of disappointment until I was faced with a messy depiction of my new life.

I popped a couple of ibuprofen from the foil before knocking them back. A young, auburn-haired nurse monitored Kai's vitals, shot me a coy smile in confirmation we weren't about to lose him just yet, then reapplied the oxygen mask that was to keep him stable for as long as it took for donor blood to become available.

Who hired her to be his fake girlfriend? I wondered, writing down the same question.

Mila had left notes condemning herself as an actress. What if Fiona had left them? But when? Had she crept in earlier whilst I was out back? Maybe she did want to make something for Kai, after all. Something she knew he'd like. And maybe I'd jumped to the most obvious assumption? Maybe both women had yellow paper too?

During my solitude, I wondered about Mila's potential involvement. If she and Lindani had fallen back into affection and were essentially now a couple, why was she always with me and my family? Wouldn't they have made time to enjoy their new relationship?

I considered who else would have a motive to hire an actress.

I'd had a couple of messages from Wendy from Spring View, offering her support at the most orchestrated times, I'd noticed. I hadn't got back to her latest message. I made a note in my pad to do just that.

If she was responsible, what would her motive be? Was it some twisted tactic to speed up my healing process?

On occasion, I'd regarded her actions towards us to be outside her arena of duties. She'd been a peripheral source of comfort for me at times, so I hadn't minded too much. It was only now that I saw her as a woman, an attractive one at that, that she became a threat. What did I really know about her, anyway? It was a chilling thought. *She knows where I live. Has she been in the house?* Yellow paper must be abundant at the therapy centre, too. I wrote down my thoughts about Wendy and how she could have orchestrated a central position within my family.

Meanwhile, Lindani hadn't so much as contacted the hospital to ask over his son, let alone visit him in person. Nor had any other woman he may be linked with. I was growing tired and increasingly humiliated at my asking the hospital staff if anyone had called the unit to ask about Kai.

Not only had Lindani been unfaithful, it seemed he had been lobotomised as a prerequisite of his new partnership. Essentially, he had no way of knowing how his son was doing and evidently didn't care either way. How could I have been so ignorant to who my husband really was as a human being?

I haven't seen her before? An athletic-looking woman, wearing a cream, button-down cardigan and fitted jeans, offered me a cursory smile as she attended the bedside opposite. *That isn't his wife!* The woman with the wavy dirty-blonde hair must have taken a day from her daughter's bedside to recuperate. It was the first day I hadn't seen her, and also the first day this new woman had taken over as 'wife' and 'mother' to the conveniently unconscious child. *That poor woman, as if she isn't going through enough.*

I swiped at the lined paper with the nib of lead until it punctured, my new observation adding fuel to my building anger. *Why are people like this?* My predominant thought was how Kai had convinced himself he was a burden to his father. *My son believes his father doesn't want to know him any more!* 'I broke my Lego when he was cooking,' he'd told me earlier that day. 'Dad told me not to and I did it anyway, so the panda broke. I broke it, Mummy.' I wrote down what he told me. I didn't know why, I just did. As if my former months in therapy had equipped me with that one and only coping skill.

I didn't know what to tell him. I didn't know myself why Lindani had remained so absent. At one time, I would have regarded his actions as implausible. The possibility of him leaving his family, even more that he would be too proud to come back to save his son's life, was just unfathomable. All of it.

The angry punching in my forehead subsided as the anaesthetic of the pills dispersed.

I considered what Alice could have meant by insinuating Lindani's troubled past. She'd said he *still* battled with demons. *What did she mean?*

Each day it was becoming more difficult to appease my son into believing his dad still loved him. I moved to the snack machine. The selection was unappetising. How had Kai interpreted our trip to South Africa? If only he'd communicated his feelings to me back then, would it have been easier to know the right thing to say?

I flicked back through my last couple of 'diary' entries and stopped at the part that questioned whether Lindani knew about Kai's anaemia.

Dad? Could he have been keeping him up to speed?

But wait, he can't have? Surely Kai wouldn't have questioned Dan's love for him if he'd called or visited when my dad had been here alone? Nevertheless, it was a possibility I wasn't about to dispel just yet. *Maybe he knew Dan was on his way to help?*

I stopped myself from asking the staff if my sentiment was correct. Had Lindani visited or called without anyone telling me? The regular staff changeovers inspired my decision to wait instead, until I had the chance to interrogate my father and finally get to the bottom of their involvement with one another.

• • •

I had sat at my son's bedside for a consecutive ten days, and had prepared for any additional longevity to our stay. So, it was with intense antipathy I acquiesced to Tom's request to meet with him at his home.

After I promised to bring back his favourite ice cream, Kai happily agreed for me to leave for an hour. I informed the nurse on duty and requested they get in touch if Kai asked for me. If he asked even once, I would come right back.

I contested the location, instead opting to meet Tom at my home so I could kill two birds with one stone and ensure Alice wasn't wholly neglected for the entirety of her visit. Mila had been keeping her company. My dad had also stopped by en route to the hospital to check in with her. I had invited Alice to accompany me on some visits, but she had flatly refused, stating she had 'been around enough of the sick to last her a lifetime'. She'd never neglected to send her well wishes, though.

Ensuring the text containing my address had sent successfully, I typed 'Tom (Mila)' above the jumble of digits and stored his phone number. I put my foot down on the accelerator all the way home, partly to allow enough time to speak with my dad in relative privacy and partly to minimise how much driving time would cut into the hour window I had allowed myself.

The top of my dad's thinning silver hair was visible from the welcome mat by the door. I scraped off invisible hospital matter before meeting him by the sofa, where I watched him sip at his Americano in relative peace.

'Mila out with Alice?' I asked, now accustomed to our unorthodox routine.

With a nod, he turned to me and asked not only about his grandson but also why I wasn't with him. *That's rich, coming from you!*

'I'm heading back in an hour. I've arranged to speak with Tom first.'

'Who's Tom?' I sensed he hoped I'd found an alternative object of affection.

He set down his Americano then dug a fingernail into the skin by his thumb. I may have been wrong.

'He and Mila dated a little while back. I'm hoping he wants to rekindle things if I'm honest. He was good to her.'

'Why would he come to you, though? Were you friends or something?'

I processed his workings out silently before shaking my head, also assessing the degree of friendship he and Dan had shared.

'He was adamant I met with him now … so here I am. Now you're all caught up!'

Curiosity had got the better of me in the end, but I figured the sooner I met him, the sooner I'd be back at the hospital.

'Sounds like you're trying to convince yourself, darlin'. I've been telling you to come home and put your feet up for a few hours, get some proper rest yourself.'

He picked up his coffee. 'You want a tea?'

Trailing him to the kitchen, I spewed out my words without thought.

'Listen, Dad, I really need to ask you something and I need you to be completely honest.'

'Baby Jesus himself, what's happened now?'

'I won't be upset or mad at you, I promise. You know I only care that Kai recovers. There's just something I need to know, to make sense of things.'

'Okay I'm all ears,' he said, returning to his chair.

A shadow of his old grin was returning.

'Are you still in contact with him? I mean is there any way you could get in contact with him now?'

'With who?'

'Who d'ya think, Dad!'

'I thought we went over this?' He set down the drink then lurched over his chair, dragging it closer to mine.

'Lois, I do not have contact with your husband. Not any more. I haven't heard from him since the day of that weird voicemail. If I'm honest, I tried to reach him more times than I can count. By text, voicemail, email, the lot. But not a peep back. That's the honest truth, I swear to god.'

'Swear on my life, Dad,' I demanded petulantly.

'Why do you still not believe me? I'm on your side. Why can't you see I'd change everything in a heartbeat if I could.'

I knew he was referring to way more than just my husband leaving us.

'Swear on my life,' I said.

'Okay, because we are five years old.'

The tornado of emotion bubbling through my pupils must have been even more unappeasable than I intended.

'I swear on my grandchild's life that I have had zero contact with your estranged husband.'

I believed him, even before he swore it.

'To be honest, I thought he might have been murdered or something so I was relieved when it was to do with another woman.'

My heart undulated the air around us.

'Sorry,' he said, noticing my rising pulse.

'I guess I was hoping you'd tell me he's been to the hospital.'

'What! Did he? When?'

'No, he hasn't, Dad, at least I don't think. I'm clearly going mad. It was just wishful thinking after the shitstorm we've had on the ward.'

'Let me make you a bite to eat. You sit down, I'll bring it over to you.'

He discreetly made his way to the pantry before revealing the apocalyptic stash of dried foods and seasoning someone had acquired on my behalf.

I picked out the carton of eggs and fresh vegetables.

'One omelette on its way!' he said, taking the items from me.

I took a quick shower before eating the lunch Dad had prepared. Allowing myself to wash and eat made me feel guilty, knowing my son was still stewing in a hospital bed on his own.

My self-allocated hour of leave had now dwindled to twenty minutes. *Come on, Tom, where are you?* A seed of doubt squirmed into my consciousness. Could something have happened to him?

Tom hadn't replied to my prompting text so I gathered my few belongings, in addition to Kai's treats and supplies, then headed towards the door, curbing my instinct to hang back just in case. Kai was my only priority right now.

Why did I tell him only one hour?

After thanking my dad, I left the house. The door locked behind me but before reaching the driver side of my car, I was distracted by a scuffle further down the street.

'What the hell's going on?' I shrieked. 'Stop before someone gets hurt!'

37

'You're not right Mila. Get the fuck away from me.'
It was Tom. His fingers were clutched around Mila's wrists. Her head was flailing back in compensation for the lack of movement in her arms.

I watched as she kneed him in the crotch, loosening his grip. She immediately rifled through his car for the few seconds his incapacitation allowed before resuming contact. Mila scanned the seats and footwells, screaming obscenities at the man she'd had growing affection for only a short time before.

'Is this what you're looking for?' Tom incited, growing tall in recovery from his injury.

Alice stood by the roadside, contributing to the conflict with incoherent criticisms. She must have sensed Tom's intention to provoke Mila into conflict.

'Give it here, Tom, you've no business getting involved.'

'Oh really. What a pity you didn't follow your own moral compass before you fucked everything up, ay!'

At some point I'd dropped my bags by the car and I found myself standing at the end of my driveway.

'What's wrong? Have I dinted your ego, Tom? I told you, I don't want you any more. Get over it!'

'Nice.' I had never seen him sneer at her before. 'Smart Mila. I always admired that about you, your intelligence, I must say it's always been an Achilles heel of mine, clearly.'

'I mean it, Tom. So I fucked you and left. You're not the first man and you won't be the last, that's for sure!'

'Don't flatter yourself, love. Now get out of my way, I need to speak with your friend.'

'What is it, Tom?' I said pressingly. I squinted to sharpen my vision of what Tom held in his hand. Only then did I recognise the sought-after item to be a smartphone.

'What is this? What's going on?'

'I think we should take this inside. I don't know about you, but I'm not into airing my dirty laundry in public like some of us seem to be,' he said.

'Please can we get a move on. I have to get back to the hospital. Mila?' I pleaded.

I guessed from her lack of movement she was considering her options.

I quickly loaded my bags into the boot of the car after guiding everyone, including Mila, back indoors where my dad sat, perplexed by the cloud of tension that had entered the house with us.

A buzz of vibration prompted me to check my phone. I retrieved it from my coat pocket as I clicked the boot shut, praying I wasn't about to receive bad news about Kai's progress.

I pinched my septum, hoping the pressure would stem the flow of emotion that I'd anticipated was to follow.

Fiona.

My heart assumed a new rhythm. It was relief, if I'd interpreted my bubbling nerves accurately. The recollection of our previous contact drew reference to the potential content of Fiona's reply.

I peered at the huddle of people through the open door of my home and experienced a sudden rush of desire for the message to have been from some stranger. Then I wouldn't have to learn who had hired Fiona. Who, upon me finding out her identity, would cause everything to change. The threat of the reveal loomed overhead like a sniper waiting for me to make a fatal move.

*You'll deal with it, Lois. Like everything else. Deal with it all then
get to your son.*

Once again, I felt trapped between what I had to do and what I
needed to know. Wasting precious seconds staring at the name on my
screen, I was lured further into my seemingly unquenchable thirst for
knowledge. Tom had added a new dimension to my desire, and it was
with his unexpected contact I was convinced into believing he held
the key to something I absolutely had to know.

I couldn't force my eyes away from the screen, despite my fears that
her response would confirm one of two things. She was either Lindani's
real girlfriend or that someone very close to me had employed her for
said role. The commotion from inside my home spilled out onto the
driveway. A male voice delivered profanities shamelessly. I craned
my neck towards the source, flaring inwardly at my having attracted
more disquiet into our lives.

A loud crash from inside demanded my attention. I couldn't see its
source from the door so ran into the hallway.

I tapped Fiona's message quickly as I entered, hoping that whatever
was happening inside would minimise the fresh trauma that lay in her
message.

• • •

I had failed in my attempt to find Lindani. If I couldn't have him,
all I'd wanted was to find the other person responsible for destroying
my family. Now that I was stood before that very person, all I wanted
was a confession, before removing her from my life for good. I was
tired of the tail-chasing and detective work. My final request was for
her to confess. No more, no less.

Something about the way I entered commanded the attention of
everyone inside.

Mila began to fill the air with indiscernible utterances, referencing
the broken camera that she insisted Tom had knocked in his violent

pursuit of her, until I added to the barrage of disruption by cutting short her declarations.

'You have thirty seconds to confess!'

Four sets of eyes stared back at me in absolute quiet.

The tan drained from Mila's face and appendages. She was no longer concerned with pointing fingers at Tom for breaking Lindani's camera.

My dad questioned what had happened in the last minute that would make me draw such a conclusion, but I was in no state to respond to anyone that wasn't her.

'We will do this the hard way then,' I said, hoping I would trigger a declaration of guilt.

'Lois, just take it easy,' I heard my dad advise as I approached Alice.

'Well, I certainly didn't expect you to be the other woman, Alice.'

She stood before me, her gaze ricocheting across the walls.

'Dear, please just say what you are on the verge of saying.'

'I know you hired Fiona to pretend to be Lindani's girlfriend. I know you kept him out of my way each time I came to look for him in South Africa. He was with you the whole time, wasn't he? You knew we would find out your sordid little plan to help Sarah and Lindani kindle their romance.'

'Eish, where on earth did you hear that trash?'

'Fiona told me everything. There's no use lying. It makes sense now. That's why you stuck up for Mila. You knew she couldn't have done it, if you did! It's why you only appeared at Sarah's B and B as we were leaving, tracking my movements to make sure we were out of your way.'

Tom searched Alice's expression, his face matching hers in its representation of disarray.

'My gut told me to stay away from you, Alice. I should have listened.'

38

'Wait a minute, Lois. If that's true, then how do we explain this?' Tom flicked through the screenshots he'd saved on Lindani's phone.

My throat burned as I fixated on the text before me.

'I don't understand, what is this?' I asked, as if we were the only people in the room.

A feral glint glittered the white of Mila's eyes as she lunged at Tom. Alice had removed herself from view entirely, to the extent that I couldn't see her anywhere.

My dad rose from his position in front of the TV and grappled Mila's waist, pulling her tight into him. 'Woah, woah, lady, just you take it down a notch.'

Tom continued, visibly grateful for Mila's human restraints.

'She left this phone in my apartment. I found it on my bathroom floor.'

'You lied to me, you bastard!'

'It wouldn't usually be something I'd do … look through her phone. But that's the thing, it isn't hers. The background picture is of you and your family.'

Mila shrieked deliriously in a bid for him to quit talking. Dad's biceps strained against her attempts for freedom before a sudden resolute jerk towards Tom succeeded in breaking one of her arms loose.

'She must have changed his passcode herself 'cos I guessed it right away. See, from what I've learned about Mila is that she's as predictable as she is calculating.'

'What's on it, Tom? Just tell me what you found,' I said impatiently.

'It's enough to make your blood run cold.'

That, I didn't need to hear.

'Is she it? The other woman?' I asked, soberly.

Tom dipped his head to one side before answering. 'In a manner of speaking.'

'What do you mean? She either is or she isn't.' *Don't piss me off, Tom. Not you, too!*

He nodded more distinctly this time, reverting my attention to the screenshots he'd so carefully collated. The first one was an image of the same message I had received back in Sarah's car after the fire.

'It doesn't prove Mila was the one who sent it ... does it? Dan would have had the phone then.'

He replied simply with, 'Keep scrolling.'

I kept scrolling. The next was of an email Mila sent to Lindani asking for him to return her message. It was the next few images that caused the hairs of my arms to stiffen.

'Fiona said Alice was the one who employed her, Tom. She said the person who made the booking, who asked her to drop by Kai's birthday party and bring a staged gift was Alice. Not Mila, Alice!'

Tom drew his thumb and forefinger across his left brow. 'That doesn't make sense,' he admitted, sweeping a wet tongue over the crust on his lower lip.

I looked back at the phone, having received no signal to stop. Doting comments littered the screen. Lindani's YouTube videos being the object of admiration. The next images displayed a one-way conversation in Mila's outbox to Dan's private inbox. There were no replies. She had logged into her account using Lindani's phone to send a reply to herself. The only replies were sent after Lindani's disappearance, not a single one before the time of the fire.

I read aloud the conclusion I had drawn from the one-way conversations before me, taking a moment to assess the gravity of my accusation.

'You're YDTNM?'

Mila spent a minute of our time privately. Her response, when it came, drew the breath from my chest.

'You deserve this not me.' The words dribbled from her lips.

'What? What did you say?'

'No, I can't. I can't do this any more,' said Mila.

I glanced at the clock. Had I been the mother that my son deserved, I would have been at his bedside forty minutes earlier. Better still, I would never have left in the first place.

'It's too late, Mila … It's far too late.'

'You deserve this, Lois. I don't! I didn't, not then.' she cried, her gaze blurring with the water coating her eyes.

The walls spun into a colourful prism, as I processed what her confession implied.

'You-Deser-T-N-M.'

'There's a sick little checklist too, if you keep going,' said Tom amidst the dancing swirls of colour that blinded my vision.

A checklist?

'Okay, Tom. Fuck. You win, congratulations. It was me. I did everything. Is that what you all want to hear?'

I sealed my mouth before Mila finished confessing. It was my body's way of preparing for an imminent attack. I'd rather she accused me of being insane.

Who the hell was she, really? I felt violated suddenly, especially since the stakes for me had been so mountainous. I'd allowed her truly and deeply into our lives.

It wasn't the moment that I wanted to recall peaks in our faux friendship. Memories of the times I would take her into the hangar at work then convince some regular flight crew to let her sit up front in the flight deck and get a feel for how it would be when she finally made it as a pilot. The times we blasted out unmelodious notes to our favourite power ballads, thrashing around as dramatically as our wheeled cage would allow, without fail, every time, whether the car journey was two or fifty miles long. The times she'd insist on singing the male verse during our duets, regarding their lyrics as 'less servile' than that of the women's. How could all of that amount to this?

Mila's limbs loosened into the dead weight of a woman clinging to life. She exhaled deeply and with added drama, sinking slightly as my dad's grip weakened around her.

'Dad?' I hoped his presence would repair my open wound.

Mila's eyes glistened with the relief of inaudible penance as the room fell into a synchronised silence.

'You did this?' I chanted between rapid breaths.

She nodded, her cheeks now dry to the touch.

'And I had *just* forgiven you.'

'The messages, the letter, the empty bank account, the actress?' The list went on.

I paused to assess Mila's stony silence.

'The wig, too. It was me, I set it all up.'

'I'd forgiven you.'

Mila sharpened her tongue enough to expel the venom running through her veins. 'You forgave me nothing, Lois. You accused me before you knew anything at all. You turned on me!'

I said nothing.

'You were left with no choice but to forgive me when Fiona showed up, that's why. You weren't truly sorry for anything.'

Her smooth, manicured brows drew into sharp focus at the centre of my vision.

'Fiona said it was Alice that booked her?' I said.

Mila's reply was unemotional. Factual. 'I gave the company the first name that came to mind.'

Her tone pained me. *Who is this woman?*

'But the note. I recognised the handwriting. It was definitely his?' I continued, spewing out anything that would exculpate her.

I can't lose her too.

She stood tall in my dad's arms, gaining a new confidence. She reminded me of a flightless bird attempting to attract a mate.

I looked over at Tom who was standing beside the door, his wide biceps folded into one another. I thought I blushed from his obvious display of solidarity. Perhaps not.

'Oh that was easy. With a bit of practice, I can forge anyone's hand-writing. And god knows I've had plenty of time to practice! I'm just glad his hasn't changed from those letters he gave me way back when.'

I circled her figure, taking in the intention behind her eyes, the way her fingers scrunched into a fist in the fabric of her blouse. How her scent shrouded my skin in a floral mist I used to like – a mist now pricked by the saltiness of sweat. A slight rise to her left cheek allowed a snigger of air to escape.

'You can't seriously be proud of yourself?' I said, reading her reaction with an accuracy I was saddened by.

'I have to admit, I was surprised how easy it all was. Once you knock over that first domino, there's no stopping the rest.'

'You *are,* aren't you? You're proud? You fucking psycho!'

The impulse to grab at her neck and stunt the oxygen flow came in one powerful wave.

'What's wrong? Have I knocked you off your pedestal, Lois?'

'You're pathetic, Mila. Too pathetic to make a life of your own, you had to steal mine.'

'Even now, you still don't realise that you're not important, do you? Not to me and especially not to Lindani. And for your information, I didn't steal anyone. We both know consenting adults aren't *stolen,* don't we?'

I allowed her words to sink in.

'You don't see him anywhere, do you? We haven't been spotted having a coffee at Starbucks or canoodling on a park bench, have we? No, I thought not!'

'What have you done to him, Mila? You owe me that much at least.'

She snapped back, 'I owe you nothing!'

I grabbed at her neck until the identifying signs of panic crept into her face. I felt nothing.

'Mila, what have you done?' said Alice, her contribution indicating she'd re-joined us in the main living area.

My dad's eyelids were pinched as he looked at me. The pleading behind them was a clear sign he was silently questioning my intentions.

'Get off me!'

Dad signalled to me he was intending to oblige. 'Pleasure,' he said.

Tom's body blocked the door intentionally, the same time as my dad folded his arm across my shoulder, drawing me closer to him.

Mila rubbed the impacted area of skin before rising tall to face her accusers. The room succumbed to a deathly silence as Mila's spectators froze in anticipation of her next move.

'What have I done to your precious boy?' she said hauntingly.

Alice pushed for a clear answer. 'Mila, dear. Look at me. What have you done to Lindani? It's more important than you probably realise.'

'Hmm, what have I done to him.' She oscillated between us, my nerves fluttering as our proximity grew. 'I have asked myself that very question for almost ten years now.' Her fingers drummed across her lips.

Mila stood before Alice, a smirk piercing through the slits of her fingers. Alice must have read something inaudible in Mila's gaze, and the thud through her chest strengthened. Her brows collected freshly formed beads of sweat and the white of her pupils expanded. Fear seeped into her demeanour, as if an eternity of secrets had escaped from the hellish prison in which they were held captive.

'The question you should be asking is, what has Lindani done to *me* ... Wouldn't you agree, Alice?'

39

lice?! What the hell is this!

'I think you need to elaborate, 'cos I'm a hair's breadth away from completely losing my shit!' I threw Mila to the ground.

'W-well, if you get the fuck up off me, I will.' Her attempt to regain control failed. 'Okay, fine. But it ain't pretty.'

I applied pressure to my stomach as if everything inside me sought an exit.

The air in the room grew still and thick.

'Dan used me. He made me fall in love with him, then tossed me aside like I was little more than a broken toy.' I listened intently. *How do you make someone fall in love with you?*

'I knew getting involved with an ex-child-soldier wouldn't be easy, but I put in the time, the energy, everything I had actually. As soon as he felt human again, guess what happened?'

I wasn't sure if she required an answer, but regardless I didn't have one to offer. Mila glanced at Alice, divulging a well-guarded secret to her too, it appeared. 'He left me.'

Wow, that was some build up. 'People leave people all the time. Shit, I've been left by my own father, but you don't see me screwing up everyone's life, do you!' There was something on the tip of Mila's tongue, I could tell by her knowing smirk and self-induced silence.

'You weren't the one who held him in the middle of the night when he'd woken you from screaming. You didn't have to fight him off when he choked you in his sleep, did you? Nor did you have to tell contractors your fake nephews had been throwing things in the house when they came to fix a fist-sized hole in the wall.'

I sat beside her on the floor attempting to process what she was telling me. *He isn't violent though, he isn't?*

I wasn't sure at which point I'd covered my ears but I was grateful for the mental dulling of my own recollections of Lindani. I too had seen the night terrors, the screams, the total emotional shutdown. I'd fleetingly wondered if his quick temper would turn its attention to me one day, but not long enough to actually fear him. For the most part though, our family was a perfectly pleasant and peaceful union. Perfectly pleasant, peaceful and repressive.

'Do you know what it's like to look in the eyes of the man you adore only for him stare right through you like you didn't exist? Or worse, like you were the very cause of his pain?'

My heart was grief-stricken for the history of the man I'd shared my bed with for the last decade, and for the lost opportunity to connect with him on the deepest level.

'Did you take him to countless therapy sessions, only to sit in the car outside and convince him he was worthy of life?'

Counselling? The Wellwish Centre. That's why he was there all those years ago. That's why he knew I'd been. Because he had too!

I searched Alice's face for confirmation that Mila wasn't spinning more lies about our family.

'Alice?'

It was a tsunami of revelation. 'It's true. It's all true,' she confirmed, staring through me as I imagined Lindani had to Mila back then.

'Child-soldier though? W-what do you mean? How?'

Alice held out her palm to me as a gesture of support. I reciprocated but felt no comfort. She guided Mila and me to the sofa, where we sat tensely beside one another, ignoring the electrical buzz that ricocheted between us.

'My dear.' She pulled out a match and a candle respectively, before sucking at her teeth. 'Ladies, let us say a prayer for his safe return.'

You've gotta be kiddin' me!

'Alice, I've prayed every goddam day for that man. Right now, it's my son I have to worry about.'

She held my gaze in silence. 'Can you just tell me what you know. Please, Alice.'

'Have you heard of the Ancestral Resistance Movement?'

Would we be here if I had?

I didn't realise I was shaking my head, but it was an honest reflection that her words sparked nothing from my memory. She lit the candle and placed it on the coffee table before us.

'Well, my dear, the A.R.M. were an occupying military unit led by one Joseph Otti.'

A drip of mucus lolled from my nostril.

'It was a guerrilla campaign that incited fear across the whole of Central Africa at the time. Lindani, well he was just a boy. As it so happened, they were more of a cult than an army. One that wasn't motivated by a political agenda per se, just one man on a power trip with a growing number of mindless followers. They destroyed anyone they claimed the ancestors told them to, which was almost everyone who crossed their path. They abducted children who had evaded execution and forced them into becoming soldiers.' My jaw loosened from the rest of my face. 'Lindani was one of those children. It was a very long time ago. There's no threat to him now, the A.R.M. are long since gone.'

Carbon monoxide must have flooded the vents that fed air directly into my trachea. The muscles coating my tubes contracted wildly.

'No … no, this is insane. It's all insane.'

Alice's gaze remained tightly fixed to my newly acquired tremor.

'He was twenty years old when he escaped the A.R.M. and found me. He was a grown man with demons far greater than his years. Mila found this out the hard way.'

It was a misplaced vote of sympathy I didn't appreciate. Tears fell from my eyes, barely grazing the skin of my cheeks this time. I felt no shame, just sharp spikes of guilt at not having been as close to him as his first wife evidently was.

'Why didn't he tell me any of this?' I appealed helplessly, my heart aching to console my absent husband.

Mila spoke up. 'Count yourself lucky it was just me he treated like shit. By the time he got to you, he was in much better shape. You should be thanking me really.'

Alice shot Mila a warning glare before she continued with her speech.

'To be fair, it made sense when I actually met you, Lois. You were just as selfish and messed up as he was. He needed someone like you, someone whose insecurities would make for a passive wife. That way he'd never be challenged on all his mistreatment. It must have been a no-brainer!'

'I didn't even know him.' I thought the words were spoken only in my head.

'Lois, my dear ...' *Why does everyone sound so fucking condescending!* 'I can only imagine his memories were too painful. After years of working through his afflictions, he was finally at a place of peace. And to taint that peace with what were – by then – only memories, well where would be the sense in that? Why would he bring that into your marriage, when it only destroyed his first one? That wouldn't make sense.'

'Is there anything he *did* tell you, Lois?'

Utter dejection engulfed me, so much that my wrists fell limply towards our once-polished floor. I couldn't help but feel the judgement Mila exuded as she sniggered noticeably beside me.

'Only that his parents had passed.' It was a solemn admission on my part.

'You really didn't know him at all, did you, Lois?' Mila said. 'You got the best version of him and you didn't even know it. How many times did you say to me that you wished he'd shown you more attention when you got fat from having his child, the one I so desperately wanted to have?'

But how does all this link to him not being here?

'You didn't deserve him, Lois.'

Alice hastened towards us. 'Didn't?' 'Why in the past tense, Mila?

Where is he?' The urgency in her eyes implanted an unexplained fear in my gut.

'There was a phone call, Alice, back when they were in South Africa.' My dad took the opportunity to join the conversation.

'What kind of call?'

'It was hard to make out. There was a scuffle of some sort I think, but it was distant. Like something was covering the receiver.'

'You didn't hear any voices? Did it sound like there was someone with him?'

'No, it cut off, then I couldn't get through.'

Alice scooped her phone from her patchwork canvas bag, passing Tom as she exited abruptly through the front door.

'He's in danger, isn't he? MILA! Is he in danger?'

Mila's face grew wildly contorted. Her nostrils flared to accommodate her increasingly rapid breathing as her eyes unmistakeably bore the answer to my question.

'The camera light,' I said. 'It was a distress sign, wasn't it! I saw on his phone, Mila, he'd activated it remotely so someone would know he needed help. It was all he could do.' My tears were free-flowing for the second time.

Mila remained nonchalant even as Tom berated her. 'You sick fuck.' He left his post by the door. 'Tell her what you did. Tell her NOW! Tell her RIGHT NOW!'

'Get off me, Tom!' she said, him having wrapped his fingers around the thick of her neck.

'Tell her where he is, you fucking bitch!'

She eyeballed me intensely, realising the extent of her cruelty. 'I didn't mean for it to go this far,' was her pathetically inept defence. 'I did, I mean at first when I found you, but then, it was too late to go back … and I needed the money for my training. To fly, to become a pilot. It's the only thing I still have that's just for me.'

You selfish bitch!

'Too far how? Where is he?' It was an allergic reaction to Mila's intentional obscurity.

'I'm sorry, Lois.'

'What are you sorry for, Mila? Come on, were friends, aren't we?' I spat bitterly. 'Are you sorry for befriending me so you could get close enough to dismantle my family?'

'He's with *them,* all right?'

A deafening silence erupted into the thick of the room, engulfing us in quilted plumes of smoggy toxicity.

My knees trembled viciously as a prerequisite for their imminent collapse, until somewhere amidst the smoke I found myself being cradled like a baby in my dad's arms.

'No ... No, he can't be, this isn't real, it's a lie, it's all a lie.'

Mila's voice became distant, indecipherable almost, yet her confession screamed through my head. My husband was with the same people who destroyed him.

Her words grew so thin I heard only my own howls.

'I actually believed he'd come crawling back home, as soon he realised he couldn't survive without me.' Mila began to explain.

I watched a bolt of red form down my left thumb as I tore away the remaining skin.

'But that day never came, Lois. Apparently, we'd drifted apart and our relationship lacked that ever so sought-after spark. It was a joke. Maybe he would have felt a goddam spark if he was capable of feeling any emotion at all.'

A mention of the L-word punctured my daze. Love. What good would that do now?

'It was all a pathetic waste of my time. All the support and effort I'd invested in us, to make him see he was special, that he was a good man. All for what? To find you!'

The contents of Mila's journal had well and truly erupted into the public domain.

'Shut up, Mila! I don't care. I couldn't care less! How could you do something so sick ... and to us, of all people?'

'The years after he left were the worst of my life. I'd never felt so lost and confused. No man ever lived up to him. He was intriguing and mysterious. Vulnerable, y'know? Don't get me wrong, I questioned if I was drawn to his dysfunction, but he was good to me for the most part.'

Nothing but time passed between us.

'It seems we're more alike than we thought, Lois, you and I.'

'My daughter is nothing like you, you vile piece of shit!'

I signalled to dad to let me handle it.

'Where's my husband, Mila? I have a dying son to get to, so even if you can't consider me in all of this then at least consider Kai. Tell me if he still has a fucking dad!' Kai's image pulsed before me, glowing in my conscience like a beacon alight for rescue. 'Cut the bullshit, Mila. I mean it.'

I caught a flicker of a flame from the coffee table.

The fire! Of course, it must have been her who started it.

'You tried to kill us all in that fire, didn't you? You did, didn't you?' I moved towards the front door just in case she made a dash for it.

'No. I wouldn't do that. I'd never put Kai in danger. The fire was just … lucky.'

'Lucky?'

'Do you want me to call the cops, Lois? Just say the word and she'll be history.'

'Tell me before I go, Mila. He needs his dad, and I need to be with my son right now. I need to be with him, do you understand?' I waited a mere few seconds for her response. 'How can you be so cruel? I need to know where he is. Tom, please, someone, find out for me,' I pleaded, scanning the faces of everyone who claimed to care about me. 'I'll be at the hospital.'

40

I never made it to the hospital. Nor did I make it outside the front door.

'Say that again. Louder so everyone can hear this time.'

This is your moment, so take it.

Mila remained stock-still, as did everyone else in the room. 'I gave them a tip-off.'

Tom was the first to react. 'You're as sick as you are insane, Mila, I swear to god! What the hell were you thinking?'

Her cheeks drained of colour as she learned for the first time how twisted her plan sounded when spoken out loud. 'Lindani was to be approached by a couple of men and led from the reception of the hotel without you knowing. I only knew he'd made it out of the fire when I received his phone in the post, as planned.' She twirled the loose black hair around her index finger, emitting a nervous energy I'd never seen before. 'I don't exactly know who sent it back, but it was the proof I'd insisted on before giving them the information they needed. You have to understand Lois, tha—'

I leapt from my position by the front door, hurtling instead onto Mila's lap. My knees splayed over her waist as I struck hard into her cheek, causing her skin to re-rouge on impact. Mila's head flapped sideways and pellets of spit flew freely through the air between us.

'What the fuck? What have you done? WHAT HAVE YOU DONE!'

My grip of her faltered, an unwelcome result of my flailing temper. I sensed no one around me, but pleaded for someone to restrain her.

I grabbed at her black ponytail as she tried to turn away. 'Get off me, you pathetic cow.'

My body contorted as her nails dug deep into the flesh beside my spine. I clawed at her arms until the sharp scrape of pain in my back dulled. Before I managed to secure both feet back onto the floor, the smell of Dad's cologne flooded my nostrils. I was harnessed against him, the back of my head nestled into his chest. I fought back as he dragged me from Mila's reach, hammering my foot hard into Mila's stomach. She fished for my heel and gasped as her flesh absorbed the impact of the kick. Breaking away from them both, I snapped away their attempts at my freedom.

Alice shot back through the front door and charged towards Mila, yelling another Africanism. 'Dom nool. He's as good as dead!'

'No, Alice. He can't be. He can't be dead.' My vision blurred from the constant swaying of my upper body.

'Dad, tell me he isn't dead. Kai, he needs hi—'

'Can we not say things like that before we know anything, Alice? She's fragile as it is.'

'Is he dead? Someone tell me now, IS MY HUSBAND DEAD?'

Mila's demeanour oozed irreverence. She side-eyed me from her new position in the corner of the room before engaging reluctantly with words.

'That wasn't our deal,' she said, spitting red peppered saliva onto the floor.

'What was the deal? What deal?' The patch of warmth from my dad's hand soothed me slightly.

Time had run out, both to resume my position at Kai's bedside and to bring my husband back home without having completely ruined any chance of requital.

Mila's words pierced the heavy ambience of the room. 'He was meant to transfer money into my account. But only if I could make Lindani accessible to him.'

Her stony disposition sent a shiver through me.

'Who, Mila? Who is *he*?'

She expended a deep cloud of air, preparing to continue. 'One of the A.R.M. soldiers forced Lindani to kill his own sister.' *He killed his sister?* 'So naturally, he wanted revenge.'

He had a sister?

'Dan befriended him so he could get close enough to kill him, and that's what he did. It was a particularly brutal attack too, if his flashbacks were anything to go by.'

No, no, stop it. You've got it all wrong. This isn't him. Not Lindani.

'That same guy he murdered, well he turned out to be the leader's son, of that faction anyway. So long story short, Lindani was an extremely wanted man.'

Why didn't he tell me any of this? My heart hurt from every angle.

'Let me get this straight. You went out of your way to track down this monster then sell my husband to him – the same man you claim to have loved. Is that what you expect me to believe?'

I gestured for the men in the room to ignore my outburst, sensing their approach towards us.

'Listen, Lois. The bottom line is, those sick bastards have been after him for over twenty years. His day was coming, whether I had a hand in it or not. Do you understand?'

'It's bullshit, Mila, all of it. How the hell could you have orchestrated something so insane?'

You orchestrated it. How could you? You've violated my life, Mila. Ruined everything. Tears pricked my eyes.

'Lindani gave me a list of numbers to look out for back when we were together. He told me if any of them were to show up on either of our phones, I was to tell him straight away then call the police. He was screening calls and messages incessantly, checking the doors and windows just as much. He was totally paranoid, and so was I in the end. At first I thought he was exaggerating, that it must be his weird OCD or something. But nope, that was our life. Two paranoid people living in fear of a phone call, a knock at the door, a frickin' nosey neighbour. That is until I got him the help he needed.'

'So, you thought, oh I don't know, I'll keep hold of these guys' contact details just in case they should come in handy one day. Is that what you thought, Mila?'

She nodded. 'Actually yeah.' *I'll fucking kill you!* 'I didn't think too much about it in the years that followed, but I guess some of his paranoia had stayed with me. I found myself checking my caller ID religiously, even after we split. After a couple of months on my own, I'd kind of forgotten about our insane looming threat, but then you came up as a suggested friend on Instagram and the thumbnail was a picture of you both together. That's when I decided to look for you.'

The energy in the room was charged and volatile, even more so than before.

I could feel it. Taste it even.

'If that's true, why the hell would he put himself in the public eye then?'

'Jesus, I don't have all the answers, do I? But everything I've said is true.'

My dad took a stride towards her. *Don't do anything, Dad.* 'Get him back now,' he demanded. 'D'ya hear!'

'I have to know he's okay. There has to be way,' I said, becoming hysterical in my thoughts.

'They promised he'd just be kept prisoner. They weren't planning on killing him.'

'They *promised*? You've really lost it, Mila. Terrorists don't keep promises. What the fuck? We have to ring the police. You have to tell them what you did.'

'Lois, Sarah's on her way to Cape Town to meet with the police there,' said Alice. 'I've just phoned her. They may be able to track the men down from security footage. There should be cameras nearby, from across the street or around the hotel. It could lead them to him.' She looked at Mila. 'I'll need the contact details you used to reach them, Mila,' demanded Alice, with a firm yet controlled sharpness to her tone.

'That won't be possible. I mean, you can have the number, but messages just bounce straight back. They've shut it down ... I started to feel bad for Kai so I tried to reverse some of the damage. I mean, he's a really special kid.'

I snapped, 'You're not fit to speak his name. Don't you dare speak that boy's name again!'

'I wanted him to have a dad, but it's too late, the number didn't work. I've had no contact since.'

Mila began to weaken to everyone's outbursts.

'You put a stop to all this now!' shouted Dad, louder than my pressing her to try harder. 'You claim to know everything about him, Mila. If it's true you know everything, you'll go and bring him back NOW!'

'Look, I know you're worried, but I had their word they wouldn't harm him.'

'They're fucking terrorists, you lunatic! You're going to find a way to bring him back, do ya hear me?'

'Listen, they sent me his phone like I asked, they'll keep their word … There's honestly nothing more I can do.'

'You'll give them back their blood money and get my husband back, that's it.'

'That's just it. There was no money. Not a penny.'

A dark human figure emerged from behind the black partition of Kai's play area. I froze on the spot, enabling panic to consume my nerves.

Its shadowy limbs unfurled into the room, revealing the same features I recognised on Wendy. I breathed a sigh of relief, a relief that was instantly replaced by the worry of what she had overheard. *She'll take my son from me!*

'Wendy, what the hell are you doing here? Who let you in?'

I detected Dad's voice in the background. 'Lois!'

'You have to leave, Wendy,' I said.

'Lois, stop. Look at me!'

'Wendy, say something. Can you hear me? Why won't you answer me?'

'Lois!'

'Why did you come here? Answer me!' I cried, growing more and more frustrated.

'Stop it, Lois. Listen to me, darling. Look at me, please listen,' continued Dad.

'Why were you hiding back there, what do you want from me?'

I was distracted by the feel of two rough hands hooked onto both shoulders. They shook my frame with a solicitation I had to acknowledge.

'Lois, you have to stop this. She isn't real, darling. This Wendy, she isn't real.'

'Wha-what are you talking about? Course she's real. She's right there. She's stood right there!' I said, pointing to the spot directly behind him.

'Listen, just do something for me. Promise me you'll do one thing and I'll never bring it up again.'

'What are you talking about?'

'Promise me?'

'I need to go, Dad. I have to find Kai … and Dan.'

'Promise?'

After a few seconds, I nodded reluctantly, seeing no immediate alternative.

He handed me his phone and dialled the number to the Spring View therapy centre.

'Ask to speak to Wendy.'

41

I scrambled together the appropriate words, ready for when it was my turn to speak.

'Good evening, Spring View Counselling Services, Gina speaking, how may I help?'

Aware of the cluster of people gathering behind me, I spoke in hushed tones into the furthest corner of the room. I prayed for the phone line to drop off, for Gina to put me on hold or to ask me to call back at a more suitable time.

'Gina, hi. It's Lois Attah, Malekai's mum.' The tremor in my hands launched an attack at my voice.

'Hello, Mrs. Attah, how may I help you?'

'Gina, I was wondering if you could maybe put me through to Wendy?' White noise crackled between my ears.

'Sorry, who? Could you confirm the name in full please?'

I peered over my shoulder, experiencing an unidentifiable affliction. Dad nodded for me to continue.

'I need to ring the hospital!'

'Lois, please do this for me, and I promise we'll both go to the hospital. Kai's doing fine, I've already checked in with his nurses.'

'Mrs. Attah?' said the voice from the phone.

'Hi, yes I'm sorry, umm, Wendy Thompson, could I speak to Wendy Thompson please?'

'Wendy Thompson?' repeated Gina. 'I'm afraid no one by that name works here. Is there anything *I* can help you with?'

'Gina, I'm sure I'm not mistaken, you were with her when I brought Kai in for assessment. Wendy Thompson,' I repeated.

'Hmm, I'm really sorry, I've been here for almost five years and I've never worked with anyone by that name. I'd be hap—'

The phone slid from my grasp, crashing heavily onto the hard floor.

'Darling, it's okay,' said Dad, approaching me from the far side of the room.

'NO! Stay there! What is this? What are you trying to do?' I felt the arches of my face morph into a horrified version of itself.

'I can explain, just come sit here, love,' he offered, palms outstretched towards me as if taming a wild beast.

I was unable to respond, trapped in the monsoon of fear and confusion I'd walked directly into. Vomit, air, and mucus gushed past my ears, rushing to find an exit, meeting in the pit of my throat and gurgling excitedly for release.

'Lois,' he persisted. 'We can talk this through together, privately.'

Wendy materialised before me like the hologram he'd claimed she was. Her head bowed to the floor, blocking my view of anything beyond.

I could detect Dad's words but struggled to identify his location. 'Everything's going to be okay,' I heard him say.

I needed him now. Just as I had when I was a little girl, all those nights when I sat wrapped in Mum's blanket at the foot of the garden on my own and wishing for him to comfort me just as potently as I wished his woman would disappear.

The room pulsed in slow motion as I watched Wendy reveal herself. A bolt of dread rendering my limbs completely immobile.

I glanced towards Dad, the same way I'd peeked over the lip of my blanket from our back garden as he approached. He wasn't the same man this time, he was smaller somehow, but the grey of his eyes was as translucent as ever. The line of dark brown was now speckled with deep threads of silver, having drawn back to reveal a shiny embankment of skin, just as a tide draws back to reveal bare, fleshy sand beneath it.

I fought against my imminent paralysis to seek my dad's protection.

Muffled recitations circled my periphery. 'Dad I'm sorry, please forgive me, forgive me. Where are you? I need you.'

Wendy's straight blonde hair had grown grizzly and terse. Purple veins throbbed through her ashen skin and her once beautiful smile made way for a sharp toothy snarl.

'No, this isn't happening. Dad, where are you?'

'He doesn't care about you, Lois. Can't you see that I'm the only one who does?' voiced the figure before me.

My limbs quivered, shaking off the salty droplets that had collected under my chin. I clasped my hands tightly over both ears to mute the feral vocalisations that surrounded me.

'Deep breaths, darling, you're okay.'

'What's happening?' I cried. 'Tell me what's going on. DAD!'

'She isn't real, Lois.' The sound of my own breathing muffled his words. 'Remember that doll, from when you were a kid? Do you remember?'

I managed a nod in acknowledgement.

'Wendy, right? And the house you used to escape to at the bottom of the garden every time you were upset.'

'Dad, what is this? Help me,' I pleaded between sobs.

'Darling, your mother, bless her soul, she was sick too. Are you listening?'

I nodded discreetly, the only movement my physiology would allow.

'The doctors told me when she had you, it changed her body so much that she started seeing things that weren't there. She personified a doll she was going to give to you, Lois. I first noticed when I brought flowers onto the ward. Your mum was telling the doll things like how important it was that you survive. She started begging the doll to make you better, darlin'. It was every time after, when she was afraid or sad, the doll became human again in her mind. Then when you were a little older and she was diagnosed with cancer, things got really bad. That's why I always tried to take you out of the way if she began behaving strangely. You see, I became really good at noticing the signs early on.'

'No … it doesn't make sense?' I whispered through the noise. 'I need to find my husband.'

'I felt useless, Lois, as your dad and as her husband. I didn't know how to help either one of you. Your mum, well she knew that too and the guilt just made everything worse.'

'But she was fine, Mum, she was happy?' I stammered, through tears.

'For the most part, darling, yes … she loved you so much. So much that she was terrified of losing you. We both were. The difference was, it consumed her entirely. I had to find a way to protect her memory and I certainly couldn't bear the thought of you worrying you'd suffer the same fate.'

'That's why you never told me?'

I covered my eyes, blocking out the twisted image of Wendy.

'I know what you thought of me back then, too. I know what you thought I'd done. It was another thing I didn't know how to handle. Your mum, well she knew about that woman you saw me with that time, at the swimming baths. Do you remember?'

I cried deeper and harder, gasping between breaths.

'I just wanted to be with you, Dad. All the time, every week, with you. You don't know how much I adored you … you broke me. Broke me in two, the same way Mum did when she died. I wanted to die too. I prayed for death all the time.'

'Oh, darlin', if I could change it all I wou—'

'And you just let me push you away, all these years? You never came for me, not really.'

'What choice did I have, love? Your mum pushed me to move on back then … for you, for us, but I—' A deep verge of grey replaced his muffled features. 'I wish you could have known her the way I did, Lois. Known how selfless she could be. She could be just as stubborn though, at times. When she was really sick, she wanted me to prove I could be happy with someone else, for both our sakes. Before she died, she begged me to show you what it meant to love someone. You were so young, and maybe I took things too literally. I know I failed. Man did I fail. I was just a stupid guy back then. Stupid but not cruel, Lois. Not to you.'

My head dizzied with growing urgency between my search for Wendy and my burning desire for my dad to make things right again.

'I was in up to my neck. I tried not to fail her again, so I met Hannah. But nothing went to plan. She wasn't your mother. I mean how could she be? And I couldn't love her the same, but I tried, Lois. I really did. I couldn't shake her off once she was in our lives. It was all just a mess, and I was hurting so bad too. I didn't have the strength to do what I should have done.'

'Why are you telling me all of this?' I said, flicking my gaze from Wendy to Mila.

An erratic commotion filled the room but I couldn't quite decipher what was happening.

'You have to know how loved you are, Lois, believe me you are.'

I picked the skin beside my fingernail, scanning the face of the woman who'd tried to ruin my life. 'I can't do this, none of it.'

'You're stronger than you think. Just look around you. You're a beautiful, accomplished woman. You're raising an amazing kid, and if Lindani didn't think the world of you he wouldn't have done what he did!'

Dizziness began to dominate my consciousness.

'What do you mean, wouldn't have done what he did?' My thoughts were fogging from a dump-load of added confusion.

'He made me feel like I was still part of the family, Dan did.'

My unbalanced demeanour and strengthening tremor were impossible to control.

'We spoke often, every week to be precise. I asked him to take care of you since you wouldn't have me around. He brought Kai to see me every chance he got too. I love that man for what he did. Don't you see?'

A cool chill swept around the collar of my blouse. The exposed flesh of my forearms gave rise to another layer of fleshy bumps that coated the outer skin of my entire body.

'Kai, he was comfortable with you that day, I saw it too, but I thought I was imagini— I need to find him, Dad. I need to but it feels so impossible!'

'We'll get him back, together, if you believe we can. Lois?'

A sentiment whipped at me then. One that simultaneously connected the figurative dots and filled me with dread.

'Kai knows, doesn't he? About me, the voices? He wouldn't talk to me, Dad. It's like he hated me after South Africa.'

Wendy remained on the same spot, a still, poster image of her newest incarnation.

'He was confused, darlin', when he saw you talking to yourself, back in South Africa and those few times at home, on the bike ride and at Spring View, he didn't know what to think. That's when he asked you to contact me. I stuck around to keep things as normal as possible for him.'

Wendy's voice masked that of my dad's. 'He left you, Lois, when you were just a girl. A girl who needed her daddy. I'll never leave you, Lois, never.'

'No, go away … please go away! You're not real, I don't need you,' I chanted, my oxygen feeling ever more replaced by delirium.

'I can't stand this any more.' The room had become devoid of all voices.

I dared to open my eyes, hopeful to confront my demons head-on. Wendy wasn't real. What was real was that my son was sick and afraid, my husband was gone, maybe for good, I'd been betrayed by my friend in the worst conceivable way, and it was up to me to fix it all.

That's when she hurtled towards me, her face a depiction of horror I had pieced together in my head. I slid from her path, dodging the reach of her pointed fingers, searching desperately for a way to stunt her approach. I called out obscenities, cursing her name and demanding she disappear.

'I'll never leave, Lois.' The words resonated with the darkest corners of my conscience.

The skin stretching from my forehead to my clavicle glistened with a coating of sweat.

'Whatever you see, ignore it. Okay, Lois, look at me.'

'She isn't going away.'

'Take it easy, Lois. Deep breaths.'

'I have to send her away.'

'You can't do this alone, Lois. We need to get you to the hospital.'

The hospital! 'I need to see my son.'

'We're going to get you some help, okay? Speak to someone who knows about these things. Can you hear me, Lois?'

His pleas were drowned out by Wendy's ceaseless taunts.

'Kai's better off dead than he is with you!'

'NO, THAT'S NOT TRUE!' I screamed.

'Eish, try to stay calm, dear.' Alice contributed to the voices.

'I'm the only one you need,' taunted Wendy.

'FIND MY HUSBAND!' I shouted into the room. 'FIND MY HUSBAND!'

The jumble of words convulsed in my skull, causing a nonsensical throbbing between my ears. Blood gushed through my sinuses, giving birth to a heavy pounding that persisted in its attempts to push through my skin.

'I DON'T NEED YOU, YOU'RE NOT REAL!' I screamed, with more assurance than I believed.

'Let's go outside, love, just me and you, okay? Lois?'

I snatched the camera from its stand.

'Everything's gonna be fine, you can trust me. C'mon, darlin'.'

The camera flew from my grasp with a force propelled by the cumulation of trauma. I expelled it directly towards the area around her face, obliterating Wendy's structure upon impact. Her cheeks exploded slowly into a mosaic of transience that caused her head to crack un-forgivingly against the granite countertop, destroying what healthy matter had remained. Wendy's descent to the hardwood floor produced a thundering crash, followed by a final outcry of raw anguish.

42

That was it, the violent end to my mental torture. At least I hoped it was. There were no voices. There was no sound. No noise. Only silence.

I expected to feel something more intense than mild relief, numbness beginning to dull my senses. Only when I scanned the room did I feel something more consuming, more insistent.

A dark crimson substance peppered Alice's clothing, its reach stretched up the walls that encased all of us, leaving no person or object between us unadorned.

A haze of white noise fizzed into action, alerting me to the real-life emergency in my family home.

'What have you done?' I heard, as a modest crowd formed around the bloody mass on the floor.

'It isn't real,' I said, not believing my own words.

Alice shoved me out of her way as she attended the invisible casualty.

'Call an ambulance!' she instructed calmly.

A buzz of panic billowed around her. My feet rooted amongst the thick of it.

'It isn't real,' I repeated, even less convinced than before. 'No, no it can't be … no … Wendy, she was right there,' I stammered, my hands shaking wildly now.

Tom and Alice arched over the body, pulling gently at the limbs to check for signs of life. Their eyes met as they took a momentary halt in their rescue attempt. The deep sadness in his stare told me what was confirmed by a subtle shake of the head. Mila took her final step backwards until she was pressed against the far wall. 'Kai needs him,' she said in a daze, her feet motioning as far away as the walls allowed.

I drank in the scene that had ended so catastrophically ill-fated.

My mask of indifference was just that, a disguise. An amateur attempt at maintaining a degree of composure that could easily be mistaken for shock, but my internal bruising was colouring through the layers until my body pulsed with the raw pain of a violent attack, similar to the violent attack I had inflicted upon the man with multiple head injuries bleeding out onto my living room floor.

My dad lay still, peaceful almost, if it was possible to look beyond the physical. All indications of pain having evaporated. It had merely changed hosts. Dad's suffering had possessed me instead.

Gone were any indications that Wendy had ever lived, in the tangible world or in my own. The timing of her absence tore at my flesh from the inside out. If only I had listened to him, believed him when he said everything was going to be okay. Perhaps if I had, I wouldn't be spending the rest of my life searching fruitlessly for an other-worldly forgiveness I was likely to never find.

• • •

My head reeled with a dialogue that was personalised in its cruelty. Thoughts of my son, his condition and how I had denied him, again, to know his grandad. How he must have felt when he woke to find no one at his bedside, broken was another promise. I speculated about Lindani and whether or not he was still alive. Whether or not I'd really just destroyed my own family and how my life would look now that I'd lost almost everything I'd had left.

I left my ex-best friend to deal with the police in my haste to leave. Determined instead to follow my dad's journey to the hospital. *Stay in the present, Lois. The past cannot be changed and the future is not yet known.* It was exactly what the professionals advised.

I would contact the authorities in South Africa and tell them what I knew, so no more time was wasted in locating Lindani. The case would still be open, and Lindani would be found, at least that's what I had to tell myself. *Focus on the present.*

We were approximately three minutes from reaching Accident and Emergency and against my better judgement, I sped up to tail the ambulance, avoiding the disapproving gaze of Alice who sat beside me in the passenger seat.

It was a journey that felt as rudderless as it did mournful. I held on to very little hope, knowing that what I'd done was nothing if not irreversible. If Dad's resuscitation had worked, he would have spoken, reassured me that everything would be okay. That we could get through this whole disaster together. But he didn't, couldn't.

Flashes of tortured recollections projected onto the car windscreen, tarring its former clarity. The transparency of the glass emulsified into a deep crimson that reflected back an insatiable symbolism of lost parental love. I couldn't save him, couldn't stem his blood flow enough to gift him the time he deserved. I had failed at a lot of things, everything really, but I couldn't give up hope. *Focus on the present, Lois.*

The sirens blared as I watched the ambulance tear through the streets of Manchester. All signs that perhaps, just perhaps, Dad was clinging to life after all. A thump of hope flared within me. Hope I knew from experience not to rely on wholeheartedly. But what else did I have?

It was only a couple of minutes until Dad could receive the care he needed. Approaching crossroads, the ambulance slowed slightly, alerting other drivers to its passing.

In my mind, I reached out, hoping and yearning to feel the warmth of Dad's hand. It would be another sign of life that I probably didn't deserve to feel. His fingers would flicker in invitation of my touch, gradually bringing a glow to his skin that told me we were still together, that we had got through the worst that life could throw at us.

A red light halted our procession. I looked over to Alice for approval of what I already knew I shouldn't do.

The ambulance began to pick up speed as it approached the far side of the junction, leaving me stranded back at the lights.

Just as I contemplated setting off, a navy-blue Ford shot out from the right side of the road. It sped recklessly across the junction before careening into the rear of the ambulance. A resounding screech of rubber preceded the ear-splitting crash of metal on metal, causing its bonnet to crumple within itself. The ambulance was knocked sideways upon impact, stunting the trajectory of the blue car.

I stared at both stationary vehicles through the mud-speckled glass of our windscreen, frozen into a stupor. Without word, Alice left the passenger side and ran across the tarmac, ignorant to its inherent dangers. Her shawl flapped in unison with her mounting speed. I clicked open the driver side door in pursuit of her, hoping the oncoming traffic would be temporarily disabled. A faint whiff of burnt chemical fluid grew stronger the nearer I approached.

I briefly scanned the crowd that had appeared from the dozens of cars occupying the tangle of surrounding streets, keeping my vision locked onto the ambulance, urging it to continue its journey to the hospital. I was just a few feet from the collision when I thought I recognised who it was that Alice was trying to drag from the blue Ford.

I could make out a thorny, elongated figure through the forest of metal. I swallowed hard, stumbling on the flat tarmac beneath me until my hand rested flatly against it, harnessing my body upright.

It can't be!

'Dan? Dan, is that you?'

A moment of clarity penetrated the junction, one which served to affiliate myself and my husband in the same moment in the same place at the same time.

Months sped between us, right there in the centre of a busy junction. The months we needn't have been separated but had, the months we'd been forced to devour ourselves from the inside out and the months that had served to alter the course of our lives forever.

'He needs your help, Lois,' said Alice, with grave sincerity.

Detecting the ever-growing distant sound of the ambulance siren, I nodded in silent reciprocation, not attributing the stream of tears gathering at my chin as that of my own.

'Stay with us, my love, please stay with us,' I pleaded shakily into the threadbare fabric against his neck, my entire body erupting into a single mass of virile emotion.

'I've called an ambulance,' Alice reported factually, remaining by Lindani's side.

His face bore the same contours as they did before South Africa, only sharper and less polished than I remembered, save the addition of some fresh grazes to the skin coating his face. I swallowed the saliva that was beginning to thicken my mouth, tell-tale signs of the weakness that was igniting by being in his presence again.

'Talk to me, Dan. Tell me you're all right. I need you to tell me.'

The clambering of white noise fluttered between us, until silence ensued at my anticipation of hearing my husband address me in person for the first time in months.

'What is it, what are you trying to say,? I pressed, impatiently.

'What… What happened to your hair, Miss Lane?'

That smile, the one I had become addicted to, churned in me the same affliction it had since our very first date. I retired the image to my memory, wondering if we could ever smile again after learning what news awaited us at the hospital.

I need you all. My boys, I need you all.

43

The hearing had been delayed by two weeks. It was another arduous fortnight, during which I'd had to hold my breath in constant fear that Mila would have a change of heart.

'Miss Mila Sanders has pleaded guilty to the involuntary manslaughter of Mr. Hudson, which occurred at approximately five thirty p.m. on Wednesday the twelfth of May 2020.'

'Do you wish to change your plea?'

Silence is key, I thought, stifling my moral desire to tell the truth. Tom and I radiated tension as we stared directly through the back of Mila's head.

'No, sir.'

'I thereby sentence you to the minimum term for involuntary manslaughter, as stated in UK law, of two years imprisonment.'

I threw my arms around Tom, exhaling an accumulation of pent-up anxiety. It was a necessary display of gratification. 'She really went through with it?' I said, smoothing down the skin by my left thumb.

'Sshh,' said Tom, subtly. 'Are you sure you're okay?' he asked, noticing my agitation.

He allowed time for me to gather my thoughts.

'I will be. In fact, we all will be. Even you,' I reassured, exhibiting my widest, sweetest smile.

'Please, it's a drop in the ocean compared to what she put you and your family through. I'll be fine. Anyway, I've already met a nice normal woman, just in case you were wondering.'

'Nice! Let's just hope you chose better than you did last time!' I teased.

'That shouldn't be hard, should it!' he said, rhetorically. 'One thing's for sure though. You certainly did.'

I eyeballed Mila, who remained momentarily in a state of shock. 'What do you mean?'

'Well, I'm already a better friend, don't you think!'

• • •

They mustn't have been there before. If they had, I'd never noticed.

An array of colour-laden butterflies danced elaborately around the stone headboard. Nature's way of celebrating reunited love.

I brushed the dirt aside, flicking clusters of moss from the names engraved beneath it. 'Emily Hudson, loving wife to Richard Hudson, loving mother of Lois.'

Beneath Mum's, read the name of the man I had grown to adore for the second time in my life. The memory of my actions intensified the pain of loss I already felt.

I sat like a child, cross-legged on the patch of grass directly in front of them, amassing an ocean full of tears I knew I deserved to cry. The regret was part of me now, as permanently etched in my blood as my parents' names on their headstones.

I hoped Dad would forgive me for allowing Mila to take the blame for what happened. Being the man that he was, I had little doubt, given the circumstances. Dad knew, first-hand, how unbearable it would be to be separated from your child. So, I knew he wouldn't wish for us to suffer the same fate.

I spread the loose floral fabric over my folded knees, before sliding out the stamped envelope from the same bag from which I had brought the flowers. I sucked in the aroma I knew was to come.

A vibrant scent of pomegranate immediately leaked into my system. The familiar fragrance temporarily stunted my flow of tears.

It was one of many letters I had grown to depend upon of late. After

Sarah's initial apology letter, begging my forgiveness for believing Mila's web of lies, she had become a consistent source of support and distraction for me. Contemplating how Sarah could ever believe that I was an unstable, abusive, unfit mother who Lindani was trying to escape from, well it was laughable. Even if there was the tiniest element of truth to it.

Carefully unfolding the scented paper, I began reading. Sarah asked for Dan to explain in our reply how he'd managed to escape the A.R.M. and find his way back to England ... again. She went on to write how Alice and Sarah had worked hard on a new joint venture, an African-English fusion restaurant, which was to open this week. She had decorated the Os with hearts, her excitement jumping from the page. I re-read the next line, trying my best to assimilate her words. Lindani's captors had been apprehended. It was over.

She signed the letter off with the usual: 'Thinking of you all and looking forward to the day we can meet again.' Then I noticed something stapled to the overleaf.

I glanced up at the names on the headstone, as if silently sharing a moment of other-worldly intrigue. Three plane tickets stared up at me from the palm of my hand, with a written message across the printout. 'What do you think, try again? We could really use a good chef!'

'You got them, I see,' came a deep voice from behind me, awakening my fight or flight instinct.

'Oh Jesus, Dan, you scared me!'

That smile! My butterflies were ignited into an electrical frenzy.

'I love you so much,' I blurted, refusing to hold anything back any more.

Lindani's natural response was interrupted by our son who, letting go of his dad's hand, threw himself to the ground beside me. He immediately folded in his legs, duplicating my exact positioning, followed by my husband, who took residence on the grass beside Kai. A surge of emotion stifled my breathing, if only for a second.

'Dad, is it really true you fighted all of them?' enquired Kai, spiritedly, a smile bigger than ever encroaching his face.

'I didn't have to, son. When word got around about the first guy, all the others didn't even bother to come near me!'

'Even the bad guys were frightened of you?' Dan shrugged. 'Wow that's so cool. *My* dad scared away the baddies. I can't wait to tell everyone at school tomorrow!'

'All right, boys,' I said, interrupting their playful rhetoric. 'You have a few more sessions at Spring View left before that happens, pumpkin!'

'Nu uh!'

Kai leapt from his grassy seat and threw himself into an array of fighting stances, antics that also served to put him out of earshot.

'How are you *really*?' I said, turning to my husband, our features illuminated with longing. I digested the relief of my observation, as if it were a cool tonic on a scorching summer's day.

There was a child-sized distance between us still, neither of us having filled the space.

'There's so much regret inside me, Lois, it's still eating away.' A contemplative quiet bristled past us, within which I offered an emphatic nod.

'I know, me too. We have each other now though … don't we?' I said, awaiting my husband's agreement. Agreement that was delivered with a promising confidence I apparently needed to hear.

'I miss him y'know, your dad.'

Lindani turned back to face the grave, resting a single finger across his top lip, his other hand across my folded knee.

'I'm so sorry, Dan, for it all. For everything. For making you feel you couldn't tell me you guys were friends, and for us both expecting Kai to keep secrets from each other.'

A white butterfly leaked from the collection of flowering stems.

'Neither of us are blameless are we, Lo. I think therapy's taught us that much.'

I smirked in agreement, folding my palm over the gravelly texture of his fingers.

'I really thought that by keeping all this shit from you, I was protecting our family. I suppose you did too, by keeping Mila secret.'

'Let's not say her name, Dan? I just want us to forget she ever existed, okay?'

'Okay.'

My arms swung into an open gesture, attempting to lure us into a shared bout of affection, but the action was stifled by the perversive reality we had created for ourselves.

He held back. 'The thought of being treated like a project, like *she* did, well that's not what I wanted.'

'I hope we work it out, Dan ... the nights are rough without you,' I said, safe in the knowledge our program wouldn't allow us to return together just yet.

'I've been spending a few evenings up in the Dales, hoping I'd see you there.' His brows crossed into each, other indicating a desire for me to continue.

'Unfortunately for me, you're part of those memories now too. Actually, come to think of it ...' An early mystery struck me. 'You never did tell me how you found out where it was, did you?'

Air snuffed from Lindani's nostrils in cadence with the same memory striking him.

'I snooped your notes when our therapist was locking up.'

'No you didn't!' I said. 'I feel violated!'

Spits of rain dusted us with a gentle dampness.

'Piss off, course you don't, you love the attention!'

In the spirit of telling the truth, I didn't disagree.

'Can you imagine how happy lil' man's gonna be when we're all back in the same house? That'll be something to tell his friends about, aye!'

Our heads drew into each other. I closed my eyes as they made contact.

'What d'ya say we tell Sarah and Alice I fought off the entire A.R.M. and caught a jet back with James Bond! Zhuzh up the story a bit!'

I spewed an uncontrollable laugh before replying, 'What, as opposed to the equally shocking truth?'

Lindani laughed with me. 'Eish! In all seriousness, I'm shocked whoever called them found the only decent police officers in Central Africa! I'd be a dead man otherwise.'

'We'll stick with the first story I reckon, yeah?'

Our therapist had advised us to lighten our experiences with laughter if we could. Being our first attempt, I'd say we hadn't done half bad.

'About that,' said Dan. 'The soldier thing. I'll tell you everything in time. I promise.'

Kai appeared suddenly between us, spreading his too-short arms around us both, drawing us closer.

'I was thinking,' he claimed.

'Oh?' I said, offering him our full attention.

'Yep. Grandad's with Nanna now, isn't he? So he'll be happy again? Like you and Dad!'

'I like to think so, son. I *really* do like to think so.'

The five of us sat side by side, intertwined forever in the same moment, residing beneath a murky pink sky. We were connected by a residual energy I was determined to carry with me for the rest of my life.

I didn't realise I was crying until Kai smoothed his finger across my cheek, wiping off the salty droplet.

'Read the poem, Mum. It will give Nanna and Grandad nice dreams too, like it did with you.'

Sleep tight my darling, for you are not alone,
For times you cannot find me, she's here to make you whole,
The dreams they will become you, enchanted is your world,
You're a star amongst the stones dear, A new page you too
shall turn,
Sleep tight my darling, for you are not alone.

I peeked over at my son, who had his head bowed too, in private solitude. My heart warmed at the sight. I was grateful Dan had been able to save him in time, and no less grateful for Kai's evident resilience.

Your Grandad had a heart attack, son. It was fatal. I'm so sorry.

'I almost forgot!'

Dan and I looked at each other with mild confusion, then back at our son.

'I brought something. Some things actually!'

He plucked out a Lego crocodile and presented it to us.

'This is you, Dad. Because you're strong like a croc,' he said, standing it at the foot of the headstone. A monkey figure followed. 'Monkeys are cheeky like Grandad was.' The sentiment brought a smile to my cheeks but it burned a little too. 'Here's Nanna!' he said, moving things around until he'd found the right piece.

'A dog?'

'A dog! Loyal and loveable ... like a dog. Just like you said!' He pressed me for affirmation.

'That's right. Your nanna was both of those things, son.' I knelt, lessening the distance between us. 'She'd do anything to be here with you, I hope you know that. They both would.' He nuzzled into my waist, just the tiniest bit.

'*There* I am!'

Dan and I stared at the opening, intrigued to learn how he saw himself these days, when two green plastic horns came into view. 'I'm getting nervous now!' said Dan. 'Horns aren't exactly what you want to see, are they?' We laughed together, with even greater ease.

'A baby dragon!'

'Why are you a dragon, dude?' Dan flared his nostrils in demonstration.

In between giggles, Kai taught us why he saw himself as a dragon now, as opposed to the plucky little Lego boy he'd seen himself as before.

'Well, you don't see dragons every day, do you? Almost no one sees one because they're roar.'

'You mean rare?'

'They're rare, like I am. But they're strong too, like Dad. And guess what? They're not scared of anything. Not even fires. Did you know that?'

'I'd say that's pretty accurate, Dragon boy,' said Dan, diving at Kai's waist.

'Wait, there's one more!' he declared.

We all sat in our original spot.

He fished out the final figure. Kai gripped it tightly between his fingers, treating it more delicately than he had the others. A few seconds passed before he reached over to place it at the centre of the headstone.

'Wait!' I said. 'Is this me?'

He nodded before a shy smile lit his face. 'You're the panda.'

From a place of curiosity and confusion I asked, 'A panda?'

'Yep, this one's broken … like you, Mum.'

My index finger made contact with the skin by my thumb, his admission reminding me how much I'd affected him during our time in South Africa. *You think I'm broken?*

'You and the panda, you're the same,' he said.

I felt the warmth from my husband's shoulder as it pressed into mine.

'Because it's broken?' I was irrationally offended by his words.

'Look on the back, Mum. Look!' I did as he instructed.

'What's this?'

'Me and Dad glued it. It's fixed now. It isn't broken any more.'

Kai stepped back to assess his offerings. He was seemingly content everything was laid out according to his own perfect image.

'Son, I need to tell you something about your grandad. About why he's here.'

• • •

Mila struck the inside of her cell door, her fists rouging on impact.

'Guard?' she called out. 'Guard? I need to speak with you! It's a matter of urgency.'

Minutes later the door unbolted, revealing her standing confidently in the opening.

'I want to change my plea.'

THE END

ACKNOWLEDGEMENTS

Thank you to everyone who has supported me during this process. To my family and friends for their constant encouragement and invaluable input.

A special thank you to my wonderful editors, Ernesto Maestre and Manda Waller, for transforming my manuscript into what it is today.

Thank you to my brilliant cover designer and typesetter, Vanessa Mendozzi.

To everyone who has sacrificed their time to brainstorm ideas with me, I really do appreciate you all.

USEFUL LINKS

Visit my blog
www.onceuponaroguewriter.com

Email me
leannemarshallauthor@gmail.com

Editor
www.mandawaller.co.uk

Typesetting/Cover Design
www.vanessamendozzidesign.com

Music Recommendation
Mr Bailey MBM
(All platforms)

Printed in Great Britain
by Amazon